Storm of Giants

Book 1: Kamiko Hoshi

DK Raney

First Edition

NEWMAN SPRINGS PUBLISHING
320 Broad Street
Red Bank, NJ 07701

First originally published by Newman Springs Publishing 2021

ISBN 978-1-63881-549-5 (Paperback)
ISBN 978-1-68498-151-9 (Hardcover)
ISBN 978-1-63881-550-1 (Digital)

Printed in the United States of America

Chapter I

It was always a surprise how small the house appeared to her, how close the woods pressed in around it. Once it had been a bastion of might, miles from the city, set in the protective embrace of a deep and primordial forest. Now she saw it as the squat little cottage it was, no more than an easy stroll from the edge of a small village. She could not recall when it had changed. It struck her as odd that childhood memories still determined her perception of home. For Kamiko, the whole of creation seemed to have turned over since she'd last seen her house. The woman she had been was gone, and she felt like a stranger, waiting uninvited outside someone else's home. Perspective was a powerful thing.

Uila tossed his head with a quiet snort and tugged at the reins. She knew he recognized this as his domain, even after more than two years abroad. She held him still, as yet unwilling to approach. The emotions flailing around in her gut needed a few more moments, not for resolution but for the simple calming effect of the quiet forest. This was her place of rest, of seclusion. The longing for home had driven her for many days, and for now, she simply needed her thoughts to rest. She wondered if the trials of recent months would ever be resolved in her mind, in her heart.

"Unlikely," she whispered.

Kamiko swung her leg over the saddlebow and dismounted, her back to the enormous warhorse. Uila nickered and chortled, his ears and eyes scanning the familiar surroundings. She could feel his unease in the sudden stillness that came over him, in the way he held himself motionless. Countless times this had been Kamiko's only warning. Uila and Kamiko were very much alike in such matters. Both were trained for war and for walking into unknown situations and unseen dangers.

A peculiar uncertainty was assailing her. Uila was no alarmist. His intuition and senses were as trustworthy and imperturbable as her own and as well honed by experience. It was telling that he sensed something she had not. Trouble has a knack for showing up in the moment of distraction. The forest was not quiet, it was silent and suddenly so.

The door of the cottage creaked and swung slowly open, sinking into the shadows of the interior, revealing nothing. The patchwork of late-afternoon sunlight on the door hadn't dispelled the darkness inside. The worries, the trials of the road, the churning uncertainties of recent months, all of the distractions in Kamiko's mind vanished as a vapor in a headwind, trailing out behind. Tranquil focus enshrouded her, the calm of lucidity. She could handle the unknown. It was routine.

Beside her, Uila shuddered gently and loosed a held breath. His head sagged and his tight lips released into a sluggish horse grin. His hips shifted as one hind leg relaxed. He was fast asleep. Such a thing had never happened, was, in fact, deemed impossible by Kamiko.

She allowed the spark of anger in her chest to grow. Someone was here, invading her home with diabolique. She held her place for several silent moments, allowing those who would attack her to take careful aim. She would kindle their fears a hundredfold. Leaving her sword sheathed and tied to her saddle, she stepped forward. Her muscles and thoughts were relaxed, empty of the distraction of anticipation. The open door was an invitation she intended to accept.

Beyond the threshold was dark and cold, unnaturally so. As she stepped through the door, the full dark shifted out the threshold behind her, and familiar candles and her single-oil lamp cast the room in the soft glow of steady firelight and warmth. An old man reclined on Kamiko's settee, his feet propped toward a small dancing fire in the hearth.

A tide of understanding and relief filled her mind and pressed all thoughts of trouble away. Her chest swelled with the long-forgotten sweetness of joy. She bent her knees to the floor and touched her forehead to the smooth wood.

"Djinnasee," she whispered.

Feet were at her head place on the floor, without the sound of movement.

"Rise, child."

His voice was the kindest sound she'd known in a half-decade since last she had heard him speak.

"I would, my friend, but for my shame," she said without lifting her face. Djinnasee had never once in her presence offered idle banter, nor had he tolerated it from her. Nothing she said had ever surprised him.

His old voice was a soft buffer against the swelling of renewed emotions in her chest. "So certain of this shame that you cannot face me, my friend." It was a statement that encompassed things only she could know. Such was the way of Djinnasee. "Rise and speak of it."

She stood and came up with his ancient hand on her shoulder. Out of necessity, his hand slid to her arm as she straightened. He was no taller than a boy coming early into manhood, while Kamiko, formed of lean corded muscle, towered over him. His hair was silver white and unruly, hers black as gleaming onyx and hanging straight upon her shoulders and down her back like fine silk.

"You have killed him then?" he said with a soft sadness in his voice.

"I have." She hesitated, trying to keep the anger dwelling in her gut out of her voice. "And all who would follow him."

His dark eyes twinkled up at Kamiko, the knowledge residing there ancient beyond the age of the kingdom of Cairistonia.

"Then the matter is done, Kamiko, let it not still be before you."

She knew to say no more, but her spirit was not yet free of it. She doubted she would ever be free of it.

"He was my father," she said.

He considered her words as one who had lived long, the passing of time only incidental and unworthy of attention.

"Granted," he said at last, "however, that does not garner him clemency for the crime which begot you. His judgment was rendered when he destroyed all that was to become your heritage. And"—he raised his hand to add weight to his words—"it is true justice that you should be the one to serve sentence."

They were standing in Kamiko's front room, once Djinnasee's own home, given to her as a father gives a daughter of his means. The silence and the darkness of the open doorway cast an otherworldly aura upon the place. Their voices seemed muffled by it, the light from the flickering candles muted.

"What have you desired from him these years, Kamiko? What do you find yourself in want of, here and now?"

She replied harshly but without disrespect, "I wanted him to die. Now? I can think of nothing I want."

"And so he has, Kamiko Hoshi, so he has. But"—he emphasized the word with a gentle squeeze of her arm and held it—"where do you direct this rage still smoldering within you? You are a creature with a hunger for the just. Has justice not prevailed for such a hideous crime against one with such a peaceful nature as your mother possessed? What more can you do?"

"There is nothing left to do," she whispered.

"Nothing," he said.

She understood her old friend. He had drawn her to the truth of the matter. There was nothing left but to accept the reality of what was and live on, carrying the burden if she must, releasing it if she could. Justice assuaged none of the destruction left in the wake of treachery. Her mother had lived only long enough for Kamiko to be born, for the rape was brutal beyond measure, and her mother's spirit had been wholly broken. From the day of her birth, Djinnasee had raised Kamiko as his own child.

She gathered resolve around her then, newly found however harsh it may have been.

"So be it," she said. Djinnasee nodded in answer and released her arm. Another silence fell between them as her eyes moved around the familiar room.

She had very little in the way of possessions and almost nothing of mementos. A small table was pressed against one wall, flanked by a pair of low chairs too compact for her size. Beyond another low table beside the settee, there was no other furniture in the room. One could easily imagine that Kamiko spent little time living in the house.

"Kamiko," Djinnasee interjected quietly, "where is your talisman?" He could no longer hide the look of mischief from her nor the look of knowledge. And she knew better than to wonder how he knew to ask. Djinnasee, the man she considered her true father, was a prophet of God.

"For the first time in twenty-five years, I don't know. I would not simply misplace it. It was in my pack, then a few days later, it wasn't." She could never hide the suspicion on her face from Djinnasee. She said, "It doesn't matter, it was a simple trinket." She knew better.

"No simple trinket, Sister." He appeared to be holding a secret and a smile in check. "I will see it returned." And with a wink at her, he added, "When next you see me. Yes, that's it, your talisman shall come into your hand." She had long since given up trying to unravel his mysterious comments about things to come.

"It is only a keepsake, my friend. Though," she admitted, "my favorite bauble."

Her attention returned to Uila's odd behavior, and her eyes cut to the pitch-dark beyond the open door. It bothered her that she could not see him. The surreal darkness concerned her less than the fact that Uila had fallen asleep, she assumed, against his will. The darkness was surely connected to Djinnasee's presence; she'd seen it more than once. The mystery of why her horse had fallen asleep would wait.

She cocked her head and asked, "Djinnasee, why are you here?"

His deep dark eyes twinkled anew, his weathered face animated with almost childlike wonder as he began unfolding the design of purpose in his mind, drawing her to sit with him on the settee.

The kingdom of Cairistonia was in the waning of her long and glorious life, a thing of much conversation between father and daughter. Centuries ago, Djinnasee had established a sisterhood of skilled warriors, an order of women dedicated to the Eternal. They were known simply as the Order.

Kamiko was one of the foremost of the sisterhood, and though undesired, her fame upon the battlefield was widespread across the vast kingdom. Her presence alone was known to dissuade the potential for war among rival clans and even neighboring nations in dispute. She was a hero to the common folk, though such was the driving nature of the sisterhood. Djinnasee had seen it so from the beginning, more than 2,500 years earlier.

"You will escort our young sister Siruis of Marjan to King Titus's throne chamber to deliver a message."

Little more than a name of slight familiarity to Kamiko, Siruis of Marjan had become gossip worthy only a few months before Kamiko's eastward departure from the kingdom. Rumors of visions and portents of desolation followed in her wake. Kamiko had dismissed the fanciful chatter offhandedly.

King Titus Phiemous XI was drunk in the common way of mighty kings, intoxicated by power and self. He was a godling of his own design, thus at constant odds with Djinnasee.

Djinnasee chuckled. "The whole of the royal court is in uproar, the king and queen at the forefront." His mirth was short-lived. As he stared into the dwindling fire, she thought she sensed a certain resignation, a foreboding in his demeanor. Such was not the way of Djinnasee. After a short silence, he whispered, "The fall of mighty Cairistonia has been marked."

Kamiko waited a few moments as the words settled in her gut. He'd spoken it as if a fact. "You are not in the habit of spreading rumors, Father."

"Indeed."

"Siruis has spoken this?"

"She has."

"What makes you think she is—"

He cut her off with a terse but gentle bark. "Who is telling you this now?"

She accepted the reprimand in the spirit it was given. If ever she had a worldly master, it was Djinnasee. "Have you seen this as well?"

He shook his head slowly. "I have not. Rather not in the prophetic sense you mean, not like Siruis has. I have anticipated the likelihood for a very long time, watched the unfolding of the inevitable. For a thousand years, the kingdom has been waxing and waning, the decline ever outpacing the increase. When Titus was first crowned, I charged him with the task of turning the state of the kingdom from its course of self-destruction." He leaned forward, picked a spit of wood from the hearth, and tossed it into the fire, then added in a quiet voice, "He has not."

Kamiko's thoughts returned to Djinnasee's directive for her. No doubt Titus greatly feared the rumors concerning Siruis.

"Are you telling me Siruis is an oracle...of God?"

"I am."

"And you believe she is in danger of reprisal from the king."

"King Titus is in league with things he cannot understand. And yes, Kamiko, Siruis is in mortal danger. Her words have stricken to the quick of the king's heart and wounded his pride."

"'In league'? What do you mean, Father? In a spiritual sense?"

He spoke in a near-whisper, "Yes, child."

Djinnasee had been Kamiko's spiritual mentor for all the days of her life. The declaration was profound in light of all he had taught her about the nature of things unseen, of powers and principalities beyond the realm of human perception. They grew silent for several long minutes.

Kamiko was one of very few sisters of the Order who had pursued a military career. She'd risen to the second-highest military position in the kingdom and, at forty-two, still held the rank of lieutenant marshal. She knew King Titus and his queen as well as anyone, having stood as the king's personal guard for half a decade.

"I have been a long time gone, my friend."

"Events move quickly," he said, nodding, though his eyes bore upon things unseen.

"What is it, Djinnasee? What is her message?"

He seemed, at first, not to hear her words. She waited patiently as his eyes glittered over countless thoughts, the darkening room and tiny flickers of near-spent candles no longer within his perception.

"She will decry his sentence and declare him an unfit monarch to his face. She will allot his death-moment to a fixed point in time." He raised his hand, again to add weight to his words. "And she will likely show him how he dies."

Kamiko felt her neck grow hot, tiny pinpricks coursing over her scalp in a sweeping wave. The dynamics of her own troubles were suddenly slight. Her mind played over the scene in the throne chamber as she imagined it.

"She will be charged as a heretic and beheaded before the tide bells ring the close of day."

"That is my belief," Djinnasee said.

Now Kamiko understood the situation, as well as her role, in greater depth.

"It will not come to pass, Old Father, this I declare before God."

His eyes flicked momentarily to the side. "That is my belief as well, Kamiko."

The quick cascade of many thoughts stirred in Kamiko's mind. "Where is High Marshal Alexander?"

"Jonathan is with King El`Thorn of the Seven Clans. There has been an incursion of savages from the clan's westing border."

This was news she did not expect. "Surely not Chief Nukto?"

"It would appear so."

"Why, Djinnasee? The Seven Clans have been at peace with the Moshue for two decades."

"I do not know, daughter."

Kamiko cast him a questioning look. She could count the times he'd spoken those words on one hand, with fingers to spare. He ignored the silent gesture and continued.

"The high marshal has gone there in support of King El`Thorn and to resolve the mystery." Djinnasee shook his head. "Alexander has chafed sore beneath King Titus's yoke of late. He has sought every opportunity for distance these many months. Our friend is not well suited for courtly drama. He is a warrior without purpose in this lingering peacetime."

"Will he oppose me to King Titus?" She thought about the question and clarified the purpose of asking. "When I bring Siruis before His Majesty under my own terms?"

"He will not. Blessed be Jonathan Alexander for hearing my counsel. He knows your heart to the core, Kamiko, and fears no harm from your hands. You, above all others, he trusts with the king's well-being."

She knew this well enough, though it bore saying aloud. The high marshal of Cairistonia's vast army was often compelled into that which he would otherwise avoid. Should King Titus command Alexander to bear his sword against Kamiko, he would not hesitate nor would he offer quarter.

Still the questions flowed unchecked in her mind. She had been removed from the cares of society for so long her normal bulwark was unprepared. She forced the thoughts from her mind and returned her attention to the present. Kamiko knew Djinnasee would leave no consideration untouched in his own mind and trusted the road to be laid with every necessity. Such was the way of Djinnasee.

"Where is Siruis of Marjan?"

CHAPTER 2

He smiled up at her and inclined his head toward the open door. Late-afternoon sunlight now bathed the threshold in golden glow, the unnatural darkness gone. At that very moment, a pale dapple-gray pony came to be framed in the doorway, bearing a small woman seated side-manner in the saddle.

Kamiko rose and offered Djinnasee her hand. They stepped to the door together, him passing through before her. Uila's flaccid pose suddenly stiffened, as if he had been caught sleeping at his post, and the dark warhorse snorted and sidestepped at the sudden presence. Kamiko gave him a quiet low whistle, barely audible but known to Uila as an assurance that no threat loomed. His assent was immediate, though he now held himself rigid and ready.

Djinnasee extended his hand toward the woman and said to Kamiko, "This is Siruis of Marjan."

Kamiko turned her attention to the rider, quickly reading the girl's manner and accoutrement, though her face was mostly hidden beneath a hooded cloak. She appeared to be a small youthful woman who carried her bearing as one wishing to remain unnoticed. Even now she showed reluctance to turn and face Kamiko, revealing only one eye with the slightest turn of her head. But as Siruis's crystal-blue eye fell on Kamiko, her perspective shifted again.

A person holds hope in the belief that those things held secret are truly hidden from all others, that only those things admitted openly are of common knowledge. It is a mantle behind which all people rightfully and fearfully dwell. In that single moment, Kamiko's barrier was gone, and standing in its place was Siruis, peering in.

The veil of Kamiko's soul tore away, the whole of who she was laid bare. An unbidden shudder rippled through her, outward, inward, nothing hidden, even to the core of her deepest recesses. Every secret and dark knowledge, every bright joy all rushed forward in a torrent of violent thriving color, the tapestry of everything woven to form Kamiko. In that one moment, she saw all of herself.

She felt her feet shifting without conscious consent. Purely on the instinct of a warrior, Kamiko deemed the intrusive presence to be an attack, sorcery bent on divulging her starkest weakness.

Siruis's eye, unable to avert itself, sparked the first fear Kamiko had known since childhood. Her careful restraints, the ironclad control over muscle and will, fell away and let loose the most deadly creature in the land. Djinnasee's voice thundered from within the maelstrom of rage and fear coiling inside as she leapt. It was a cord of familiarity connecting her to reality.

The pony shied from Kamiko and reared, prancing backward on hind legs. As the young woman reined over, the motion broke the terrible soul-wrenching gaze, and Kamiko felt an immediate tightening of the cord. Kamiko saw the frail young woman, Siruis of Marjan, lose her place in the saddle and begin to fall.

The fury and confusion sweeping through Kamiko's chest abated only a small measure before movement caught her eye, fast and fluid from the cover of the forest. This brought her to a hard stop three short hops from the pony, as Uila's dark mass came into her field of view with a leap and an angry grumble.

An avalanche of pale flesh sailed in a low fast arch, coming not toward Kamiko but to the ground beside the dappled pony. Huge hands reached out and caught the falling woman, before she came fully clear of the saddle, and drew her into a broad chest, bulging with power.

A true-blood giant rose to his feet beyond the frightened pony, the woman enfolded within his mass. Kamiko held herself in check, shuddering with the fiery wrath still storming in all her being, physical and spiritual. The warrior was fully awake, fierce and ready and loath to withdraw without spending much energy.

So it was that one corner of Kamiko's mouth twitched when she saw that the giant kept to his toes, his momentum already shifting in her direction. She chose a single-strike tactic and set her feet, twisting her soft boots against the ground to gain that tiny edge of traction. She would have to drop him with her first move or face more trouble than she was prepared for.

Beyond the fact that he was easily half again taller than Kamiko, he appeared to be simply a strong man in the plain clothing common to the area. He wore the garb of a woodsman, loose breeches, a woven shirt stretched tight across the bulge of his chest, and a loose tunic with a hood thrown back, revealing long locks of golden hair which enshrouded his face almost entirely. His build was thick in every proportion, even considering his enormous size.

With gentle care, the giant set Siruis on her feet. Then with speed which belied his mass, he lunged at Kamiko, the headlong charge of a giant bull, massive fists out to either side. This was Kamiko's primary language, and fast, though, he was, her violence was ready.

She leaned a finger's breadth leftward and saw the tell in his bright eyes and the inclination to meet her there. She drew rightward with split-second reflex, noting the oncoming giant's readiness to follow. He took both feints to heart. Then without giving away her intention to do so, she sprang straight up and snapped her feet up tightly beneath her.

The giant wailed as he passed under her, realizing too late that he had missed the target. Kamiko shouted high and clear and stabbed both leather-booted heels into the thick base of the giant's muscled neck.

The force of the kick was sufficient to send Kamiko higher into the air in a long arch and the giant onto the hard ground face-first. His thick legs flew up behind him, and his bare feet slapped like big slabs of meat against his rump. She sailed away, turning as she flew so that she landed facing him at the ready. All motion ceased on the instant she touched the ground. The giant lay sprawled on his face and chest, unmoving but for his heaving back, his legs now straight out on the ground.

A high fear-laced wail of desperation tore from Siruis's mouth. Uila leapt to stand over the prone giant, hooves coming to bear, and Djinnasee howled a command to cease. Kamiko chirped a piercing whistle to still the warhorse, belaying the imminent hoof thrashing. The dappling pony skittered to the woods' edge with nostrils flaring and eyes rolling in panic, dancing like a child too frightened to run.

Uila obeyed but with obvious reluctance, drawing a sharp command from Kamiko.

"Uila," she called. "Avert!"

He slung his head and backed away.

"Retrieve." Kamiko raised her open palm toward the dappling. Uila trotted to the pony, bickering deep and quiet to still the frightened animal, which, in turn, lowered her head with a snort. She followed the warhorse back to the clearing and fell to a nervous quiet.

Siruis moved to the giant, her small voice on the verge of hysteria, though laced with anger. "What have you done?" She fell to her knees beside his massive head, whispering to his face in breathless terror, "Jerim, Jerim!"

The giant lay unmoving, though his breath was now slower, less frantic. One arm had been pulled hard beneath the fall and lay twisted at his shoulder. With the other he had reached for Kamiko, and it lay straight out from his body like a fallen tree trunk. The field of rolling muscle across his back strained against his clothing, even at rest. By Kamiko's estimation, he easily outweighed her by triple, his shoulders nearly as broad as the whole of her arm span. He was the natural-born opposite of the small woman at his side.

Kamiko knew of only one other true-blood giant, Bartolamew Kane. Massive, dark, and old, Bartol knew ways no man could fathom, save the only man he named master—Djinnasee. Beyond Djinnasee, Kamiko counted Bartol as her only true friend. She drew several deep breaths, calming the last of her fury as Djinnasee knelt at Siruis's side, speaking kindly words.

"He is not hurt, child. His nerves will awaken shortly."

Siruis yanked the cloak tie at her throat, pulled the wrap from her shoulders, and threw it to the ground. A thick mane of reddish-blond hair partially concealed her face and was bound into a long tail down her back. Her hands moved gently over Jerim's face and eased his long golden hair aside. Kamiko could see the youthful silkiness of his skin, flushed crimson from exertion. Djinnasee turned to look at Kamiko and nodded down at the giant, silently asking for her help.

She felt hesitancy rising in her chest, a constricting tightness in her throat. The flood of memories was still rife with sharp heat. Once long buried and dulled by passing years, she now held the whole of them in one moment. The failures and losses weighed heavily against the joys. She'd never imagined such a stark tally possible. The harsh perspective sent a wave of despair through her, and pain flared in her chest.

Her memories were of battle, of quenching the lives of men and no few women, of blood stench and the wails of death beneath her sword and fists. Her mind reckoned the outriding wave of good from her actions, but her eyes rarely—if ever—beheld it. Her legend was that of holy knight, benefactor of the innocent masses; she was their stronghold, their moat of fierce strength against evil men. She was death incarnate, relentless and brutal. The good she had seen with her own eyes was no more than a cup of water weighed against that deluge of horror.

"It will be a few moments before he is able to rise," she said. "He is not injured."

*****

Kamiko had no reason to stay any longer. She was still packed from more than two years on the road. The last few months had been easy, returning home because nothing else had demanded her attention. Uila was well rested and anxious to be underway; the brief excitement after so long at ease had sparked his warrior blood anew, and his feet were restless beneath him. Djinnasee had brought provisions enough to allow the trio immediate departure, and it had taken Kamiko less than ten minutes to pack the food and water into the empty stores of her travel gear.

Jerim managed to shake the stinging numbness from his limbs and get Siruis back onto the pony. Both held a nervous silence as they readied to continue their long journey. Not a single word was spoken until Kamiko and Siruis were seated atop their respective mounts. Jerim was standing like a tower over Siruis, somehow managing to scowl at Kamiko without looking at her.

Only Djinnasee felt the need to speak, his old hands lifted upward and his eyes sparkling with what Kamiko recognized as pure joy.

"So it begins, my friends." He chuckled. "Let those principalities who thrive on fear be well fed henceforth, for never has a troika such as this been released upon the world! And I pray before God Almighty that each of you retain mercy and compassion within your core." His eyes came to rest on Kamiko. "Without compassion, the world and all that dwell upon it shall perish."

Kamiko heard the inflection clearly. Djinnasee was not stating what he believed could happen; he was declaring what *would* transpire. He was warning her. There was nothing remotely metaphorical about his words. He considered the destruction of the world to be a definable possibility, and by the way he held her in his gaze as she mulled over it, he intended the warning to be taken as fact. Coming from any other living human, it would not have felt like a mule kick to her chest. But Djinnasee was a prophet.

A hard shudder rippled through her body and her mouth went suddenly dry. Jerim's head came up and turned toward her, a curious look on his face. The motion reminded her of Bartol, who could sense someone drawing a breath through the feel of the ground beneath his feet.

Djinnasee offered her a knowing look and turned toward Siruis. He walked over to the pony and placed his old hand on hers. They shared a silent but deep conversation before he stepped away and strolled to the door of the cottage. As he crossed the threshold, the door drifted silently closed behind him, as if nudged by a low gentle breeze.

Kamiko could easily imagine opening the door to find the cottage empty, but she eased Uila into a slow trot, turning him directly into the lowering sun.

CHAPTER 3

King Titus's throne chamber was a half-year journey to the southwest, across the entire breadth of the vast land under the sole reign of the errant monarch. Siruis and Jerim were staying a steady hundred paces behind Kamiko and Uila. The young sister was clearly intimidated by Kamiko, and both women carefully averted their eyes from each other. Kamiko wondered how Siruis would manage, being privy to all Kamiko had seen. No doubt she would have troubled dreams for months. *Serves her right*, Kamiko thought.

The giant bore what seemed a permanent angry scowl on his boyish face and kept his eyes on Kamiko, almost without relent. And though they kept their mounts at a slow run through the long dusk, Jerim maintained an easy trot close to Siruis's side. Kamiko set their course in a direct line to the southwest, cutting through the forest-veined plains of the wilds. The well-traveled roads of the kingdom would offer nothing they required, be it hearth or stores. In truth, Kamiko had no desire to be among people for a while longer; she still needed open spaces around her.

The seed Siruis had planted in Kamiko was growing, a sharp awareness held at bay until now. It was a truth she'd known for all her years but had not seen in so stark a light. Kamiko was a woman as a natural fact, but she was in no manner *womanly*. Her hands were callous and weathered dark, her strength impressive, even when weighed against the most capable men in Alexander's famed military. And though she had once reveled in the knowledge that she had bested Alexander's champions in the royal games, she had grown to feel a sharp revulsion in the fact.

She had long since retired the armor, helm, gauntlets, and weapons array of her knighthood. Such was the garb of the battlefield. At times she still wore her leather breastplate and her longsword, but in truth, she considered them to be overkill. Fist and fury had served with sufficiency against all but one. Her armor was well oiled and carefully kept, scarred with the nicks and repairs of long service and many battles. Now she only wore it when necessity dictated and kept it secured in her pack. Her traveling garb was much the same as Jerim's, loose fit, comfortable, and in the natural tones of the wild.

Her thoughts again brushed over the scene forever burned into her mind—her father's band of brigands, scattered in hundreds of bloody heaps, with him on his hands and knees as she took his head. She had walked into their midst in full sight, sword and fist and burning rage unfettered.

Uila lunged forward with a start, ears erect, nostrils flaring. Kamiko felt her legs drawn tight against his ribs, in reaction to her returning anger, and forced the dark memory away with a deep breath. She patted his thick neck and spoke in whispers until they both settled.

What had the young sister done to her? Her thoughts had never been so distracted, her peace so tainted. She felt disoriented to the very core. As if drawn by the need for distraction, her eyes rose and found the western sky. The beauty of it pulled at her and calmed her a little.

A line of distant clouds hung low across the horizon, draped like a silken veil of light coral enfolded with the shades of a faded rose. The southern tail stretched away beyond sight in a wispy train, but the mass grew thicker and darker by degrees toward the north. Above them was clear sky, deepening azure. The sun was only minutes below the veiled horizon when Kamiko brought them to a stop at the edge of a small forest grove and dismounted.

As Siruis reined the pony to a stop, Kamiko could see Jerim had not been tapping his strength in the slightest during the long run. His breath was slow and easy, his muscles at rest yet as solid as carved granite. Such was no surprise. Bartol had once run the entire breadth of the kingdom, five hundred leagues, from the Black River to the Antarius River, without stopping for food, rest, or water.

Kamiko could see in the gentle way Jerim helped Siruis from the pony that he cared a great deal for her. He was no servant, no guard assigned to watch over her. The young giant was personally committed to her and deeply entrenched with love for the woman. Kamiko could only recognize such a thing from a distance. Love was a foreign land to her, as frozen and uncharted as the northern wastelands beyond the great mountains.

He kept himself between Kamiko and Siruis, as the young sister went into the privacy of thick undergrowth nearby. When she returned, he hovered close by her as she worked the girth loose, and then he lifted the saddle clear of the pony. It was tiny in his fingers, weightless. All the while, he kept a watchful eye on Kamiko, as if she were a bandit waiting for an opportune moment to strike.

Kamiko turned her attention to Uila, removed his tack, and curried him down. This was her favorite part of each day, to pay service back to her handsome companion. She took her time with his care, checking old scars and looking for new ones.

In some parts of the kingdom, Castlehaven in particular, Uila was as well known as Kamiko. He was easy to remember, not only because he was so big but by the odd markings of his dark coat. He was a deep dark brown for the most part, but his withers, back, and down his shoulders were brindled with black, his massive face a black mask from nose to crown. The only marking anywhere not rendered in dark brown or jet black was a small shock of pink skin resembling a lightning bolt on the end of his nose, between nostril and lip. Thus his name, Uila—lightning—a perfect fit for his manner. Uila required neither tether nor hobbles, rather he served as sentinel as he grazed the perimeter of the campsite.

Kamiko busied herself with the preparations of their camp, and soon a small fire crackled and popped, and the scent of woodsmoke drifted into the windless warmth of the summer night. The faintest whisper of dusk remained, west of the darkening sky, and stars were beginning to flourish onto its stage with their slow march.

Siruis and Jerim were still set apart, conversing in hushed tones, hers a quiet imploring voice, his full of deep unhappy grumbles. Kamiko rose from the fire and stepped toward the pair. She would break the tension between them and be done with it. No more traveling alone.

Jerim rose to his full height and tried to look as menacing as his young face allowed. Kamiko ignored him and walked straight to Siruis standing at his side. She towered over the small woman and felt her presence to be too domineering, so she knelt to one knee and nodded her head in a slight bow, as yet unable to meet her eyes. Her own reluctance, that odd feeling of fear, troubled her to the core.

"Sister, please join me at the fire. I will prepare a meal. We have much to discuss."

*****

The simple meal was taken in silence, save for a civil *thank you*. Siruis sipped down the small bowl of meatless soup with obvious hunger and ate the heavy black bread quickly. Jerim sat on his haunches to one side of her and tried to keep his face bent into a constant glare meant for Kamiko. He succeeded only to a point. Kamiko had arranged a folded blanket for Siruis to sit on, while Kamiko occupied her own low camp seat, a three-legged stool stretched with soft deer hide. It was her only luxury. The intensity of Jerim's scowl proved difficult to maintain, and soon enough, his features softened behind a curtain of golden hair. He ate nothing.

The pair looked oddly well matched; Jerim's muscled bulk drew a sharp contrast to Siruis's small delicacy, his fine golden hair a mane of natural boyish curls, hers a barely contained bush of henna. Both were beautiful. Apart from the drastic difference in size, both had faces of youthful whiteness, blush of cheek, features smooth and round. Kamiko felt at odds with that. Her face was slim and pallid, framed in black hair, straight and limp from the root. Beauty was certainly not part of her legend.

"Thank you, Kamiko Hoshi, for the meal," Siruis said. "I was more famished than I allowed myself to admit. I have not taken food today."

Kamiko felt the strain of her smile as she replied, "Forgive me riding so far, Sister. Had I known you were hungry, we would have stopped much sooner." Still she could not meet those crystal blue eyes. "Would you like a bit more?"

"Oh, yes, thank you, Kamiko Hoshi." She held out her bowl as Kamiko extended the dripping spoon ladle.

"Please, Sister, call me Kamiko." How could this small woman be the cause of the fear she was feeling? Was her hand trembling?

"Kamiko, it is I who should be seeking your forgiveness."

Kamiko almost missed the bowl entirely, spilling half the soup on the ground.

"Oh, excuse me," she said, as the thought *avoid those eyes* screamed in her mind. Her hands found a towel, and she reached to catch the soup dribble on Siruis's fingers.

"Kamiko," Siruis spoke again, this time imploring, "Sister." And she touched Kamiko's hand with her own.

Kamiko visibly flinched as her heart pounded suddenly in her chest, a sensation all but forgotten in her life. The wooden spoon fell at the edge of the fire, but only for an instant. She plucked it up with a battle-quickened blur of her hand. Her honed instincts were fully engaged, adrenaline pulsing in her veins. She felt Jerim lean forward.

"Kamiko." Came the soft voice again, filled with kindness, with longing. In her mind, Kamiko knew no attack was coming and held herself in shuddering stillness, breathing short silent gasps.

"What have you done to me?" she asked the question not of Siruis but to unseen demons, unhinged thoughts.

"She has done nothing, warrior!" said Jerim. His first words in Kamiko's presence were filled not only with defiance but also with compassion. The texture of his voice was deep, yet it held the tightness of lingering youth. "It be her bane. That which makes her prey, hunted…a criminal by declaration of the king."

The statement struck Kamiko. Something in the way Jerim had spoken touched a familiar part of her. She had no doubt he was colored by the presence of Bartol in his life. He spoke with Bartol's odd dialect, as one unfamiliar with societal influence. Jerim would lose the white cleanliness of smooth skin and golden hair, and like Bartol, he would become dark and wild, beyond the fierce of nature's creatures, his voice a dreadful rumble.

Siruis had fallen silent and was peering up at Kamiko. She was no sorcerer. Kamiko's perspective was shifting again, she could feel the approaching wave. But it was not an attack; her fear was unfounded, and the churning of distress in her heart began to settle.

"Please, explain," Kamiko said, as she looked up at Jerim's face, aglow in the faint light of the fire. His anger was gone, replaced with deep sadness as he gazed down at the top of Siruis's head. He leaned back to the ground beside her, sitting cross-legged, with his thick arms resting on his knees.

The night was still and quiet. The crackling of the small fire, the summer song of insects, and the distant whisper of night winds across the grass plains offered the only relief from silence. The sky was a black ocean dotted with silvery stars, moonless, but with an opaque brightness. Kamiko's own private constellation, Koralilia, was just appearing in the east. Days were on the wane, a full month beyond equinox, another hot summer in retreat.

Siruis placed her tiny hand on Jerim's arm, offering her own explanation.

"It is something I have no control over, Sister," she said.

Kamiko looked at the whiteness of Siruis's throat. It was the best she could manage.

"Try to *not* feel the breath of wind on your skin or to *not* hear the sound of night birds. Even if you close your ears, their song rings in your mind, and the winds call from your desires when you are beneath the hot sun."

Kamiko could feel Siruis's gaze on her face, a force drawing her into the oblivion that had struck her to the core with fear. It would be impossible to resist Siruis's eyes for long.

"I am drawn down, my Sister. My eyes see the horror of people's deepest secrets, like their eyes see the color of my hair. They loathe, they hate, and they despise *me* for what *they* have become. They will kill me if they can." She paused and took a deep shuddering breath. Jerim was motionless at her side, staring at the ground. Siruis continued, "I do not ask for it, and I am no sorcerer, as many have come to believe. The spirit of God speaks to me. Sometimes in the form of a man with sweat on his brow and dust on his feet, sometimes within my own thoughts. I simply obey."

Siruis's voice was mesmerizing. Kamiko felt the gates opening against her will, the gates of fear and pain, the agony of an empty life, kept safely behind a fortress of knowledge. The knowledge that she was doing right, that emptiness was a worthy cost. She raised her eyes to meet Siruis's.

"I now know everything about you, and this knowledge is the source of your great fear. You are Child of the Star Tortoise, the ancient meaning of your name, Kamiko Hoshi." She pointed to the glittering sky, toward the center of Koralilia. "It is not a true constellation. Only you, Djinnasee, and Bartol even see it. I tell you this so you will know I speak the unseen truth." Kamiko's gaze was drawn to the stars. Koralilia was formed of three celestial triangles depicting roughly half of a sea turtle, as if it was rising from the ocean into the sky.

"I have seen your deepest dreams go into the past without coming true, felt the void where your mother belongs as my own emptiness. I now carry the vision of your father in my heart, an aching wound, forever bleeding." She dropped her hand.

"I understand the longing, Kamiko, the ugly disfigured self. There is a constant nagging that cries against who you are, what you have become."

Kamiko was not falling away. Visions were not sweeping her soul into that hell of self she'd been impaled upon earlier. Siruis was inside her as a silent beacon, speaking to the Woman long lost within the Warrior. In a remote corner of her mind, she felt cool wetness on her face and the swell of her throat, her chest constricted. So long forgotten.

"You wear your armor in full view, and you will stand fast. You shun what would be, what *could* be, for what *must* be. Your heart is tempered by fire so that you need not fear the flames of despair. Yet despair is an insidious poison, slow and subtle. It crawls beneath the surface—the tendrils wrap around the whole of your being." Siruis was leaning forward now, her soft hands on Kamiko's wrists. Her breath brushed Kamiko's face as she spoke. Kamiko watched glistening trails slipping down from Siruis's eyes.

"Sister Kamiko, in you I have seen that one spark, that willingness to see yourself as you are, and accept it at face value. You do not and will not hate me. Djinnasee has placed us together on this road, lead where it may, that you and I be whole."

Kamiko's breath was still coming in short gasps. Her chest trembled as the fortress fell away and tears streamed down her cheeks. She felt she had known the depth of those blue eyes for all of her life.

"And now, I must stand before the king..." Siruis's voice trailed away, her hands trembled on Kamiko's wrists, her eyes closed.

Kamiko tried to speak. Words did not come, only deep feelings, a new flame awakening. Siruis looked suddenly back into Kamiko's eyes, crystal blue orbs seeking the depth of Kamiko's dark emerald. A smooth calm swept over them, a flood of sweet water to cool the burn. Breathless seconds passed. Kamiko felt a vast power in Siruis's spirit pour thundering into her own body, felt her own spirit bellowing inside Siruis, also vast and powerful. The night song of the plains vanished as all things physical drew to an immediate silent stop, as if time itself had paused.

A mountain rose silent and swift beneath them, thrusting them upward through the high clouds of some unknown distant land. In Kamiko's right hand, a sword writhed, shrieking violence. With it, she touched the face of the mountain and cracked it from crown to root.

Both sisters jumped where they sat, now back over the small fire in the darkness. Night winds were stirring, and myriad insects still sang without relent. The two sisters of the Order were clasping hands, physically holding to the bond that had linked their spirits together. Jerim did not move in the slightest.

"What was that, Sister? What did we see?"

Siruis's hands were calm. "What will be."

Chapter 4

They had twenty-three days of quiet riding after the strange vision. The shriek was still in her ears, and the heavy jolt still tingled in her hand. More than once, she'd awakened during the small hours of the morning from a deep troubled sleep, unable to recall the dark dream that woke her but with the lingering reverberation of some powerful thing in her hand.

Kamiko cycled around a wide gambit of emotions, time and again, through what was mostly solitude, with only Uila's quiet presence beneath her. Jerim had spoken enough words within her earshot to fill a glove, and Siruis was in almost-constant whispered conversation with someone Kamiko could not see. That was well enough; solitude was what she wanted. It gave her time to think.

She spent a lot of that time thinking about Bartol. Jerim's presence brought many reminders to her. The two were so alike in their bearing and physical grace.

The end of another day was fast approaching, and once set, the sun would mark the point on the horizon that the morning's course would follow. They were making for the ancient temple ruins of Ferith-Dale. From there, they would follow a more direct westerly course, keeping the setting sun some degrees south of their track. Kamiko had kept their path bearing just south of a wide forest, skirting the slower yet more direct route through the woods, thereby avoiding a line of settlements and villages which had sprung up along one of the well-traveled roads connecting east and west. Siruis should be kept out of sight as long as possible.

Kamiko was grateful for the task at hand, yet the constant ruminations over her father had long since grown maddening and served no purpose she could conjure. Djinnasee's directive was no small affair, and her thoughts were muddled with the complexity of it. She held no illusions as to the depths the king was willing to go to set his way upon the order of things. Without a doubt, Titus had already ordered Siruis's capture.

She glanced over her shoulder, thinking how the motion had become a new habit, to constantly check on her odd traveling companions. Her eyes met Jerim's for the thousandth time and avoided Siruis's in like number. They were steady at fifty paces behind. Siruis was standing in his cupped palm, her feet near his waist, with her back leaning against his shoulder. Her eyes were closed, and her mouth was not moving. She looked like a small finely crafted porcelain doll. The sun shone on her face and lit Jerim's mass and golden hair with a bright glow. The pony trotted sleepily, as if entranced, at his side.

Kamiko had played out every scenario she could conceive of each approaching encounter with the king's Royal Militia. They would have several such meetings before reaching King Titus's throne chamber, of that she had no doubt.

And therein lay the real dilemma; she could not raise her hand to Titus, certainly not against his person or even to those under his command. She was fairly certain Jerim felt no such restraint. If anyone attempted to lay a hand on Siruis, be it militia or mercenary, Jerim would not go easy on them. To think otherwise would be folly.

And once in the throne room, this would be no simple petition of the king. Even if Kamiko went in under parley, Titus would have an entire legion crammed into the throne chamber to keep them from leaving once Siruis delivered the message. They needed to be in Titus's presence suddenly, inside his impenetrable security unawares, a thing of no small concern.

Kamiko's approach to the great city of Castlehaven would need to be well planned. They would cross the central wilds to the westernmost edge of the plains, pass through the southern arm of the Great Cairistonian Jungle, and turn south into civilization at Flavin Township, an area considered the outskirts of the northwest.

She would seek out the sisterhood in Flavin, a return to Mars Knoll. There they would rest for a week and recover from the journey before they make the last leg of the trip. It would give Kamiko a chance to adjust her senses to the bustle of city life and the press of people all around her. Just thinking of the constant droning of senseless chatter made her tremble.

What a reaction to have—Kamiko Hoshi, Paladial Protector of the people, shuddering at the thought of having to touch someone and much the more for a crowd of lethargic marketers and drifting noonday drunkards. The more disturbing thought in her mind was that she'd once felt full at ease in a crowded market or a noisy pub, but now her patience had fully waned.

She shook the distraction from her thoughts and turned in the saddle, expecting to see Jerim and Siruis at the usual fifty paces behind but found them stopped. Siruis was again seated sidesaddle on the pony, and Jerim was crouched yet still towering near her side. A small dark bird was fluttering, frantic, right in front of Jerim's face, and for all Kamiko could tell, she was watching a conversation unfold, the tiny bird bickering shrill and fast. Jerim was nodding throughout, obviously drawing a real-world conclusion from the chattering bird. He turned suddenly to Siruis and spoke, then cast Kamiko a dark foreboding look before he bounded off. Around him, the tall grasses came momentarily alive with the breathy sound of wings as a small flock of dark field birds rose into his fast wake and gave chase. He landed on his toes and fingertips for an instant and sprang again. In moments, he was gone from sight, plunging into the forest thicket three hundred paces away.

Siruis reined her pony over and nudged her into a quick trot, bringing her toward Kamiko, and spoke as she drew to a halt.

"There is trouble to the north," she said, pointing the direction Jerim had gone. "Something big is moving through the forest. He thinks it may be men on horses. He will return shortly." Her voice trailed off as her eyes came to rest—on what Kamiko could not tell. She followed Siruis's gaze to an unremarkable place on the ground.

"Sister?" Kamiko asked.

"A veil is being lifted," Siruis said. "Even as the king searches the breadth of the kingdom."

Now Kamiko's attention was abruptly divided. The question on her lips shifted from Jerim's actions. "What do you mean the veil is being lifted?" She guided Uila around in front of Siruis to place herself in Siruis's line of sight. "Sister, please tell me what you mean." The possibility of a band of men moving through the forest on horseback had taken on an entirely different flavor with Siruis's odd statement. Kamiko's first thought was that the band would be Royal Militia, combing the territory for Siruis. Now she was uncertain.

"No, Kamiko, not *the* veil, the Lord has not yet come. There are many veils which dwell in the realm of knowledge, this is but one being drawn aside," she said. "It is *your* veil, Sister, the one covering you these few years. You have been hidden from friend and foe alike, and you are about to be revealed." Her eyes came up to meet Kamiko's gaze with the last word.

Myriad thoughts burst into Kamiko's mind, all of which were vying for her undivided attention. The simple statement defined the last few years of her life with perfect accuracy. She'd been totally alone. It had not occurred to her until now that Djinnasee was the first friendly face she'd laid eyes upon in years.

"I have been traveling all over, Siruis. I saw no one of consequence. Most of that time, I was in the wilds of the Ten Nations, leagues beyond the Antarius."

"It is as you say. Yet here you are, returned to the kingdom. And the veil," Siruis said as she lifted her hand to point, "is being drawn."

Kamiko turned to look where Siruis was pointing and, for a moment, saw nothing. Then Jerim's mass appeared at the forest's edge, coming down from the higher reaches of the canopy in a great leap. A dark swirling cloud was trailing out behind him as he built speed, running for several powerful strides, then leaping, then running. He crossed the strip of grassy field and came to a quick stop near Siruis. The cloud was still heading their direction but had made it only halfway by the time Jerim spoke.

"A company of brigands makes haste for a human settlement just westward." He rumbled, deep and quiet.

"Essen," Kamiko added.

"I believe they are heavy with the spoils of thievery." As he spoke the last, the trailing cloud descended fully on the trio and chaos ensued. It came on them so quickly, Kamiko had only just begun to hear the shrill howl and the breathy roar of thousands of beating wings. Birds! And the flock had grown much bigger.

They swarmed overhead like a storm as Kamiko spent precious moments unstrapping her traveling gear and armor and letting them fall.

She had to shout to Jerim to be heard. "I leave her in your protection." The giant youth cocked his head in what looked like mild confusion. And then she was on Uila's back and was away. She gave him full rein, offering no guidance as the powerful warhorse drove toward the forest at a hard gallop. He knew how to thread his way through the jungle wilds without her help.

Dusk was coming more quickly beneath the canopy, the darkness deepening with every step. Uila's pace slowed as he came to a tighter grouping of smaller trees. He dodged through the grove with shallow hops and long, smooth lunges. Kamiko held herself draped over the saddlebow, her face low near the base of Uila's thick neck, her knees, hands, and elbows in tight, following his rhythm, his moves. She was a small weightless ball, centered one hand behind the crown of his withers, Uila a thundering, dancing terror beneath her.

They broke through the grove into a long narrow clearing, and Uila pressed ahead. Kamiko saw the clutter of ground fodder a moment before the horse's hooves left the ground in flight. But in that moment, she lifted her weight with a slight shove on her feet and rose upward in concert with his dark mass. In the sudden quiet of the long jump, both horse and rider heard the dull rumbling of many hoofbeats just ahead to the right. They touched ground at a full gallop, and Uila continued his headlong powerful charge. Soon he eased the pace to a fast run, lifting his head slightly as a signal to Kamiko to assume command. They were upon their quarry.

She drew the reins in just enough for him to feel the tug on the bit, letting him know she was in control. They veered rightward out of the clearing and again bounded into the forest, dropping to near half the pace when Kamiko reined him back. Once inside the canopy shadow, she slowed him again. It was too dark for more than a quick walk, but it was a short-lived frustration. They emerged onto the road Kamiko had been heading for, the air still thick with settling dust. She called the command for Uila to give unrestrained pursuit, let the bit slacken in his mouth once again, and leaned into the force of his stride.

In all their years together, Kamiko never lost the thrill of being atop the powerful warhorse when he gave chase. He could smell those they pursued, sense their fatigue. She could feel it in the way his hooves struck the ground with urgent and fierce energy. He'd been out of action too long.

The darkening road curved sharp to the right and down an easy slope, the first mark of local familiarity Kamiko had yet seen. She lay low against the saddlebow as Uila took the curve without slowing. The sun was gone, the sky a deep blue coming swiftly into full dark in the narrow clearing above her. The forest was thick on both sides and, over many short stretches of the road, formed near-black tunnels.

The settlement of Essen was just ahead. Kamiko had been through the small township many times over the years, and as everywhere in the span of the kingdom, she was well known to the people who lived there. A half-century ago, three large families had grown weary of the way of things in the kingdom, sold all of their holdings, and moved to just beyond the northern border, into the wilds, to start anew. They had dedicated their lives to the service of God and raised their children accordingly. Djinnasee had been elemental in helping to establish a working relationship between the people of Essen and the kingship. King Titus demanded only a single tribute per year to be paid at Hallows Eve and agreed to leave the settlement to its own devices. Essen had grown to more than three hundred souls. Now those souls were being threatened.

Kamiko's chest began to tighten as the rage inside her changed, growing into something entirely new to her. She could feel it roiling in her gut like an angry viper trapped inside a sack. She was no longer detached and in control. It felt alive.

Uila's head rose. His ears swiveled forward before he pressed them back against his head. Seconds later, Kamiko heard it too—hooves rumbling across a long wooden bridge, the last marker before arriving in Essen. She was too late to intercept the bandits before they reached the township.

"Uila." She growled. "Push it...*hard*!"

From deep inside the amazing horse, new strength awakened, and her call was answered. The wide bridge came into view as the jungle opened to the river, and the remnants of the waning light outlined the blackness of the tree line in the deepest darkest blue. The trailing end of the band was midway across when Uila's hooves struck board.

She saw shadows of men turning in their saddles, the telltale glinting of spear tip, sword, and helm. Their mounts were fatigued from travel, moving at a slow run and biting their bits against the commands of the riders. She knew the ways of highwayman, always expecting ambush. Instinct and experience told her these were not traveling merchants.

The calm focus did not come. Kamiko's thoughts did not fall into hushed silence, and her being did not find the familiar balance, the perfect center; the viper thrashed inside her gut, wild and violent. She had no intention of keeping it contained. As she engaged the fight, her senses became a cluttered jumble of flashing dark images, broken by cut-off shrieks and blood spray. Uila held himself under control, staying beneath Kamiko on dancing hooves. Then, and suddenly, silence.

Kamiko's head swam with the power of blind unfettered rage, nowhere near satiated. Fevered and hungry, the rage grew hotter as her thoughts were drawn to Essen. She was unable to think clearly, furious that these thieves would presume to destroy all that these people had worked so hard to build. Go to them! Let be what will be. She did not recall dismounting, but she was on her feet, standing near the embrasure of the stone wall. Below, the River Voerde swept by in its quiet rumble, only just coming into the realm of what she was aware of. It was high and swift and sounded angry to her, yet she managed to be calmed by it. She forced her mind and body to settle and allowed her years of training to engage. Her fury subsided to anger. In moments, she was atop Uila, once again coaxing him into a hard run.

As Uila stormed ahead into the full dark, a small voice in the depth of Kamiko's heart began to whisper. It was quiet and small, and it was not telling her to stop. Whether imagined or real, she perceived the presence of Siruis.

Essen came abruptly into view; a small field of sparkling points of firelight perched near the top of a low rise. The founders had chosen the location carefully. Essen was situated on the southern lee of the rise to keep the harsh winter winds at bay. The town was set at the edge of the great jungle where the plains began and spread southward for many leagues, bordered on the northeast by the Voerde. Hunting, farming, fishing, and timber were at the settlement's doorstep.

And now, trouble had crossed that threshold. Evil men were about to take at sword point what these people had worked their lives to gain. The sharp pain of anger again flared in Kamiko's gut as the fiery rage redoubled. Visions of her father's stronghold assailed her mind, and at the edge of awareness, she felt her voice rumbling a wild animal growl.

The main road led to the center of the township and continued straight out the other side. Men were running down the street, fear in all their movements but still weaponless. The town guard was not where it should have been. Some were shouting into open storefronts, which were immediately slammed shut and darkened. They heard Uila's thundering mass and leapt aside, shouting all the more as she passed by. It took only moments to traverse the distance between the edge of the town and the centermost courtyard.

She realized she was about to butcher more than fifty men right in front of the peaceful citizens of Essen, and the Woman lost in the dark clamor of her soul shrieked for mercy. The deep rage waned, and she felt an odd lightness descend, sufficient to confuse the Warrior within. And during that single moment, a point silently suspended in time between Uila's pounding hooves, she felt the separation in full. Two separate beings were residing in her body, at silent war with each other—Woman and Warrior. The din of passing time returned. She reined Uila to a hard stop out near the edge of the central open courtyard. Confusion flooded Kamiko's mind.

A great bonfire was burning in the center of the courtyard, just as she had seen in years past for midyear festivals, harvest celebrations, and weddings. Several long tables were lined up along one side, laden with carafes, mounds of bread, large platters of fruits and steaming meats, wedges of golden cheese, and all manner of stacked plates and mugs waiting to be filled. Torches mounted on long poles burned brightly in a ring all the way around the perimeter, many adorned with colorful streamers.

Kamiko's mind immediately recalled the seven men she'd left dead on the bridge, and a cold nausea curdled in her stomach. Doubt and dread washed into her mind. The shock of knowing the men she'd slaughtered could be innocent paralyzed her where she sat on the saddle.

Yet something wasn't right. It didn't add up in the light of reason. Those men had turned and attacked. The men of Essen would not have attacked; they would have defended. They would have demanded she identify herself and declare her intentions. Urgency flared anew in her chest, and her eyes scanned the finer details in a single sweep of the courtyard.

It was obvious that a party had been prepared, a great feast, but there was only a sparse crowd. No children could be seen anywhere and only a handful of the women. Rather than the lively festive chatter and noisy commotion she expected, the courtyard was still, and the gathering was quiet. Kamiko thought it strange that no one had marked her arrival, but then she heard a single voice rise above the murmur. "Hoshi!"

A wave of notice commenced and spread across the whole of the assembly, turning every pair of eyes to where she sat atop Uila. The hush was absolute. One face in particular drew her attention. It was as out of place in the gathering as a coyote in the henhouse.

"Broga Kipp," she whispered. Every doubt vanished from her mind, and a strange mix of relief and dread rose suddenly, her assessment finally settling on actual facts. The relief was now not having to guess or doubt. The dread was realizing that a brutal killer was indeed standing in their midst. Beyond that it was obvious the townsfolk were prepared for his arrival, that instead of coming in for a raid, he was returning. In that silent span, Kamiko assembled the whole of the puzzle into a cohesive picture in her mind.

Three wagons were lined up opposite the bonfire from the tables. The loads of two were bulging beneath enormous canvas sheets and were hitched to six-horse teams. Several of the rough dirty brigands were overseeing a group of younger townsmen, who had just begun tending the lathered teams. The horses were stamping and snorting, and their heads sagged to the ground from fatigue. The third was a carriage of a quality that Kamiko knew to be far beyond the norm of most highwaymen, obviously stolen, the rightful owners most likely dead. The road-worn brigands stood in stark contrast against the townsmen, which made it easy for Kamiko to pick them out. With the slightest flex of her legs, she moved Uila forward to get closer to the center of the gathering, to get closer to Broga Kipp.

She knew the people of the town, knew their faces and many of their names. She became aware of the faces missing from the crowd, ones who would not have been elsewhere in a situation such as this. One in particular was the administrator of Essen, Fredan Berg, great-grandson of the original founders, an elderly gentleman of peace and much wisdom. Another was Captain Willet, the appointed leader of the town guard. That neither of these men were present spoke volumes of trouble. The viper roiled in her gut, but she gave it no quarter and kept her calm. Now she felt the harmonic center of her being come into equilibrium, the rage balanced by purpose and necessity.

As the crowd parted before Uila, the brigands gravitated toward Kipp. Some rested their hands on sword hilts, some eased up behind unsuspecting citizens. The only sounds came from the crackling fire and the crowd of exhausted horses shuffling and complaining that they had not been relieved of their tack. The hush of voices was complete.

Kamiko knew exactly what to expect from the band of thieves, malicious and cowardly by nature. Their fear was her greatest weapon. The legendary Kamiko Hoshi was needed in abundance. She felt the Woman grow silent and still inside her spirit, allowing the Warrior to have full presence. Some part of her wished to blind the people to what was about to happen, to spare them the memory of it.

Kipp was an enormous man. His bare head glistened with dirty sweat. Thick long braids of mustache and beard hung around his mouth, adorned with trinkets and beads. His broad bare chest and fat gut stuck out from an open leather vest, the dirty skin cluttered with fading tattoos. At his hip hung both sword and dagger, and his eyes burned with malice and arrogance.

Kamiko knew a band of outlaws such as this would never follow someone who could be easily bested. Kipp was widely known to be brutal beyond measure, murderous as a way of life. Once, many years ago, Kipp had raided an outlying town. The citizens were warned of his approach, but instead of showing resistance, they offered him free run of the town and piled as much loot as they could gather into his wagon. He was so taken aback that he left without taking a single life. Months later, the rumor reached his ears that he had shown mercy to a bunch of common villagers, that he was going soft. He returned with a war party and butchered every living thing in the town—man, woman, child, and beast. Then he burned it to the ground. The rumor was never spoken again. From that point on, he always killed. It was easy for Kamiko to conclude he was here to do the same. God had delivered the elusive butcher into her hands.

Visions of her father danced in Kamiko's mind. He had been only slightly less brutal than Kipp. The viper writhed and twisted, angry for being held in check.

With another gentle nudge of her legs, she brought Uila to a stop, swung her leg over the saddlebow, and slipped to the ground. With slow deliberation, she slid her sword from the saddle, still in the scabbard. She whispered to Uila, "Guard," and walked toward Kipp.

All around the courtyard, weapons rang in the air. Quiet gasps escaped in a wave across the townsfolk, and every person in Kamiko's sight moved, stepping back on impulse. To her delight, even Kipp took a precautionary step back. His mouth formed an unspoken *O* as the last of his doubt vanished. He knew who she was. Thick fear permeated the air.

Behind her, Uila growled deep and followed at exactly five paces. She knew his eyes were taking in every detail, his ears scanning for even the slightest sound, his nose smelling their fear like dank animal musk. She was free to focus wholly upon Broga Kipp and to set the order in which the brigands would die.

Kipp would not be the first. One of his lackeys, a burly man of short stature, was behind an unsuspecting farmer, heavy dagger already poised to come up to the farmer's throat, to hold him hostage against Kamiko. He would be the first.

As Kamiko came to a stop three paces from Kipp, the brigand leader raised his left hand and beckoned to another of his filthy lackeys. This one stepped from the crowd of men and grabbed a younger man from behind. He propelled the lad forward with a rough shove that sent him to the ground near Kipp's feet, then drew a long curved sword. He would be second.

She spared a brief glance over the men of Essen who were standing nearby and saw them drawing courage and readiness from their guts and knew they would act. One in particular caught her attention, an old comrade from her infantry days, Randel Bowater, formerly a lieutenant. Their eyes met briefly.

Behind her, Uila spread his front hooves and lowered his great head. He required no further commands to know his role. Kamiko had been gathering her energy into that center point within her being as she stepped up to Kipp, holding it like a sizzling, popping caldron of electric rage. Her movements were choreographed to the last.

Broga Kipp opened his mouth to speak.

Kamiko moved.

She leapt forward and kicked straight out with a high shriek, sword hilt in her left hand, scabbard in her right. Her foot impacted Kipp's chin and lifted his mass from the ground. Teeth and blood geysered from his mouth. With her right hand, she launched the scabbard from her sword, sending it into the throat of her first mark, crushing it and knocking him backward before he could raise his deadly blade. Her sword simply whipped to her left. The doomed man standing over the boy never even flinched. His head tilted sickly to one side and rolled from his shoulders, just as Kipp landed flat on his back. His breath exploded out in a short roar.

The sudden momentary hush and the panic that followed were no surprise. A short-lived assault ensued which left Kamiko standing alone with several dead bodies at her feet. Kipp had rolled aside and scampered out of her reach. The townsfolk scattered. Many of the men had snatched up dropped weapons and joined Kamiko in the fight. Uila also entered the foray, offering Kamiko safety from being flanked. One of the attackers writhed beneath the warhorse, a nasty bleeding gash across his forehead, his arms holding crushed ribs.

Kipp's voice boomed. "Hold yer weapons! To me! *To me*!"

The band responded immediately, forming a tight circle around their leader. The few townsmen who had stayed to fight subdued those who were unable to reach Kipp. Several more citizens rushed out and offered help, both to the injured and to the ones now holding weapons upon the brigands. Those who ran did not go far and were forming into groups and clusters around the edges of the courtyard. They would bear witness to the history of Essen unfolding before them. The frantic motion dwindled quickly, and everyone stopped where they stood. Uila held his station behind Kamiko, Bowater several paces to her right.

When she turned and saw Kipp, the viper howled inside. Kipp held his sword to the throat of the youth who had been thrown at his feet. He had tried to get away when Kipp went down but only managed to scamper in frightened circles in the sudden chaos. Kamiko stepped to within reach of the foremost of the brigand circle and stopped. The boy's name was Terence Dul, sixteen summers into his life. He was the great-grandling of one of Kamiko's many friends in Essen. Like several others, Hattie Mae had offered Kamiko lodging in the past. She was an elderly woman who was raising Terence and his younger sister, Clarie-Ann, in their mother's stead.

Kipp heaved a great gob of bloody spittle to one side. The burning rage in his eyes belied the deep chuckle rumbling from his chest.

"Kamiko Hoshi," he said. Blood dripped in a steady stream from the long braids framing his mouth. "You will disarm, and you will do it right now!" To stress his intent, he drew the sword lightly across Terence's neck, leaving a bloody line which immediately began to run in thin rivulets. She felt the full weight of Terence's life on her spirit. As soon as she was no longer a threat, Kipp would kill him. To think otherwise was madness.

Kamiko addressed the brigands standing at the ready around Kipp. "If that boy dies, we will slaughter you to the last man." To emphasize her point, she stepped forward and snapped her sword out and back. The motion was so fast that no one seemed to think she had done anything beyond taking that one step. For a moment, nothing happened. Then the brigand directly in front of her coughed and dropped to his knees. Bright blood flowed from a narrow slit directly over his windpipe. He flopped on his backside and looked around, his hands going to his throat. Everyone understood the message with perfect clarity. It would take him a long time to die and that in great pain.

The strike had surgical accuracy. She had carefully avoided the vein that would bring a quick death. Best she could tell, as the man began writhing in pain, everyone in sight shifted their feet and bounced their weapons, except Bowater. He simply called out in a loud voice, "*Archers*! To the fore!" Several townsmen bolted away. He then called out again, "*Pikemen*! To the fore!" Several more ran to retrieve their weapons. The old warrior stood at the ready with a group of ten men, all armed with swords but without armor.

Fear was their greatest weapon.

Kamiko stepped to her right, coming face-to-face with the next man in line. She stared directly into his eyes.

"Damn you, Hoshi, I will kill this child," Kipp said. But she heard the hint of despair he was trying to conceal.

She called out to him but never took her icy gaze from the man in front of her. "No, Broga Kipp, you will not. If you do, then I will gut you where you stand." The man in front of her was shaking hard, his clenched teeth showing yellow beneath an unkempt mustache. He held his sword so tight his knuckles strained to white.

She addressed him directly in a voice of quiet menace. "Lower your weapon and step aside."

"Stand fast, fool, or I shall kill you myself and feed your flesh to the—"

Kamiko interrupted Kipp with a lightning-fast vertical sweep of her sword, and the man fell straight backward with a howl. The whole of his abdomen was open from just below the belt up to his breastbone. This would be a painful death.

The gathering of townsfolk was growing, and an audible gasp rose all around her as, again, everyone shifted involuntarily. She kept her focus fixed upon the Warrior, refusing to allow the Woman even a slight voice. The remaining brigands were quickly reaching their point to fight and escape, exchanging nervous glances all around. They still numbered just over thirty armed fighting men and, if not for Kamiko's presence, could have fought their way to freedom. Bowater's archers would return in moments with the pike-bearers soon to follow.

She sidled slowly to the right, coming to stand before the next man in line. Uila moved likewise, still five paces behind her, keeping the whole of the scene under watch.

She looked directly into the man's eyes. "Lay down your weapon and live," she said, this time a genuine request.

Kamiko heard Siruis's small voice at her left elbow.

"He sees his life in full at this moment, Sister." With a slight turn of her head, Kamiko found the young woman standing right beside her. Siruis's hood was back, and the thick mantle of hair was drawn into a loose tail behind her head. She was looking up at the brigand's face.

"The pain and fear inside him are not of his own making. He would respond to compassion if given the chance."

Kamiko immediately raised her weapon defensively between Siruis and the man. Siruis was easily within his weapon's reach. He made no move to either advance or retreat. He made no move at all. The staunch fear on his face was frozen in place, and his head no longer darted nervously from side to side. Even the dirty beads of sweat ceased running down his face and hung motionless on his skin, like tainted jewels on a lifeless statue.

Silence and an all-encompassing stillness like nothing Kamiko had ever imagined surrounded her and Siruis. The light of the bonfire no longer played on their faces, replaced with a soft ethereal whiteness which came from everywhere and from nowhere.

"See him as he is, Kamiko," Siruis said and touched Kamiko's elbow.

A young man, barely beyond childhood, stood where the brigand had been. Kamiko recognized the fear-etched face. He was cowering now, trapped inside a darkened room, blood oozing from wounds on his face and chest. He was clutching his hands around his head with all his might, trying in vain to keep out the sounds from beyond the door of his prison. And Kamiko knew the truth of it, unsure as to how she knew, that the boy's mother was being beaten by a man the child believed to be a demon—his own father.

She jerked her elbow away from Siruis and momentarily reeled aside. The fear on the boy's face had once again become panic-induced anger on the man's face. Siruis was gone. The sights and sounds of the firelit courtyard returned. He stepped forward and swung a desperate chop at Kamiko's head. She dropped below the clumsy move and spun on the ball of her right foot, striking him in the meat of his thigh with her left heel. The impact drove his legs together and out to the side, and he slammed to the ground with a wail of pain. Bedlam broke over the courtyard anew.

Wisely Bowater pulled back, instead of lunging forward, and drew his men with him. The brigands rushed out at Bowater just as the archers returned, running fast, bows coming to bear. The tactic had the effect of breaking the brigand force into smaller parts. The timely arrival of the pike-bearers sealed the conflict, and one by one, the brigands threw down their weapons. To his credit, Bowater did not have them killed to the man.

While the short battle took place, Kamiko confronted Kipp. She felt no compulsion toward mercy, nor did she desire further conversation. He could see the judgment in her eyes.

Kamiko knew her quandary. Kipp now had his foot planted firmly in the middle of Terence's chest and was pressing hard. The tip of his heavy sword rested just below the boy's sternum, poised to make the killing plunge. The window of possibility was too narrow. Kipp knew he was about to die, and Kamiko knew he would kill the boy as his last act. She kept her eyes glued to his as she approached, watching for his break point.

Siruis's small voice returned to Kamiko's head, "*Be still, Sister.* Without hesitation, she stopped. She was still too far from Kipp to do anything effective before he could kill Terence. Her mind tried to calculate the possibilities, to weigh the options and determine the best outcome. It was meaningless, the boy would be killed regardless.

Kipp's solution was also his problem. She could see in his eyes that he was coming to the same conclusion; his break point had arrived. Kipp's filthy face was smiling as his master drew nigh. His lord was death, and he welcomed it. His eyes were locked with hers as he leaned his weight onto the sword and drove it through the boy's frail body.

Violent fury erupted inside Kamiko. She saw the face of her father in his last moment, felt the heat of his blood on her face. The world ceased to exist but for the vile creature in her sight as she lunged with all of her might. Once again, her vision became a series of disjointed flashes.

Siruis was kneeling at the boy's head, her hand on his face. There was a blur of motion to Kamiko's left as Jerim slammed into Kipp and drove him high into the darkness. Then everything was still. Her target was no longer in sight.

Hattie Mae's high wail tore the rage away and brought Kamiko's mind reeling back to the whole of the scene. The elderly woman stumbled to Terence, on his back in the street. Her mouth was open, and her weathered hands pressed against her face in disbelief. Siruis was still there, kneeling beside Terence, gently caressing his face. The front of his shirt was bright red.

Deep sadness flooded into the void where the viper had been, and the Woman she held at bay wailed for release. Kamiko allowed neither to turn her from necessity. She scanned the dark perimeter for Jerim, even as her chest pumped hard, her heartbeat redoubled. From a hundred paces away, his wide face peered back at her like a wild animal, his mass barely visible as a dark fire-tinted glow. But she could see he was crouched low to the ground over a black mound. He had waited until Siruis appeared at Kipp's feet before he attacked. *Could he have saved Terence's life?* she wondered. *Perhaps.*

She drove the thoughts away with a growl, snatched her scabbard from the ground, and sheathed her sword as she trotted down the street to Jerim. The look on his face stopped her in her tracks. Kipp was dead, still partially hanging from Jerim's massive fist. The brigand was facing the dark sky, but his body was front-down in the street, his back and neck a flimsy rope of shattered bones. Jerim's face was expressionless, his eyes hollow orbs now fixed on the body in his fist. Uila trotted dutifully up behind her, his nostrils flaring, snorting.

Kamiko had seen the look far too many times and knew there were no words for Jerim. He had never before taken a human life. Bartol would have done all he could to prepare Jerim for this moment, but it made little difference once the time arrived. She stepped up and placed her blood-flecked hand on his wrist.

"Jerim," she said. "Such is the way of the warrior. Release him, my friend."

He hesitated and then lowered Kipp's twisted body to the street. When he raised his eyes to Kamiko's, his face had hardened once again. He nodded his assent and repeated her words.

"Such is the way of the warrior."

His face was grim, but his eyes shone clear with understanding and the first gleam of acceptance of what he was. And though the street was packed solid from years of constant travel, he easily plunged his fingers into the ground and scooped out a handful of dirt. He vigorously scrubbed his hands until all the dirt had sifted through his fingers. It was a symbolic act. Kamiko caught a handful and did likewise, but scrubbed away as much of the blood as she could with only dirt. They crouched together beside Kipp's broken body.

She felt a relief at being out on the edge of the shadow, while the horror was sinking into the people of Essen. The boy was so young. She slapped her hands together a few times and brushed the clinging dirt from her fingers.

"Why did you wait, Jerim?" she asked quietly. "You could have taken Kipp before he killed the boy. Why did you wait?"

His eyes were peering over her shoulder toward the courtyard. He spoke first. "Siruis bid me so." Then he looked down at Kamiko.

"Siruis?" she said doubtfully. "Told you to wait." This she spoke as a statement. Jerim simply nodded. "Why?"

"I do not know, Sister Kamiko. I did not understand the meaning of her words."

"What did she tell you?"

"That she must remove her veil."

"Her veil?" The earlier conversation with Siruis came abruptly to her mind but was cut short by another long cry from the midst of the gathering of townsfolk. Hattie Mae's shrill voice again, mixed with—laughter?

Kamiko and Jerim sat looking at each other, questioning. Then they rose together, and as Kamiko led Uila toward the lighted courtyard, Jerim moved further out into the darkness.

Chapter 5

The crowd had formed into an unbroken mass, encircling a small clearing in the center. Instead of stepping through, Kamiko moved around the outer edge to where several armed men held the surviving brigands under guard. The outlaws' hands and feet were bound, and they were seated in a line, backs against the wall of Pherson's livery. She found the younger man she'd encountered uninjured, his head hanging down with his chin against his chest. Kamiko imagined he was trying to retrace the steps that had brought him to this place in his life.

She placed her hand on Uila's face and whispered the words he understood—to stand down. He visibly relaxed his posture and shook his head before nuzzling the back of Kamiko's head with his nose.

She hung the sword on Uila's saddle as Bowater walked up to her. "Sister," he said, "thank you." He held a weathered short sword in his hand. Kamiko nodded to him, her chest too thick with emotion to speak easily. She was distracted by the odd reactions coming from the gathering. Had someone just laughed aloud?

"Where is Fredan Berg?" Her throat ached with unspent anger, and her voice was breathy.

Bowater's lips tightened beneath a full but trimmed gray mustache, speckled through with the waning remnants of dark reddish brown. His already serious eyes took on the look of anger held at bay. He spat the word *Kipp*!

Kamiko held him with a knowing look and placed her hand on his shoulder. "And Captain Willet?"

He only nodded his response. Kamiko noticed the sword bounce in his hand.

"I am sorry, Bowater," she said with sincerity. "Would that I had come sooner."

"It wouldn't have changed anything. Kipp slew Fredan before either man even spoke. Then he turned on the captain and ran him through. Just like that, it was done."

"How did this happen, Bowater? Why?"

Bowater's fiery gaze settled on the captive brigands for a moment before he spoke. "They took several hostages, Sister, children mostly." His sword bounced again. "Kipp intended to take Essen for himself, to enslave the whole town." The captives glanced up at this, then shared worried looks among themselves. "We tried to figure a way out of it but came up short. They were due back today." He placed the tip of his sword under the chin of one and lifted the man's face.

"How long?" she asked.

"Three weeks." He moved the tip of the sword to the man's cheek just below one eye, his silent promise of a terrible interrogation, one already begun. Several of the brigands groaned aloud. "So we prayed, Sister Kamiko. We prayed." Then he snapped the sword back and slipped it into the sheath. "And by God in heaven, you arrived right on Kipp's heels." A trickle of blood oozed from a shallow cut on the brigand's face. The man shook visibly, and his chest heaved.

Kamiko reached out with both hands and lifted the younger man she'd spared earlier, all the way clear of the ground, pressed his back to the wall, and stared hard into his eyes as she spoke to Bowater. "This one will tell you all you want to know." Then she offered the dangling man a question, "Will you not?" He nodded vigorously and stuttered the word *yes* several times.

A soft wave of gasps flowed over the crowd, followed by several bright laughs. Then silence returned. Through that silence, she could just hear the soft imploring voice of Siruis saying Kamiko's name. Every head she could see turned and began searching the courtyard, soon coming to rest on her. The gathering opened with a wave of motion that reminded Kamiko of water parting before the prow of a slow-moving ship. They found her still holding the man aloft, pressed forcibly against the rough wall. Still holding him in the air, she turned and dropped the man on the ground in front of Bowater.

The faces she saw were nothing like what she'd expected. There was no sadness or shock drawing their features downward. Their eyes were bright and searching, and though many were glistening with tears, none looked stricken with the darkness of grief.

She could see Siruis standing with a second smaller cluster of people to one side of the bonfire. Three of them had dark bloodstains coloring their clothes. One in particular demanded her attention. After a sidelong look at Bowater, she strode to the center of the gathering, Uila close behind.

Terence was standing, tall and whole. Hattie Mae clung to him, her face wet with tears. The elder woman immediately released Terence and shuffled to meet Kamiko, hands waving in the air above her head. She cackled softly as she reached up and placed her hands on Kamiko's face.

"Bless you, child! O may the God of all creation be praised! Bless you, bless you!"

She leaned forward as Hattie Mae pulled her face down to kiss her on each cheek. But Kamiko could not take her eyes from Terence. He was alive, but he couldn't be. Kipp had pierced the boy's heart. Then Jerim had crushed every bone in the brigand leader's neck. It happened. Kipp was dead. Terence was dead.

Kamiko's head spun with the oddness of seeing the boy's bushy head and his broad smile, while his shirt was soaked with his own lifeblood. These sights did not belong in the same picture. Even Hattie Mae's hands felt like strange distant things only painted across the surface of what was real.

Uila's soft chortle brushed across her awareness and slowed her growing uneasiness. The muffled silence was simply that, a gathering of people standing in speechless wonder, silently waiting to see what would happen next. Kamiko understood; she was speechless as well. As her eyes came to rest on Siruis's calm face, she was struck with an odd familiarity she had not felt before. Something had changed about the young sister that Kamiko could not put her finger on. She seemed more real, as if she'd been enshrouded in mist. No, not mist. A veil.

"Sister," Kamiko asked, "what happened here?"

For a moment, Siruis appeared to have aged, and she gazed up at Kamiko through eyes of wisdom, ancient and deep. Then the odd sensation passed, and Siruis's soft youth returned to her cheeks.

Terence could no longer hold his energy in check, and his mouth began to move without pause. He began the story when Broga Kipp first arrived at Essen, three weeks earlier. The rapid-fire soliloquy then ended abruptly, with the last of the words stuck in his mouth. Hattie Mae finished the sentence for him.

"She healed him, Sister Kamiko!" She opened her palm toward Siruis as she spoke. "She was kneeling there whence Kipp—"

Now it was Hattie Mae who could not speak words to describe the killing plunge.

Two of the other men who had been wounded stepped forward with eager joy on their faces. "Me as well, and him too, Sister," one of the men said, hooking his thumb toward the other. "We was dead for sure but for the dyin'. She whispered something over me and then—" He stopped and looked at the other man. "Here we stand."

Murmurs began waving through the gathering as the gap slowly closed behind Kamiko. The clearing in the center of the crowd was large enough to allow for the brigands still lying where they had fallen. Over the heads of the townsfolk, she could see Broga Kipp's lifeless mound heaped at the edge of the light. The dead man was the connection to Kamiko's reality. He was the one who forced Kamiko to acknowledge what could not be real.

Uila was at Kamiko's back. Pieces of broken thoughts began falling into order in her mind, and a strong notion filled her thoughts.

The veil had been lifted. News of this would sweep across the kingdom. She spun around, leapt onto Uila's back, and extended her hand toward Siruis without a word.

"Down, Uila," Kamiko said, and he immediately lowered one front knee to the ground so Siruis could easily reach the stirrup. The young sister stepped forward and took her hand, and Kamiko lifted her onto Uila's broad rump as the warhorse stood upright again. Without word or warning, Kamiko reined him over and carefully made her way through the throng. As soon as they were clear of the crowd, she leaned forward and urged Uila into a gallop. She caught a brief sight of Bowater and made eye contact, for only a moment. He held his sword aloft in silent farewell and sincere thanks as Kamiko and Siruis made straight west out of Essen, into the dark of full night.

*****

Once out of the town, she slowed Uila to an easy run and stayed on the westward road. Kamiko's heart raced, pounding in her head. She could feel Siruis's arms around her waist and felt a newly found sensation rising. It was that wavering cringe which comes from such proximity to raw power, like leaping with all one's might just after a nearby lightning strike.

If Siruis had indeed healed Terence, then Kamiko knew she possessed an immense well of power. She also knew from experience that anything vast was terrible. And if that power did come from God, then nothing more titanic or dreadful could be conjured in all of nature.

She could feel Uila's growing tension in the way he was slowing his pace at regular increments, stepping higher than normal in his stride. He knew better than to run in the dark even on a well-kept road such as this one. He was right. She drew in slightly on the reins and brought him to a stop. Uila had put in a hard day's work without complaint or pause, and Kamiko scratched and rubbed at his withers. She took a few slow deliberate moments to show the warhorse her appreciation, while her mind stormed over everything that had happened.

No conclusions awaited Kamiko, only the small woman sitting in silence behind her. She felt certain that Siruis would have the answer to any question that could be asked.

She reined Uila to the side of the dark roadway, definable only by a strip of star field overhead. Siruis's presence was like a boulder resting on her shoulders. Then she felt the sister's hand close gently on her arm, just above the elbow. At first, Kamiko thought she saw a flash of light out in the forest, in the direction they were facing. But it was not a flash, it was simply illumination, soft and white and barely perceptible.

Uila's head came up, his ears facing forward, soft snorts of uncertainty.

Kamiko turned her head and looked down at Siruis.

"I borrowed a little bit of light, Sister."

Kamiko almost asked where she'd borrowed the light from but could only dump the statement into the swirl of thoughts and odd possibilities already churning in her brain. She nudged Uila with her knees and started through the ghostly glow at a walk.

Chapter 6

Kamiko patted Uila's broad rump and left him to eat and to rest, then walked back to the small fire. Siruis was slowly pacing in a wide circle around the perimeter of the campsite, which was no more than a couple of big stones for sitting around the crackling fire. Kamiko had nothing but her sword with her. Pack, provisions, and her armor were lying beside the trail where she'd dropped them earlier.

She had not spoken a single word nor had her eyes fallen on Siruis since they had set out through the dark forest. All she needed was to lie down in the grass and let her body relax. She wanted out of her layers of traveling clothes and boots, much like Uila had wanted out of his saddle and bit. Her skin needed to feel the cool air.

She opened the clasps of her cloak and slung it aside, then worked open the buckle of her shoulder harness and belt and dropped them beside Uila's saddle and her sword. Then she quickly unbuttoned her tunic and shirt and all but flung them away. Her thin undershirt gave off hazy tendrils of steam reeking of sweat. She dug her fingertips into her scarp and scrubbed her head vigorously for several moments. Then she dropped onto her backside in the grass to free her feet.

Removing her boots proved to be more of a chore than she'd expected. Her fingers twitched with nervous energy as she worked at the stubborn laces. She looked up when Siruis began feeding more wood into the fire, only then realizing that she was shivering, not just from nerves but also from cold. The muscles across her back were knotted and aching, and the tightness had traveled up her neck to the base of her skull. From there it became a mass of dull pain that filled her head and made her eyes throb in time with her heartbeat. Finally the boots and thin stockings fell aside.

She was shaking harder now, more from the chill than anything. The heat of the growing fire drew her closer, and she knelt with her back toward the blaze. Relief came quickly. Warmth spread across her back like an invisible blanket. She wrapped her arms around her knees, and perched on the balls of her bare feet, she began stretching and flexing her muscles. A small measure of calm returned, and at last her thoughts began to settle.

Kamiko could sense that Siruis was now sitting near the fire and could feel the woman's eyes on her back. The night was not cold, only chill against her damp shirt. She turned, still on the balls of her feet, and readjusted her crouch to bring her front around to the warmth. She pushed her knees outward while sitting on her heels. It occurred to her how improper the pose may appear to Siruis, unaccustomed as she likely was to the brutish etiquette of soldiers.

Siruis nodded and smiled when Kamiko looked at her, a gesture Kamiko returned, though words remained lost. For all the confusion and impossibilities Kamiko had just seen unfold, the final outcome had been astounding. A strange joy was hovering just below the surface of Kamiko's conscious thoughts. Something more had transpired than was detectable by the senses.

"You are having trouble quantifying what has happened."

The statement caught Kamiko off guard for a moment, and her mouth shifted to an uncertain half-smile. The animated look on Siruis's face drew the chuckle building in Kamiko's chest all the way to the surface. Siruis's bright smile tilted to one side, her eyes sparkling in the dancing firelight. The levity was refreshing after so much turmoil. Kamiko stayed crouched beside the fire and let the laughter come. It was one of those giddy moments borne of weariness, hunger, and too much stress. It passed too quickly but left Kamiko in a much better state of mind.

As the chuckles dwindled, she said, "It shows, does it?"

"Ha! You look fit to pop, Sister," Siruis assured her, absently poking the fire with a long stick. Her young face was aglow from the dancing firelight.

Kamiko nodded and wiped both hands up across her face, combing her hair back with spread fingers. "I imagine so."

She could only guess at how ragged she must look. She could remember a time not long ago when she would not have cared. It made her wonder what had changed, though the reality was that everything was changing. The small flourish of levity dissipated as the memory of her father surfaced again, reminding her of how radical, how absolute that change truly was. She felt her face turn harder and her mouth draw tight, and it struck her that this was her true face. Hard and angry, a scowling threat to all who would cross her. She fought the loathing with logic. Her appearance was of little consequence where her duty was concerned. She was not, and would never be, one of the ridiculous beauties depicted in literature, battling the minions of evil while maintaining a stunning figure and perfect hair. It was much easier being ordinary and dirty from the road, people tended to take her seriously.

The words came out of her mouth without conscious effort. "Siruis, what happened back there?"

"Why do you ask? You already know what happened." The answer sounded so much like Djinnasee.

"Did you save the boy?"

"Technically? No, I was only a conduit. I have no power beyond what God sees fit to give. But yes, it was the result of my hands touching him and my prayer that he be healed, as with all of the injured." She gazed at Kamiko's face as she spoke, tracing the form of her cheeks and forehead with her eyes. "You know why too, Sister, but have yet to look at it fully." Her eyes came to rest on Kamiko's.

Kamiko replied, "So that God be glorified." At best the statement sounded ambiguous, nothing more than the blind recital of Kamiko's childhood schooling, empty of meaning. The words should have been powerful but fell out of her mouth as hollow doldrums.

After a moment of reflection, Kamiko continued, "No, that is not it. At least not all of it." She tried to recall the way Siruis looked when they'd first met but could make no clear picture come into her head. It was almost as though Siruis had been a ghost. Then she remembered Jerim's odd answer. "The veil," she said. "Now the veil has been lifted."

"Yes, Kamiko. Now *my* veil has been lifted."

"King Titus will hear about this."

"By the time we reach Flavin, yes, most certainly," agreed Siruis.

Kamiko shook her head. "I was hoping to avoid that, Sister."

"Why?"

"Now we will have droves of not only Royal Militia looking for us but mercenaries and greedy opportunists as well. I had hoped to get you into Castlehaven unnoticed. King Titus may not know who you are, but he certainly knows me. I expect he plans to command me to hunt you down, Siruis." Kamiko shifted but remained crouched. "And I know beyond a shadow of a doubt that he will order me to give report on my whereabouts for the last two years. When I tell him I have slain Garret without royal leave to do so, he may have me jailed instead." She shook her head again, her eyes still on Siruis.

"He does not know Garret was your father."

"No, he doesn't. And he will not be happy to hear it."

"So now we will have to make a run for it to get to Castlehaven before he expects us," Siruis said. "Which is why we left Essen in such a hurry."

It was not lost on Kamiko that Siruis spoke in statements, rarely asking a question. She caught herself wondering if there was anything her young sister did *not* know.

"Why did you stop me—"

"From killing Kipp?" Siruis completed Kamiko's thought. Another statement, though framed as a question.

"Yes."

"Sister, Cairistonia has long turned away from the voice of God. You know well enough that the king is fascinated with all things arcane. He has come to regard the edicts of God as simply another cultic progeny of a fickle society."

Kamiko recalled one of the enormous paintings King Titus had procured of the mythical faerie king, Krall Devish, riding into battle atop a fiery beast, flaming sword in his mighty fist.

"Essen was established as a stronghold for the seed of belief," Siruis went on. "Here the Word of God still holds true in the hearts and minds of the people. Djinnasee has been nurturing that belief and will lead them out of this kingdom. We have reinforced their hope a hundredfold."

"You make it sound like all this was predestined," Kamiko said, waving her hand in the general direction of Essen.

"And what can be said to be otherwise, Kamiko, in the eyes of God? What thing does he not know in the fullest measure?" Siruis tossed the stick into the fire and folded her hands, her arms resting on her knees.

"That is simply knowing what will happen," Kamiko said.

"Then what is the difference?"

"Between prediction and predestination?"

"Yes, between knowing the future and *setting* the future."

Kamiko thought in silence again, knowing the surface answer was not what Siruis was digging for. "One allows for people to strive to improve and to hope for goodness, the other takes the human will away." She let her thoughts continue aloud. "If everything has been set to order ahead of time, then what is the purpose of living? What would be the point?" She stood and walked around the fire, her eyes searching inward.

"Then what of Titus? Do you think his path was set before he was born, before the world was created? Or was he doomed merely by the circumstances of his upbringing?"

"King Titus made his own choices, same as you and I," Kamiko said.

"Yes," Siruis conceded. "Just as you chose to go after Kipp, knowing you would be seen by the people of Essen, knowing your secrecy would be lost. But choosing to eat chicken rather than fish is not the freedom of will we are talking about, Sister. Titus may have sufficient worldly power to command many millions to bend to his desires, to fulfill his will, but beyond that, he has nothing."

Kamiko nodded her assent as she thought about what Siruis had just said. Her sister was correct. Kamiko had known she would be seen, but she had not expected Siruis and Jerim to follow. And she certainly had no idea that Siruis was going to cause such a memorable scene right out in front of everyone.

"I didn't really have a choice, Siruis, I could not turn a blind eye on them. And it is not known that we are traveling together." Then she added, "At least not until now."

"But you could have decided that our secrecy was more important. You acted based upon what you felt to be the right thing to do. That is free will, is it not?"

"Maybe. I guess I'm not convinced this can be worked out to a single answer." She lowered herself to sit near Siruis. "Could I have killed you back at my home when I thought you were attacking me? Some part of me certainly set out to."

Siruis held Kamiko's eyes for a long moment. "You would not have succeeded."

"How can you know that? Because Jerim was there?"

"No, Sister, Jerim would prove to be inadequate defense against you. It was because it was not within your will to do so. We are now talking about the will of God, not ours."

Kamiko chuckled to herself. "You've been talking to Djinnasee. He would be chastising me for asking the question in the first place."

"Kamiko, we were placed together because of your will, not in spite of it. We are here because you would not turn your back on common folks in need, and so our path will be true to the end. What does it matter that this was known by God before you knew it for yourself? But more so, who among us may overshadow the will of God?"

Something occurred to Kamiko. "What of Kipp? Where is his will in all of this?"

"Kipp, like Garret, would never acknowledge any higher authority than himself, be it king, court, or God. It is a deep conundrum based in spiritual blindness. Kipp was in league with demons, Sister, and once in that state, he could see neither the hand of God nor the hand of the deceiver."

The mention of her father, Garret, reminded Kamiko that Siruis knew everything that had entered her thoughts since her birth into Djinnasee's hands.

Something seemed to catch Siruis's notice, and she stood, though without alarm. Kamiko's guard came up, and she immediately scanned their surroundings, holding her hand up near her face to shield the soft glow of the fire from her eyes. To her surprise, because she had not seen or heard them come, there were several small dark birds perched around the perimeter of the campsite. She now began to hear the soft breathy whisper of moving air out in the night.

"Kipp would have killed them all," Kamiko added.

"Yes."

"That is why I could not resist."

"Yes."

"Then God be praised!"

"Yes, Sister." Siruis looked over her shoulder and locked her eyes on Kamiko's. "Now you know what happened back there."

Kamiko nodded her response as she thought of the joy Hattie Mae would know all the days of her life. Inside her mind, she perceived the Warrior and the Woman standing together in peace but, oddly, still separate. Kamiko needed food and rest, but tonight would have to settle for only rest. She tried not to think too much about the feast they'd left behind in Essen.

Then she saw Uila heading toward her at a slow trot, his head close to the ground. He was looking alternately at the glow of the fire and the star-washed sky, his ears darting around. The breathy whisper was growing into an airy tumult, getting stronger by the moment.

"Jerim?" Kamiko asked as a dark swarm of fast-moving birds overtook them in full force.

Uila came to a stop within arm's reach of Kamiko and cast her a worried look. His head was low to the ground, and his thick cropped tail was tucked in tight. It appeared as though he was trying to be a very small thing. Kamiko dropped low, following much the same instinct as Uila. But the horde of dark missiles flew by well overhead with never a peep of voice. The effect was eerie and unnerving, to say the least. Kamiko would have guessed that thousands of fleet birds were passing above their heads. The moonless night darkened further by their sheer mass blotting out the field of stars.

Siruis pointed out into the night and spoke above the din. "Jerim."

Chapter 7

The twelve days it took to cross the plains would have been mundane but for Jerim's constant entourage of wildlife and the rolling rumbling storms in the west. Kamiko had been driving them long and hard throughout the days, striking out before dawn and continuing beyond sunset. The days fell into numb repetition, each unremarkable from the others but for gradual variations in the terrain and subtle differences in the vast horizon. The days were growing shorter, and it had rained on them often. Jerim had retrieved Kamiko's gear and Siruis's nameless pony before they left Essen.

Neither Siruis nor Jerim could explain why, but all things animal were drawn to the giant youth, like cubs to a mother, and had been since his birth. The birds were a constant presence day and night, a hectic swirl of motion that only rarely settled. The busy chatter of the birds wore on Kamiko's nerves, and the large jungle beasts had her feeling ill at ease to say the least. At one point, she reckoned roughly two hundred wolves had them completely surrounded but did little more than keep pace for a full day before vanishing back into the wild at nightfall.

Another day, it was a pride of enormous golden jungle cats. Jerim would run with them all. Almost daily, he would secure Siruis on the saddle, shed all but his breeches, and charge headlong into whatever group of beasts happened to be nearby, be it gazelle or jackal, mountain lion or monkey, wildebeest or elephant troop. He would clap his hands and roar like thunder, and his cries of joy would roll out over the plains. Uila was no more immune to the odd effect than the animals of the wild and tended to drift into Jerim's company at every opportunity. The bearing of the great warhorse would change to that of a yearling stallion when Jerim would charge away at a lope, leading Uila and several others in a ferocious game of tag, wild animals, all.

They watched great storms race across the sky in the west for several days, as the cooler air sweeping down from the northern mountains collided with the moist southern air of the sun-warmed grasslands, heated across the table of the plains as it drew northward. That timeless battle was waged before their eyes, day and night. When at last the weathering balance was drawn, the lightning ceased, the wind subsided, and the rain became snaking ribbons of falling slate-blue water.

After days' gray with mist and nights black as pitch, they finally witnessed a stunning sunset. The clouds were strewn across the horizon in long sharp-edged swaths that caught every shade of fiery tones the sun could create, a vast river of golden-red flames in the sky.

Kamiko had stopped midway through the afternoon, declaring that a longer break would serve body, mind, and spirit with equal benefit. She easily found the old campsite known only to her, Bartol, and Djinnasee—the ancient temple ruins of Ferith-Dale, from the age before the kingdom was founded. She had been setting their course by keeping just south of the border of the lesser jungle.

A small stone-hewn deck, octagonal with finely carved pillars at each peak, was set on the gentle side of a valley shoulder. The tops of the pillars were all jagged, long since broken and crumbled away beneath the weight of the stone roof. Centuries ago, Djinnasee had cleared the floor of the rubble and set simple stone seats around the center point of the platform. Using bricks from fallen roof stones, he'd built a fire ring with a stone oven and a cooking griddle. Jungle growth had long since hidden the whole of the ruined gazebo from being seen afield. And since the time Djinnasee had cleared and arranged the sanctuary, the jungle had ceased the slow relentless destruction of the site.

A bed of coals was all that remained of the fire they had used to cook their evening meal. As with every evening meal for the past two weeks, Kamiko prepared flatbread, a light vegetable stew, and pullings from a parcel of peppered venison jerky she'd purchased from a hunting party shortly after leaving Essen. The provisions had lasted much longer than Kamiko would have imagined, another mystery in what was becoming a life filled with unknowns. Even Uila's feed rations seemed to be holding out.

Kamiko and Siruis watched the day's exercise in awe as Jerim took Uila through his game. Today's lesson would be one-on-one. It was becoming obvious that Jerim was reaching Uila at a much deeper level of communication than either of the sisters had seen before. He had recently added the use of several deep guttural barks when calling Uila to bear, and the horse had taken to answering.

"I feel change coming. A fundamental shift in everything." Kamiko heard the words come out of her mouth even as they formed in her mind. "Watching Jerim out there with Uila"—she paused as the words veered from what she was trying to say—"I do not mind mystery, but I hate being ignorant. I would rather live without sight than without knowledge."

"I agree."

The two sisters were sitting in the low grass near the top of the sloping rise leading to the ruins. Fifty paces behind them, the face of the jungle awaited, their new adversary. There the forest grew in size and depth, and the travel would be slow. At dawn they would begin to pass through.

Out beyond the sisters' bare toes, the land fell away at a gentle slope into an open field, a remnant of the nearby plains the jungle had surrounded but had not yet overthrown. It snaked away southward beyond sight. The air was humid from the rains, and the day still felt cool from the slow breeze drifting up from the south.

Jerim was leading Uila at a fast run, easily outpacing the warhorse. They had made a long circuit around the northern end of the grassy island. Uila thundered with all of his considerable might behind Jerim. Kamiko had never seen Uila run as fast and wild in all their years together, and she could tell he was growing stronger. But Kamiko knew something deeper was going on. Uila was not simply attracted to Jerim with animal instinct. Jerim was in his head somehow, affecting Uila's behavior.

The chase had taken them to the eastern edge of the field to where the jungle's ancient assault had been slowed by a wide deep ravine. Although normally dry, it was now laden with flowing brown water from the several days of heavy rain. On the jungle side of the ravine, erosion had undercut the bank at several points, causing many of the trees to falter in the steady march. And though many of the trees were tilted only a few degrees over the ravine, no few were laid to the ground, roots clinging to the bank, crowns resting in the field on the opposite side.

One of these was an aged sentinel whose girth could hold a freight wagon and whose length could contain the wagon and a team of six draft horses. It had the look of having been the first to fall long years past. The sign of decay was evident in the thick bark that hung from below it in broken weather-grayed sheets. Kamiko had used it to bridge the ravine just before they'd stopped to rest.

Jerim bounded high into the air, a giant featherless raptor soaring up and away from Uila. His flight took him to the midpoint of the prone tree where, for a moment, the giant youth and the giant tree appeared more normal in relative size. He shot immediately into the sky again and landed on the jungle side of the ravine. Uila followed headlong until the last moment, then tried without success to stop and instead dove for the tree from the very edge of the bank. By the time Uila's hooves slammed home on the fat trunk, Jerim had reversed course and was lunging once again, back toward Uila.

Uila's hooves lost purchase on the brittle bark, and the great warhorse bounded off the tree and fell headlong toward the churning muddy water. He struck Jerim midfall, chest to chest. The suddenness of the situation drove a bolt of shock into Kamiko as she watched Jerim and Uila plunge beneath the surface and out of sight. With a loud yelp, she was up and running.

Panic grew quickly, another sensation lost in Kamiko's distant past. A slight rise, hidden beneath the grass, stole her footing, and she pitched forward. She dove into the motion, spinning instead of falling. Though her mind was a blank, her body moved of its own accord, and she rolled to her feet without slowing. The great tree seemed a hundred leagues away. She ran without thinking. If she allowed thought, she may falter.

She tore past the crown of the massive tree to the jagged edge of the ravine, expecting to find Jerim and Uila being swept away, no doubt thrashing but still alive. When Jerim's deep bark struck her ears from behind, she dug in her heels and spun toward the sound and realized that Jerim was laughing.

At first she saw only churning water and the bank where the massive lower limbs lay buried in the mud. When a great mound of the bank moved, she realized she was looking directly at the duo. Uila's head lifted from Jerim's shoulder with a quiet deep grumble. They were completely covered with dark ruddy mud. Jerim was lying on his back with his right arm wrapped around Uila's middle, hugging him close. Both of Uila's front legs were draped over Jerim's shoulder, belly to belly with the giant. The lower halves of their bodies, up to Jerim's chest, were beneath the surface of the rushing water, which was trying to pull them from the bank and take them further downstream. Jerim's left hand was clamped onto one of the thick limbs, where it met the tree trunk, securing them in place.

Kamiko bolted to their aid but could see no way to adequately help them. She dropped down near Jerim's head, frantically doing nothing. "What can I do?" Her voice revealed little of the racing of her heart.

Uila was not struggling to get out of the water. He was laying atop Jerim as if he had no care in the world. Even considering Jerim's enormous mass, Uila still buried the young giant beneath muddy horseflesh, pinning him against the bank. If Jerim released his hold on the tree, the water would most likely pull them in again. If Uila tried to climb out, he would trample Jerim in the process. Though Kamiko was possessed of great strength, it was simply human strength, and she could, in no way, offer the assistance of enough muscle to affect the outcome.

As Kamiko's panic subsided, sudden relief flooded into its wake. Triggered by Jerim's chuckle and Uila's quiet mumbling, Kamiko dropped to sit in the damp grass, her bare feet still in the mud above Jerim's head, and let the laughter rise in her chest. Somewhere in the recesses of her mind, she realized that she'd almost forgotten how to laugh. She felt the old habitual urge to stifle the laughter behind the mask of her Warrior bearing, lest it distract her from the darkness of living in a world of evil men.

But the laughter would not be denied and rolled out over the rushing water in waves of bright music Kamiko had forgotten she possessed. The waves echoed inward as well, washing over the dry treeless landscape that had become her spirit. She had no claim to joy, no right to be at peace. Too many had died by her hand, and countless more would follow. The flame cooled. The laughter trailed off. But the sweet wash of joy lingered, leaving her heart lighter than it had been in a very long time.

"What are we going to do, Jerim? We don't have time to wait for the river to run dry."

He turned his head to peer at Kamiko, his wet muddy hair a mask nearly covering his face. Kamiko leaned forward and parted his hair down the middle, drawing it to either side like a great muddy curtain. She dried the moisture from her fingertips and wiped her hands across Jerim's face, carefully clearing the dirty water from his eyes and forehead. Uila nudged and nuzzled Kamiko's arm with his nose to draw the brief scratching and pats of affection he sought.

Jerim looked to his left and right as far as he was able to turn his head. "Back away, Sister. Give me some room."

Kamiko drew her feet up and stood, backing away as he'd requested but uncertain as to why. Jerim relaxed, drew several deep, chest-swelling breaths, and let them out slowly. Uila went still and quiet, his head resting next to Jerim's. The only sounds were of flowing water and sparse but piercing bird calls from deeper inside the jungle. Kamiko's eyes were momentarily drawn to the canopy across the deep ravine by motion at the periphery of her sight.

The dark jungle face was dotted with a vast array of colored feathers, as well as hundreds of furry faces and the overlarge curious eyes of a troop of tree monkeys. Attempts at stillness and silence were a wasted effort for the monkeys, as wave after wave of jumping and bright chitters swept through their numbers. Below them, several enormous jungle cats paced, tails twitching with nervous energy, their eyes never leaving Jerim for more than a moment.

Then almost too slow to perceive, Jerim's muscles began to flex. The smooth rolling slopes of definition began to sharpen and divide into cords and strands and clusters of smaller bulges. Kamiko stepped farther away but kept her eyes riveted on Jerim, thoughts of the mighty Bartol flitting through her mind. Yet Bartol was dark and old, while Jerim was still blush and pale with youth. She realized that she'd never imagined Bartol being like Jerim, young and beautiful.

Jerim leaned his head forward and simply pulled with the hand clamped to the tree limb. Though the rippling field of muscle across his back swelled and flexed, he seemed to be affording very little effort. He began pushing with his feet, still chest-deep in the flowing torrent, Uila lying silent and still against his chest. He began taking small calculated steps backward, again without any evidence of strain. With his hand still grasping the thick limb, he was soon standing thigh-deep in the muddy water.

Many times Kamiko had witnessed Bartol as he performed feats of wonder, lifting things which could not be lifted, felling trees with a single blow of his fist, leaping a river gorge it took Kamiko a sixty-count to bridge, riding Uila at a full run. Yet she would never tire of seeing such wonders, and she felt her heart churning anew.

Jerim turned at the waist and began lowering Uila to the bank, using the tree as an anchor to keep him upright. Kamiko could not help but reach for the warhorse; she stopped short of touching him and instead backed away and allowed him an open path.

For a moment, it appeared that Jerim had come to a point of strain on his strength, his left hand locked around the limb, his right arm just beginning to extend beneath the fullness of Uila's weight. As the giant paused in his slow procession, Kamiko noticed something she'd never witnessed with Bartol. Jerim's corded muscles were not simply rolling and flexing, they were growing before her eyes. After a moment, he lowered Uila gently to his hooves, back legs in the water to his hocks, front feet on the ground.

Kamiko watched as the warhorse stepped carefully from the ravine onto solid ground. He lowered his head and shook the mass of his body, throwing much of the sluicing water off in a raining torrent that showered Kamiko with muddy specks. Then he trotted out into the grass and rolled to his back, flopping from side to side to further dry himself. Seeing nothing about Uila that suggested he was injured, Kamiko looked back to where Jerim was standing thigh-deep in the water.

Without warning, a cold shudder rippled up the length of Kamiko's spine. She spun all the way around, expecting to see someone standing close by but saw only Uila, the open plains and the jungle. All of her instincts told her that trouble had arrived, but, in what form, she could not discern. She turned back to Jerim with her hackles standing sharp, while her eyes kept the periphery in focus.

Chapter 8

Jerim had not moved. His left hand still grasped the fat limb, and his right arm was still extended to where Uila had come free of his hold. The whole of his body began shuddering as if under a weight mightier than even Uila's heavy mass. The shroud of silence which fell over the jungle was only a tiny pause between a drawn breath and the release of a storm. It was a momentary herald Kamiko caught, almost too late. She crouched into a ready stance, and again, as countless times before, it saved her life.

The jungle erupted with sound and motion—angry, violent, frightening. Uila bolted out into the grassy field, unhinged and wild, thrashing the ground and kicking at unseen pursuers, his mind seemingly lost. The monkeys fell immediately to war among the boughs of the higher canopy, as the great colorful birds scattered in every direction. Droves of smaller darker birds, hidden by the inherent shadows of the jungle heights, converged, becoming a single shrieking moving shape, tearing through the treetops.

Kamiko saw Jerim move. He spun at the waist and, with no more effort than snapping a twig, broke the fat limb from the trunk of the downed tree. Kamiko was already in the air. She landed atop the tree trunk just as Jerim's empty right fist flashed through the space where she'd been. His momentum slung his long muddy hair across his face, blinding him. Kamiko knew better than to think it would detract from his abilities, for Bartol had mentored him. She leapt again, flipping off the tree to land opposite from Jerim, all the while gathering the surroundings into her awareness.

If she broke across the field, Jerim would be on her instantly, if his intentions were indeed to take her down. If she dove into the rushing water, the outcome would be the same. She had to stay ahead of his thoughts, to be where he would not expect and to find that quickly moving place in full flight. She had no clue about his behavior, no idea what set him off. But she was not yet convinced he was trying to attack her. Again the odd sensation that someone else was present assailed her mind.

She leapt away again as he smashed his open palm into the thick of the tree. Kamiko came down several feet away from the trunk of the tree and farther from the bank, landing amid the sprawling dead limbs, and dropped to her belly.

Jerim threw his head back and bellowed up into the open sky. He still held the heavy limb to one side, as though it was no more than a hollow length of cane. The muscles in his neck and along his back and shoulders bulged and rolled and, to her amazement, began to grow.

Again the wild reacted, and the fighting was replaced by some thousand odd voices of every timbre, howling and wailing with the same mournful agony as Jerim. It was not mimicry; it was real to them. They were engaged in Jerim's misery, just as they had been in his joy and rage.

The din was unnerving. Kamiko felt a wave of despair strike her heart, and his deep pain became hers as well. Not directly from Jerim, the way it seemed to work with the animals, but from her own knowledge of human suffering. She knew then and there that Jerim had suffered beyond what she could comprehend. Even so, the Warrior within her held absolute sway over her thoughts and emotions, keeping the Woman quietly at bay. Kamiko felt completely helpless.

Jerim's voice wailed long and fierce and showed no sign of weakening. His arms and legs visibly thickened. His tunic tore from the strain of his swelling chest, his waistband snapped, the forgotten limb in his fist crackled and popped and fell in two pieces to the ground. Kamiko half-imagined, half-expected his skin to tear under the strain as well, for Jerim's body began to darken with a flushing crimson.

A tiny whisper from just behind her startled Kamiko.

"Beloved!" Siruis's voice was both the slightest breeze through a summer willow and a sharp clap of thunder.

Kamiko whipped her head around only to find no one there. Instead Siruis was standing in the place where Kamiko had left her, near the top of the rise just below the ruins. Uila was standing at her side. Even from the distance, Kamiko could see his great chest heaving for breath. Otherwise he stood at the full readiness that Kamiko recognized as his guard.

"Beloved, hear me!" Came the breathy thunderclap again just as Siruis took a tentative step forward, drawing Uila with her.

Jerim's roar clipped off as though he was struck in the chest. Kamiko snapped her eyes back to him. She rose to a low crouch within the crown of the tree, watching Jerim's head turn slowly from side to side, as if something of great import lay just beyond his sight. Overly thick hands came up to his face, great knots of muscle curling his fingers into misshapen claws. At first, Kamiko thought it only her imagination when she felt the thrumming of his great heart against her feet and through the air, fast and heavy like a deep frantic war drum.

"Jerim!" Siruis said, again sounding so near, Kamiko would have thought Siruis was speaking into her ear from an arm's length. On impulse, she turned to mark Siruis's passage across the field, only to find her standing nearby, among the sprawling limbs. What had been a long hard sprint for Kamiko had taken only seconds for Siruis and Uila. Kamiko rotated on the balls of her feet to turn more fully toward her sister, dividing her attention between Siruis and Jerim.

"Beloved, hear my voice. Turn your heart to me, open your mind."

It seemed to Kamiko that Siruis's words were for Jerim, but she was speaking to Uila. His great head was at her feet, her hand resting, delicate and calming, on his neck. He was perfectly still, even to his breathing. The odd doubling of Siruis's voice, the barest whisper from her lips in concert with the thunder of her voice in Kamiko's head, was unsettling.

Kamiko looked back over her shoulder and saw that Jerim was also breathless, now as still as a statue. His hands were pressed to his face, his skin shades darker and taut with knotted muscle. The next was a command, all whispers gone. Kamiko felt the foundation of the world shudder against her feet.

"Jerim, hear me!"

Siruis's presence washed over Kamiko in a single wave of bright power and cooling peaceful comfort. In that moment, all of her nagging and struggles, her new-found fears and old wounds of the spirit sluiced away like dried sweat in a sudden downpour. Though the call was for Jerim, Kamiko felt herself respond as, for the smallest of moments, all else fell away but Siruis.

Uila's head came up with a start, snorting confusion and fear, but then he held himself silent and still. His ears and eyes found and momentarily locked upon Kamiko. She could see his anxiety dissolve as he shifted his feet to guarded readiness and squared his broad mud-stained chest. Siruis was still under his guardianship. Her hand was on Uila's shoulder, her face now toward Jerim.

The thunder was gone from Siruis's small voice as she spoke Jerim's name again. The jungle across the ravine seemed void of life, though Kamiko had not noticed the exodus, only the silent aftermath. The sharp tang of blood was in the air.

She turned back toward Jerim as she rose. A small nagging voice in her mind told her she would never know normalcy again. Those things in her past that had seemed extraordinary would be forever mundane.

Jerim's great mass began to smooth even as Kamiko watched, the knotted bulges across his neck and shoulders losing the sharpened relief of ridged valleys, of deep clefts. She could not see his face from her line of sight, but his hands spoke volumes. They shook with the strain of squeezing his own skull, then trembled and came to rest where they lay against his head, his fingers entangled in mud and hair. He'd still drawn no breath, and though his bulging muscles continued to relax, the darker crimson of his skin and the size of his mass remained unchanged. Jerim could be no less than two full hands taller, broader across his chest and thicker in every aspect of limb and torso.

The only sounds were those of whispering wind and swift water. Jerim's body shuddered hard. He drew a slow deep breath and began swaying to and fro like a drunkard, his hands once again clamping his skull with staggering force.

Kamiko imagined that she felt the deep rumble before she could hear it, against her feet and through the air. Jerim's voice rose up suddenly in a loud but deep shout—the sound of violence at war inside Jerim. It tore at Kamiko's heart. She had seen anguish, had lived with it enough for a lifetime already, but held no such wail in her soul. This was something boundless and ancient. Primeval. Jerim could no longer be taken for a simple young man with a stormy past as his youthful face had declared. There was an uncommon darkness in him.

He fell backward with a slump that left him lying in the grass, his feet buried well past his ankles in the mudbank. His voice wavered and fell low, as his hands came away from his head and dropped to his sides. Though he went limp, it took a few quiet moments before he grew still. Only the slight rise and fall of his chest told Kamiko he was alive.

*****

The night air was chill, with a damp slow breeze moving down from the jungle. The only indication of air moving at all was in the tilt of the narrow line of smoke, twisting upward from a small fire she'd kept since nightfall. Jerim had not moved. Siruis sat at his shoulder with her head bowed in whispered meditation. Even the night calls were silent, which, given the reaction of the jungle creatures to Jerim, made Kamiko imagine thousands of eyes fixed on his still body.

After Kamiko had moved their camp necessities from the ruins down to where Jerim lay, they spent the better part of an hour trying to clean him up in some small measure. Kamiko had dipped brown water from the ravine and carefully rinsed the dirty film from his face and eyes. With clean water from her stores, Siruis bathed his face, neck, and what hair she could reach without moving his head.

Kamiko felt as though she worked on an enormous carved bust, odd having so thick a set of features under her fingertips. Odd too that those features held an almost metallic sheen of burnished crimson, dark gray in the thin moonlight. Heat poured off his body from some well-stoked furnace deep inside, drying the moisture from their washing within seconds.

She'd covered Jerim with a thin blanket from waist to crown and set two sticks into the ground on either side of his head to form a low tent above his face. The morning would be heavy with dew.

They then turned their attention to dislodging his legs from where they were buried past midcalf in the mud. Each was greater in girth than Kamiko's waist, and she had no doubt that each weighed half her own significant mass.

By the time the task was complete, her arms were leaden, and her back was a knotted field of tired, sore muscles. The damp grass felt cold against her skin when she at last lay back to take a few moments' rest. She was almost as dirty as Jerim, and Uila had not yet been brushed out. The three of them were a sodden mess, with nothing but the dirty swirl of runoff water to bathe in. Three days into the jungle, the River Perinaldi would be in a swollen rage, the next source of clean water, and the earliest possibility of a good bath.

Chapter 9

Kamiko felt her body flex, and she sat up abruptly as she came out of an unexpected doze. Siruis was seated in the grass beside her and, as soon as Kamiko's eyes came open, laid her hand on Kamiko's shoulder.

"Come with me, Sister."

Everything within the perceptible range of Kamiko's senses drained first of color, then of substance. The sensation of being submerged in gray light swept over her then, just as suddenly, ceased. As her eyes came into focus, she could see they were high on a mountain, perched on the precipice of a great sliver of stone. She knelt beside Siruis and peered over the edge of their outcropping and looked down upon nothing but vast white depths. Ice-laden wind howled in her face, every gust an attempt to throw her down, yet she felt neither cold nor threat. At her side, Siruis stood facing west in perfect stillness, her eyes upon some distant point.

Kamiko could see no shade of color, only degrees of gray and pristine white. And though the night was moonless and dark, she could easily see everything before them. Even her sister's bright blue eyes shone like polished silver. She followed Siruis's gaze to a distant peak and easily recognized where they were. They stood on the towering eastern peak of Mount Elan. Immediately to their west stood the tall mass of Mount Oman, mountain twins overlooking

Ravencroft City. Between them lay the only passage through the mountains to the prosperous northern lands beyond. This was the capitol city of Baron Riplin's domain, 350 leagues north of the kingdom of Cairistonia. Siruis's attention was fixed on Mount Oman's icy peak.

"What is this, Siruis?" Kamiko asked in a low whisper.

"Be still and watch. This is real, Sister, we are seeing no vision. We are here...now." Siruis's voice had grown stern. She lifted her hand and pointed toward the peak of Mount Oman and spoke, "See there, Kamiko, the face of our enemy." As Siruis's finger came level with the top of Mount Oman, a man appeared. He too was standing on a great prominence of stone and, like the sisters, was perched at the very edge, looking down. Even with the great span of darkness and distance between them, Kamiko could see him in fine detail, as if near and far were one thing.

Kamiko's eyes fell first on his hands. His left hand was a twisted wreck of coiled knotted fingers, hanging from a bone-thin wrist. He held it out over the valley below them under a great and painful strain. A dark shadow flowed from his wretched palm, flooding down the face of the mountain. In his right hand hung a massive hilt, a sword with no blade. The sheer weight of the hilt and crosspiece bent his back in a perpetual rightward lean. Where his fist gripped the hilt, sword and flesh were melded into one, his hand as blackened as the sword.

The very sight of him filled her with an unexpected dread, and she rose to stand beside Siruis. Her hand moved instinctively to her shoulder, seeking the familiar assurance of steel strapped to her back. But it was not there. Her sword was with her gear beside a small fire four hundred leagues southeast. Something told her that steel would be useless against this being, even though he appeared to be simply a strong man.

"Do not look upon his face, Sister," Siruis said, "and never speak a word to him, lest you give him a foothold." Kamiko lowered her eyes with a curt nod to Siruis.

Far below them, the unbroken shroud of white parted, revealing the great wide valley where Ravencroft City lay sprawled. The shadow issuing from the man's withered hand had covered the mountainside entirely and was just passing into the northern edge of the great city, spilling an unnatural darkness into the streets like a fast-moving flood. The whole of the valley shuddered and moaned.

"He is Luthain," Siruis said. "Do not fear him, Sister, fear only God."

The sound of Siruis's words triggered a mild jolt inside Kamiko. Time, breath, and heartbeat all began anew but with the dull ache of an old wound. She couldn't recall when they'd stopped.

"He is second of the Faleen Dre'Gothe…Perfidious Daemonis."

Siruis's voice was calm and soft, completely devoid of fear. There was a certain familiarity in the words, but their meaning escaped Kamiko. She forced her heart to slow and locked her eyes on Siruis's calm face. The highland winds wailed around them, waves of thick snow blowing in every direction but downward.

Kamiko found her voice. "What is that? Daemonis? Is he… what did you say?"

Siruis's face was still fixed on the distant peak as she said, "He is an angel, Sister, though deceived by the usurper and cast out. He is cursed beyond what you and I can imagine."

The mysteries of old, angels and demons, the heavenly realms—Kamiko had learned of these things from the days of her earliest youth. Djinnasee had taught her of the living God with such regularity and vigor that she had never considered any other way possible. Until this very moment, she thought she had lived with that knowledge as the very fabric of her life. Now she saw that it was not so, that she had laid that garment aside somewhere along the journey.

"Yes, Sister, see and believe." Siruis touched Kamiko's arm again, and movement flourished around them. Dark wisps of shadowy forms materialized, and for a moment, Kamiko could see they were surrounded by what appeared to be men. She heard their voices in her mind, speaking sinister thoughts but with the sweetness one would expect from a close friend. They wanted her to be angry and afraid.

Then a slight tremor rippled up her arm as heat bloomed in her palm and instantly engulfed her entire hand. The shock of the unexpected sensation stunned her mind and took her breath, and for a few moments, she was unable to move. She was holding a silver sword. It was the same one she'd held in the vision weeks ago, the sword she would one day destroy a mountain with. The world around her had grown still and quiet, as if she and the sword were the only two things in existence. Kamiko felt a presence about the sword which caused both emotions to rise in her chest—fear and elation.

The moment of disjointed serenity ended. The wind wailed around her, and the icy mountain was once again under her feet, Siruis at her side. Luthain still poured his vile taint into the physical realm of man and beast. As if by Luthain's command, the highland gale turned downward in full, driving an icy storm into the sprawl of Ravencroft City.

The sword called to her, a voiceless cry for release, for havoc. She simply raised it skyward, and a bright clear voice rang out from the blade, like a silver bell, reverberating in her hand and down her arm. She held fast to the sword and peered across the chasm at Luthain, her eyes carefully fixed to his chest.

His perfect form twisted in agony, his mouth opened with silent rage. Black spittle flew from his mouth as he writhed, shaking his head and body with such violence that even Siruis took a step backward. The great dark angel lunged forward and dove from the precipice, disappearing into the very blackness he had released into the physical realm.

The sword's silvery voice clipped off, but the sound rang through the heavens for several moments. As the bright resonance diminished, the sword vanished. However, the memory of the being that had taken up the brief occupancy in her hand was burned into her soul. She could feel the name as clearly as her own but could not connect it to any word she had ever heard.

Hun'jotzimon.

She could feel the vast nature of the sword's power, like a bottomless pit looming at her feet, threatening to draw her into its depth. It was exhilarating to think she'd held such a being in her hand.

Down in the wide valley, the shadow continued to move across the city, filling every space. The entire valley rumbled and shook as the very foundation of nature reeled from the tainted darkness. Kamiko and Siruis watched in silence as the frigid mountain storm dropped into the ancient upper city.

"It seems winter will be early this year, Kamiko."

"Much more than winter has come to Ravencroft City. Siruis," Kamiko asked, "what have we just seen?"

"Luthain has been given jurisdiction over all these lands. He has begun his imperative."

"What do you mean his imperative? He is bound. All daemon are bound."

"Bound, yes, but not without function, Sister. Luthain is powerful beyond human measure. He has been preparing for centuries, answering the ever-increasing call from the people of these great kingdoms. He is here at their insistence. Were he not bound, we would be watching the destruction of Ravencroft."

"No, Siruis, that cannot be. God would not abandon Ravencroft to the whims of Luthain."

"Both Cairistonia and Ravencroft have been granted to Luthain's petition before the Council of the Host. God has not abandoned them, Kamiko, he has granted the people's collective wish. It could be said that he has answered even their darkest prayers. Luthain is here by their own invitation. But God will move in might over the land, have no doubt." After a moment of reflection, Siruis added, "Luthain's request to crush King Per El`Thorn was denied, Sister, with a single provision."

Kamiko's brow furrowed slightly. "What provision, Sister?"

The highland storm was building around them, below them, driving a deep spike of frigid cold into the heart of the vast city. Siruis was silent for a few-count, then spoke with a questioning voice, "I have not been made privy to that, Kamiko." Below them, the storm seemed alive, set on a purpose. It did not move as a storm so much as it writhed like an angry, hungry serpent loosed upon a field of unsuspecting prey.

Kamiko moved her open right hand out over the city. She could feel the unrest already rising like heat from a newly built fire. And even from the lofty height, she could hear individual voices, fleeting chirps of anger and fear, barks of surprise at the sudden cold, feet running, doors slamming in the wind as well as against it.

She gazed into her empty right hand and saw only skin pulled tight over muscle and bone. She tried to see herself as the Warrior in that moment and failed. The being she had held in her hand made such a notion moot. She knew if she wielded the sword, as a warrior, the land and all living in it would perish. "I have no compassion, Siruis. It is not in me. I am a butcher." She dropped her hand and turned to face Siruis. And froze.

The young sister held her hand out toward the north and whispered to Kamiko, "More to see…still the *now*, Sister. This is no vision, this is sight."

Just beyond Siruis, not fifty paces, a man knelt in the blowing snow, his gloved hands resting heavy on a newly built stone sepulcher. His brother, Kamiko somehow knows. Yet the man was deep in the mountains, far to the north from her and Siruis. He wept openly. "I will know this man," she spoke the thought aloud.

A woman's whispered voice drifted across her shoulder, a voice Kamiko recognized as the master of all thieves. Trouble! Dairei Parzon was back. Kamiko turned on the balls of her feet, ready to move, to defend.

There was movement far to the west, beyond the river, in King El`Thorn's land. Another great shadow loomed in the savage wilds even further west. It pressed the mighty king to the foot of his own mountain. This shadow was that of men bent on war. Bartol's thundering bellow marked the onset of battle as the Seven Clans made their stand. Again the cool feminine whisper, one forever marked by mischief, and Kamiko's swift reaction, spinning at the ready. Dairei! The only person to have defeated Kamiko in a fight.

Yet at Kamiko's feet lay only a giant, his head and shoulders draped in a funeral shroud, dried brown flowers scattered across his chest. The familiarity struck her as odd, as though she was seeing the projection of a dusty memory. The snow and blistering wind were gone, the highland vista above Ravencroft a sharp memory. She turned to look back toward the man kneeling at the grave but saw only scattered tree limbs, a grassy field, and a horse.

Uila! And Jerim.

Her senses flooded her mind with so much information that it took several moments to draw a breath. She saw a slow cyclone of images until her knees touched the grass. Then the weight of the physical world came upon Kamiko in a rush, as the sight dimmed away. She lay back as sleep took her. The last thing she saw was Siruis sitting in the grass at Jerim's head.

Chapter 10

Be still. The fear of the Lord is the beginning of wisdom.

Djinnasee's words were so familiar, the sound of his voice in her head so strong, that at first Kamiko imagined he stood over her as he spoke. She opened her eyes to a black sky filled with stars and the feeling of cool night air on her face. She felt no urgency for the present moment, so she stayed where she was, stretched in the grass, half-covered with dried mud. Jerim was where she'd left him, his breath so slow she had to listen carefully to hear him at all.

In all the wash of stars, her eyes fell directly upon Koralilia, her personal guardian of the heavens, rising from the east. On the clearer nights, the star formation was hard to find because the overall sight of celestial wonder was overwhelming, but Kamiko could point to it with her eyes closed. Her hand had almost ceased longing for the feel of her talisman and the worry stone habit. It was strongest when she was lying beneath the stars. The talisman was made in the depiction of the sea turtle constellation and was her connection to Delia Mars, her ancestor.

Her eyes lingered on the heavens, but her thoughts began dancing among El`Thorn, Siruis, Luthain, Djinnasee, and the sword, each driving her focus to the next in a quick loop. She had seen what mere humans are not supposed to see. Beings such as Luthain are hidden from people for good reason. Beings such as the sword were too vast and too powerful to reside in the physical realm. People could not easily dwell beneath the shadow of such giants, be it lords of chaos or of order. The result was the same. The will to exist, the *need* to exist, dwindles and dies. Meaning and purpose become insignificant in the face of the colossal. She felt small in the face of that storm.

She was on her back beneath an unending field of stars. The grass beneath her was sharp and icy cold, her breath thick as water. For the first time, her body felt like nothing more than a container, her soul a thing trapped inside the minuscule space.

She tried to focus her thoughts, to find one thing she could connect her heart to. The attempt left her feeling empty. She had no one beyond Djinnasee who was truly a part of her life. She had not felt kindness, desire, kinship, or even a relatively close friendship since her younger days. Since El`Thorn. Everyone she had known for two decades had been part of her warrior world, brothers and sisters but only at arms.

A small voice slipped into her awareness, a whisper of fear. Siruis. It rose quickly to a clipped-off cry, "Leave him be! Bartol, *no*!"

Bartol was here? Something was happening. She rolled from her back to her hands and knees. Her movements were slow, even as her thoughts were racing. Bartol's presence always meant big trouble was afoot. Always.

But Bartol was not nearby. Kamiko knew exactly where he was, a few hundred leagues to the west, engaged in a newly sprung war. He would be at King El`Thorn's side for months to come. She was not sure how she knew this, but it was a fixed certainty in her mind. The sound of his mighty roar was still in her head. That she could recall his voice, all the way from the barbarian lands, left her confused.

Siruis sat in the grass a few steps away. Her legs were out to one side, and she leaned heavily upon her hands. Her head hung low and slowly shook from side to side. Fear and disbelief radiated from the motion, from her posture. Kamiko had thought Siruis was immune to such things. She could barely tell Siruis was speaking, her voice was so thin and weak, but as she crawled closer, she could hear Bartol's name on Siruis's lips again and again, pleading and desperate.

Feeling and strength returned to Kamiko's limbs slowly. The cool damp of night mingled with the warm sweat trailing down her face in itching rivulets that felt like a battalion of tiny ants. Uila sniggered and stepped carefully to Kamiko's side, his hot breath brushing the nape of her neck. The familiarity of the sensation helped clear her head, and she rose, leaning into Uila's solid mass.

She moved to Siruis's side and lowered to one knee. Siruis's thick mane of hair was unbound and shrouded her face and shoulders completely.

"Sister," Kamiko whispered. No response. Kamiko reached down, touched her shoulder, and said a little louder, "Siruis!"

The young sister's entire body jerked hard, a quiet gasp of surprise breaking from her lips. From her reaction, Kamiko could easily imagine that a live coal had been set on her shoulder. She moved faster than Kamiko thought possible, scampering away on her hands and feet. Even in the dim firelight, Siruis's white face was a mask of fear, flashing over her shoulder again and again. She was running for her life, running from Kamiko.

Siruis dove into the shaggy grass beside the downed tree and pressed her back against the trunk. When she looked at Kamiko, there was no measure of recognition evident, only panic. Her crystalline eyes darted past Kamiko several times in quick flashes as she scanned and rescanned the surroundings. On instinct, Kamiko scanned the area as well—sight, sound, and scent. No one. Just the same, Kamiko divided her attention, keeping the greater part of her awareness on their surroundings. Nothing stirred.

She approached Siruis slowly, making no quick movements, as if she was stepping toward a frightened animal on the verge of bolting. Siruis turned her full attention toward Kamiko and grew as still as a badger backed into a hole. Her flight effort was spent; fight was now the only option. Kamiko saw Siruis's tiny fists knotting into the only weapons she could muster.

The sight of her sister in such a wretched state released a wave of compassion into Kamiko's heart. The hopelessness and fear of the innocent always turned Kamiko from her path, without exception. They were enemies Kamiko could not strike with sword or fist.

She could not have avoided coming to love this frail woman. The opposing forces of strength and weakness at work inside Siruis were beginning to stagger Kamiko's mind. She sensed an ancient depth in Siruis, a well of knowledge beyond human term and capacity. Yet here she was, facing down Kamiko with small white fists, shivering with fearful rage.

Kamiko bent her knees to the ground within an arm's length of Siruis. The small fists lost all strength and fell apart and a soft moan escaped her colorless lips. Then came that moment of recognition, the dawning of truth, evident in the sudden change in Siruis's body language. She fell forward to her hands, her breath coarse and quick. Her muscles went slack, and she swayed to one side. Kamiko's quick hands caught and drew her into a gentle embrace.

Siruis collapsed against Kamiko's chest, her body limp but trembling. She spoke so quietly Kamiko could not understand her words, only pick out the names of Bartol and Jerim.

Kamiko spoke quietly. "Rest here with me, Sister. We are both tired to the bone."

Siruis drew a deep clearing breath, her trembling beginning to settle.

"It is Bartol. He is lost to us. He and Jerim were—" She stopped midsentence, lifted her face from Kamiko's chest, and looked around them in bewilderment, shaking her head as if in denial of what she was seeing. "Where are we?"

"The ruins of Ferith-Dale."

Siruis was still shaking her head as she pulled further back from Kamiko. Her shock was waning, but the comfort of closeness was something she was slow to relinquish.

"No," she said. "That cannot be true. We passed through Ferith-Dale before winter solstice, last…"

Siruis's eyes became busy with nervous energy, darting from point to point without slowing to even gain focus. Kamiko could see that she was not looking for details, she was looking for something big. She was looking for Bartol. Her searching stopped upon Jerim.

"Bartol is not here, Siruis. He is with King El`Thorn, many leagues to the west."

"No, it cannot be so. We have been with him for months." Her voice deepened and softened. "And King El`Thorn is…" Her voice trailed away, and she became very still.

Kamiko waited with her. She could feel her own body giving in to exhaustion in waves. She needed sleep, if only for a short while longer. Her mind was teetering on delusion, her ability to reason clearly now clouded with weariness. She imagined the pressure of eyes on her back but resisted the urge to look behind her.

"Ravencroft, Kamiko, we are in Ravencroft." Siruis's own disbelief was obvious to Kamiko. She was trying to convince herself of that which was obviously not true.

"Siruis, look at me." Kamiko raised her palm toward Siruis's face, drawing her attention to where their gazes met. Siruis's eyes locked onto Kamiko's with fierce intensity and the fear drained away to sudden weariness. The trust she showed Kamiko was without reservation, complete from the very beginning. Such a thing was a rare treasure to Kamiko.

She felt a renewed determination rise in her chest. Siruis deserved to be protected here among men. She was waging war, the like and kind Kamiko could not comprehend. She knew then that nothing of this world would harm Siruis without first getting past Kamiko. With a flutter in her chest, she felt the birth of kinship, of a wholeness of spirit between two people. Her sister. In that moment, Kamiko knew she was capable of committing war the likes of which had never been seen.

Stray cords of matted hair were stuck to Siruis's face and neck by the sheen of sticky sweat covering her skin. The only light besides the glittering mass of stars overhead came from the small fire near Jerim, a source quickly dwindling. Even so, the flames cast a dancing miasma of fire-hued shadows across Siruis's face and distorted those features into something Kamiko could barely recognize. Her thick loose mane seemed to have a life all its own, waving about in frustrated captivity, every movement an attempt at gaining freedom. She appeared no less disheveled and dirty than the witches of Eten and no less maniacal. Kamiko had no doubt that while in her current state, Siruis could walk into their midst unnoticed.

Kamiko reached to gently brush the strands from Siruis's face and could see the young woman was returning to her center, calming in waves of recognition. Her skin was cool and clammy to the touch, and Kamiko had to lift the strands away from the stickiness of her face. She bundled Siruis's wild mane by sweeping her hands down each side of her head, drawing the gathered mass away from her face. This she twisted and gently stuffed into Siruis's cloak at the nape of her neck, a temporary solution at best. Kamiko was certain the mass was alive.

She could feel the tension in Siruis's body begin to drain away as she leaned back against her chest. By the time Kamiko had the unruly mane secured, Siruis had gone completely limp, exhausted and asleep.

The overwhelming sensation of being watched itched along her spine. She turned her head and shoulders to look, already suspecting the source. Jerim's darkened face and bloodshot eyes peered at her from where he lay, Uila standing silent, now near his shoulder. He had moved the thin blanket from his face, and with effort, he drew his massive arm out from his side. It was a request that Kamiko fully understood. She moved with as much delicacy as she could manage, trying not to jostle the sleeping sister in her arms as she rose. Siruis held almost no weight as Kamiko carried her to Jerim and lowered her to the crook of his arm.

She stood to turn, but to her surprise, Jerim spoke, "Sister."

She turned back and looked down at him. "Jerim."

His first question to her in all the weeks since they had met completely surprised her. "Why are you called Kamiko Hoshi?"

His face was calm to the point of being serene. He looked at peace. When she did not answer immediately, he continued, "Such is not a name from this part of the world, it does not match your race." He smiled with one side of his mouth, but his entire face brightened, though his skin was still darker than before. His beauty was stunning.

She returned the smile and sat on the ground where they could easily keep eye contact. "I was named by my ancestor, 2,500 years ago. She was orphaned when she was ten and raised by a woman of the race you refer to. They were an honorable people who placed great value in their heritage and their traditions." Then she added, "They are still a strong and viable race, one of the purest still in the world."

"Siruis called you a turtle?"

At this Kamiko laughed out loud. "Well, she called me the Child of the Tortoise Star, a loose meaning of my name. But," she said, still chuckling under her breath, "yes, my friend…I am a turtle."

"I must offer you an apology, Turtle Star," he said. Kamiko cocked her head slightly in question and let the twist of the name go. "It was me who took Uila from you on the day we met. I felt his heart, and it was fierce and bore the mark of great intelligence."

It took her a few moments to figure out what he meant. "Ah… it was you who put him to sleep. How did you do that?" He turned his head toward her slightly and simply looked at her face, seeming to weigh the question for several moments.

"Yes, Sister Kamiko, Turtle Star, but I cannot explain. I feel them in my mind, a primitive sort of emotion that people can't hear or understand. I…understand. They…" He paused and thought a moment. "Understand me. I don't know how." Kamiko thought about the small bird that Jerim had seemed to listen to coming into Essen and how Siruis had been speaking to Uila. Jerim must have been thinking similar thoughts, for he said, "I am able to hear what they hear, see what they see, and to a small degree, I can feel their sensations. I don't feel the pain when they are hurt, but I know they are in pain."

She knew there was much more to it, but now she understood the nature of what was going on. She finally had Jerim in a conversation of more than four words and had other questions, so she changed the subject. "What just happened to you, my friend?"

He held her gaze for a few moments before turning his eyes back to the stars. "Again, Sister, I can tell you only that my body reacts to great physical stress, but I do not know how or why. I know that I can now lift Uila without strain."

"Your body…grew larger, Jerim, right before my eyes."

"Yes."

"You were in a lot of pain," she said flatly. He closed his eyes for a moment, then turned and looked at her.

"Yes, Sister." He thought another moment and continued, "Bartolamew told me such would happen. It is part of my maturing physically. In terms of our race of giant-kin, I am still considered to be only a boy. I, like Bartol, am able to heal myself. When I attempted to release Uila, his weight overbore my muscles and caused them to tear. This caused a wave of spasms over my whole body which, in turn, because I was torn, began to tear more muscle. My body's ability to heal struggled to keep apace but managed to break the cascade. Djinnasee very carefully explained it to me once." His voice had softened, and his words were gradually slowing. "I shall be fine once I sleep."

Kamiko knew of Bartol's ability to heal, but she had never seen him endure what Jerim had just gone through. It made sense that he had because the top of Jerim's head was roughly even with the top of Bartol's shoulder or, at least, until this happened. She could see his eyes drifting shut and his struggle to keep them open.

"Sleep, Jerim…giant-kin," she said quietly and drew the thin blanket over them both even as Jerim's heavy eyes closed.

Kamiko rose on legs that felt like wet rope and looked around the makeshift campsite. The fire was little more than a small pile of bright coals. Uila had fallen into sound sleep, standing motionless at Jerim's shoulder.

"Rest well, my friend," she whispered to Uila. "Tomorrow you will need to keep me astride while I sleep."

She would stand watch. The edge of the deep jungle was no place to sleep unguarded. The first thing to do was stoke the fire back to life. Her mind felt like mud as she began searching for firewood. She had taken only a few steps down the riverbank when the thought occurred to her. She did not even try to suppress the chuckle that rose in her chest and stood beneath an ocean of stars, giggling like a schoolchild. The massive tree was directly behind her, enough firewood to last a half-year.

*****

Jerim left them for the first two days to eat and to heal. When Kamiko asked if he would hunt, he'd lowered his eyes and answered quietly, "Yes, Sister. To be a predator in the wild is natural to all creatures. They fear me only when they know I come as a hunter."

"You warn the animals before you go hunting?"

"No, Turtle Star, they are aware of my intent, as they are with the lion. They see and smell...and they fear." Kamiko could tell Uila was nervous and kept Jerim at a greater distance than usual, his eyes never leaving the giant until he was gone. Siruis's nameless pony had been lost in the brief war Jerim triggered before they entered the jungle. She had bolted into the foray and was taken down in the natural way of the wild.

Three days into the jungle trek, the sweltering still air beneath the thick canopy was driven away by a wash of cold north wind and renewed rains that sent Kamiko and Siruis digging out their hooded cloaks and gloves. Jerim appeared completely unaware of the abrupt drop in temperature and was oblivious to the pouring rain.

The extreme oddity of a cold spell in the southern reaches of the jungle drove Kamiko's thoughts to a memory, the vision of a highlands vista and the unleashing of winter upon an unsuspecting city. She had seen Luthain. And she was left with an odd-sounding word on her tongue, one that would not hold in her thoughts long enough to speak it—a name.

Kamiko knew the ways of survival. She'd been sleeping on the ground for years, living on what could be hunted, trapped, or harvested from nature. Passing through the jungle would be a slow undertaking, over one hundred leagues at a walk. She made a makeshift bow and arrows sufficient for small game, and a pair of heavy wooden spears as the days progressed. And she used a simple lodestone, dangled from a string, to determine north so she could keep a westward bearing.

Jerim would leave to hunt only once every ten days or so, and when he returned, he always brought food. As always, the birds were ever-present, but they had become less noisy and kept more at a distance. But anytime Jerim was near, the jungle was alive with animated shapes and musical calls.

Near the end of their jungle passage, Jerim remarked that very few animals were around them. He believed they were reacting to someone else being in the jungle and were hiding. Such was not unusual as men were commonly out in the southern jungle wilds.

At long last, Kamiko, Siruis, Jerim, and Uila stood looking out over the first distant horizon they had seen for fifty-two days. The cold dark of the jungle had become maddeningly oppressive so that when the lowering sun first fell on their faces, they all but swooned from the sudden relief.

They stopped at a small unnamed river that bordered the jungle's westward edge. Beyond the river spread a less foreboding forest of puffy-topped hardwood groves, lacking the colossal evergreen giants and aged fat sentinels.

Kamiko and Siruis sat side by side on a large flat outcropping of sun-warmed stone. Both were naked beneath light blankets covering each to their shoulders. The stone was set in the bank of the burbling river and extended out over the surface half a dozen paces. The flat of the stone was narrow but fifty-odd strides long and slightly wider where it hung out over the water. Spread behind them, every scrap of clothing and every piece of gear lay drying in the sun, newly washed. They were doing much the same, drying in the warm sun after a hard cold scrubbing. The icy water had made even the chill air seem warm.

The eastern edge of civilization lay seven easy days ahead, the township of Flavin another two days beyond that. Siruis had been distracted for most of the journey, lost to places, events, and people only she could see. But she had not lost contact with the present again. She was always aware of her physical surroundings when her mind regained lucidity.

Kamiko could not decide what unnerved her more, Siruis's persistent chatter of things she could not understand or the fact that much of that chatter was in a language she had never heard. It had apparently become so commonplace with Jerim that he no longer noticed.

He and Uila were two hours gone on a scouting trek and would not be back until after sunset. And though Uila was showing signs of fatigue, he seemed more than pleased to follow Jerim across to the opposite bank and across a wide clearing at a dead run. There had been little opportunity to really stretch his legs in the cluttered bramble of the jungle floor, and Kamiko suspected that lack of use was among the chief causes for his weariness.

The expansive growth of Jerim's body had not decreased in the slightest, though the crimson flush of his skin had faded to a shade slightly darker than he was before. Darker and bigger, like Bartol.

"It takes you a while to stop, Kamiko Hoshi, but you do pick beautiful places to rest," Siruis said quietly, breaking Kamiko's revelry.

Kamiko smiled at Siruis. "This is likely to be the last of it." She let the fiery low vista draw her eyes back to the horizon. "Things are about to get crazy, Sister," Kamiko said.

She closed her eyes, feeling the warmth of the low sun through the chill air on her face and eyelids. Her breath was slow and meditative, her spirit calm and easy. The cool air was simply drifting. The burbling voices of the shallows were whispering of creation, of perfection made by the hand of God.

For the first time in what seemed like years, her thoughts drifted toward her mother, the most beloved to her of any creature. She had no memory of her beyond the vision rendered by her own imagination, borne of Djinnasee's words. The moment was fleet.

"We will begin to run across woodsmen and hunting parties soon and droves of brigands," Kamiko said. She shook her head and opened her eyes to no more than a squint. Inwardly she felt the Warrior standing at ease beside the woman. With calm resolve, the woman prepared to retreat but lingered. The viper was nowhere to be seen or felt. For the time, her rage was contained. It would not remain thus.

"And Royal Militia," added Siruis quietly.

"Yes, and Royal Militia."

"They are the greater problem, aren't they?"

Kamiko nodded. "Against thieves and murderers, I have no need for restraint."

"Whereas officers of King Titus need only tell you of the summons."

"They need not even bear arms, Sister. I cannot refuse an order to go before the king. They know this all too well."

"What about me? Would they try to take me by force?"

Kamiko's eyes flared, and she wondered if Siruis saw the reaction. "If they do, I will break them of that habit on the very first attempt, have no doubt." The heated flush passed completely through her body. "To my reckoning, Djinnasee's words carry more weight than the king's." She thought about it for a moment. "It is a tight spot to be sure. I can easily imagine being forced to choose between the king and…well, you."

The calm air shifted slightly, a momentary eddy in the lazy current. The wet dankness of a wild furry animal drifted across Kamiko's nose. The Warrior stepped abruptly forward, even as the Woman began moving back. The hackles stood from the top of her head to the base of her spine.

"I believe you have already resolved the issue," Siruis said.

"Djinnasee charged me with your safety, Siruis. Let us pray that I am not forced to commit war on Cairistonia."

Kamiko heard no sound of movement. She felt it. No more than a slight tremor in the air to her left. Siruis was to her right, eyes closed.

Kamiko rolled instantly to her back and thrust her feet straight into the air above her. Shoving hard against the stone face with her shoulders gave her all the momentum she needed to spring upward and land on her feet in full battle readiness. The thin blanket billowed down to cover Siruis completely as Kamiko thrust her open palm out to her left, into the middle of the dark mass springing from the cover there. The heel of her hand impacted a solid bulk of thick muscle and heavy bone beneath a wrapping of tightly wound leather and cloth. She snapped her fist closed and heaved with all her might, dragging the attacker upward, redirecting his momentum. She recognized him immediately and determined to hold her attack in check. When her arm was straight overhead, she turned his considerable weight and dropped his back to the rock directly in front of her instead of slamming him hard.

Before he impacted, however, his knee stuck out and grazed the back of her skull, and his broad fist clipped her midchest. He had presence of mind to catch most of the impact with his feet but still roared when he hit the unforgiving stone. He jerked his head to one side as Kamiko's fist came down, narrowly avoiding a heavy blow to his forehead, one that would have been fatal had Kamiko desired it. Her control was tight, so she held the full force of the strike just shy of punching the rock and instead dropped her weight onto his chest with her elbow.

His breath exploded again, but he never slowed his assault. Much as Kamiko had done, he kicked his legs upward but with a wide scissor twist and spin that jerked him from beneath her weight and brought him to his feet, gasping for air and still bringing the battle in full. As he dove over Kamiko's kneeling mass, he hooked his arm across her throat, meaning to drive her backward, howling like a madman. She allowed his momentum to aid her move and simply spun with him. Instead of being driven to her back, she rolled him under her own body, twisted out of the neck hold by stabbing her thumb into the nerve cluster just above his elbow, then delivered a stiff-fingered stab into his gut just below the rib cage. His momentum faltered from the blow, and he paused where he lay. With the twinkle of a mischievous smile in her eyes, Kamiko jerked his heavy mass into the air with both hands and threw him out over the end of the stone slab and into the river with a great splash.

Siruis peeked out from under Kamiko's blanket as the icy river water rained down around them but otherwise remained very still. Kamiko followed Siruis's gaze to where it rested on a group of men standing in silence and at ease, hands and weapons relaxed. They were all of similar size, lean with corded muscle, and dressed suitably for trekking the jungle unseen.

At first sight, they only looked ragged and surly, like fool brigands lost in the jungle. Their easy manner and predatory stance spoke otherwise to Kamiko. Their captain was well known to her as High Marshal Alexander's lifelong friend, Bentaub Rath, chief officer of the team of recon scouts. Captain Rath rose from the cold water with a laughing snarl. Wisely he kept his eyes on the water swirling lazily across his thighs.

The men were painted with dirt, sticks, mud, grass, leaves, patches of fur, and dung. Nine armed men had snuck into an easy ambush stance without her notice. They were good.

The lot of them stared openly at Kamiko's nakedness, save one who had averted his eyes and was shaking his head in silent reproach. Captain Rath knew Kamiko's temper all too well and stayed where he'd risen, seeming to be waiting on something to appear in the water, his eyes also carefully averted.

Kamiko's attention was first drawn across the river to where Uila was standing at watchful attention, then to the presence of the birds sitting in silence outside the perimeter all around them. As good as the unit was, they were no match for Jerim. As for the gawkers, it was time for her to teach them to respect a woman's body, so in her nakedness, she lunged at the closest.

CHAPTER 11

The night was to be a dark one. The moon would be late rising, and a covering of clouds blocked any possible starlight. Once Kamiko had finished her lesson with the seven scouts and had draped her body in her blanket, Jerim appeared. He seemed to pop out of thin air and was standing at his full height in full view. The scouts had resisted Kamiko's "soft attack" to their best, as was expected, and were still breathing hard from it. Jerim had stood from a crouch, and everyone in sight, but Siruis, leapt in their tracks, including Kamiko. Then every warrior except Kamiko drew a weapon and made ready to fight.

Jerim appeared not to have noticed. He stepped to Siruis with one stride and scooped her up, blanket, clothes, and all, and they withdrew to a small grove across the river. Kamiko dismissed the scout unit from the rock, dressed in her clean clothes, and laced up her boots. Then she joined her old acquaintance at arms, her friend from the bad places.

Two of the scouts had dug an arm-deep hole for the fire, large enough to stand inside. Another drove a spear into the ground at an angle aimed at the bottom of the void, while they piled in thick chunks of wood and small broken limbs. Once the spear was pulled free, the small tunnel allowed air to draw to the bottom of the fire. The purpose was to avoid the fire being seen from afar. They'd not cooked food for the previous fifteen days to avoid the telltales of an open fire. With flint and steel, the fire was going in moments, and a soft smoky glow arose. Another of the captain's men prepared game and forage for cooking. Kamiko and Captain Rath sat side by side near the fire yet in darkness. The sunken blaze cast very little light on the campsite.

Kamiko looked around at the seven men that now carried a reminder to avert their eyes should they find themselves in such a situation again. They had taken the thrashing well, but each came away nursing a black eye, the worst of the injuries. In spite of that, they were in fair spirits, relishing the thought of cooked meat straight from the pit, and seemed to hold no ill feelings for Kamiko.

They were having no small amount of fun at the captain's expense. Rath would likely never live his own attempt down. He was quick to remind them that he had tried it on his own but that she had taken them down as a whole unit. Save one. As far as any of them knew, they now held the collective distinction of having battled a very naked Kamiko Hoshi, outcome notwithstanding. The bruises were a small cost.

The mirth lapsed. Kamiko suspected the unit was carrying something deep and serious among them. Their moments of levity passed quickly. Their countenance was serious.

After a long silence, Kamiko asked, "What is your unit doing out here, Captain?"

Thick dark curls that looked to have been kept trimmed with a knife capped Captain Rath's broad face. In the indirect hue of the fire, he appeared dark red, the sharp weather creases across his brow and around his eyes etched in shadow. Unlike the lean runners of his unit, he was thick across his chest, arms, and neck. She could see that his mind was racing, and it seemed as though the question had interrupted his train of thought.

He inclined his head toward her slightly, as if about to divulge a secret, but paused for a moment. Finally he asked, "How long has it been, Sister, since you were last here?"

"I have not been west of the river Antarius for two years and a handful of months," she said. "I was last in Flavin some four or five years ago. I lost track. It has been a long time."

"Why?" His voice rumbled kindly. "Where have you been?"

His tone changed. He was questioning her as an interrogator, not as an old friend. It occurred to her that even though she'd thrown him into the river, the captain had bathed, scrubbing all his dirty masking away. The deep scouts never bathed when they were on maneuvers, it ruined their scent mask. That realization, coupled with the fact that they had built their first fire in a half-month, made Kamiko wary. She ignored his question.

"Are you here looking for me, Captain?"

His brow furrowed into a deeper scowl than usual as he turned to look at her. Again the captain, carefully deliberating, was slow to speak, but at last he said simply, "No."

He turned back to the fire and began talking to Kamiko as if they were trusted comrades, all pretense of questioning passed.

"Much has happened, Sister. And you will not recognize Flavin." He drew his knife, a long, thick-bladed affair with a fat leather-bound hilt. As he spoke, he worked one end of the leather binding free and began unwrapping it.

"We hail from the western barbarian front, where High Marshal Alexander has come to the aid of King El'Thorn. Chief Nukto has—"

"Attacked the Seven Clans." Kamiko knew it as fact. She continued in a low quiet voice, turning to speak into his ear from a handbreadth. "Bartol is among them, was with them at the outset." A single thought flashed in her mind. "Nukto is dead, Captain." The memory flourished fully—the vision. She could see *through* the events, scroll through the moments of what she'd seen. "Bartol has the tribal mother of the Moshue in safety, but Nukto is dead." She returned his steely gaze as he turned to face her. His eyes skipped back and forth between Kamiko's, attempting, she knew, to weigh her soul in light of what he had just heard.

"How can you…" His voice wheezed. "How do you know this?"

Now Kamiko was the interrogator. "Captain, tell me why you are all the way out here."

He took it in stride. “We are giving chase.” He shook his head and corrected himself. “We *were* giving chase. We picked up two runners coming out of Nukto’s back line, moving northeast. The high marshal said don’t come back without ’em.”

The camp was otherwise silent. The men of the unit had formed a rough circle and listened intently.

“We were twelve when we engaged the trail. Now,” he said, and peered across at the unit, “we are nine.”

Kamiko found it hard to believe someone could give Captain Rath the slip. She waited for him to gather his thoughts.

“They grabbed Sakie.” He looked at Kamiko and clarified, “My first lieutenant.” His voice was an angry cauldron. “They impaled him on a broken tree limb two hundred hands up into the canopy. Alive. We were a long time bringing him down.” He looked over at Kamiko with an apologetic smile, sympathy for her having to hear it. “We never got the trail back.” He was slowly winding the leather back into place on the hilt, taking care to lay the edge in a perfect lap, thereby gaining slight ridges for his grip. He was careful even in his anger. “We picked you up a ten-day ago.”

Kamiko knew then why they had not been surprised to see Jerim and why their glances at Siruis were laced with suspect. Jerim had been right, someone was following them.

“We set to watch your flank and trail you across, just in case. I thought the runners might circle around, start playing with us. I have never seen the like, Sister Kamiko. They strung us out, took three from us, and never showed one single time. They tipped their hand, though, when they tried to backtrack and flank us. We could tell they were leading us, but we had no choice. We had to keep trying to track ’em down.” Nods and quiet murmurs from the circle punctuated the short tale.

“They timed the kills, Sister,” one of the men in the circle added. She needed no explanation, she knew what it meant.

“One each day, at the same time of day,” she said to the young man who had spoken. “Followed with precision for twelve days, ending with you, Captain.” She turned to peer at the man beside her. “You were wise to heed the warning.”

"Only after three of my men are dead." He growled. They were keeping their voices pitched deep, speaking slow and quiet. The circle had tightened conspiratorially around Kamiko and Captain Rath.

"But you have learned something about your enemy as well. They are not from any of the races of Nukto's savages."

"This we have established beyond question, yes, Sister. Nukto's plainsmen know little of the jungle."

"And they are traveling northeast?"

"I'd say more northward with a slight lean to the east, bearing fairly on for Ravencroft."

"What is your next thought, Captain?"

He spoke flat and dry. "Dairei Parzon."

"My first thought as well. But the thief did not kill your men, Captain, nor would she allow anyone of her league to commit assassination such as befell Sakie."

Dairei Parzon, the greatest anomaly of the modern-day kingdom. She was the single most prolific and wildly popular outlaw in the land. In her two and a half decades of activity, she had not taken a life, until she had engaged in wholesale war against the pirate lords a half-decade past. Of those she left hundreds dead. Her ways were somehow above and beyond what could be defined as normal. The populace in general believed she was in league with things arcane.

"But honestly, my good Captain," Kamiko said and rested her hand on his shoulder, "I cannot think of anyone alive but her able to give you the slip."

"I do not disagree, Sister. Perhaps in these past two years, Parzon has changed her method and has taken to butchering soldiers." His quiet voice dripped with sarcasm and tightly held anger. The captain did not believe his words any more than Kamiko did.

She dropped the line of thought. "What now, Captain?" She noticed the wave of unrest that swept around the unit. More than one of the scout's hands twitched with the need to locate weapons. She was not surprised by what Captain Rath said.

"*If*," he barked, his steel gaze settling on the men around them, "we were to find Kamiko Hoshi, which would be unlikely this deep in the wilds, we would relay orders from the throne." Half the group wore poorly hidden humor on their faces. The others looked more nervous than ever. They were split on the matter. Soldiers divided between loyalty and reason.

"However," he continued, "for the life of me, I cannot recall the exact wording of the order, and I dare not misrepresent the word of King Titus in such matters. So until I am able to review the order, I would likely hold my tongue. I and those I command." He growled the word *command* and pointed a thick finger at two of the men standing together, his meaning clear. They nodded assent, but their furrowed scowls stayed in place.

So the order had been given to summon Kamiko Hoshi to the throne. She was now aware of the order and should go directly to King Titus. It was the law, though with less teeth than an arrest order. From her perspective, she was already on her way there, with Siruis in tow.

"By order of Jonathan Alexander," he added, "we have not seen you, my friend."

"The high marshal has increased my debt to him tenfold. He has always been a champion of reason, Captain."

She focused on the two doubters but spoke to Captain Rath, "However, if you are able to affix at least one manacle *anywhere* on my body, I will follow you to the throne room without resistance." The look smoldering in her eyes left no room for doubt.

Complete silence. Sweat broke across the two faces that were under Kamiko's gaze. She could tell by the body language of the group that the split was no longer even; these two were the only detractors. No one moved or breathed.

"May we then call the matter settled?"

Captain Rath chuckled under his breath. "Of what matter do you speak, traveler?"

A few tense silent moments passed before the captain flashed a subtle hand signal dismissing the unit. The two detractors shared a nervous look before turning back to Kamiko, offering nods of affirmation.

While the others dispersed out into the dark to set a perimeter, one of the men stayed to tend the fire. He unceremoniously dropped the fat bundle of food into the pit, an assortment of game meats, wild tubers, berries, chopped gourd pulp, and various nuts and seeds gathered from the jungle, all tightly wrapped in wide green leaves. This he buried beneath a layer of chopped greenwood bits and chunks of larger dried wood, the makings of a slow-burning fire that would last well beyond dawn. The meal would be hours cooking. This done, he cleared and smoothed a narrow strip of ground a few feet from the pit, laid down on his back with a breathy groan of relief, and was asleep in moments.

Of all the branches of the Royal Militia, Kamiko was most impressed by the captain's scouting unit. Theirs was the most demanding of all the military disciplines. She was fully aware of the severity of Captain Rath's losses. To her knowledge, he had lost only four of his men in the twenty-five years of his command. For three to have been killed in as many days would weigh heavily on any man, a burden tripled in the captain.

The quiet of night felt like a tangible thickness around them. The firelight was buried beneath the new layer of wood and redoubled the darkness. Captain Rath's voice sounded distant when he spoke.

"How did you know, Kamiko?"

She needed no clarification. The question was burned into her own mind.

"I'm not sure I can explain it, Rath. I have...seen it."

"Well, you are correct," he said. "Chief Nukto has taken leave of his senses and comes against King El`Thorn. The old chief gathered all the savage nations under his banner, Sister. They field over one hundred thousand warriors. If not for High Marshal Alexander, the Seven Clans may already have fallen." The pit glowed as the fire overtook the covering of new wood. The captain rose in a fluid motion that belied his age and stepped to the edge of the pit, speaking as he moved. "But for Nukto, I accept your words. You could not know of his death, Sister. Such is not known outside the immediate command structure. Unless—"

He paused as he pushed a mound of the dugout dirt onto the top of the fire, partially covering it to slow the burn. He shook his head as the thought tried to form into a logical conclusion. Kamiko could easily see the unspoken implication that would follow the word.

"*Unless*," she said, picking up where the captain had left off, "I have been in contact with those you were tracking."

Even in the slight glow rising from the deep pit, Kamiko could see that he was doubtful. He lifted his spear from his neatly piled gear and plunged the blunt end of the shaft into the pit's breather hole, tamping it down to reopen the draw of air.

"Or those you are traveling with," he concluded, turning to face her as he spoke. "How well do you know your companions?"

"I know them well enough, Rath." The memory of the vision filled her thoughts anew. The captain had confirmed what she had tried to believe was nothing more than a dream. She had seen Nukto's broken body with her own eyes. The knowledge that she had seen him from hundreds of leagues did not change that. "But I did not learn of this from them, I saw it for myself." It sounded impossible, even to her. How could the captain believe her to be anything but delusional?

He seemed to accept her word for the moment and pressed on to the next subject in his mind. "Who are they, Sister?" he asked, as he leaned his spear across his gear and regained his seat beside her. "I never imagined another colossus such as Bartol, especially with such a boyish likeness."

Kamiko thought about how best to answer but lead with a question.

"Have you been given any other orders from the throne of late? Any arrest-on-sight commands?"

The look of surprise that appeared momentarily on Captain Rath's face answered the question for her. The glow of the fire was only slight but cast dull illumination on the smoke rolling up from the smoldering greenwood. He was too slow to answer.

"There are always such orders from the throne, Sister," he said with more grit than was necessary. He drew his heavy knife again, thumbed the edge at several points along the blade, then pulled a smooth stone from a pocket near his waist. He set stone to blade with long easy strokes.

"Speak plainly, Captain Rath. I have been out of the loop a long time. I need to know what is happening."

The *shink* of the whetstone paused when he looked at her, his dark eyes smoldering as hot as the firepit. Again he was slow to answer.

"The days of sanity are behind us, Kamiko. I do not know where to begin to explain. So I will start with now," he said with yet another growl of distaste. His voice was no longer pitched low and quiet.

So she thought, *This is for the benefit of his men as well. Perhaps they are beginning to doubt his motives.*

"We are indeed ordered to bring the young seer Sirious Martain before King Titus." The name, even incorrectly spoken, fell on the ground like a heavy rock. "She is to be bound and gagged, Kamiko"—he growled—"and caged like an animal." A seething rage burned in the man. "She is little more than a child, Sister, a child!" The heavy knife was now poised to strike some unseen villain, as if it were stalking them from the dark. "What is the point of kingship if the words of a child strike him with madness?"

The words of a child. He could not begin to imagine the depth of madness dwelling there. Kamiko's mind lunged forward, covering the next hundred-count in a single instant. She saw the sudden result—Captain Rath and eight royal scouts dead at her feet.

He meant to take Siruis. His unit was not on the perimeter, they were setting for ambush, awaiting his word. She and Jerim were about to have innocent blood on their hands. The elite unit had been tracking them for a ten-day, no doubt coming to the conclusion that they had stumbled upon Sirious Martain. It had taken ten full days for them to consider taking on Kamiko and, obviously, Jerim. She admired their bravery.

"Alexander offered no repose from that order, though, did he, Captain?"

"No, Sister. I have no choice in the matter." His gaze was fixed at the edge of the pit, as if mesmerized by the dancing fire-tinted smoke. Kamiko now realized the man stretched out near the fire was not sleeping. His breath was too steady, and his hands were not lax; they were simply calm. He was ready to move.

Kamiko knew then that she had indeed made up her mind to place Siruis's well-being above the commands of the king. Her sister was correct.

"I recommend you reconsider your blind devotion to King Titus, Captain Rath. Spending your remaining life in the next sixty seconds will not deliver this woman to him. A good captain knows when retreat is in order, knows how to preserve the lives of his men. Your chance of success does not exist." Her voice was smooth darkness and pitched to carry out into the night. "If you try this, Captain Rath, I will kill you to the man." It was spoken as a simple promise, with no inflection of intimidation or boast. She waited for his response without moving from his side. Her eyes were on the dagger in his fist, watching for signs of predetermined action.

Her gut told her Rath wanted no part of the king's order, else he would have attempted the ambush while they were still unseen and out in the jungle. She knew the moment had passed, his decision made. He was a wise man. She was grateful for the reprieve. She had just declared that she would kill them to the man, an act she'd sworn never to do.

He drew the flat of the blade slowly across his forearm, seeming to contemplate the sheen of the polished steel for a moment before dropping it atop his gear. She recognized it as the better of two possible signals. The order had been silently given to abate and set the perimeter. Kamiko's chest swelled with admiration for the good captain. He had determined to be the first to die by her hand.

His question was both the simplest and most complicated of all possible questions. "Why?"

The answers were many. She picked one. "Because it was not given to you to bring her before King Titus."

He shifted his thick mass to turn toward Kamiko before he spoke, his eyes alight with question and, she thought, a glimmer of hope.

"You are taking the seer to the king? Are you certain, Sister?" His body language mirrored the concern in his voice. "Do you know why Titus wants her? Much has happened since you were hereabouts. He will execute her on sight."

Now it was Kamiko who uttered the simple question, "Why?"

"His decree has named her a sorceress, a witch of descent from Eten. She has cast a blood curse meant to bring about His Majesty's death. That is why she must be gagged and delivered in a coffer, lest she curse again."

Kamiko could only stare at the captain. Indeed, madness reigned from the throne. After a cold silence, Kamiko found her voice.

"Things are much worse than I could have imagined."

"Can these things be true, Sister?"

"What do you think, Captain?"

His one-sided grin was confined to his lips. His face was as hard as ever. Silence settled over them once more. Kamiko let the silence fill her mind as well, unwilling to ponder anything for the time being. After several minutes, he spoke again.

"Thank you, Sister. You have spared my life twice this night, mine and the lives of my men." She looked from him to the man lying near the fire, who was now sound asleep and snoring softly. Captain Rath continued unprompted, "Once when you spoke sense to me and allowed me to think, to choose. The other is that you are taking the seer to the king."

They both knew that the captain might have garnered the death penalty when he chose to stand down from arresting Siruis. But until Kamiko was ordered otherwise, she was still an officer of the court and, as such, held authority over the captain and right of warrant for Siruis. She simply nodded.

"My name, good Captain Rath, is Siruis of Marjan."

The soft words seemed to peal from above, coming down from the black sky, as though from the heavens. The captain's hand snapped instinctively for his dagger as Jerim's white mass formed out of nothing, within easy reach of Kamiko. The darkness surrounding them was suddenly alive with the movement of stunned warriors, as spear tips and worried faces appeared in a circle around the firepit. The sleeper was on his feet in an instant.

Siruis was seated in the crook of Jerim's elbow. "And I am certainly not a witch."

Chapter 12

Over the seven-day journey, the captain took the scout unit into cover but shadowed Kamiko's route to Flavin Township. Compared to traversing the tangle of the jungle passage, their progress was quick and easy. Jerim stayed close to Siruis at all times, and a large black wolf joined the party, running right at Jerim's heel. His dark eyes and busy nose never stopped searching.

The fifth night was under clouds and ever-chilling winds which came in gusts, mostly from the north. They had taken refuge in the lea of a boulder pile at the edge of a long stretch of foothills. The old wolf was lying atop the boulder in watchful vigilance. Siruis was dozing, leaned with her back against Jerim's thigh, with her head lying back slightly. Her eyes were glazed and partially closed with sleep, and her mouth was slightly open. The fire would be out in minutes, as the wind kept it stoked to a bright fast blaze. Uila had chosen to stay in close and had worked his way next to the boulder where he stood in horse slumber, tired from a long day of running.

Conversation had become easier between them, and she learned much about Jerim. Like Kamiko, his mother died giving birth to him, but Jerim had been taken into slavery and kept there until he was thirteen. Even now, being twenty-four years old, he'd spent more than half his life in chains. Therein lay the source of Jerim's darkness. Djinnasee found him, and Jonathan Alexander had rescued him and almost a hundred other slaves. And then, in what Kamiko was learning to be Jerim's conversational fashion, he changed directions.

"Sister, why did you kill your father? I know what he did to become your father, and I feel that you and I are bound by our mothers by how they died," he said. "I am curious if it was vengeance or justice?"

She didn't have to think about it long to answer, she'd mulled it over countless times already. "Well, my giant-kin friend, that point shifted back and forth a lot. It was vengeance that burned in me all those years, but it was justice that sent me after him. By the time it was done, both were served equally. And now, I am an orphan."

Jerim nodded and said quietly, "As I am," and, looking down at Siruis, added, "As she is."

After a long pause, he asked, "Are you glad for having done it, Turtle Star?"

Again the answer required no pondering. "Yes, I am very glad of it. I count it a good deed."

"Do you believe the same about Broga Kipp?"

She did not need to think about that question either. "Yes, my friend, that was a good deed."

*****

Two days later, they broke over the top of a long ridge line, which snaked down from the low mountains to the north. The stench was almost unbearable. Taken together, the scene spreading across the long valley and the stink of deep rot had stopped Kamiko's breath. Below their vantage, a newly formed village, for all appearances, had risen at one end of a massive trash dump. Captain Rath had rejoined them and led them here.

Some thirty-odd villagers were spread out over one section of the refuse sprawl, harvesting as if in a garden. A handful of children were gathered around a makeshift fort near one edge of the rubble, a mock battle fully engaged, sticks and mud balls flying in a steady barrage. The surrealism was stark and disconcerting. A lowering gray sky had darkened Kamiko's mood since a reluctant dawn barely defeated the night a few hours earlier.

"I take my leave, Sisters." Captain Rath's voice was tight with emotion. He had joined them, intending to separate here once Kamiko had seen this valley. It was important to him that Kamiko see this scene, that he could see her reaction. Some part of her was glad she could not read his thoughts at that moment. Kamiko simply nodded to him, her voice lost. He left without another word. Siruis seemed oblivious to his presence, enthralled by what her eyes and her heart beheld. The captain moved away in silence and was gone.

The details of the scene were slow in coming to Kamiko's benumbed awareness. They stood at the northernmost end of a long valley. The cold air moving down from the mountains pressed lightly against their backs. A bluish haze seeped from the heaped mass and wafted southward, obscuring the farther reaches from their sight. Ghostly figures stirred about all across the field of trash, harvesting. They moved in tightly knotted groups, in what appeared to Kamiko as slow motion. The crisp white silhouettes of long-legged birds floated around them in silent droves. They followed in the wake of the harvesters, foraging in the newly turned rubble. Their motion never ceased as they flocked to and fro in waves of brief flight and, likewise, faded in the smoldering haze as they grew more distant.

Nearby a dark and wrinkled old woman, wearing layer upon layer of once-colorful clothes, pulled at a mound of rubble with a long hooked cane. Her efforts were rewarded with a small avalanche as the top of the pile tumbled down the slope of the mound to break apart near her feet. The old woman fell quickly to the ground and drew her tattered mass of rags up over her head just as a dark cloud, of what Kamiko assumed were bees, swarmed up out of the protective cover of the pile.

A dark lanky boy, dressed in only a pair of tattered shorts, scampered to her aid, wielding a long limb with a fat bundle of smoking trash tied to one end. He thrust the smoking end into the swirling mass and waved it slowly around the old woman until the frenzy of the swarm broke, and one angry mass became hundreds of confused individual bees. The old woman peered out from beneath her protective shroud before she stood, drawing the rags around her head and face so that only her eyes were uncovered. She assaulted the trash pile once more with happy vigor, plunging the hooked tool into the same spot over and over. The bees regrouped and swarmed again, and again the youngster came to her aid with the smoking limb.

"This is the total sum of her life, Kamiko, to dig in the trash for bits of colored cloth."

Kamiko had to fight for words. "We are in Cairistonia, Siruis. How can this be?"

She expected no answer. None came.

Movement at the opposite edge of the field caught her attention as a line of men came into view from out of the smoky haze. Silvery helms and waving spears marked a few of them as Royal Militia. The rest were big husky men of labor. Even with the distance and the obscuring haze, Kamiko could tell that this was a prison labor detail. They all wore dark-green work suits adorned with a pair of wide bright-red stripes, one capping the shoulders and one encircling the waist. They were far better off than the inhabitants of the garbage-dump village.

The men were divided into three gangs, each forming a loose ring around one of three enormous wagons. The wagons were so overloaded Kamiko expected them to buckle beneath the weight with every bump they crossed. Teams of mismatched oxen, horses, and mules struggled for every step as the slow parade climbed a long slope, which would bring them to the top of one of many large mounds. Once in place, the men scrambled up onto the wagons and began pitching trash, some by hand, while others were using large long-tined forks. Below them, the villagers gathered like ants upon a fallen insect.

A light snow of tiny flakes began falling as the gray sky descended further.

Kamiko lowered her eyes, looking down at the ground between her feet. Anger threatened to consume her entirely but for the sheer grief that quelled the rage. Every fiber of her being wanted to descend into the trash to pull them out, to set them right. But she knew it was not the old woman digging for bits of colored cloths or the scrawny lad keeping the bees at bay or any of the countless others. They had been driven here by forces beyond their control and would be relentlessly driven back. All Kamiko could do was turn and lead Uila and Siruis back into the forest and make for Flavin.

Jerim waited a hundred paces inside the tree line, his face somber and hard. He was perched in a tree too flimsy to hold even Kamiko's weight, yet the tree showed little sign of bearing the giant's mass. He was covered almost entirely in small brown birds so that he appeared to have a constantly moving, living cloak draped over his shoulders. When he grew still, he all but disappeared from sight.

No one spoke as Kamiko led Uila, with Siruis seated side manner on the saddle, back into the still forest. The snowflakes grew in size and number, and the sky darkened, setting down closer and closer to their heads. It was just past midday.

By the time they made it to the edge of Flavin, the snow fell in thick drifting waves. Passage through the forest had taken hours longer because Kamiko made a wide circuit around the north end of the populated areas, staying in the cover of woods as long as possible. By the time they emerged from the trees, the grayness of the day had long since given way to what would have been a pitch-black night. The ever-present glow of Flavin shone bright against the underside of the cloud blanket so that the whole of the town was bathed again in its own light. Even so, Kamiko could see no more than twenty paces through the curtains of falling snow.

Jerim spoke quietly to Siruis for a moment, bowed to Kamiko, and gave her a worried look that soon melted to a sincere smile, then he leapt back into the forest in a single bound that took him completely out of sight. He would enter Flavin in his own way, in the way of Bartol—silent and unseen but never far away.

Chapter 13

Kamiko would be ever grateful for that snowy gale, for no better cover could have been conjured. Siruis appeared to be a bundle of blankets atop Uila, lying curled in the saddle beneath the folded layers. Kamiko was covered head to foot in her inadequate traveling robe, head and shoulders wrapped in her bedroll. She walked pressed against Uila's flank as they traversed the township, for all intents, unseen. She was doubly grateful that most of Flavin was hidden from her sight as well. What little she could see was disheartening. This was no longer a well-kept town.

By the time she rapped on the gate pad of the sisterhood, it was pressing toward midnight. The complex that housed the Order was among the oldest structures in the whole area, almost one hundred years older than Flavin. It was built just after a long and grueling war the Crown fought with one of many nomadic warlords from the western savage lands. The Order had maintained one of the battlefield hospitals all through the war. They also fought as a tactical strike unit under the command of Delia Mars and were responsible for tipping the balance in many of the heaviest battles. Delia Mars, the only sister in history to equal Kamiko's fame, fought her way through the mass of savage warriors and took the warlord's head, thereby setting the final rout into motion.

To show its gratitude, the Crown built a permanent dwelling for the sisterhood of the Order, a compact walled fortress complete with dormitories, a heavily fortified keep of hewn granite, stone outbuildings for food and seed storage, and an impressive stable house for livestock and horses. Subsequent decades saw the people swarm to the sisterhood for the protection of her walls many times.

By the time Flavin was formed into a viable township, the complex had a reputation for being battle-hardened and the sisters who resided there of no less acclaim. The walls had never been breached by force, nor had the doors had ever been closed to those in need. It was dubbed Mars Knoll, even though the sisterhood had a way of leaving things unnamed.

Over the years, Kamiko had been to the Knoll countless times, but she had interned there from four years old until she was almost nine. She remembered little more than the endless hours of work, the prevailing kindness, and the rarity of sleep. Yet she developed her abilities quickly, achieving the proficiency of master by nine years old. The legend of Kamiko Hoshi began moving across the land. She never apprenticed again. She went to work at ten years old, training to survive the things you cannot fight with steel.

Kamiko rapped the gate pad again and was immediately answered by a click-clack, just before the entire door began to rise. Soft yellow light spilled across the gray black of the wintery bluster enshrouding them, washing first the stone walk, then rising to Kamiko's face. She'd chosen the livery gate without even thinking, following the deep grooves of old habits. Only visitors petitioned at the front gate.

The first sound they heard was that of an oddly human yowl, which seemed, to Kamiko, a joyous expression, almost a laugh. A young girl stood framed in warbling firelight, a short bundling of hastily gathered robes and blankets atop two skinny legs that disappeared into the tops of overlarge woolen boots. Her face was shadowed, but Kamiko could see her bright expression, eyes wide open, staring up at Siruis.

Kamiko glanced over her shoulder to see Siruis still on the saddle but seated and peering out from beneath the edge of her cover.

Her blue eyes were glistening more crystalline than usual, and her face was flawlessly white. She would not have looked real except that she was visibly shaking from the cold.

Kamiko led Uila into the livery. The young girl lowered the big door by spinning a large brass wheel mounted in the wall, closing out the bluster with a solid thump. With that sound, heavy wood thudding against thick stone, Kamiko felt the rush of familiarity, a flood of peace, of home. Uila snorted and stomped, shuddering from head to rump and creating a miniature momentary snowstorm. The scene had unfolded in close exactness again and again in this very room. It had been so long.

It was a long stone-built room attached to the inside of the perimeter wall. At most the size could accommodate five horses at any one time, but a second large door could be opened to allow an entire troop to pass from the street to the courtyard of the fortress. There were currently no horses in any of the five stalls, and only one set of saddle and riding tack was waiting on the rack. This was only a ready room; the horses were kept in the stable.

In the center of the room, a recently built fire crackled and popped atop a raised stone fire bowl, beneath a low-hanging steel-wrought hood designed to spread the heat. It had not had time to warm the room much, but simply getting out of the wind had made the cold at least bearable.

Siruis was too stiff from the cold ride and too heavily bundled to negotiate climbing down from Uila's lofty back without Kamiko's help. Once on her feet, she moved across the room to where the fire burned, shedding layers as she moved. The young girl was right at Siruis's heels, her own layering of covers coming off in one great mound, now that the cold no longer pressed. She was a skinny youth who appeared to be gaining her womanly height in one fast growth streak. And she had not made any attempt at talk, content to drift into Siruis's wake. Kamiko could not be sure if the quiet girl was even aware of her presence for all the notice she'd given.

Kamiko dropped her bedroll and cloak to one side, then turned her attention to Uila. She had just lifted the saddle from Uila's back to the saddle rack when the door leading into the courtyard swung open. A woman of Kamiko's height and build filled the doorway. Her shoulders and short brown hair were flecked with snow and glistening moisture. She stepped briskly through and pushed the door closed behind her, then turned her attention to Kamiko, threw back her head, and laughed aloud. A wide smile broke across Kamiko's face as she met the woman halfway across the livery room. They stopped just short of embracing for a moment and simply gazed upon each other, then fell into an embrace of strength and the laughter of sisters long separated.

Felene was dressed in comfortable loose clothes that appeared hastily donned, with a woolen cloak draped over her shoulders.

"Blessed be, Sister Kamiko. I have missed you sorely."

"Felene, dear Felene, God be praised, it is good to see you, Sister."

To have such a jolt of unexpected joy threatened to unhinge Kamiko. She recalled that weeks ago, she'd reckoned her true friends on one hand, a lie she'd convinced herself of during her secluded travels. Felene bore much of the responsibility for who Kamiko was. And likewise, Felene's mastery of fighting held a strong resemblance to Kamiko's own style, for they had sparred for many hours over the years. And with Felene's sudden presence came the rest of Kamiko's worldly family into her thoughts, the sisterhood, and more specifically, Sister Grace. Felene and Grace were longtime crime-fighting partners in Ravencroft City, working for Baron Vladimir Riplin, the ruler of the northern lands.

She shook it aside for the moment and turned both her and Felene to face where Siruis stood leaning over the fire, the young girl anxious and ready at her side.

"Felene Dresdle," she said, extending her hand toward Siruis, who turned to face them at the sound of Kamiko's voice. "This is our sister, Siruis of Marjan. She is in my care." She knew Felene understood the depth of that simple statement, "*in my care.*" As Kamiko moved nearer to the warmth of the fire, she cast a short glance to Uila. His head was drooping.

Felene smiled at Siruis. "Welcome to Flavin, Sister. At last you have found a place of safety and comfort. I trust Kamiko stopped at least twice on the journey here," she said and turned a sour look toward Kamiko, followed by a wink at the young girl. Felene's hands worked through a short expressive dance, drawing a snicker from the girl.

"Sisters, this is Danae," and, with a smile for Kamiko, added, "She is in *my* care. If you wish to speak with her, please let her see your face or use your hands." She signed the words for Danae as she spoke them. Kamiko knew the girl was deaf when Siruis bid Danae greetings with a slow fluidity in her hands, clarifying her name as Siruis. The young girl's smile was so bright, Kamiko thought she may ignite. She was already fully drawn into Siruis's world, forever captive there.

The slightest hint of color was beginning to enliven Siruis's complexion, the blaze in the hearth doing its job on her. She drew off her cloak and hood and released her hair out into the warming room. It billowed around her shoulders to her white cheeks and partially covered her face. Danae flashed some words with her hands far too quickly for Kamiko to keep up, which brought a smile to Siruis's white face.

Danae turned her attention, for the first time, to Kamiko in obvious and innocent expectation of the same from her. Kamiko looked down at her hands and began searching her memory for those few elusive simple letters.

"Um, well, I haven't had much opportunity for keeping this working too well." She looked from her hands to Felene for help, then held her hand up and spelled out K-a-m-i-k-o, the benefit of rote teachings of her youth.

Danae's face lost the animate brightness of her expression. Her eyes darted side to side for a moment under a furrowed brow. Her short hair looked to have been styled by her own hand and forgotten. Her head spun toward Felene, and her hands blurred a short question. Felene simply smiled and nodded once.

Fear and wonder washed across her young face as she looked back to where Kamiko was standing at the hearth. Danae's eyes found and fixed on Kamiko's with hesitancy, as if something dangerous could befall. Kamiko felt old feelings stir in her gut. She remembered the stares and fearful whispers that once followed her every step. It was one of several reasons she'd left. And here, in a small girl, in Kamiko's sanctuary, her very first encounter, the look had returned. She breathed slowly, deeply, her face as passive as she could manage while the young girl displayed another message to Felene.

Siruis stepped past Kamiko and spoke with her voice and her hands. "Ask her, Danae."

Felene nodded her assent and placed her hands palm flat together, then nodded toward Kamiko while keeping her eyes on Danae.

For the span of a few heartbeats, nothing in the room moved. Then the young girl turned and strode purposefully to Kamiko and spoke in the only tongue she knew. Kamiko was familiar enough to get the gist of what Danae was saying but had the benefit of Felene's aural transcription as well. Nothing could have prepared her.

"Please forgive, I am very nervous. I am Danae, and you are Kamiko Hoshi." She looked aside to Felene but continued quickly, "Djinnasee told me to ask you about Karak-Tan, bid me implore you for instruction. When first I meet you, said Djinnasee."

Both Danae and Felene's faces were bright with anticipation. Kamiko was stunned for several quiet moments. She had misread Danae completely. For Djinnasee to pass that message through Danae spoke very highly of her. Never in all their years had he done this. She would honor her father's request without reservation.

She remembered a few of the shorter expressions and signed the word *maybe* to Danae but offered a quick covert wink to Felene. She watched Danae's body language very carefully. The surrogate apprenticeship had already begun. The girl did not budge either in stance or attitude, and Kamiko thought she saw a flair of determination build behind her big brown eyes. She would not be denied.

"Care for Uila," Kamiko spoke without using her hands. Danae's head snapped around to see Felene's dictation. When she turned back to Kamiko, the look of bright wonder had returned multifold. She momentarily laid her small hand on Kamiko's arm before she sprang into motion. Her careful approach to Uila's drooping head showed she had at least a smattering of horsemanship. When Uila nickered deep and quiet and nuzzled Danae's shoulder, Kamiko knew they would get along. That was Uila's way of asking for a good rubdown. Danae led him to the opposite end of the stable room, to where the implements of equine care were hanging on the wall. Satisfied, Kamiko turned back to Felene with a look that must have spoken of being bone-weary and ravenously hungry. Felene shook her head, a thin smile of kindheartedness on her face.

"Come inside," she said and led them to the door she'd entered earlier. Kamiko lifted her pack to her shoulder and tucked her sword under her arm before she fell in line behind Siruis and followed them into the newly whitened courtyard.

Felene was as tall as Kamiko and, at first glance, just as well muscled. Normally her garb was worn but well-maintained leather boots, breeches, and vest which were dark with years of weathering, oil treatments, and repair stitching. She moved with more power than grace and was widely known as being vicious with a great sword. Yet Kamiko knew well enough that Felene would draw steel only when the need to do so had reached the utmost. She had never taken a life outside full battle, even when hunting down the most villainous criminals. She would beat them beyond repair, holding nothing in reserve but the killing strike, but if they did not press her to it, she would spare their lives. That compassion, the concern for every single life, had skipped Kamiko entirely, and she found herself wondering how Felene would have handled Broga Kipp.

*****

Stepping into the silent courtyard of Mars Knoll was like stepping backward into Kamiko's youth. They were inside the safety of the tall heavy walls that served to keep out not only a pressing enemy but also the ever-present sounds of Flavin's bustle. The muffling effect of the snow blanket and the mild fury of the snowstorm reduced the noise further, and an eerie hush lay over the complex. Her body fairly ached for the hot bath and warm bed she knew waited just across the courtyard.

An odd flush of alarm washed over Kamiko. Every pore of her skin opened at once, every nerve firing from a common trigger. Adrenaline dumped into her veins, and the fatigue of many weeks of travel evaporated. Yet she could not see or hear anything to cause such a reaction.

The sharp breath of the blustery wind died suddenly against her face. The swift swirl of the snow slowed midplummet before stopping entirely to hang suspended on nothing. She was back atop the mountain, as before in her vision, in Siruis's vision. But it was so brief it could not be reckoned as a full moment. The whisper she'd heard on the mountain, a woman's voice at her shoulder, flourished as a single point of thought in her mind—the thief Dairei Parzon. She heard that same voice in her head now, whispering her name, but this time with clarity.

She was again walking through the silent courtyard, one step behind Siruis but six long paces behind Felene, the cold bite back in her cheeks. She let her traveling pack drop from her hand but kept her sword tucked beneath her arm.

A dark but gleeful intent rose out of the whiteness of the night to meet her, a tangible emotion Kamiko could all but taste. Someone was waiting, someone audacious enough to trespass among the sisterhood. The clues needed neither arranging nor contemplation. It could be none other. Dairei was here.

Her eyes were drawn to an oddly placed low mound, as if by some outside compulsion. Even as her eyes fixed on the mound, it moved, exploding outward. Kamiko charged.

She intercepted Dairei Parzon with an open-handed palm-punch to the middle of her chest that sent the brigand careening aside with a throaty growl. She had moved on Felene, approaching in her blind spot. Dairei rolled with her momentum and came easily to her feet and was—to Kamiko's surprise—laughing softly.

It happened so quickly that Felene simply froze in her tracks and divided her attention between Siruis and the infamous thief. The only sound was Dairei's quiet mirth. She stepped forward a few easy paces and stopped, casually shaking her head, all aggression gone.

"I must admit, Hoshi, that was fast and nicely executed. You saved your sister a world of hurt."

Even though Dairei was standing in full sight, not ten paces from Kamiko, she was still difficult to see. Her garb was tattered rags, all mottled shades of gray spots and wide jagged stripes of white. The fluff of snow covered her entirely, having melted and refrozen into a furry coating of perfect camouflage. The swirl of falling snow was unbroken motion and served to further break the lines of distinction of Dairei's form.

"I'm taking the girl." Her eyes rested momentarily upon Siruis.

"Not tonight." Kamiko drew her sword and dropped the scabbard at her feet. Felene's feet shifted in the snow, and Kamiko thought she heard a stifled sharp breath. The sword was ice in her hand, a bulky weight on her arm. For the first time in Kamiko's life, it felt cumbrous, a sensation so at odds with her that she paused, her eyes on the lump of unruly steel in her fist.

"Hoshi, you haven't changed at all, have you, child?" Dairei stepped forward two careful strides and stopped. "That," she said, pointing at Kamiko's sword, "is why I took you down when last we met. You hesitate when you should not and fail to hesitate when you should." She chuckled. "You are ever backward, Sister, born confused." Dairei took two more easy steps forward. "Are you not the *good* sister? Would that Felene had a fraction of your goodness, that she too could wear the mantle of butcher without remorse."

Kamiko could see no single bit of Dairei that was not fully masked. Even her eyes were veiled. Kamiko needed little reminding. They'd met in the past, both recent and distant. Dairei spoke the truth. Kamiko had tasted Dairei's wrath and felt her strength on three separate occasions. And each time, Dairei had spared her the killing blow but left her wounded of body and spirit. Kamiko knew she would have never offered Dairei the same mercy.

Yet Kamiko had spoken her peace and had no intention of repartee with Dairei. She gathered her resolve into a single point of focus, as she'd always done, and sloughed the accusation aside. The brigand was also legend in the land of Cairistonia, known for her daring, for her disdain of all things royal, and, Kamiko knew all too well, for her compassion.

In at least one thing, Dairei was wrong. Kamiko had not lived her life confused and backward, such was a recent development. She could trace the transformation to a single easily definable moment. For the first time in her life, her sword had paused for a breath of doubt. Then she slew her father with it. The seed was planted and had been growing into a thorny vine of self-doubt and inward loathing since he bled out at her feet.

And now, in Kamiko's sanctuary, the most notorious criminal in the entire kingdom was scolding her for being a butcher. Sarcasm was not Kamiko's way, so when the words came out of her mouth, she too was surprised.

"Perhaps I should be more like you, a common thief, strong-armed and spineless. If you tire of picking at the wealthy man's trash pile to fill your coffers, maybe you could buy your own kingdom, set your own rules."

Behind her, Felene quietly closed the gap between her and Siruis. Somewhere within the main building, a voice rang out and lights sprang to life.

"Why would I?" Dairei asked. "I enjoy these freedoms already. And stealing is ever so much more entertaining than anything else I have found to whistle away my life with." She stepped closer, two easy strides. She still held no weapon but her gloved hands in full sight. "But we digress. The girl comes with me. If she comes willfully, Sister Felene need not suffer. Try to stop me, and she will never walk again, this I promise."

Felene stepped forward and said, "Try it, thief."

Kamiko felt the Warrior inside her chest swell with rage and imagined the part of her spirit holding the viper in check however loosely. Dairei was baiting her into acting on her anger, into abandoning reason for violence. But as far as Kamiko knew, Dairei was not in the habit of making empty threats. Felene was in a great deal of danger.

Kamiko asked, "Why? What could you possibly want her for?"

Dairei cocked her head slightly, a gesture Kamiko sensed was meant to project humor. "Money!" She purred. "Pure and simple. She has become a high-commodity item. Have you not heard?"

"What?" Felene fairly well barked. "Money? Are you daft, thief? What could you possibly need—" Her words were cut off when the double doors of the main building swung open and a dozen women and men poured out. There was no single weapon among the whole group other than a pair of wooden staves.

The elder sister, Rachel, was at their lead and spoke loud and clear, obviously and fully agitated. "Because there is a bounty on her head and a large one at that. She undoubtedly means to ransom our sister, hoping to quadruple the take from the king. Am I correct, Parzon?" The small troop fanned out and formed a circle around them.

Dairei only bowed slightly in Sister Rachel's general direction. Her stance declared she was completely unconcerned with the sudden swell in numbers. She kept her attention fixed on Siruis, ignoring the fact that she was surrounded. Kamiko understood—their numbers would count for little once Dairei engaged the battle.

Behind Kamiko, Felene spoke, stepping toward Dairei without hesitation. "Well, then, charmin' lass that ye are. Ye may as well get on with it. How 'bout startin' with me, *darlin*!" She'd slipped into the rough guttural dialect of her island homeland.

"Stand easy, Felene." Elder Rachel's voice commanded respect and obedience, even when she spoke softly. Kamiko had witnessed the elder pass from a sword-wielding woman of ferocity to the arbiter of peace as her middle years had waned.

Felene complied only after coming to within reach of Dairei, having positioned her body to block Dairei's sight line of Siruis. She made it very clear that threats meant nothing to her, that Dairei would indeed have to pass through her to get to Siruis. Siruis had not moved at all.

For all the banter, Kamiko knew Dairei was not one for much talking. The break point approached rapidly. Sister Rachel crossed the whitened courtyard and stopped within reach of Dairei.

Even in her elder years, her skin was both smooth and sharp of feature, eight decades of healthy living keeping the inevitable wrinkles at bay. Her age-silvered hair was loosely drawn into a tied bundle on the back of her head, a thick blanket wrapped about her entire length, shoulder to ankles. She still maintained a warrior's confidence of stride and bearing. With her eyes glued to Dairei's masked face, Rachel ordered, loud and bright, "Clear this courtyard, now! Telitha, secure the main building." To Felene, she said quietly, "Stand your ground, Sister."

Chapter 14

To Kamiko's relief, their compliance was immediate, and in moments only, the five of them remained. Even so, the rage was building in Kamiko's gut, and all the focusing and inner reprimanding she could muster was doing little to assuage it. She was being called upon by *Hun'jotzimon.* It wanted her to release the rage, a force of will driving her to unbridle her own strength and draw upon the strength of the sword. But she would not. She would hold her bearing in check. She could feel the smallest fraction of the well of power dwelling in the sword and shied from it.

But now she felt a coiling of anger in that presence. It was as though someone of great importance had been summoned but was being made to wait as lesser beings languished in indecision. The power to level mountains had been called to remove a splinter, and anger was growing as the result. It was directed at Kamiko and at the icy steel in her fist.

In a wash of realization, Kamiko remembered and understood. She had broken one of the few edicts of Mars Knoll. She had drawn steel while inside the sanctuary. Such was forbidden outside a time of war. But it was too late, the deed was done and penance would be paid.

"Dairei," Kamiko implored, "don't do this. You don't need the bounty. And you would be handing her over to the executioner." She lowered her sword and stepped back to stand beside Siruis. "Why do you think Titus offered the bounty in the first place? If you want to be a burr in his saddle, leave her be. Trust me when I say she is going to bring him sleepless nights like you never could."

That seemed to respark Dairei's interest. In a gesture that made it look as though she was standing down, she hooked a thumb under her chin and pulled her mask up into a bunch at the top of her forehead. And there, framed in tattered cloth and swirling snow, was the essence of stunning beauty. Her skin was cold-bleached white as Siruis's but with a light dust of fine freckles on her cheeks. Her eyes were a deep sky blue with a shading of tiny green flecks. They were unwavering on Felene's face.

"What do you mean, Hoshi? What offense could she possibly offer King Titus?"

Dairei possessed a physique that was both the bane and the boon of every woman of elegant standing in the kingdom. Like everything related to the thief, Dairei had received a double portion of sheer beauty. Yet as Kamiko had seen on one occasion before, Dairei was scarred. Her left cheek bore an ugly white starburst just below her eye that snaked down her jawbone and disappeared beneath her clothing. Kamiko knew it continued across her shoulder and down her ribcage, ending in a deep jag near her left elbow. Kamiko had seen it many years ago. As far as Kamiko could tell, no one alive knew when or how Dairei had been so severely injured.

Siruis's voice was soft, but Dairei seemed to hear her clearly. "She means to use me as bait, Sister Kamiko. She has no intention of taking me to King Titus."

The look on Dairei's face changed so slightly Kamiko almost missed it.

"She needs me in order to flush out Terel Boatman's crew. But she is reconsidering that plan because she thinks you are hiding something about me, something she could exploit." As if to clarify for Kamiko and Rachel, she continued, "Boatman is dead, you see. She left him at the bottom of the Bos`Jin Sea, a league down the coastline from Selli's Shipworks."

Both Dairei and Felene turned to look at Siruis, who stepped up to where they faced off, coming to stand across from Rachel. Kamiko stepped in behind her but stood to the side near Dairei, where she could easily interpose her body between Dairei and Siruis if the need arose. Her sword was still in her hand, but it hung like a deadweight on the end of her arm. Dairei showed no sign that she even noticed Kamiko standing so close with a weapon in her hand. Her brow had creased ever so slightly.

"Dairei," Siruis addressed the woman, "you will not make it from this courtyard alive if you try the thing brewing in your mind at this moment. I implore you to reconsider and return to your original plan. Boatman is dead, and his crew will not hold together. You have accomplished what you set out to do, and you are needed in Ravencroft."

Dairei's scowl deepened from the classic battle of disbelief when the truth is breathing down your neck, but it is too strange a truth to readily accept. Yet Dairei was not a simple thief and had never been one to wallow in uncertainty. She chose not to dig.

"Well, *youngster*," she chided, "You certainly have a knack for guesswork."

"Baron Riplin has your second in custody," Siruis continued, "and will soon wrest the location of your stronghold from him. Yannis is about to give you up, Master Thief. He is chafing under your absentee methods, thinking he could better lead your outfit. When the good Baron offers him amnesty and cash, well, you know Yannis better than anyone. What do you think he will do...*La `Rouge*?"

Dairei's face had gradually knotted into an angry glare, though Kamiko could see the same stunned uncertainty she'd felt time and again while in Siruis's world. And even after having been in the constant company of her young sister for many weeks, Kamiko could not reckon how Siruis was able to know the things she knew. Judging by the silence and the look on Dairei's face, Siruis had spoken every word true, down to the derogatory nickname her crew used behind her back—La `Rouge, the Red! Years past, Kamiko had learned of the endearing tag during a fairly brutal interrogation with one of Dairei's lackeys.

"If you do not believe me," Siruis said, without scorn or taunt, "then make your move."

Kamiko felt both Felene and Rachel tense in anticipation of Dairei's response to Siruis's quiet challenge. The break point had arrived. Dairei's eyes burned with the promise of violence, but she made no move.

"Impressive, child," she retorted derisively. "A witch in the midst of the sisterhood. Whatever bewitchment you employed to take Hoshi's spirit will not work on me. I have been to the coven temple in Eten and was not moved by their sorcery any more than I am yours." She shifted her attention from Siruis, and her face returned to the same impassive mask of disregard Kamiko knew. "Keep her then, I have no energy for the annoyance. But," she declared, her voice as cold as ice, "I never break a promise."

The hiss of the word *promise* was still in Kamiko's ears when Dairei snapped her ridged hand into Felene's gut. The move was so quick that Dairei was already into a diving backflip before Felene began to fall, before Rachel even blinked, before Kamiko snapped her sword up and into play.

As unnaturally potent as Dairei's speed and strength may have been, Kamiko was no trifling apprentice still gaining her feet. She understood the dance of death. Dairei twisted midflight and came down on the move. As her feet touched ground, Kamiko was on her, sword trailing high behind her. She would try to bring her down without killing her. As much as she'd hated to hear the truth, she had heard it. It was there at the base of her mind, changing her perspective yet again. She body slammed Dairei and drove her face-first into the snow.

She was vaguely aware that the double oaken doors swung open again, that the courtyard began to fill. She knew they considered themselves combatants coming to the aid of one of their own, but they were little more than weapons to be wielded in the hands of Dairei.

Kamiko felt their combined mass continue the forward motion, felt the muscles in Dairei's back harden. Dairei jerked her knees under her as they landed and kicked hard. Her face, chest, and open palms against the ground gave her the braking effect she needed to flip Kamiko off her back and into the air. But Kamiko's empty hand shot out and grabbed a fistful of Dairei's garb at the nape of the neck as Kamiko tucked her knees, letting the momentum flip her over Dairei's anchoring mass. Although Kamiko had managed to stay close to the thief, she'd not been able to control how her body impacted the frozen stony ground. She found herself facedown as well, her anchoring arm painfully overextended.

Then Dairei was no longer there in the snow, and all Kamiko held was the woman's tattered hooded cloak. Others were shouting and running toward her. She sprang to her feet, with her arm a tingling mess at her side, hot pain spreading across her back and shoulder. Her eyes fell on Felene, and try as she might, she could not tear them away for a long moment. Her sister was not moving. Siruis knelt over Felene's body with her hands on Felene's young weathered face.

Elder Rachel had not joined Siruis. Her blanket wrap lay in a bundle where she'd been standing. When Kamiko's eyes found her, Rachel was just releasing Kamiko's scabbard with a sharp yelp. She threw it like a long wooden dagger and scored a solid stabbing hit on Dairei's right buttock, spinning her briefly as the brigand made a run for the wall. Rachel's silver hair had come unbound and waved about her head in the swirling, lifting breeze. Together with the billowing of her silken nightdress, she looked as angelic as anything Kamiko had imagined. And obviously her aim was still flawless.

But Dairei simply twisted with the direction of her spin and, though slowed, was nearing the wall at a run. Her fiery namesake was now free of the hood—La `Rouge. Bright flames of rich red hair trailed out behind her an arm's length, twisting and dancing as if alive and angry.

Kamiko bolted after her, rage welling inside, boiling anew at seeing Felene lying on her back in the snow. Dairei raised one hand and fired an unseen device with a muffled pop and a brief flash of light and smoke. A long thin line sailed up and over the wall, seemingly weighted at the leading end, though Kamiko could not see well enough in the nightglow to tell. The line went taut as Dairei came to within ten paces of the base of the wall, and then she was airborne.

Now it was Kamiko who let fly. As Dairei's feet touched the rampart, Kamiko's sword overtook her and sliced across her left shoulder. It had been a long throw, a last-ditch attempt to slow the woman. Whether Dairei saw or sensed it coming, Kamiko could not know, but she dropped the shoulder at the last moment, narrowly avoiding a direct hit. Such was the way of Dairei Parzon.

Kamiko had closed half the distance to the wall when Dairei stopped cold and spun around. A thick round muzzle came up from the folds of her garb and leveled upon Kamiko's chest. A moment passed as a wracking twist of pain from the new wound in her shoulder stole Dairei's breath. Kamiko had seen and felt it countless times. Dairei reeled for an instant but forced her body to obey her command with a hard growl and centered the weapon.

And Dairei froze, her eyes resting out in the center of the courtyard where Felene had fallen.

Kamiko dove into the cover of the low stone hedge encircling the courtyard well, meaning to gain the top of the wall near the livery. She had no such grappling device and was forced to use the stair passage.

Dairei was no longer tracking Kamiko with the weapon, she was staring back into the yard. Keeping low and moving fast, Kamiko bolted to the base of the stair leading up to the deck of the wall and leapt for the landing midway up the stair.

The motion was not lost on the thief. Tearing her eyes from the yard, Dairei turned and stepped over the outer edge of the wall, dropping to the street in a tight roll that brought her to her feet on the run. Kamiko moved to follow when she saw Uila waiting on the street outside the fortress, Danae astride his broad bare back. Her face showed no fear, only the anxious determination of someone ready to enter the fight. The dancing glow of the open stable door shone across the street and upon the wall of the building opposite.

A momentary vision of Dairei standing over Danae's body assailed Kamiko's mind like a battering ram, jolting her senses with enough force to ease the building anger and allow a smattering of reason to return. As Dairei ducked around the corner of an alleyway across from the fortress, Kamiko knew it would be futile to continue the chase. Besides her charge was Siruis, and she must not leave her unguarded. She'd seen no evidence of Jerim's presence.

She became acutely aware of the mistake she had been about to make. Had Danae not distracted her, she would still be on the chase, and Siruis, though inside the keep, would be under the protection of less capable sisters. The thought rekindled the flaring of anger in her gut, but she quickly checked it. It was well enough to let the woman go; Kamiko had no doubt the chance would arise again soon.

The whitened street below her was not entirely deserted. Even with the onset of a wintery blast, the sizable township never fully slept. The pubs, hash dens, and brothels drew men and women alike, regardless of the conditions of war or weather. A cluster of revelers stood a short way up the street, leaning against one another for support and warmth. By the look of it, they had been making their way down the street and stopped to watch the strange scene unfold atop the fortress wall. Their heads huddled together while one pointed toward where Dairei had been standing, obviously confirming what their drunken eyes had seen. Another was attempting to draw their collective attention further down the lane to something on the ground—Kamiko's sword.

By Danae's reaction, Kamiko knew the girl to be possessed of a quick intellect. She flipped gracefully down from Uila's back and darted to where Kamiko's sword was partially buried in the snow. It had landed flatwise and slid halfway down the block, coming to rest against the leeward side of the low building where the snow had yet to thicken enough to cover the ground.

Just as Danae was trotting back to Uila, another cluster of nightlife dwellers came sauntering around the very street corner where Dairei had escaped. These wore the gaudy livery of the local Royal Militia, a trio of heavily bundled patrolmen making their rounds.

Against all her instincts, Kamiko dropped to the rampart, hiding behind the low parapet. She had no doubt that the sight of a girl brandishing a drawn sword in the middle of the night would bring the soldiers to investigate. She also knew that because they were certain to have imbibed themselves and were likely bored with the mundane routine, they would harass the situation mercilessly. They would make full opportunity of the chance to return to the warmth of the station with Danae in tow.

Kamiko was just beginning to rise to offer herself as the greater prize when she heard Rachel's insistent and demanding voice bark a sharp reprimand at Danae, echoing from the walls of the buildings across the street. She peered carefully through the embrasure to see Danae take a sudden pause, not only at Rachel's presence but at the elder's confusing actions—barking orders to a deaf girl. To her credit, Danae cast a quick glance behind her before springing in one great stride atop Uila's bare back, Kamiko's sword in hand. Rachel's chastisement continued unbroken until the great warhorse passed through the gateway and into the stable house. Rachel stepped gracefully toward the trio with an explanation of exasperation at the folly of teaching anything worthwhile to youngsters of the current age.

Two of the three chuckled and guffawed graciously, offered a brief appraisal of their own sons and daughters in that same light, and promptly lost all interest. The third stood staring into the fire-lit doorway, seeming to draw some unspoken conclusion before he joined his fellows. They sidled up the street and dispersed the onlookers gently, bidding them head for home. The third guard cast one more glance at the door as Rachel drew it closed from the inside, as if there were some certainty he could not put his finger on.

By now the heat of Kamiko's adrenaline had subsided, and a hard cold shudder wracked her body from crown to heel and set her shivering so hard she felt her spine must certainly crack from the strain of it. Still crouched low, she backed toward the stair landing and turned to make her way down to the yard.

Siruis was as still as a frozen ice sculpture. Fat flakes of crystalline snow drifted in slow circles, reluctant to light on her. To Kamiko's amazement, Felene was standing! She was silent and unmoving, looking down at Siruis, a carved post of solid muscle. Her strong face was unusually slack and flush with the heat of excited wonder. Yet even from the distance, Kamiko could see Felene's eyes ablaze with an inner fierce passion.

The whole of the scene was set in vivid contrast. The refuge of the sisterhood, the fortress and all in it, were the design and construct of men, dark granite cut in sharp angles and dramatic bas-relief carvings meant to depict strength and dominance. Yet every top surface was inches deep in pristine snow, whiter for the nightglow of the surrounding township. Felene's bright cheeks were the lone color within Kamiko's sight, all else was perfect white set upon the dark of mottled granite. The half dozen who had again stormed into the courtyard were in frozen stillness as well, every eye fixed upon Siruis, every breath short and every expression that of pure wonder.

Just as Kamiko's heart soared, overwhelmed by the still silent magnificence, it dropped into the pit of her gut. Without preamble, her first meeting with Siruis filled her thoughts, and the unadorned truth assailed her with renewed strength. She was wholly out of place here. By simply descending the stairs, she would break the spell, not heighten it. The unmasked wonder on all their faces would morph into disdain at her approach so that even having seen Siruis heal Felene, the sight would diminish, and they would return to their mundane existence. Some part of her could not bear it, though be it the Warrior or the Woman, she could not tell.

She had drawn steel in a place set wholly upon the benevolence of God. And she had felt the rising of the kind of rage that has limitless depth. She knew now that Hun'jotzimon was jealous, unaccustomed to being set aside for lesser preferences. It was not Kamiko's anger that had flared, it was the sword, and that presence was totally gone from her spirit.

Her emptiness felt complete. There remained no single *right* thing in all of her being. Odd that here, in the fortress of the sisterhood of the Order, did she see herself in the true light and that it was full darkness staring back at her.

Movement at the livery door drew her thoughts and eyes away from the surreal scene. Rachel glided across the snow toward Siruis but cast a brief glance up to where Kamiko knelt, shivering hard. There appeared to be no mercy in those eyes—remorse, but no mercy. Several of the others followed Rachel's gaze but lingered longer, watching Kamiko as if expecting her to stoop further than she'd already fallen. Kamiko's sword hung like a dead animal in Rachel's fist.

So she need not even descend the stairs to break the spell. The moment was gone, the magic depleted by little more than looks of judgment. She forced her legs to move down the stair instead of over the wall and into the bright night. By the time she made the yard, she already regretted the choice. In truth it mattered little, the outcome would be much the same.

Rachel spoke softly to Siruis, who, in turn, nodded as if in understanding and assent. Danae was standing inside the open livery doorway, cinching Uila's saddle and checking his bridle for travel. For a moment, Kamiko feared insanity had taken her mind without her knowledge but shunned the notion immediately. Such would be an easy route, and she had little doubt that "ease" was forever behind her.

Kamiko Hoshi was dead.

It remained to been seen who had taken her place.

Chapter 15

Rivulets of sweat traced itchy lines down Kamiko's face without relent. Deliciously hot water all but cooked her like a boiled chicken in stew, the broth of which was soapy and fragrant with herbs meant to open pores and leach the layered grime away. She could remember the last time she'd been wholly submerged in steaming hot water, but the span of months was too long to bother counting. Besides she had nowhere near enough fingers and toes.

The small room was dark with aged cedar paneling and filled with myriad smells of wood and smoke, herbs, and soaps, all thickened by the musty reek of soaked-in moisture. A small woodburning stove kept the compact room stifling hot, even though the world outside was washed entirely white with ice and snow. The deep tub occupied one end of the rectangular room, opposite the stove. Near the tub, an ornate dressing screen offered the only privacy to be had. A narrow doorway was centered on one of the long walls, flanked on either side with low wooden benches built into the wall. Opposite the doorway, a single longer bench took half the wall in length, this flanked on either side by glass-fronted cabinets built floor to ceiling. One of these held freshly laundered towels and washcloths neatly folded and stacked. The other was stuffed with bottles of oil, boxes of soap, and pouches, bundles, and bound clutches of herbs and fragrant flower caps.

Kamiko wondered if she could work things to never leave the room again and was inwardly pleased that at least some smattering of her humor still existed. A quiet rapping on the door sounded just as Felene pushed it open and stepped inside. Frigid air brushed across Kamiko's face for a moment, igniting the itchy streaks across her skin, so she released her foothold on the opposite end of the tub and slid forward enough to submerge her head.

She guessed it was the silent hum of the water that helped trigger a cascade of recent memories. The foremost was that of the impromptu village which had spontaneously grown at the massive garbage dump. The second most was that Rachel had kept her sword, a thing which both rankled and relieved. Though the sword's absence cast her bearing off balance, she could not help but hope change was in the making.

She swept her hands forcefully across her face and scrubbed at her hairline and behind her ears with calloused fingers, scouring the already-clean skin again. She dug her nails into her scalp and massaged, as if she could wash her thoughts away with the dirt. Again. The dirt was long gone; the thoughts, of course, remained.

Kamiko gently shoved with her feet, and her head and shoulders rose from the water. With pruney hands, she pressed the sluicing moisture from her face and eyes, then swept her hair into a soaked bundle at the back of her head.

"You gonna stay in there all night?"

"Maybe. Probably."

Felene's voice had always held what Kamiko could only describe as a blush of joy. Even when she was angry, and especially when in the heat of battle, Felene never seemed to lose her brightness of character. Kamiko opened her eyes and turned her best comical glare toward her younger sister and was more than a little surprised to see that Rachel was seated on the low bench opposite the doorway.

The tension she had so carefully worked out of her spine climbed from base to crown in a single rush, ending in her jaw. It was another old habit borne of a jangled history between them.

"Hello, Sister Kamiko." Tension was in Rachel's spine too and projected in her terse voice. Rachel made no effort to hide the look on her face; she did not want to be here.

"Greetings, Elder." Kamiko did not want Rachel there either, but that she had followed Siruis and Kamiko into the wretched night spoke of a great need.

"You did not come here to chastise me, did you?"

"No, I did not."

"Right. Throwing us out into the freezing night has made that point with prime efficiency."

"Good!"

"Keeping my sword was just a simple insult."

"Hold your tongue, child. I have neither time nor energy for such witless banter."

Kamiko could feel the elder sister keeping an iron grip on her own tongue, holding her frustration carefully at bay. Something greater was amiss. Kamiko felt the same as Rachel; she had no energy for argument. In truth, she had no right to rankle. She had committed a real infraction against the sisterhood by drawing her sword.

"Sisters, please avert your eyes. I am shriveling from prune to raisin."

Felene's smile had been contained to one side of her mouth but spread all across her face at Kamiko's gentle and willing retreat. Once out of the tub and wrapped in one of the overlarge towels, Kamiko addressed Rachel with the respect due the elder sister of the Order.

"Greetings, Sister Rachel. May God bless you and guide your ways in peace." She felt it and meant it. She sat beside the elder woman and wrapped one arm around her strong shoulders. "Please forgive me, Sister. I have been out of the loop for a long while. And seeing Parzon..." She paused as the viper coiled. "Well, she really—" Words left her.

"She makes you want to spit flaming daggers!"

Both Kamiko and Felene felt their mouths drop at Rachel's statement. She continued, reminding Kamiko of the warrior this woman had been.

"She does the same with me, Kamiko. I would have you cut her down first and seek forgiveness later were it up to me." She leaned into Kamiko. "But there is no need to seek my forgiveness, Sister. We walk the path as it passes beneath our feet, come what may."

Felene retrieved another towel from the cabinet and tossed it to Kamiko. Rachel disengaged from Kamiko's embrace, stood, and continued with a question.

"Do you know where we are?" Rachel indicated with a sweep of her hand that she referred to the establishment they now occupied.

Kamiko ventured an educated guess. "I believe this is Lord Merritt's estate." She began toweling her face and neck, squeezing the water from her hair. Fatigue drove the tension from her back but left her with a dull ache at the temples. "It was difficult to tell where we eventually stopped. Felene seemed intent on leading us all over this town, despite the blizzard."

Rachel and Felene shared a look that held both humor and concern, the latter being stronger. Kamiko eyed them with open suspicion. She knew well enough where she was and had been curious about the wandering nature of their route once she realized the destination.

"You feared we were being shadowed," Kamiko said.

Both women began to speak at once, but neither did.

"You *think* we were being shadowed."

Felene's face was devoid of humor, but it was not replaced with concern. She simply nodded, hands on her hips, a warrior's slouch at the shoulders. And there being no decree against weapons being wielded in Lord Merritt's estate, a broadsword hung from her shoulder, slung low on her back. Kamiko saw that Felene was again dressed in her leathers, with a small breastplate of worked and hardened hide.

"Well," Kamiko continued, "we were being shadowed but not by any enemy. His name is Jerim, Siruis's other guardian. He will not let anyone come close to her, nor would you know he was there unless he wished it. He is very hard to find when he wants to be." She scrubbed her head vigorously, knowing well enough she was tangling her hair into knots that would require severe work with a stiff brush. Sleep was calling her like a long-lost friend.

"Why are we at Lord Merritt's estate home, Sister Rachel?" Kamiko asked. She rose and stepped behind the dressing screen where freshly washed bedclothes and a thick robe were folded and waiting. "And why was it necessary that Siruis be ejected from Mars

Knoll? Such was wholly undeserved. She was half-frozen, Sister, and beyond exhaustion." Kamiko's voice was kind but to the point.

"It was an unavoidable precaution," Rachel retorted with obvious control over her tone. The elder sister had never grown used to Kamiko's authoritative manner and met Kamiko's steely gaze over the top of the screen with her own. Yet Kamiko knew there was no measure of spite or meanness in Rachel that would cause her to send Siruis into the frozen night without well-founded intentions.

She pulled the nightshirt on over her head and drew the soft fleece pants up over her legs. As she tied the waistband, she was both surprised and pleased to see that they fit. She stepped from behind the screen, eyeing Felene with a wink of gratitude and a slight smile.

"Thanks for the bedclothes."

Felene chuckled. "Try finding a fit for you around here. You're lucky we didn't just wrap you in a sheet and shove you under the covers."

A loud thud sounded at the door which made Kamiko jump in her tracks. Felene opened it to reveal Danae, bearing a small tray of food perched on one hand and a large cloth-covered mug in the other. The lithe girl fairly skipped into the room to escape the cold and the swirl of flakes still falling outside. Beyond her pants and shirt, she was wrapped in only a thin blanket and seemed to have simply stepped into the boots closest to the backdoor of Lord Merritt's great house. She could have easily fit both feet into only one of them.

The wash of cold air chilled Kamiko's feet instantly and sent a shiver up her body in a wave of gooseflesh. She unfurled the robe and stuffed her arms into the thick sleeves while searching the floor for Felene's proffered woolen house shoes. She could see Rachel's patience quickly waning by the set of her feet and hands on her hips.

While Kamiko pulled the shoes on, she repeated Rachel's last statement in the form of a question. "An unavoidable precaution, Sister?"

Danae placed the plate and mug on the bench beside her and flopped down on the opposite bench, facing Kamiko but positioned where she could watch every mouth in the room. When Rachel continued without dismissing the young girl, Kamiko knew she was already party to what was about to be revealed. It was obvious to Kamiko that Rachel opened her comment with a statement meant to stun.

"Lord Merritt has offered his estate to the sisterhood as refuge," she began. "We have been losing Mars Knoll to the Crown. And tonight, you may have sealed that end as an absolute."

In the silent moments that passed, Kamiko imagined never feeling warmth again. Rachel held Kamiko's gaze as she'd always done, without flinching or apology, and let the silence linger. And in just the same way the elder sister had, for years, answered Kamiko's queries with silence, the truth bubbled to the surface in her thoughts. Rachel waited with a patience which seemed ancient.

"Siruis," Kamiko whispered. "I brought Siruis to Mars Knoll."

Rachel closed her eyes and nodded a single affirmation. When she opened them again, it was with the most subtle of changes. Any accusation Kamiko had perceived was gone. In Kamiko's younger days as a warrior, she'd once had the honor of following Rachel into battle. It was a historically minor war fought on behalf of the frontier landowners to the east of the Antarius River. Kamiko had been at Rachel's right flank, her strong guard. The bearing Rachel carried on that day was once again on her features in full.

A look to Felene, and then Danae, revealed to Kamiko that they too shared that fierce resolve. She had no doubt more was happening than had been revealed. She also had little doubt that the conversation would unfold here in the seclusion and privacy of the bathhouse, thus the food. Her appetite gone, Kamiko mechanically lifted a wedge of cheese, wrapped in a nutty flatbread, to her mouth and took a bite. Rachel needed no questioning to prompt her into an explanation.

She took her seat beside Kamiko as she spoke. "Do not worry over it, Sister, King Titus has been laying this trap for some time. I suppose it is both fitting and foretold that it be triggered at Mars Knoll."

Kamiko's head tilted in silent inquiry, her mouth still chewing.

"Djinnasee," Rachel answered. The single name was sufficient for Kamiko's understanding. And even with questions dancing around in her thoughts, she awaited Rachel with learned, practiced patience. She washed the first bite down with a familiar concoction, one of Rachel's herbal brews meant to induce restful sleep.

"We have seen it coming and have taken what steps we can. By now, word of Siruis's appearance at Mars Knoll is on its way to Titus. Yours too."

Felene interjected in stark terms. "We have a royal spy in our midst." She unbuckled the barding and lowered her sword as she took a seat beside Danae.

The declaration prompted a spark of sorrow in Kamiko's chest, but she was only a little surprised. Corruption could be minimized but never eliminated. She took a mouthful of dried blueberries, a sure sign she was there to listen, her eyes returning to Rachel.

"For some months now, we have been moving our base to Lord Merritt's, with as much secrecy as possible." The look on Rachel's face told Kamiko that she was drawing toward the crux of the conversation with care. "He is putting himself at great risk, but he is a man of exceptional integrity and would not be refused the task. There are so few godly men left to the world, sometimes I fear for the sanctity of this kingdom."

A troubling thought occurred to Kamiko in almost the same instant she spoke it. "Suppose you turned Siruis and me over to King Titus. Would that salvage this situation?"

Danae sat upright and snapped out a quick question with her hands. Felene simply nodded in the affirmative, the look on both their faces serious. Felene answered, "Don't even think about it, Kamiko. Our course is set, and upon it we will stay."

Rachel held up a calming hand toward the two and said to Kamiko, "Yes, it would, and we would claim an enormous reward for our troubles and possibly keep the sisterhood intact."

Danae's fingers flew again, but Felene laid her hand gently over them, quieting the girl with a subtle look of reproach, big sister to little sister. Danae's face flared hot with anger and no small measure of anxiety.

"But you know the answer to that, Sister," Rachel continued.

"Do I? And what do you mean, 'keep the sisterhood intact?' There is more to that. I want to hear it. The Order is not dependent on Mars Knoll for survival."

Rachel nodded to Kamiko and flashed a message to Danae, who looked like she'd been poked unexpectedly in the ribs. She hopped up and moved to the woodstove, at last kicking the overlarge boots from her feet as she passed the door. She stoked the fire, added a couple of thick wedges of wood from the stack, and then hurried back to her place beside Felene. Kamiko imagined the youth seldom slowed her pace to what was considered normal.

With another nod, Rachel reminded Kamiko of the plate of food sitting on the bench between them. Kamiko lifted the cheese and flatbread to her mouth and shoved the remainder of it in at once, her eyes locked with Rachel's.

"We intend to disband." The gleam of mischief twinkled in Rachel's eyes as the mouthful of food turned to dry stone on Kamiko's tongue. She'd done that on purpose. Rachel continued speaking while Kamiko attempted to chew, effectively silenced. "I would personally lead the assault on the Crown should King Titus try to take either of you by force. Especially, Sister, after what I saw in that courtyard." She chanced a brief look at Felene. "Siruis must be protected at all cost, king and country aside. Do you understand what happened, what Siruis did?"

With no chance of speaking, Kamiko simply nodded her answer.

"Well, I do not fully understand it and have yet to stop long enough to think it out. However, I do know well enough that we need to get her away from here. If Titus does succeed in getting his hands on her, I fear for her life." Rachel's face grew a shade darker. "He must not."

Suddenly Kamiko was near to choking on the unruly gob of food in her mouth and wondered if her own face had darkened noticeably. And Rachel thought she was delivering difficult news. Kamiko's stomach hardened. In the silence that fell over the bathhouse, Kamiko stood abruptly, moved to the door, stepped out into the icy cold, and expelled the food out into the snow. Rachel's declaration was echoing around in her head like a newly rung bell. Behind her, Felene's quiet voice was full of concern.

"Are you okay? You should take smaller bites." She placed her hand on Kamiko's shoulder. "We won't let it happen. This is all about making certain Titus does not find Siruis. Or you, for that matter." She leaned around to draw Kamiko's eyes but without success.

The frigid night air only heightened the tingling in her face, the weariness in her bones. She let Felene pull her inside and dropped back to the bench beside Rachel. She felt hardened, confused, depleted. Her gaze fixed upon her hands lying in her lap. They were sacrificing everything in their world to keep Siruis out of Titus's murderous hands, a plan come to fullness in the last hour. A plan that went directly against Djinnasee's decree for Kamiko. A sharp pinging rifled through her ears, and she felt a sudden falling sensation. Strong hands were on her shoulders and arms as she fell, as her vision and her thoughts went dark.

Chapter 16

She awoke hard, like a punch in the face. Uila was thundering beneath her, a blast of cold wind on her face, a brutal enemy at her heels. It was an enemy unknown to her, newly wrought from the core of the mountains and forged by the fires of slaughter the likes of which Kamiko had never faced. Even Uila's great strength was not enough to outpace those giving chase. She did not question how she knew this.

The falling sun was ahead and to her right, low and fat and blazing. She was heading southwest then, but from where and to what end she could not recall. Stark rocky ridges were high on her left, the tall grasses of open plains on her right, down the slope. Uila had his head and was staying in the narrows between rock and grass, making his way at breakneck speed.

Kamiko lifted her hands to gain control of the warhorse, to rein him into an approaching gap in the tall grass, take the enemy into cover where she could stop and make a stand. She could feel the shudder of fatigue in Uila's body and knew the chase must end soon, lest he die beneath her. Her hands came up empty and slow, as if moving through an invisible yet thick morass.

She was aware of something heavy and solid around her waist and discovered it to be a single muscle-bound arm, covered wrist to elbow with a thick hide gauntlet. Recognition erupted in her mind. The gauntlet was inscribed with twisting vine and time-faded flowering depictions of ancestral runes, names of previous kings and warlords of the Seven Clans. King Per El`Thorn was the mass behind her, and she was, in fact, his burden. She felt his massive heart pounding against her back, his breath fast and labored. They were *both* riding Uila; shock filled her. She held no recollection of what had transpired.

She heard his voice then, the mad roaring of a mighty man in the throes of combat. He was singing. Even without seeing his bright and beautiful face, she knew it was a mask of enraged joy. He sang the song of his bride's glorious favor, her many years ahead in crossing to the next life. He would see her this very day, or so he sang and laughed and raged. She felt his left knee press gently into Uila's forerib and leaned into the turn on instinct, as they plunged down the slope toward the grasslands.

Many thundering hoofbeats followed close behind. To her horror, King El`Thorn kicked Uila all the harder, demanding the beast give his life for this one moment. His free arm swung over her head with his battle-ax at the outermost reach; it flashed out of his hand and beyond her vision in an instant. Sounds of death and the squeals and shrieks of tumbling horses answered his attack, and fewer of the enemy gave chase. By Kamiko's reckoning, three fell from his single blow.

His arm tightening around her ribcage was the only warning. The mighty warrior king lunged off Uila and flew out into the tall heavy grass, cradling her like his own beloved child. He would die for her. He *was* dying for her. How she knew this, she could not tell.

The impact of the ground blew his breath out in a howl. Kamiko felt the hot sting of an arrowhead pierce her shoulder, driven through his chest from behind by the hard ground against his back. He'd been carrying the arrow all through the chase. The force of impact newly stunned her, and her eyes again swam in darkness.

Her own fury had been slow to awaken but, at last, came rushing into her chest as she tumbled out of his arms. When her eyes came open, she had the distinct sensation of being smothered by a thick blanket of fog and stifling heat. The Warrior inside became enraged and struck her to the heart with pure violence.

Her fist closed on the first solid thing she found—a heavily muscled arm. The adrenaline of melee coursed through her veins as her senses came fully alive. From lying on her back, she jerked the arm toward the ground beside her and propelled her own mass upward, while holding the meaty flesh in the steel vise of her fingers.

The shriek of pain and surprise was not what she'd expected. It was the voice of a woman. Yet the momentum was begun, and Kamiko's bare feet touched down on cold stone floor before her mind could order her fist to loosen its grip. Bed sheets and a thick blanket billowed around her and partially hid the woman who slammed to the floor at her feet, but the voice was distinctly Felene's.

Rachel and Danae skittered away on tiptoe, mouths open in shock yet stunned to silence. The frantic motion stopped as the sheet settled to the floor atop Felene. Kamiko immediately released her arm, dropped to her knees, and began trying to untangle the bedding. When Felene's face came into view, it was red and held the look of someone who'd ignored a warning to stand clear of a growling dog and been bitten as a result.

She made no move to rise but smiled up at Kamiko and exclaimed, "You are fast, woman!" Then she winked and said in a low suspect voice, "Are you going to help me, or should I expect an elbow to the sternum as a follow-up?"

Kamiko's heart still raced, but her stance relaxed, and she sat back onto her heels. Her mind was torn between Felene and the lingering impression of King El`Thorn. Her body was quivering from unspent strength. She pushed her mass up with her toes, reached down to take hold of Felene by both sides of her leather breastplate, and then lifted her full weight into the air, settling her down on her feet with ease. Her eyes moved around the room, and only when her eyes fell upon Siruis did she think to release her hold on Felene.

It was a dream—that place and not this room. Yet the one seemed to hold as full a place in reality as the other, her own presence just as complete. The Warrior rallied against Kamiko's willingness to calm down, demanding she follow her instinct to distrust a situation until all possibility of foul play was investigated.

Siruis was seated on the edge of an ornate throne-like chair at the far end of the massive room. Her feet dangled almost at arm's length from the floor. Danae, Rachel, and Felene were the only other occupants and appeared to have been at Kamiko's bedside. On second look, she saw movement at Siruis's feet and realized that a great furry lynx was curled beside the chair, looking back at her with regal confidence.

Kamiko's gaze moved once around the room before being drawn, as if by force, back to Siruis. Lord Merritt's library, judging from the sheer volume of heavily laden shelves, beheld a vast wealth in not only books but antiques of every bent imaginable. Weapons and curious artifacts of civilizations vanished millennia past adorned the walls and shelves in an array meant to stagger the mind. But Kamiko had spent no small span of years at King Titus's side, and such wealth had long since lost the pull on her senses. The whole of Lord Merritt's estate could be nestled within the halls of Titus's personal library.

She took a step toward Siruis but stopped and turned toward Felene, her actions now returning to her mind. Felene seemed unconscious of the fact that she was clutching her arm or that a measure of awe was on her face.

"Please, Sister, forgive me," Kamiko said. "I certainly meant you no harm."

"I get that. I should have listened to Rachel, I guess." Felene raised one brow as she spoke.

"I tried to warn her," Rachel said as she stepped toward the two.

Danae's quiet yowl drew their attention, and she replied with a quick hand sweep that she agreed with Rachel. Her face was bright with animate humor, one eyebrow raised slightly in a gesture Kamiko recognized as borrowed from Felene.

Rachel looked at the back of Felene's head, gingerly touching it to probe for a bump.

"Are you hurt?" she asked.

"No, Sister. Didn't you hear her say she meant me no harm?" Yet when Felene pushed her sleeve up, there was a bruise in the shape of Kamiko's hand. It was already a deeper bluing blush where her fingertips had gripped. "Strong too," Felene said as she flexed her fist and arm.

Rachel flashed a message to Danae, who, in turn, trotted across the room and out through the broad double doors. Rachel cast a brief look toward Siruis before turning to Kamiko.

"You should get dressed," she said and lifted a neatly folded set of clothes from a low end table at the foot of Kamiko's bed. Only then did Kamiko realize that she had been given lodging inside the library, that her bed was simply a table with a mattress on it. Rachel continued, "Danae is fetching Lord Merritt. We still have much to talk about, Sister. But it is necessary that Lord Merritt be party to all we do and say. It is likely that he is risking more than the lot of us." She added with a nod, "He wishes to meet with you."

Rachel motioned toward a doorway between two of the towering bookshelves, indicating that Kamiko should change clothes in the room beyond. As Kamiko reached the door and pulled it open, she noticed both Felene and Rachel cast what appeared to be furtive glances to where Siruis sat. She could think of many reasons why they would be uncomfortable with Siruis and felt the inward twisting in her gut at the recollection of her own first contact with the young sister. It made her wonder what Rachel's accumulated past must look like, if the good outweighed the bad, if Rachel held the same view of self that Kamiko did.

The thick door closed behind her with a quiet thump, leaving her in a miniature version of the bathhouse, minus the tub. The dark stone floor and the lower half of the walls were the same, a marbling of deep green, black, and shades of dark gray veined through with glistening white crystal as fine as spiderweb. The upper part of the walls, ceiling, door and single window frame were of the same rare cedar as in the bathhouse.

She had never met the elderly Lord Merritt personally but was familiar with his name and his exploits. His family heritage was traceable at least a thousand years back, hundreds of generations deep in

Cairistonia's history. It was believed that his ancestors were present at the founding of First Colony, when the charter of kingship was originally penned. Yet such claims were simply legend; information of that nature had long since been under the careful keep of the Crown.

She dressed, avoiding the mirror mounted to the wall above the washbasin. Her hair was less tangled than expected, though she could not imagine having slept through even a light brushing. Her own toiletry kit lay to one side of the basin, and beside that was a wooden box with a small note card bearing her name. Inside she found the common items she would have soon hoped to replenish with a trip to the market, all newly acquired: a bone-and-bristle toothbrush, a bottle of lightly scented oil, two bars of soap wrapped in waxed paper, and a jar of tooth powder, no doubt blended with crushed willow bark.

As she cleaned her teeth, she could not avoid the mirror without feeling as though she was loath to see her own face. She held little concern for whether or not she was considered beautiful or homely, such was a thing of perception more than fact or function. She was not pining for a mate and had no reason to doll herself up.

Yet she could not help but notice how weathered she appeared, even to her own eyes. Her face was plain of feature—thin lips, narrow eyes, and a smallish nose and high cheekbones. She had aged since the last time she had seen her own face in a real mirror. Her skin was darker than she'd realized, and faint crease lines had formed at the corners of her eyes and across her forehead. And though she was not manly to look at, neither was she overtly womanish. She imagined that few people outside the sisterhood had ever seen her without her breastplate, and that it was plainly obvious her armor needed very little in the way of extra space where her natural form was concerned.

She rinsed her mouth and cleaned the bristle brush thoroughly. She meant to make the small luxury last as long as possible. She'd forgotten how much she disliked cleaning her teeth with a frayed stick. She had forgotten luxuries almost entirely: hot running water, indoor toilets, a soft mattress with fresh linens, laundered clothes, and to her notion, the greatest luxury of all—a hot bath with soap.

It occurred to her that her inner duo had switched places. The Woman was standing in full view for the first time in her recollection, and the Warrior was the one withdrawn. It was a little unnerving, she had kept them so distinctly separated that she had conjured the dichotomy at all. Yet as she stood gazing into the face in the glass, she realized that the Woman inside her, the one she had formed a mental picture of, held very little resemblance to Kamiko Hoshi.

She had never been frail, even in her youth. The woman always retreated behind the Warrior out of necessity, out of weakness, even at the slightest confrontation. And the Warrior, the imagined embodiment of what Kamiko believed she must be, was invincible and strong to a ridiculous measure. She could see it more clearly now than ever before.

It was with a sudden flush of embarrassment that she recalled how she played out her earliest encounter with Dairei in her mind again and again, yet with the Warrior slapping the thief down with ease. She could remember it with greater clarity than the actual outcome. She had limped around her campsite with a badly bruised face, broken ribs, and a devastated ego, reliving the vicious battle over and over, unable to sleep until she'd convinced herself that Dairei had bested her by a simple fluke. She'd laughed aloud that she gave as good as she got, that Dairei was nursing the greater of the wounds. She was a fool. Parzon had given her a sound beating and only spared her life because there was no need to take it. For all Kamiko's skill and strength, Dairei had held back. The brigand's strength was far greater than her frame and muscle mass should allow. And her control in a fight was purely natural motion for her, as though she'd never needed to be trained.

The anger that flared in Kamiko was not for Dairei. It was not really directed anywhere specific; it was just a churn of unrest fueled by a small measure of rage. Kamiko had been in the practice of creating an illusionary life, playing games in her own mind to convince herself of—what? That she was better than everyone else? Worse than everyone else? She had obviously concluded, in some part of her mind, that Woman was weak, and Warrior was strong.

Both were staring back from the mirror as a single thing: a woman of strength. Part of her felt silly for coming to such a simple awareness so late in her life, but the thought led to another—she had taken her first life at only twelve years old. As the memory swept over her, the face in the mirror looked suddenly foreign, unrecognizable as Kamiko Hoshi. She felt like a child in the presence of a stranger, a dangerous callous brigand come into a town of simple folk.

Chapter 17

She had only been twelve years old. She was still twelve years old! Perhaps she had never grown beyond that day in any way other than size and strength. Djinnasee had been weeks gone then, people had been killed. The children were being taken from the town. Her town. Slavers. The harvesting season labor hands were butchering the old, bagging the young, and enslaving the people. They'd never imagined one such as Kamiko could be in their midst. That tiny fragment of youth, of childhood innocence that had remained inside her, was destroyed. She hadn't simply taken a life, she had committed war on the brigands and she'd won. There was never any choice in the matter. She simply defended the town as best she knew how, holding nothing in reserve.

She'd formed a picture of herself while still standing among the bodies, and it was not the woman she was now looking at in the mirror nor the one she had seen only moments ago, brushing her teeth. She was the foreigner. Kamiko was the impostor, the Warrior simply a construct built by a twelve-year-old mind grappling for sanity. It was there in the center of town, with blood up to her elbows and streaked across her face, that Woman and Warrior had emerged as separate beings from the deeper recesses of her mind.

It was on that very day that she had first seen Bartol.

The remote thudding at the base of her skull resolved into loud banging on the door. A stranger's voice demanded as to her well-being, asking if everything was okay, with more concern than Kamiko imagined necessary. A quick glance around the room revealed nothing familiar. She quelled the need to panic, confused and a little angered that she would lose touch with where she was. She held no recollection as to how she'd arrived in what appeared to be someone's bathroom. Someone of extreme wealth judging by—her blood froze. Reality and memory unfolded in a single moment. The door opened, and Felene's bright face peered around the doorframe, concern etched in the lines at the corners of her eyes. Her smile was uncertain at best.

"I guess it's my week to keep tabs on you, Sister," Felene said quietly.

She stepped inside with a glance over her shoulder and shut the door behind her. Judging by the odd look on her face, Felene had something important to say that would be for Kamiko's ears only.

Instead she said, "I know it has been a long time, but you are acting a bit peculiar, even for you, Kamiko." She lifted her chin in a gesture of inquiry, her brow furrowed. "What's going on, Sister? You look like you don't feel well."

Kamiko drew a deep, surprisingly shaky, breath and said, "Nothing, Felene." After a moment of reflection, she corrected the lie. "Actually everything is going on, and all of it is bad." She shook her head, remembering to whom she was speaking, and decided to trust. "Well, most of it is bad. Some of it is good. I just met someone I did not expect."

Felene's eyes flicked to the window for the tiniest of moments. This brought a small smile to Kamiko's face.

"No, nothing like that. I'm talking about me, Sister." When Felene's brow lifted on one side, Kamiko grinned again, looked directly into her eyes, and asked, "Do you know when my birthday is?"

The brow lifted further as Felene answered, "Of course. You were born—"

"I wasn't born on the eve of Fall Harvest. That is only the day we acknowledge my birth."

"Well, okay, when is your—"

"I don't know." She looked back to the mirror, still seeing the stranger where her own face should have been. "I have never seen my mother, and I can only assume to have met my father." She lifted her hand and studied the skin and knuckles, scars and lines exactly where she knew they should be, the memory of each mark clear in her mind. She asked Felene absently, "Do I seem different to you, Sister?" Everything about Kamiko's life felt remote, a story she'd read long ago. Her hands and voice were distinct, but her face was a mask.

"What do you mean different? Can't really say you do, but I haven't seen you for…" She paused and thought before continuing. "Well, for a good while." The odd look deepened.

Kamiko's memories were there as she sorted through the last months.

"Sorry, Felene," she whispered. "I'm just feeling a bit odd at the moment. I'll be fine."

"Speak for yourself, Sister." Felene's voice held an edge Kamiko did not recognize. Her face appeared over Kamiko's shoulder in the mirror wearing an expression of despair Kamiko did not know Felene was able to manage. Or was it fear? When Felene continued, her voice was low and dark and held the essence of searching. Kamiko was uncertain if Felene spoke in statements or questions.

"Dairei," she said. "I was down, my back broken beyond question. I felt it go, felt my gut explode, and tasted bile. For that one tiny moment, the pain was so hot I could not move. Then nothing." Her eyes burned from the memory of it, the intensity reborn as she spoke it aloud. "It seemed as though I was frozen in place, but the whole of everything had only slowed, and then I felt my head slam. I thought someone had hit me from behind, Kamiko. I didn't know I was already on the ground."

Although Felene's dark eyes were locked with hers in the mirror, Kamiko knew she was watching the scene unfold again and knew she would see it a thousand times over in the weeks to follow. Kamiko did not move, did not turn to face her sister. Instead she kept the picture framed in the mirror so she could see her own odd face through the telling.

"How could I not know I was on the ground?" Felene's hand came to rest gently on Kamiko's shoulder. "I could not get my eyes to focus, couldn't find where gravity was drawing me. I wasn't cold or hot." Kamiko could feel Felene's weight beginning to bear on her shoulder. "And I guess I must have…" She paused as her eyes watered and her grip tightened. "I dreamed, Sister. I don't know what else to call it."

Kamiko knew it was her time to listen, to keep her own cascading troubles inside. They would wait.

"I knew it was over," Felene continued. "Dairei promised she would do it. She said I would never walk again, and she made good on it. She was so fast I didn't even know she'd moved."

"What did you dream?" Kamiko was relieved to hear her own familiar voice. It brought the faintest twinge of recognition to her face. The question seemed to have surprised Felene as the focus of her eyes returned to the mirror, to Kamiko.

She shook her head and released Kamiko's shoulder. "I saw myself infirm, bedridden for all the decades of my life, a spoon-fed invalid. And, Sister, I did not just see it. I lived it. I was there. When first I felt Siruis's hand, I had been lying in that bed for some forty years."

Felene turned from the mirror and sat down in an ornate dressing chair. Kamiko followed but stood at her side, leaning against a small sturdy table, the only other free-standing item in the room. Kamiko understood with more clarity than Felene realized. She had seen the whole of her past stacked into a handful of moments.

"I was there, and then I was back, lying in the snow, everything moving so slowly. Some part of me refuses to believe any of it happened, that Dairei did not break my back, that I only imagined the rest of it." Her shoulders rose, and her chest swelled as she drew a deep breath and let it out slowly. "But it happened, didn't it, Sister?"

"Dairei broke your back, Felene, and likely ruptured your gut in the process." Kamiko could feel the presence in the mirror beckoning her to return, to reconcile. "And you are now whole, at Siruis's hand." She placed her own hand on Felene's broad shoulder and closed it with gentle strength. She knew it was as much for her own sense of anchoring as it was for Felene. "As for what you experienced, I cannot say. But know this, Sister, I no longer doubt anything that comes to me as a result of being around Siruis. Make of it what you will but accept the resultant *now* as truth. You are here now and you are whole, even though you were broken. Beyond that, I don't know."

Felene rose, her voice darker and more insistent than Kamiko had ever heard it.

"You don't understand, Kamiko. I have lived out my entire life as an invalid, a useless mass of numb flesh. I could speak, and I could swallow, Sister…that's it! For forty years!"

She'd not pulled from Kamiko's grasp when she stood but stared across the small room at her face framed in the mirror.

"Danae stayed with me for near-on fifteen years. They moved me to the east, all the way to Cartha`dul and kept me in an ancient priory near the coast. I heard news and rumors that Cairistonia was at war and that Titus was dead. They told me you had been lost, either taken captive or killed, no one knew."

Felene's words began to take hold in Kamiko's mind. Felene had not seen those years compressed into a whole; she'd lived them in real time. Less than sixty seconds had passed for Kamiko during which forty years had unfolded for Felene. Her thoughts reeled as understanding at last unfurled. For out of that bottomless well of despair had come an awakening for Felene.

Kamiko's thoughts returned to the courtyard at Mars Knoll and Felene's figure, frozen in stunned silence, having just been healed. She tried but could not imagine what her sister must have been feeling in that moment.

"Felene, *bear with me the burden of the ages.*" It was an old song of the Order, a promise of unity and of helping one another through difficulties or coming to aid in battle. Kamiko sang it from the original verse with Djinnasee's ancient inflections and odd melody, the way Felene would best recognize it.

"*When comfort flees and madness rages.*" Her voice was soft and raspy, unaccustomed to singing. Felene's head sagged a small degree.

"I barely recognize myself. To look at my own reflection is to look upon a stranger."

Kamiko blinked from the mild shock of hearing the statement from Felene's mouth instead of her own.

"Which is the dream, Sister?" Felene asked, her voice barely a whisper. "Which of these two lives am I truly living? Has my mind finally snapped? Am I still lying in bed in a small dank room on the east coast of Cartha`dul, dreaming all this?"

By the tone of her voice and the hard inflections in her words, Kamiko imagined that Felene was truly considering such as a possibility.

"Madness!" There was no mirth in Felene's voice. "I have become madness, Sister. Should I now become Rage?" Felene was again facing the stranger in the mirror. Kamiko knew the answer to that question.

"Absolutely. You should *become* Rage, Felene." Visions of her father bleeding out at her feet danced in Kamiko's mind. He was the sole cause of thousands of deaths among the innocent and honorable—a devil in flesh. "We are in the beginning of an age of madness. Death will claim millions, Felene. It will claim you and me, Danae and Rachel, and many more in its headlong avalanche. So"—she squeezed Felene's shoulder hard—"prepare your spirit and the madness in your mind, let the mystery subside and get ready to fight for all you are worth. I do not know what to make of what you have experienced. I have been unable to make sense of my own mysteries. Based upon what I have seen, it likely happened just as you recall. Which means it is behind you now. You are not dreaming this, Sister. You and I are here, now. And you are as strong in spirit and body as ever." Felene did not look convinced.

Kamiko barely recognized Felene, never having seen her in such a state. That thought brought a twinge of understanding to the queer nature of the mirror. Kamiko had never been in such a condition either and found comfort in the fact that she was not a babbling fool, trussed up in rags and begging on the street or digging through the trash dump for bits of colored cloth.

Felene's face was swollen with emotion, dark with that smoldering angst of confusion. It was not lost on Kamiko that her sister kept it all held at bay, submerged and hidden from everyone until now.

The trust Felene showed her touched Kamiko in the deepest part of her spirit and had the effect of a cup of cool water on her parched tongue.

"There is nothing for it but to press on, Felene."

"Yes, I know, Kamiko. Lose it if you can, live with it if you must."

Felene's countenance firmed as she reined her emotions back into control and drew the mantle of a warrior back over her bearing. Kamiko knew she would never see her sister the same way again, that Felene had been born as something entirely new. In that, they were the same. Felene's eyes came close but stopped short of meeting Kamiko's directly. The mask of her bearing almost hid her exhaustion.

"You have not slept."

"No," Felene said as she moved toward the door. "Come on, Sister. Lord Merritt waits."

Kamiko touched her arm. "Why was I in the library?"

The twinkle of knowledge flashed in Felene's eyes. "Because I assumed you would appreciate a little privacy." She drew the door open. "Lord Merritt's estate is full."

Chapter 18

Kamiko was more impressed with the elderly gentleman than she cared to admit. Lord Anton Merritt was nothing like the wealthy land barons or merchant lords she'd encountered in the past. Even though in his eighties, she and Felene were pressed to keep stride with him as they passed through the estate wing. Tall and lean with a clean-shaven face and close-cropped hair of shimmering silver, his face held a kindness that the silvered hair and trimmed but full brows only heightened. He had the bearing of a man who had lived his life as a diplomat rather than a warrior. Kamiko could see that his attire was suited to spending the day outdoors, with the addition of a heavy coat, warm hat, and gloves. And she'd noticed the distinct absence of the smell of cologne or even scented soap, another of his oddities, considering his social peers. Lord Merritt did not act wealthy. He seemed to be simply a man. The lack of pretense was refreshing.

Felene was correct that the estate was full. Lord Merritt's only explanation had been that he could not leave them outside to freeze. There were hundreds. And every set of eyes tracked the rapid passage of Lord Merritt, Kamiko, and Felene. It was midmorning, and pale daylight seemed reluctant to drift in through the high windows, holding warmth in check. The long broad hallway of what turned out to be the east wing was lined on both sides with people who appeared to be simply camping indoors. Kamiko recognized them. Not individually but as a group. They were the indigent, the dwellers in the street, benefactors of the insanity of extreme wealth. They were society's backwash. Their collective fleshy reek overfilled the hallway.

It was difficult for Kamiko to think of Lord Merritt as the exception to that causality; the rich were the rich, good and bad alike. Vast layers of wealth lay in his stores as surely as any of his peers. The thing that made Lord Merritt unique was his willingness and indeed his desire to give a great portion of it back. That and his abiding belief that mankind was not the greatest mode of existence. He believed in God Almighty and lived his life as witness to that.

Kamiko also liked him for the simple fact that he had met Bartol and considered him a friend. To her notion of things, Lord Merritt was fully vetted by that simple fact. No one alive, with the possible exception of Djinnasee, was more adept at reading the depth of a man than Bartol. Her giant friend could smell deceit from a hundred paces and sense a quickening heartbeat through the ground.

Lord Merritt turned left into a short hallway that opened abruptly into a large round anteroom. Kamiko surmised that the contents of the room had been cleared to make space for the droves of homeless commoners filling it. A honeycomb of temporary walls had been assembled in an attempt to bring order where chaos threatened. Dispersed throughout the entire wing were the armor-clad militiamen of Lord Merritt's private security force.

As yet, Lord Merritt had shown no interest in conversation beyond the initial introductions. He had been genuinely pleased to finally meet Kamiko after so long following her exploits through not only the common news but through Djinnasee as well. He had made certain that Kamiko saw the ring on the pinky of his left hand, had waited with twinkling eyes until he was sure she'd recognized it as having come from Baron Vladimir Riplin. Then without further preamble, he'd turned and strode away, bidding Kamiko and Felene to follow.

Baron Riplin, the single wealthiest man alive outside royalty, was a man Kamiko knew well. The signet ring was a message to

Kamiko that Baron Riplin was here, if only by proxy, and that something was definitely afoul.

Kamiko thought she could sense a need in the elder gentleman to increase their walk to a paced run. She was pleased he did not. The chatter in the room dampened slightly as they rushed through. The name Hoshi wafted from more than one direction, drawing a strained look over Lord Merritt's shoulder. Kamiko understood his concern; she was supposed to be a secret.

As they approached an ornately carved double door at the opposite side of the room, two heavily muscled guardsmen stepped forward and pulled the doors open. They wore no armor, nor did they openly carry weapons. Kamiko suspected they had no real need for either judging by the fluidity of their movements and the confidence of their manner. Kamiko understood the language.

The men followed the trio into the room and locked the doors behind them. Lord Merritt's personal guard saw fit to accompany them now when his safety within the general populace was not an issue. Kamiko's mind marked the thought, her perspective altered however slightly. She cast a wary and brief glance over her shoulder and noted the dour look on Felene's face. The seed of suspicion rumbled in her gut, but she shoved it down and shrugged it off.

She remembered Bartol's first words to her when she was twelve and smattered with drying blood. "Doubt is a most compelling disruptor of potential and of clarity."

Oddly the room was both plush and sparse. The walls were lined with dark paneling, the expansive floor a wooden patchwork mosaic. As in the long hallway, the windows were high so that the room was dark of texture but bathed in soft light. It looked to have no more function than to be passed through, a large hub connecting wings. Kamiko found it interesting that none of the abundant crowd of refugees had been allowed to spill into this unused and quiet space.

One of the two guardsmen quick-trotted across the expanse of the room and took up station at the opposite doorway. The other lagged behind near the door they had entered. Kamiko and Felene were left alone with Lord Merritt midway across the great floor. Only then did she notice that a large round section of thick carpet was recessed a hand's width down into the floor. Lord Merritt led them into the shallow pit and stopped, turning abruptly to face the sisters.

Kamiko could hear the faintest hiss of what sounded like steam slipping slowly from an ill-fit furnace pipe. But it was not until Lord Merritt began speaking in low even tones that the puzzlement evaporated, and the purpose of the room's odd design became clear. The sound of their voices would not travel beyond a few paces from the center of the room. It was a place where plans could be made in secrecy. That the elder gentleman felt the need for such measures in his own home spoke volumes to Kamiko.

"Please forgive the secrecy, my friends, much is at stake. Would that there were a clear beginning for me to make a logical start, but need dictates otherwise." He acknowledged Felene with a smile and a curt nod and turned his full attention to Kamiko. "And though I promise not to grovel, I must once again tell you, Sister Kamiko, that you honor my home with your very presence." He winked at Felene and pressed on without hesitation. Kamiko got the sense that Felene was no longer considered a guest, rather an integral part of the lord's daily life.

"Trouble presses from every corner, from without and from within the royal sanctuary, from within my own household, from the ranks of the sisterhood, and most definitely from the throne of Cairistonia. Baron Riplin holds Ravencroft together by sheer force of will. He has been in the throes of battling a sudden upturn in criminal activities that has lasted two years."

"Sister Rachel informed me that Dairei Parzon has returned, which I am hoping will result in a measure of control returning to the streets of the Baron's fair city. There have been inexplicable crimes of violence and murder, brutal in the extreme. Parzon would never stand idle for such atrocities."

Nodding toward Felene, he said, "Grace sends her greeting. She said to assure you that she is getting at least one night's sleep a week. Sister Grace, by choice, and Baron Riplin, by decree, are doing great deeds for the citizens of that city."

Kamiko's senses were trained in full measure upon Lord Merritt. He filled in all the blanket information first, saving the main topic for last. His posturing suggested he was reacting to an inner fear. He would be bearing ill tidings and was hesitant.

"I suppose you are aware of the kingdom-wide decree of arrest posted upon our young sister, Siruis of Marjan. The reward is substantial enough to have gained Parzon's notice, is it not?" He lifted his hand in Kamiko's direction. "You will be served a summons to appear and will be escorted to King Titus forthwith, if you are seen out in the open. But I know of no arrest or detainment order issued on your behalf."

She shook her head as she considered her quandary. It seemed her only choice was to arrest Siruis and take her in. Protect her with court-recognized authority. The thought almost made her chuckle. Instead it caused a curling knot to form in her stomach.

"And we have been seen," Kamiko said.

"Best I can surmise? Yes. You are not the only one with a recognizable face, Kamiko. Word is spreading outside the Order that Uila was seen at the Knoll, and that news will make it to the king quickly enough. Sister Rachel told me of the events that took place inside the Knoll. Certainly word will reach the king about your traveling companion."

"What of King El`Thorn? Do you have news?"

He tilted his head. "What news of King El`Thorn do you seek?"

She considered the lengthy explanation that would result from telling Lord Merritt of the vision. "I have been told of the war, my lord. We encountered one of High Marshal Alexander's scouting parties in the jungle. Captain Rath told me all he knew."

"Rath, good man," Lord Merritt said. "I trust him to have been thorough in his assessment." He rubbed his forehead, obviously letting the thoughts congeal. "Ah, but news is a thing full of mystery, is it not? It goes as in all warfare when a larger force presses a small one. Were it not for Bartol, methinks the Seven Clans would be doomed. High Marshal Alexander has been elemental, to be sure, even with the sparse allotment given him by Titus." Lord Merritt took a deep breath and continued, "But we have yet to affix any logic as to why Chief Nukto would commit war, or why he would bring the entire continental populace of savages and barbarians into the picture. The death toll is staggering, Kamiko."

"Are you in contact with the high marshal?"

He nodded and said in a low voice, "I am his supply coordinator for Flavin Precinct. We send two loads a week from here. A small number of his men are currently in my infirmary. Their wounds were catastrophic. If they survive, they will need long-term assistance and a lifetime of rehabilitation, so Jonathan sent them to me. Though it is doubtful they will live much longer."

Felene shifted on her feet and came near speaking, but held quiet. Kamiko wondered if they had shared the same thought. Siruis could help those men.

Lord Merritt continued, "There is some unseen element at work here, Kamiko. Of this, High Marshal Alexander is convinced." His voice was rough and quiet. By the nature of his body language, Kamiko imagined the hackles were standing on his neck. "As am I."

After a reflective pause, he said, "But that is not the most pressing thing at the moment, is it, Sister Kamiko?"

He'd just given it to her. That thing she was determined to avoid—knowledge. She looked at Felene and said quietly, "I must prepare for my audience with King Titus. I now have knowledge of his summons and must answer it."

Lord Merritt said, "It is better to have come by it this way than to be served a warrant. You have safe passage due to your rank. I checked and you still retain your commission. High Marshal Alexander is the only man in the kingdom, outside royalty of course, who may give you an order, my friend."

Felene lifted an eyebrow. Kamiko guessed she'd never heard it put like that before. The familiarity of that look reminded Kamiko again of Sister Grace, and in that odd moment, she remembered that Felene's perspective would have a forty-year breach. She appeared to be accepting what she was seeing and hearing as truth, or she was completely numb.

"I agree, Lord Merritt, and I am blessed that Alexander is a friend. I will not bring trouble upon your estate with untimeliness."

He leaned closer to Kamiko and Felene. "I will 'deliver' the summons over dinner tonight. Until then, meditate on these things, take food and rest, and feel free to visit my armory. I can see that you are, for whatever reason, weaponless." He said to Kamiko, "I would be in a constant state of delight knowing one of my swords adorned your personage."

"I may have need of that fine offer if I am to present arms to our king."

"Good, good! If I may be so bold, I have well-sourced knowledge as to your combat'aunce etiquette and will choose a sword I believe fitted to your needs. We shall see how observant an old man may still be."

*****

Lord Merritt continued his delivery in hushed tones, laying out a soliloquy of events and situations in single factual sentences so that, in under a minute, Kamiko felt she had a firm grasp of the state of affairs across the vast kingdom. She also got a good sense of the man's diplomatic persona. He was a master of communication and a tremendous vault of knowledge.

Felene listened with rapt interest, nodding her acknowledgment at many of the points, shifting her brow at those she did not yet know. Kamiko shuddered, and her heart ached anew every time Felene's strange circumstance entered her thoughts. That which was yesterday was also forty years removed. What must that effect have on her memories?

The kingdom of Cairistonia was in disarray. The weave of society had been warped beyond reasonable repair. The wealthy caste was shrinking in numbers but had swollen in sheer net worth. The current trend lay in the acquisition of enormous landmasses outside the borders of the kingdom—

Abruptly, as if whispered by an unseen intruder, Kamiko could feel the return of something familiar and the forgotten pressure in her chest. The queasy churning in her gut was borne of Lord Merritt's oration in the "higher language" of the privileged class. She'd once been immersed, then once been set free, and was now going back under the vicious gaze of that distraught slice of Cairistonian society.

And though Lord Merritt continued, his voice was breathy and slow, and Kamiko's attention faltered. The room they occupied grew less distinct, as if she were looking through a dew-covered window. The two standing with her in quiet conversation seemed to have been painted with a too-narrow assortment of colors. She sensed everything physical as if it were rendered upon a gossamer wing being shaken by a slight breeze, too thin a veil to withstand anything more. She could easily imagine that if the breeze stopped, physicality would end.

So too seemed the voracity and complexity of the state of the kingdom—thin and fragile, a simple thing painted over with majesty and towering scenes. She could see the whole of Cairistonia, an overlarge beast crowned with countless twinkling jewels and aglow with streaming gold, but a dark smelly beast just the same. It laid spread upon the land like a living shimmering blanket, trapping the heat of angst and the ever-present stench of greed and despair. In every pore of the great beast, many millions languished so that mere thousands could thrive. Her only glimpses of beauty were those single faces appearing briefly now and again—a good father, a mother and child at the hearth, an honorable judge, all of them hungry and all pulling at her awareness like a field of blinking nightjar on a dark morning. They were all in need. Where to begin?

This gossamer veil, the ethereal canvas upon which the physical elements floated, began to waver, the precursor to a hard shudder rippling through the very fabric of existence. Kamiko's eyes were drawn to Siruis, the epicenter of the disturbance, no longer sitting plaintively in Lord Merritt's cathedral library. She was a long walk down many corridors, through doorways and crowded rooms, but Kamiko felt her presence as if she were standing near enough to touch. She looked up at Kamiko with a slight smile, then spread her hands upon the chest of a man lying infirm, and whispered three words.

The ether around Siruis stirred, and at the head of the bed, a knot of white liquescent vapor formed into the visage of a man. But the sighting was fleet, and only his upper body appeared as his hand extended to touch a finger upon the infirm man's forehead. His departure was swift and set off a sharp thunderclap that made Kamiko jump and had the effect of snapping her out of the reverie.

The sound of Lord Merritt's voice returned, at first, with the sharp force of a trumpet blast, which made her jump again. But Kamiko could sense someone—the man Siruis had healed—approaching the door. She could feel him walking up the hallway beyond and knew she would recognize his name when she heard it. He'd been badly burned in combat. That he'd simply refused to die was likely the only reason he survived.

During that breathless moment, when the angelic finger had touched his flesh, Kamiko too had seen the man's essence. The spirit of the man, that part shaped by thought, intention, and deed, was as dark as any other human, but it was upright and was carefully held in true form. His life was fully vested as a warrior. An honorable man among the warrior class was a rarity.

She felt him lean his weight against the doors and hesitate. His mind was only beginning to grapple with the fact that he was walking, whole, and healthy, his life energy crackling with excitement. Joy and fear mingled and agreed to coexist within his chest. He pushed the door open and strode inside.

The guardsman standing watch snapped around when the doors he'd carefully locked swung open. It was the doorway opposite where they had entered, and the hallway beyond was empty and silent. The moment froze as two men forged in the furnace of violence and war faced off, uncertain. Both held the balance of reason in tight control, and the tension soon fled.

The man framed in the doorway still wore the gauzy infirmary garb of the hospice, stained from a field of seeping wounds. He was thick and broad of stature, tall and brimming with calm power. His head and face were shaved clean but for a tuft of blond fur capping his chin and fine brow of light gold. His eyes, though blue as a still lake, burned with purpose. He would allow the proper protocol but would not be refused entry.

The burly guardsman blocked the man's progress just long enough for a short whispered conversation before he turned toward

Lord Merritt, who flashed a hand signal. The guard stepped aside and motioned the man to enter. As he approached the center of the room, the guardsman inspected the lock and door handle, shook his head, then closed and re-bolted the doors.

The man came to tower over Lord Merritt but only looked down at him in silence. Both men stood as if in shock. Lord Merritt's face was slack, his mouth slightly open, breath shallow and quick. The younger man's breath came deep and slow. The man, who Kamiko knew to be named Kim Doran Carthage II, was only a few short minutes beyond hard and terrible pain. He had been burned over half of his body, from his waist up, a charred mass of blackened flesh. Some part of him would not relinquish the hold on life.

Lord Merritt was the first to speak, though not without searching for his voice. "I…I'm…" He cleared his throat. "Beyond words, Captain." His voice was soft and deep.

"Lord Merritt," Captain Carthage said, also quiet and breathy, and extended his heavy hand toward the elderly gentleman. The lord clapped his hand inside the captain's, an act which had the effect of eliciting a sudden wash of moisture in the eyes of both men and a whisper from Felene, standing just behind Kamiko's shoulder.

"God be praised!"

The big captain's head turned slowly toward Felene, recognition in his bearing and renewed joy upon his face.

"You!" he exclaimed.

Felene's homeland accent came to fullness. "Aye, me friend, I been with ye for no small measure." Kamiko knew that from Felene's perspective, she had not seen the infirmary for forty years, and she was feeling a kinship far beyond anything Captain Carthage could yet imagine. To the captain, though, only a few days had likely passed since he'd last heard her bright island lilt. "Ye've been black and mottled something fierce, never thought ye'd be such a handsome lad." Kamiko could hear Felene's emotions running hard in the rasp of her voice. She sounded to be the weariest person alive.

Even as the thought passed through Kamiko's mind, she felt Felene's hand close on her shoulder, tighten suddenly, then grow completely limp. The captain caught her before she made it to the ground, moving so quickly he had her in his arms before Kamiko managed to turn. Yet he did not lower her immediately to the carpet but held her upright, cradling her head against his thick shoulder for a moment.

"She was there, my lord, with us?"

"She was."

"Aye, she read the whole of *The Cantlefalgen Tales* as we lay invalid."

"Thrice, she did."

At last Captain Carthage lowered Felene gently to the floor, disquiet and wonder on his young face. Kamiko answered his unspoken concern as she knelt beside them.

"She is exhausted, Captain, that is all. She has been sorely tested of late and needs rest." She brushed the back of her fingers across Felene's cheek, only then noticing a tear stream trailing from the corner of her eye. Kamiko wondered how long it would take before the fear of waking into a living nightmare would subside for Felene. Perhaps it never would.

"Captain," Lord Merritt said. "Bring her to the infirmary."

But as the captain bent to lift her, Kamiko's hand on his shoulder stopped him, and for the first time, their eyes came together. For a brief moment, they searched there, both intent on bearing the unconscious woman without help, as an act of honor and of kindness. Kamiko saw, in that moment, that Captain Carthage's need was greater than her own. She scooped Felene into her embrace, stood with her full weight, and placed her gently into his able arms.

"It is well, Lieutenant Marshal," he said to Kamiko. "I am instructed to bring you to the young healer. She is waiting in the hospice."

Hearing her old title for the first time in years caught Kamiko off guard. Lord Merritt had just told her that she retained her commission, which meant she was, technically, still lieutenant marshal by rank. But always in that past life, a demand was attached to the title, just as now.

The queasiness in her gut grew again. She felt the old way rushing at her, the manacles of servitude clanging in her spirit. The irony of leadership thickened in her mind. Anyone, no matter how small, could command her into action by compelling her to duty. If things progressed now as they had then, she would soon be pulled in a hundred directions at once and would accomplish little or nothing in the process of answering those demands.

She shook the thoughts away and focused on Felene. "Let's go then, Captain, Lord Merritt."

Without further word, the elder gentleman turned on his heels and made for the doorway where Captain Carthage had entered. Before he'd taken three long strides, a muted but insistent knocking erupted from the opposite door. The guardsman paid no heed to the knocking when Lord Merritt glanced over his shoulder but gave no signal. Momentarily the knocking ceased, but only long enough to allow them a few more quick steps in the opposite direction. The knock returned with a heavy clanging thud, which resounded through the room like a dull gong being struck by an angry commoner unaccustomed to lordly decorum. Everyone in the room turned and froze until Lord Merritt offered the guard a single nod. He opened only one of the double doors, caution and readiness defining his every move.

There framed in the dark wood of the lush room, backlit by a roomful of concerned faces of the commoners, stood Danae, a short spade wielded in both hands and a look of pure determination on her face. Kamiko barely stifled the laugh.

By the strained look on Lord Merritt's face and the way the guard spread his feet and planted his hands on his hips, Kamiko understood that this was likely an oft-repeated situation. She mused that the sisterhood tended to attract those of strong will who were less inclined to acknowledge the workings of aristocratic protocols. She was just raising her hand toward the elderly lord to ask his patience while she dealt with Danae when the guardsman took his leave to act. Though to his credit, he had waited until Danae prompted his action.

She set the spade gently at her feet and sent it sliding with an easy kick, presumably back to the rightful owner camping near the door. Then with her typical quickness, she was inside and making past the guard with enough haste to cause him to move with a start.

Kamiko held her tongue, wanting to see how the lithe girl handled the situation. She was not displeased in the least when Danae suddenly appeared behind the burly man. She'd tricked him by feinting into his grasp and projecting her intended movement, as if to drop below his hand, which he fell for without reserve. She was, in fact, simply bending her knees for a hop, which brought her now-beaming smile to within a mere inch of his calm face. With one hand on the top of his head and her legs split into a perfect horizontal line, she sailed over him, landed on her toe tips behind him, and seemed to simply bounce on impact, gaining another five paces in the air.

When his head snapped around, the sheepish look on his face told all. He'd been bested by a child. Mild disappointment colored the smiling faces of the people watching from the common room as the man closed and bolted the door. Danae stood with her hand on Felene's face, who, to Kamiko's surprise, was smiling at her sleepily. Lord Merritt was looking at something on the ceiling, the grin plain on his face in spite of his efforts to the contrary. The other guard was guffawing openly, and the big captain's eyes were moving from person to person, uncertainty and mirth contending with each other. Danae appeared to take no notice.

Just before Captain Carthage's gaze settled on Felene, her eyes snapped shut, and her face went blank. Danae's face froze in a mask of feigned concern, though Kamiko could tell she was holding herself very still. Kamiko allowed a slight grin at one corner of her mouth as she placed her hand on the captain's shoulder and turned him back toward the opposite doorway.

Lord Merritt turned, muttering under his breath, "Yes, well…"

As they passed into the quiet hallway beyond, the two guardsmen secured the door behind and trotted into positions just ahead and just behind the elder lord.

Chapter 19

Of all the aspects of the infirmary commanding notice—the crowd gathered in silence, the men, women, and children still in hospice garb standing around Siruis, the empty disheveled beds lining the walls and corridors, and the attendants standing with their hands in their pockets—all eyes in their small entourage were drawn first to the great lynx sitting by Siruis's side.

His face was a mask of fiercely edged serenity. Thick tufts, which held the appearance of furry jowls, hung beneath a short chin and small gray nose, streaked with jet black against pure white. His mouth was formed into an ever-present smile that looked more akin to a thin dark mustache. His angular upright ears were topped with thick strands of black hair that formed long spikes, giving him the look of a horned beast. His eyes, glistening orbs of brilliant light green, were locked upon Kamiko's face, a mischievous intelligence she could not mistake. She tilted her head to one side and was pleased when the great cat mimicked the motion exactly. She nodded knowingly and was answered in exact likeness. This was Jerim's doing. *Wonder of wonders*, she thought, the young man was wholly unique, even compared with Bartol. Jerim was hidden somewhere nearby, using this lynx to stand guard over Siruis.

At the edge of her vision, Kamiko saw Felene's hand rise to Captain Carthage's shoulder and saw her nod to be released. She thought she sensed a measured reluctance in the captain's assent, but he at last placed Felene's feet on the floor and stood her up.

As Danae stepped forward, Kamiko knew the girl would forever be the icebreaker in frozen moments. She completely lacked the restraining grip of fear. She walked lightly to Siruis's side and knelt before the great cat, as if he was nothing more than a common mouser, and buried her hands in the thick mantle of fur behind his ears. He growled quietly and licked his chops, momentarily revealing thick white teeth, but never took his gaze from Kamiko.

A few whispers further broke the silence, and Lord Merritt stepped forward, his face flush with what Kamiko could only reckon as boyish wonder. His eyes were first drawn to Siruis, who was seated on a low orderly's stool at the foot of an empty bed. One corner of her mouth turned up, but otherwise her face was wistful and worn. Kamiko imagined Siruis had not slept any more than Felene had.

Breathy but speechless, the elder gentleman looked around the room. He seemed to recognize every single face, a further declaration to Kamiko that he was personally vested in their lives and not simply a remote provider. This had nothing to do with the duties of lordship. Her respect for the man flourished anew.

Recognition pulled at her peripheral vision, and she turned to see Sister Rachel standing at the very back of the gathering, her golden face streaming with tears. She stood behind a young woman in a wrinkled hospice gown, enveloping her in a full embrace. She met Kamiko's eyes with her distinctive firm bearing, but with softness only perceivable by those closest to her heart of hearts. She offered Kamiko a single wink before motioning with the tilt of her head that Kamiko should watch what was beginning to unfold.

Captain Carthage stepped forward as five burly men moved from the rear of the gathering to the open space around Siruis. Nothing above a quiet whisper had been spoken, but now the room fell silent. They formed a rank of three and three on both sides of Siruis, the lynx, and Danae. Kamiko saw Siruis offer a simple hand gesture to Danae, not a request but a command, to join the six men now standing at military rest, facing Kamiko. There was nothing comical about how she hopped to her feet, glanced over at the captain, and attempted to mimic the stance. Her smooth young face was just as stern and her eyes just as locked upon Kamiko's, as were the veteran warriors in her company. Captain Carthage growled. *"Teh-chun!"* And the men snapped into rigid attention. Danae was fast to follow.

Up to this moment, Kamiko realized her feelings had been oddly inert. She knew well what had transpired. Siruis had healed every single person in the hospice ward. It was a place of dying. Anyone who found themselves in the care of hospice knew they were being comforted and kept from pain until death called, nothing more. The infirmary, housed in the adjoining wing, was the place of healing and recovery.

Yet her spirit had been overwhelmed again and again, filled and overfilled, and she could take nothing more into her being. The dawning of what had happened to Felene had been the point at which her emotions would no longer respond, lest she give way to a flood of despair for Felene's suffering. She could feel the expectant quickness of her dear sister's breath at her shoulder.

She slid her feet together, drew her chest out, and returned the honor by flexing every muscle in her body into perfect stillness, her eyes locked upon the highest ranking officer in the file, Captain Carthage. There Kamiko waited for the mandatory count of seconds before speaking, the signal for the procession to proceed. "Captain!" she said. She already recognized what was about to happen, and the lost feeling of longing, of belonging, blossomed to life.

He stepped forward, his blue eyes wild with the fire of purpose, yet he did not offer Kamiko the required obeisance of military protocol. He dropped his attitude of full attention, relaxed his shoulders, and lowered himself first to his knees, then bent at the waist, and bowed his forehead to the floor, with his hands lying flat on both sides of his face. Kamiko had never imagined such a thing would happen. The line of men behind him followed suit.

Danae cast a worried look at Siruis, who signed that she should not follow their example. It dawned on Kamiko that this entire event had been planned, that something new was occurring. She slowly swept her eyes around, meeting Lord Merritt's, Felene's, and, at last,

Sister Rachel's gaze. Only Rachel offered a knowing look, the others were as taken as Kamiko. Siruis rose to her feet and drew Kamiko's attention back.

"Kamiko Hoshi," she began. "Such is the way of things that we are drawn off our intended course, that our feet are bogged by duty and honor to people and places deserving neither. The great deceiver of the world has won, if he may only turn your eyes from that path, though you live a life of belief and dedication to the good. Yet the One who lives in us is greater than the sum of all parts. The Eternal would not have it so and calls you back to the path set aside for you."

The sight of the men bowing at her feet disturbed Kamiko to the core. She felt her head shaking back and forth slowly, words forming on her tongue that would stop this madness. The longing churned into cool anger in waves. As she moved to raise her hands and step forward to lift the captain, she felt her arms disobey, felt that her legs did not even flinch. Her mouth could utter nothing of her protest.

Somewhere deep in her mind, she heard a call to be still and to listen. It was a voice she knew as intimately as her own yet had never heard with her ears. It was not the gentle call of Siruis, rather it swelled from a depth no rod could fathom. This was the Spirit of God. She obeyed without hesitation but tested the movement of her hands just the same. Her fingers, wrists, and elbows flexed easily.

Siruis continued, "These few are as dead men, Kamiko Hoshi, already forgotten by the world, their mortal bodies buried and in decay. For what is this physical reality if not human perception? We are but images projected onto a gossamer wing, set in motion by the breath of God."

Had Kamiko not spent the previous weeks with Siruis, the accuracy of the description would have struck her with awe. It was simply a reminder of who Siruis was—a being still deep in mystery.

"Why do you bow before Djinnasee in this same way?" Siruis asked.

"He is my master, the anointed prophet of the Eternal God." As Kamiko spoke, the memory of seeing Djinnasee in her cottage sprang to life in her mind.

"Do you bow thus before Titus, king of Cairistonia?"

Her mind raced to unravel the point Siruis was leading her toward. "No, I do not. That is not royal protocol."

"Yet he is the anointed of God, chosen by blood to rule this kingdom as he sees fit."

There it was! Kamiko cast a quick look at Rachel. The elder woman's eyes blazed with expectation, but her face was a stone mask. Now Kamiko's feet moved upon her will, and she took one purposeful stride forward, her fists clenched at her side.

"No," she spoke softly. "Not as he sees fit. It is God's will he has been ordained to follow, not his own." Her thoughts fled to the frustration she'd felt only minutes earlier, that her rank as lieutenant marshal was the chain binding her to duty, that she was by no means freed by it. "The king, in all his glory, is bound all the more by his worldly power over men. His charge to serve their well-being is the highest in all the land." It was a charge that had long since been laid aside.

"Whom do you serve?" Siruis asked, leading quickly to the next layer.

"God Almighty!" Kamiko declared.

"Not Djinnasee?" Siruis's head tilted slightly with the question.

The ready answer on Kamiko's tongue was instantly forgotten. She had anticipated the question but had expected the subject to still be King Titus. She could feel the presence of the kneeling warriors like a physical pressure against her legs. She was not certain why the hackles were suddenly standing like quills on her neck. The men offered no threat of danger.

At the moment, she did not have the capacity for figuring out what seemed, to her, another of Siruis's circling logic lessons. Her nerves were tattered, and her mind was distracted by the avalanche of visions she'd seen and thoughts she'd had since coming into Siruis's strange existence. In spite of the fact that there had been ample time to sort it all out, it had not sorted. Kamiko felt certain that she'd forgotten the greater part of it all anyway.

She answered with what she knew was not heartfelt conviction, rather what she deemed to be correct. "No, not Djinnasee. I serve the God of our fathers, Siruis. Djinnasee is my teacher, as is Sister Rachel."

Kamiko's hand became suddenly hot with the need for her sword. She got the distinct feeling that something was amiss.

Siruis continued, appearing not to notice Kamiko's growing agitation. "It is the same with these few." She placed her hand on Danae's shoulder, as if to make certain Kamiko understood the girl's inclusion in the group. "They will be an extension of your fist, to be in places you cannot, to exert your influence in the coming war. They will call you master, as you call Djinnasee master, but have no doubt—they serve God Almighty."

Siruis had Kamiko's undivided attention.

"What do you mean an extension of my fist? And what war are you referring to, Sister?" She felt Felene move forward, pulled more firmly into the conversation by this declaration. The room remained silent.

Aside from a few hands going to cover open mouths, Danae was the only person who actually moved at all. Her brow knotted, her head tilting slightly, as if listening to a faint distant noise. She began sniffing the air.

Siruis ignored Kamiko's questions. "They will be waiting for you, Sister Kamiko. They are known as *Ʒu Kalem*, the Dead Fist. Seek them out when you reach King El'Thorn." And to the kneeling men, she said, "Arise, my friends, and go directly to High Marshal Alexander. Tell him everything I have instructed, to the smallest detail. Turn aside for nothing."

The men rose at once, each pausing just long enough to smile broadly at Kamiko and punch his right fist into his left palm with a sharp slap. Every observation of military protocol was gone; the salute, the slight inclination of the head, the stiff-legged cadence as they turned to depart, and the marching formation until they were out of line of sight. Instead they turned and broke into a quick trot, making for the door at the far end of the hospice ward. Each of the men stopped at the door just long enough to grab a tightly packed knapsack, weapons belt, sword, warm clothes, and food-ration pack.

Six outfit rigs had obviously been prepared ahead of time. Kamiko felt conspired against.

Captain Carthage was the last to turn, offering Kamiko a simple handshake, which she hesitatingly afforded him. She felt not only real strength in his hand but also a wave of the power of his spirit flow outward like an unseen explosion of presence, bright and fierce.

"We will wait for you, Sister, and prepare the way. The God of creation be with you."

She was still speechless from the sheer mass of sensory and emotional input, so she simply shook his hand and dipped her head. It was the best she could manage.

He then extended his hand to Felene, who took it immediately. He spoke no words and offered no gesture of friendship, as he'd done with Kamiko, rather he bent down and kissed the back of her hand. Her mouth was open slightly and moisture formed in her eyes as his gaze came back up to meet hers. Kamiko had the feeling they could have stayed that way for the remainder of the hour. But the captain nodded at Felene with a broad smile and released her hand. He turned to Lord Merritt with a heartfelt thank you, and then trotted after his troop, snapping up his gear and warm clothes almost without slowing.

*****

Even as the captain closed the door behind him, the world came rushing back to Kamiko's immediate awareness. Danae was wholly distracted by something she appeared to smell in the air. Stepping forward, she located, first, Felene's eyes, then Kamiko's. She brushed her fingertips across her nose and mouthed the strange sounding word—*moe*!

Felene clapped her hands, the motion drawing Danae's attention back to her, and then signed for a question.

Danae's hand flashed the letters S-M-O-K-E.

"I smell it too," Rachel interjected as she stepped forward, moving the young woman in her arms gently aside.

Kamiko had smelled the faint twinge of woodsmoke since she first arrived in the wee hours, stronger in some parts of the estate. Fireplaces were in practically every room. Her nose had grown accustomed to it. What she could now just begin to smell was indeed different, more of an oily smoke.

By the looks on their faces, the others in the room could now smell it as well. Awareness, confusion, and the onset of panic spread in a quick wave, and the still silence gave way to the noise of shuffling feet as elemental fear struck like a thunderclap. They spread in every direction at once.

Lord Merritt reacted immediately, speaking with all the authority he could muster. "*Hold*! Everyone, stop, now! Be still, people. Silence!"

One of his guardsmen was already trotting to the door leading to the infirmary; the other stayed close to Lord Merritt. Everyone stopped in their tracks and turned to face the elder man.

Felene had not moved from Kamiko's shoulder and was signing to Danae. "From what direction? Can you tell?"

Danae ran a short way opposite the infirmary with her nose working furiously, spun, and pointed back toward where the guard had just opened the door leading into the infirmary.

Lord Merritt was calmly giving orders, first to Rachel. "Get them out of here," he said with forced quiet and pointed to the door Danae was nearing, "out through the northern gate."

Rachel burst into fluid motion, snapping her finger at Felene to draw her into her wake as Lord Merritt barked the simple command—"Follow her"—to the small crowd. They moved as one, Rachel leading and Felene herding them like sheep as they spoke sharp but calming instructions to not panic, not run, move quickly, no pushing.

Danae had thrown the doors open but turned to look back at Kamiko as if for instruction. Only Kamiko and Siruis held still. Lord Merritt ran to the infirmary where the smoke was visibly building and where muffled shouts and screams of fear could now be heard. The mild din from the open door was growing rapidly but was washed away by the sudden howl of a loud quick trumpet blast that warned the entire estate to take immediate emergency action.

Kamiko made no move to follow. Siruis had shown her the hand sign to stand still and wait and was staring hard into Kamiko's eyes as if to pin her in place. Danae's silent presence appeared at Kamiko's right, her delicate hand finding Kamiko's forearm, as if grasping for an anchor against the brunt of a setting storm. The lynx had been flat on the floor, growling deeply in obvious and expected agitation, but, without warning, up and ran for the open door, keeping a low hunker, with his ears flat against his head.

Still Siruis made no move, nor did she give any indication that Kamiko should act. And though Danae's hand tightened on her arm, Kamiko could not feel the slightest tremor of fear in the girl's grasp.

By the waning sounds of the infirmary that filtered through the wailing trumpet, it seemed the evacuation was proceeding quickly. Smoke was now pouring into the hospice ward through the open door, dark and thick, roiling across the ceiling and filling the room. If the speed with which the smoke rolled and twisted were any indicator, the fire was close. The smoke had somehow failed to assault them, with only the faintest scent still clinging to their noses. Danae's face was wide and bright with worried wonder. For all Kamiko could tell, they were in a bubble of clear air.

If the rigid hackles running in waves up and down Kamiko's spine were indicative, the fire was no accident. She held little doubt that someone was making a move for Siruis, for a king's ransom. Dairei Parzon was not the only thief with enough moxie to attempt such a stunt. Kamiko was certain Parzon was not behind whatever was coming to bear. She would never set a building on fire that was filled with innocent people, though she would likely be skirting the periphery for any opportunity she could glean.

Kamiko's suspicions were confirmed in the form of a room-shuddering thud from above, followed by a second and third in quick succession. An entire section of the ceiling where the rooms joined, hospice to infirmary, exploded downward in an avalanche of stone, splintered timbers, swirling mounds of snow, dull sunlight, and Jerim!

He landed lightly on his toes in a half-crouch, his eyes already locked on Siruis, and a brief stillness returned. Jerim had punched through the roof from above.

The thickening smoke immediately began pouring up and out of the enormous hole, driven by the gathering heat from the next room. Likewise a blast of frigid air cascaded into the room, bringing a torrent of fresh unhindered oxygen to the hungry flames. The smoke would clear in moments, but the flames would soon sweep through the door in an angry firestorm, following the supply of fresh air.

Kamiko could no longer force her feet to remain still. She stepped forward to take hold of Siruis and head for the door, but the young sister backed away and drew her arm from Kamiko's reach.

"Wait, Kamiko," she said. "Just a moment longer." Her eyes were wide and possessed of an excited joy. "Nothing is yet what it seems."

The fire was now beginning to howl from the infirmary. Flames were dancing in the open doorway and through the broken wall, and heat was filling the hospice ward like a newly lit oven.

Siruis looked over at Danae, who was now showing her fear openly, and spoke with her hands. "Do not fear what is to come, young sister. Trust in the Lord. Trust in Kamiko. Remember the *Karak-Tan*." She then nodded once to Jerim, who quickly scooped her up into his arms.

Only then did she speak to Kamiko. "They are not here for me." Just as Jerim bounded back toward the rubble of the collapsed ceiling, Siruis called, "I will find you!" With no more effort than an easy hop, Jerim leapt up through the hole and was gone, black smoke roiling and billowing up behind them.

Kamiko felt glued to the spot. Her mind reeled with layer upon layer of images, memories, and information which all seemed to belong to someone else. And while she could not get it organized into anything useful, neither could she set it aside to allow her mind clear unhindered thought. It made her feel dull and befuddled. She'd not spoken a word since her unanswered question, and now the building was burning down with her and Danae still in it. Time felt thick and cumbersome, confining her to living a dirge-like existence; everything moving in slow motion, everything painted over in dark colors.

She felt no fear of the fire, no excitement borne of what was certainly serious danger. Her purpose was set, her path protected until she reached some predetermined destination. And it took no cryptic confirmation from Siruis to know the same was true for Danae. They were in no danger, regardless of how strong the appearance to the contrary. The *Karak-Tan* seemed wholly irrelevant in that light.

Strange-sounding words broke her reverie, and the near-frantic motion of Danae hopping nervously from foot to foot, one eye on the growing pyre and one on the opposite door. Still Kamiko did not move. Siruis's words echoed in her head, *They are not here for me.*

Do not fear…

Remember the Karak-Tan…

Trust in Kamiko…

The heat was growing to a dangerous intensity, now igniting the ceiling rubble that had fallen through with Jerim.

Then she could feel them, as clearly as if they had stepped out of some other plane of existence and into her sight. Danae easily caught the slight inflection in Kamiko's hand signal to readiness and acknowledged by drawing her body still and closing her eyes. Kamiko followed suit once Danae was fully in form.

The *Karak-Tan,* the sisterhood's own trial by fire had begun in earnest. Master and student, playing rough. Fitting that it should begin within actual flames. Yet *Karak-Tan* was a thing borne of the spirit, specifically the fire of the soul, just beyond the veil of physicality.

Kamiko trusted Rachel to have prepared a capable student. Her eyes opened upon that other realm to find Danae's spirit roaring like a blast furnace beneath an overzealous bellows.

Danae

Danae did nothing beyond focusing her mind on her own spiritual *self,* dwelling in her body. Rachel had drilled her for hours on achieving and maintaining a calm center, where her spirit could take the forestage between body and mind. What happened next was wholly new to Danae and came as the result of a much greater spirit acting on her behalf. One layer of the physical veil was drawn aside, and Danae could suddenly and clearly hear, as a wash of sound flooded her from all directions at once—from stark silence to a world of noise, as though stepping from one room to another. And in this room, several people were present. She could feel their malicious intent.

She heard the guttural sound of a chuckle from her right. She and Kamiko were undefended, eyes closed, heads down. Any warrior worth his salt would think that was funny.

He's not going to think that for long, Danae mused silently.

They were overconfident, revealing their numbers too soon by the movement of their feet, by the vibrating tsunami of sound washing over her, marking their passage. To Danae's senses, those of her awakened spirit, they were as clear as in broad daylight.

Rachel's teaching ricocheted around her brain, and her thoughts abruptly veered. She focused her senses beyond the obvious and found more. A second set of hidden bodies in motion, shadowing the first, more subtle and more controlled. They were the real threat.

She could feel Kamiko standing beside her, one pace ahead, her breath so steady and slow Danae could barely tell she was moving at all. But her energy, her raging spirit, her intent at wild abandon, those formed a more tangible being than Kamiko's physical mass. Danae felt Kamiko's presence much like being submerged in deep hot water, flowing with gentle but unmistakable pressure on her skin.

She heard words. A deep angry voice—the chuckler again. All motion shifted from coming straight in to spreading out. Those shadowing drew still and silent. No matter. Danae could hear them, even down to the air whistling through their nose hairs.

She wondered absently if they knew it was Kamiko Hoshi they faced, if they were counting these few breaths as their last. They had only until each found their position, then each, in turn, would die. It mattered not one wit that Kamiko held no weapons of steel, they were bringing everything she would need where steel was concerned.

Danae instinctively set the order Kamiko would follow, thirteen men, starting with the chuckler. There would likely be more of the silent ones holding back. She felt Kamiko's resolve solidify and knew the moments of waiting had passed.

Kamiko did not make a move—she was simply gone. The breath exploded from the chuckler as Kamiko released her building rage with a fist strike to his chest, crushing everything beneath his sternum with enough force to crack his backbone. Danae felt it. The ferocity of that first attack caused her to involuntarily flinch and snapped her out of her state of spirit focus. Silence returned, and with it came the wash of physical heat and the anxiety of uncertainty.

Her eyes popped open just as Kamiko let fly a short curved sword with enough force to drive it through a studded leather breastplate, knocking the man straight to the floor. It was the second deep shock in as many seconds. Danae's feet were rooted in place, and her eyes would not close. She'd failed the first and most vital part of the Karak-Tan, the spirit focus.

Panic rose in her throat. Kamiko would be counting on her to help. But she had never been engaged in full battle and certainly not against the likes of these men.

They recovered quickly, as a single unit, and converged upon Kamiko in a single mass. Only two of the thirteen were down. They encircled her in two layers. The inner circle wielded short wide blades and bucklers bristling with nasty-looking spikes. Those forming the outer circle were setting up to stab at Kamiko with javelin-styled spears from behind the front line.

The whole of the process took only seconds.

Danae felt completely useless.

The third, fourth, and fifth bodies collapsed to the floor at Kamiko's feet, and she now held a bloody short sword in each hand. Yet she was forced to go into a fully defensive posturing before she could continue her assault. Were there too many? Even for Kamiko? Spear stabs and sword slices fell at her from all directions in a steady rain meant to overtax her defenses with sheer numbers. It would take only one solid blow getting through to trigger the cascade of death.

The two swords formed what appeared to Danae as a near-unbroken canopy of whirling steel around the woman, so far turning every attack. Yet Kamiko's face appeared relaxed, unconcerned, even shaded with what Danae could only imagine as mirth.

Then it struck Danae. They were totally ignoring her. She offered no threat to them, not in the slightest. That single thought prompted a sudden and all-encompassing shift in her gut. Panic vanished beneath an explosion of anger. Djinnasee had considered her sufficient to undergo the *Karak-Tan*. She'd been Rachel's understudy for years. Who were these butchers to ignore her? She leapt into motion.

*****

Kamiko

About time, Kamiko thought.

One of the spearmen dropped back and skipped over a prone body, setting his feet to deliver a throw into the melee at what he likely imagined her weak flank. He'd been fighting in unison with one of the swordsmen, helping to keep her partially occupied while the other pressed in closer. She would now break the circle and go on the attack. She was counting on the spearman to deliver an accurate fast throw to her midmass.

He was ready.

She was ready. All she needed was Danae.

*****

Danae

Danae recognized the maneuver. She no longer held any doubt that the squad knew who they were there for. They had been carefully trained to fight the greatest sword fighter in the land and were about to spring the kill. The spear-wielder was the triggerman.

She'd retrieved a glass vial of simple alcohol from a supply shelf and a flaming brand from the edge of the fire. By her reckoning, her clothes had almost ignited in that single moment so close to the inferno. She threw the vial at the feet of one of the swordsmen, shattering the glass and splattering the liquid onto his feet and legs. She knew it would do little damage as an attack but would serve to break the man's concentration for a moment. She tossed the brand, igniting the alcohol.

In the moments it took him to realize he was on fire, Danae's heart skipped a pair of beats. However, the effect was exactly what she'd been hoping for, and Kamiko's movements abruptly changed. The enflamed warrior was the first to go. A short thick blade burst through the backplate of his armor midway through his first leap to escape the flames running up his legs. In another moment, Danae's eyes found Kamiko already coming up behind the line, and their numbers fell once again.

*****

Kamiko

Kamiko left the sword buried hilt-deep in his chest, spun, and snapped the spear out of the air midshank.

Then she danced. She fell into a groove of fluid ease. Her heart was easy in her chest, and her hands felt as insubstantial as ever, weightless, floating in slurry of slow time. And the weapons of her enemy circled in slow arches, all bearing down upon Kamiko Hoshi as though submerged in water.

She saw the slightest whisper of a shadow drop from the cover of the thick smoke still pouring into the room. In the next blink, Danae was simply gone from sight.

Just then, the five remaining of the squad pressed wildly ahead. She danced backward, spinning, the deadly javelin, snapping out four precise times. Then only one remained. However, his gain was short-lived.

A thick timber crashed to the floor in a flaming heap, drawing with it a large swath of the roof. A bright storm of swirling flames rushed out from the infirmary ward, now fully engulfed and seeking to expel the heat.

Kamiko leapt over the bodies to where Danae had been and quickly scanned the surroundings. There was only one possible exit from the room—opposite the boiling inferno. She bolted with all her strength.

Chapter 20

Kamiko burst into blinding sunlight and a throng of people. They were gathering against the inside of the perimeter walls, their numbers growing rapidly as they poured out of the burning complex. It was midmorning, and the snow was deep beneath a clear blue sky. The frigid air was a sharp bite and a welcome relief against Kamiko's oven-baked skin. She'd not realized how hot the hospice ward had become, and her lungs burned from the sudden cold.

Her heart pounded in her chest, the musings of only a few moments ago completely gone. Fear threatened to run rampant in her chest. She stifled the automatic urge to begin shouting for her deaf sister, as if she could hear, as if she could answer. She lost precious moments scanning the crowd with her eyes before she thought to engage her mind. How would she have planned her egress? She spun back to face the building and activated that small part of her makeup that could be an assassin.

A thousand possible covers lined the wall of the estate—trees of various shape and size, long hedges of manicured shrubbery, and section after section of vine-covered lattice stretched ground to roofline. *It would take the better part of an hour…*

She dropped the thought and broke into a hard sprint, heading toward the far corner of the building. It was the only option for someone bearing the burden of a body, if they meant to leave unseen. Rachel's voice thundered through the tempest of fear and rage in Kamiko's mind and brought her to a sudden stop.

The elder and Felene had been only faces in the crowd but were now running quickly toward Kamiko. Rachel billowed with robes and a thick woolen blanket clasped at her throat. As always, Felene was in loose dark leather and a studded breastplate, a cloak thrown over her shoulders. She arrived first and all but shouted, "What happened? Where's Danae?"

Rachel drew up beside her a moment later, her eyes busy between the door and Kamiko's apparent destination. Thick black smoke now billowed out the door, rising to join the churning mass pouring into the sky.

Until she spoke, her voice a hard growl, Kamiko did not know she was breathing hard. "She has been taken! This was no accident. We are under attack!"

Only Rachel was in control of her bearing and spoke with the calm of reason. "Parzon?"

Kamiko considered the question for a moment and answered with certainty, "No, Sister, Dairei would not do this." Rachel accepted Kamiko's assessment at face value and pressed on immediately.

"Felene, go find Lord Merritt and do not leave his side." She clapped her hands sharply when Felene hesitated, admonishing her like an errant novice. "Quickly now, go!"

With one hand, Felene unclasped her woolen cloak and tossed it to Kamiko, then bolted away at a dead run, repositioning her sword to allow for an easier draw. Kamiko could not have missed the look of pure longing Felene cast over her shoulder as she turned to go.

Rachel turned back to Kamiko but said nothing. She held her gaze for an eternal moment, the look on her weathered face demanding that Kamiko recall every single word of her training, the countless hours of study and all of the cumulative wisdom of the life of a warrior of the Order. Then, and still without speaking a word, she slung the woolen blanket aside and opened her cloak. She unbuckled the barding holding Kamiko's sword to her waist and held it out.

As Kamiko's hand closed around the scabbard, that familiar calm settled in her gut. The rage dissipated and left cool silence down in her spirit. She was surprised when neither Warrior nor woman stepped forward in that inner space. She found only the empty construct of their dwelling, the tower, and the courtyard. Even the more recent aspect, the viper, was absent.

The quiet of that inner sanctum was overbearing, but the emptiness was not complete. Something, rather someone, was waiting there just out of sight. She reached to it but felt only refusal, gentle but unrelenting—Hun'jotzimon. The steel sword felt heavy in her hand, but so real and so certain.

She slung Felene's cloak over her shoulders and fixed the clasp at her throat, then strapped the sword low on her back in her own odd combat configuration and checked the draw.

"Any chance my plate is hiding under there too?" Kamiko asked, rapping her unarmored chest with her knuckles.

Rachel simply smiled and took a step back. "Let's go find Danae," she said, then nodded toward the corner of the building and added, "Your lead."

Before she moved, Kamiko drew from the well of training and wisdom she had garnered from spending years on and off with Rachel. In spite of the pressing need to act as quickly as possible and amid the rampant chaos of blaring trumpets and shouting people, with the backdrop of a raging fire belching a fat black cloud into the sky, Kamiko took Rachel's hands in hers and leaned forward until their foreheads came gently together, and they prayed.

Rachel

As Rachel listened to the sound of Kamiko's voice, it seemed to grow almost distant, as if they were no longer within the confines of physical space. Her words were not echoing back from the snow around their feet or the estate walls towering nearby, they were being drawn outward into the heavens, like fallen petals upon flowing water. With seamless and perfect ease, Kamiko had drawn their very spirits forward to a point where they predominated their physical bodies. The spirit of God had taken them the step further. Rachel had no need to open her eyes to see, her ears to hear.

She smiled to herself when Kamiko asked for fierce power and brutal reckoning. A shudder passed up Rachel's spine as Kamiko petitioned the very throne of God for destruction upon their enemies, the likes of which had never been felt. Her eyes welled slightly as the young warrior all but demanded a legion of wild angels be dispatched to stand guard over Danae until she should arrive.

Rachel reveled in the thought of one such as Kamiko coming to her rescue. She prayed inwardly that she could live up to Kamiko's ferocity.

She opened her eyes amid the total chaos running rampant in the courtyard and met Kamiko's emerald gaze.

Kamiko

The look on Rachel's face further bolstered Kamiko's spirit. The thought of them going after Danae together sparked a hot flare of excitement in her chest. She brushed the moisture from one of Rachel's cheeks and savored the moment an instant longer before turning back to her course.

Upon seeing the very first telltale, Kamiko sensed more than just a kidnapping. Rachel echoed Kamiko's thought when she said, "Now that is just too obvious."

Right at the corner of the building, a pair of imprints, unmistakably Danae's feet, were pressed lightly into otherwise undisturbed snow.

Siruis's parting warning rang in Kamiko's mind and out of her mouth, "They are not here for me."

Confusion colored Rachel's face. "No, they were after Danae," she said.

Kamiko turned it over in her head quickly, coming to what seemed an obvious conclusion. They were not after Danae; she was only an acolyte.

"They are here for me," she said, without noticing Rachel's peculiar expression. Only when Rachel tilted her head and held her hands out in question did Kamiko realize what she'd said. From the swirl in her mind, the only explanation that surfaced was, "Siruis."

Rachel only shook her head and pointed in the direction the footprints were tracking, to the west toward the Black River, and directly toward one of several small but heavily fortified passages leading through the outer estate wall. These were too low and narrow to allow a horse, meant only for personnel to pass in single file. The thick portcullis appeared to have been simply melted through, and the solid granite doorway lay in shattered pieces inside the courtyard.

The two sisters broke into a run. They didn't have to go far. Kamiko and Rachel saw it at the same moment. It was a strip of Danae's shirt hanging in plain sight from the edge of a roofline.

The township of Flavin had long since outgrown the descriptive designation of township. It was, by every measure, a fully developed city. Lacking the towering ornate structures amassed in cities such as Castlehaven and First Colony, this smaller city was covered with a layer of clay-tile rooftops, haphazardly strewn about and effectively unbroken for miles. The buildings beneath them were just as randomly designed and puzzle-fit into every square foot of space not maintained as a walkway or road and, all of which were anywhere from three to ten stories, tightly packed. In some areas of town, the sky was almost totally blocked by a seeming infinite number of signs and banners in every language known. Most had been dulled by weather and neglect, and the all-encompassing reality that there were simply far too many to keep up with. It gave Flavin the pervasive look of being worn down, a weary old man in ragged clothes sitting in an ill-kept garden. Today it was a garden covered over by a clean white sheet of snow.

Due to the original town having been built nestled in a narrow valley within dwindling mountain fingers, the expansion had grown as a tangle of streets and byways, rising and falling hodgepodge across the broken terrain. It was rare to find passage in any direction which followed a straight bearing for more than a couple of blocks. Hemmed on three sides by this terrain and by the deep canyon of the Black River on the western edge, Flavin had no choice but to build upward.

Kamiko spoke first. "He's on the rooftops."

"Still heading west," Rachel said. "We'll split up. You go topside, I'll stay down here."

"You will not be able to keep up once we reach the market."

"I will go around the north side, hit Bricks Avenue. Nothing there but beggars and thieves, Sister."

Kamiko was about to object, to say she had a feeling in her gut that it would take them both to wrest Danae from her abductor. They needed to stay together. Before she could speak, a piercing bright flash flittered across both their faces, drawing both their heads around in a concerted snap. It came from the top corner of a building three blocks ahead, blinking rapidly for another moment before going out.

Even at that distance, the distinct form and fiery red mane of Dairei Parzon was obvious. The small mirror in her hand flashed once more before she stashed it away, then she waved one arm overhead while pointing northwest with the other.

"Big surprise," Rachel said.

"Yes, Sister, like we didn't expect *her* to be hanging around."

Dairei turned and trotted back away from the northernmost edge of the building, staying near the eastern edge and within their line of sight. The sisters shared a questioning look. When Dairei reversed her course and broke into a hard sprint, they watched in a moment of expectant dread. Kamiko felt Rachel's hand close on her forearm and tighten as Dairei leapt out over the wide street, obviously meaning to make it to the building on the opposite side.

On her best day, Kamiko knew she could not jump half the distance herself. Yet Dairei was not in the habit of foolery. She dove with her arms stretched forward, a fat tube extended ahead in both hands. The sisters heard a faint pop echoing down the sides of the buildings lining the avenue and saw what appeared to be a small dark ball shoot out and impact the side of the building, only a few feet from the top corner. Then Dairei pulled the tube in tight against her chest and fell in a steep arch—but only a few feet. The line was too thin and too distant for the sisters to see, but the effect was unmistakable. Dairei's course snapped into a sudden change of direction, her feet whipping forward beneath her, her trajectory now a speed-building curve.

Kamiko's breath stopped short when Dairei tore past the corner of the building, feet straight up, and disappeared behind the edge of the shorter neighboring structure. A moment later, she popped into sight above the roofline, in a tight momentum-defeating spin, and landed as gracefully as a bird gliding to perch on the very edge of the building.

Rachel's hand was now painfully clamped on Kamiko's arm. She whispered *wow* and released her grip.

Kamiko could only nod and say, "She is good."

"I think she wants us to follow." Rachel looked doubtful as she spoke.

"Figures," Kamiko said ruefully.

Word had already spread about Lord Merritt's estate, as most of the foot traffic was moving toward the fire. Kamiko's eyes darted around the immediate area, expecting to find any one of hundreds of militiamen currently seeking to gain kingly favor by delivering Kamiko the summons to appear. She looked back at Dairei standing near the edge of the building, three blocks down, returning the silent gaze.

"I'm going up, Sister," Kamiko said.

"Yes, get off the streets. See you on the other side." Just as Kamiko gave a start to step away, Rachel grasped her by the elbow and gently drew their faces together. "You watch her close."

Rachel

Rachel watched Kamiko make the three-block sprint to the base of the building. Dairei stood at the very front corner, with one foot perched upon the edge of the wall. As Kamiko looked up, Dairei drew an odd fat pistol from the folds of her loose garb, aimed it at the ground, and fired. A long thin tether-line projected all the way to the street.

They were right out in the open, people watching from up and down the street, murmuring and pointing. The building was flat-topped with a low retaining wall encircling the perimeter of the roof.

Dairei appeared to simply hook the grip to the top edge of the building, then stepped to one side and watched as Kamiko secured her hold on the tether. Dairei slapped the top of the device, then turned and sprinted across the roof, immediately out of Rachel's sight. Kamiko leapt up and outward, just as the tension grabbed the line. She came against the wall on her feet and at a dead run, Dairei's device reeling her quickly toward the top.

"Running up the side of a three-story building," Rachel whispered.

She turned and headed toward the growing gaggle of people who were anxious to see if wanton destruction had indeed taken a rich man's property and possibly some lives. They were giddy with it, already recreating the story as they walked. She spotted a trio on horseback, and thereby marked them as royalty or, at least, nobility. Two handsome young men and a frilly girl were riding three well-groomed chestnuts. Because of who Rachel was, the eldest of the young men would give his horse willingly.

Otherwise I shall knock him from it and take it anyway, she mused.

When she saw the man's look of smug self-import, she felt herself hoping for just such an outcome. *Kamiko has too much of an influence on me*, she thought as she headed for the trio at a run.

Chapter 21

Kamiko's prevailing thought was that she was being blatantly led into a trap. They were not even trying to hide the fact. Danae was bait, plain and simple. The greater mystery was Dairei's role, even if she was simply acting as the ultimate opportunist. She would not help Kamiko in anything unless it served her own purpose. It mattered little. She would follow the carefully placed tracks to Danae and deal with whomever was waiting for her there.

She pressed on at a careful but fast run. The snow-covered rooftops were set beneath a bright blue sky, the sun glaring yellow and cold above her head, white and harsh beneath her feet. Felene's borrowed cloak billowed out behind her and, for a brief moment, reminded her of the days of her youth, when the cape was the most important part of her garb. It had made her faster, more agile, and far more ferocious.

Dairei was keeping out ahead of Kamiko a few hundred paces. The thief had obviously pieced the scenario together by watching Lord Merritt's estate. Kamiko wondered if Dairei knew this was Danae and not Siruis they were chasing.

The signs were placed, the tracking easy. It would take near to an hour to negotiate the variegated terrain across the top. She needed down. She needed Uila. But she could not abandon the trail.

They were nearing the bulge of the city center, where the roofscape rose suddenly atop larger buildings, and the gaps between them opened. The main market center was marked by the low uniformly rectangular strips of long white rooftops, side by side and fifteen deep. The huge dispersal warehouse stretched breadth-wise across the far ends of the market houses proper, the back side of which was against one of the broadest streets in Flavin. Here massive caravans of heavy wagons entered the dispersal house, where the freight was unloaded, unpacked, and dispersed by droves of dirty laborers. The wagons then departed through the opposite end to return to the river and be filled again in an endless cycle. A single merchant lord would earn far more for that labor than the combined income of them all.

The streets would be too crowded to make good time on foot. Without Uila's fury bearing down on them, the people would present too much natural slow resistance. Yet Dairei was following the blatant trail directly toward the huge swath of low flat rooftops.

Again Kamiko considered that Danae was simply bait. The intent could be one of only two possibilities by her reckoning: to lead her into something or to lead her away from something. Her gut told her it was the first, though the potential for both was strong.

She was also confident that Rachel would come to the same conclusions. To a much lesser degree, Rachel seemed, at times, to gain insight from outside her own purview, just as Siruis always appeared to do. Such was a gift apparently lost on Kamiko. She was often aware of the fullness of a situation only after finding that she was fully engaged in it. It occurred to her that she was doing so now, running into the furnace unawares.

The *Karak-Tan*. It was a word in an ancient tongue known only to Djinnasee, the language of a dead race annihilated by war. Loosely translated, it meant to be thrown into the furnace, crucible, or trial by fire, depending on the subject of its use. Djinnasee had used the word often enough but had only implemented it once during Kamiko's life. She remembered her crucible with great clarity.

The distraction of her thoughts almost cost her dearly. Her left foot lost traction as she was charging along the snow-covered ridge of a building with a particularly steep pitch to the roof. As her foot shot out to the side, her full weight came down on her right leg, causing it to slip from beneath her as well. Her natural momentum brought her down like a whip, her legs going out to the left while her upper body jerked to the right bringing her rib cage down on the ridge. Her only recourse was to spin to disperse some of the momentum and lessen the brunt of the impact as much as possible.

To a degree, the attempt worked. None of her ribs snapped. However, the bulk of her weight and the remaining forward motion drew her over the ridge cap, headfirst and onto her back, and would have sent her sliding down the slope. On instinct, by impulse, in desperation, she hooked her right leg on the ridge at the knee and checked what would have been a headfirst plunge down the steep roof and off the edge for a three-story drop.

For a few moments, all she could do was lay still. The strike had been much like a kick she'd received from Uila way back when she was still training him, when he resisted the process. It hurt.

Suddenly Kamiko was not alone. A man was standing on the ridgeline of the roof, looking down at her. He could have been any common man, dressed in loose-fit clothes, which could have been a baker's or a cabinet maker's. His features were handsome but unremarkable. Kamiko simply accepted that she knew him to be an angel. He lifted his hand and pointed to the west, directly at the lighthouse fortress above the river.

For a single moment and far below her, the thick snaking body of the Black River slipped silently by, nothing but open air between Kamiko and the dark rolling waters. Then she was again alone on the snowy rooftop.

Kamiko's head snapped up, and she was on her feet in an instant. In spite of the pain burning in her side, which threatened to fold her over, she was moving with every bit of her power. She knew where Danae was with as much clarity as if she'd just seen her. Dairei was on a false trail. Kamiko could see her standing at the corner of a lower flat building, looking back her way with one hand on her hip, disdain in her stance. Behind and below Dairei, the market district lay as a mass of churning noise.

Right, Kamiko thought, *like you've never fallen flat on your back in the middle of a chase.*

Dairei gathered her mane into a bundle at the nape of her neck and held it with one hand, while with the other, she drew a hood over her head. She tapped her forehead once in a salute to Kamiko, turned, and stepped off the corner of the building and into the rush and bustle at the edge of the busy market.

Kamiko let the mystery fall immediately away and set her course once more across the top of the city. She spared a single look back toward Lord Merritt's estate. The column of dark smoke had lightened considerably, a sign the fire was being brought under control. It also served to remind her that those responsible would not hesitate to use wanton destruction with as much readiness as she would use her fists.

Chapter 22

Flavin, the northernmost of the big cities along the western river-bound border of the kingdom, had grown up inside a tilted bowl. The higher ridge curved around behind Kamiko to the east. The lower ridge to the west demarked the snaking canyon of the Black River. Flavin was packed into the depressed valley region between the two.

From Kamiko's vantage, she could see all the way to the great stone structure of the lighthouse perched atop the edge of the canyon wall. It was one of more than a hundred lighthouses placed along the length of the mighty river, designed to illuminate the canyon walls and the river itself. They allowed the barge pilots to operate around the clock as far north as Flavin. Their points of light could also be seen for leagues across the land in many directions.

She no longer needed to follow any signs or tracks in the snow, she knew Danae had been taken to that lighthouse. Yet another of the collecting mysteries—how had they gained a half-hour on her? She had allowed no more than a fistful of minutes from the moment Danae was grabbed until she and Rachel were running all out. If anything, she should have gained on them. The sense that she was missing something important rang in her head like Lord Merritt's trumpeter.

Danae

The cold was harsh and biting, and the wind whipped her skin with frozen quills and caused her to swing around in slow circles. This told Danae she was tethered by a long rope. She could feel the rasp of the hood against her face and the squeeze of the cord around her throat. They had wound her into what felt like a canvas cocoon from waist to shoulder, affixed the rope to the canvas between her shoulder blades, and thrown her over the edge of the great wall of the lighthouse overlooking the water. The fall was mercifully short before the rope caught, although she felt her weight slacken and grab, slacken and grab, as they lowered her farther. The ultimate bitter silence and dark gray of her hooded sight had returned, but so had her command of her body.

At least one of her captors now nursed a heavy bruise somewhere on his leg. She felt certain there were at least three of them. Two had held her still while a third had secured her bindings. She'd fought them like a wild beast.

Now she was dangling from the side of the lighthouse, high above the river. She was the bait. Kamiko was the prey. Danae had to work hard to focus her will beyond the rage and fear, to calm her spirit with prayer, and to release her desire to live and thereby overcome the fear of death.

But at long last, the lightness returned to her body. It felt like someone pulled her into it. Her ears and eyes opened to find a humanlike being standing midair beside her, clothed in the style of a commoner but who held a hurricane in its fist. Danae knew it was there as her protector.

It was in quiet conversation with another being of the same manner but with a tongue of fire dancing in its palm. She believed this one was a messenger. She knew, without doubt, that both were angels. Questions were being asked, a request her protector denied without quarter. The fire grew animated in the angel's palm, and Danae's protector turned its attention fully upon the flame.

"That," it said, "is not for this one. She belongs to me. You will withdraw until the designee arrives. Only then will I allow you to serve that decree." The messenger nodded its approval and slipped from sight.

The words bounded around in Danae's head. She knew Kamiko was coming for her. The angel messenger was here for Kamiko. Danae's spirit shuddered through and through, leaving her feeling all the more helpless for the knowledge that she could in no way intervene.

The being turned to Danae and spoke, "Remember the Karak-Tan…it is about belief in God, my friend, for I am sent to watch over you." For a few moments, the hurricane in its hand grew. Then it stepped back and was hidden from Danae's sight.

Human voices began to roll down from over the ledge of the lighthouse, high above Danae. One was barking orders, the others acknowledging with guttural cries that sounded darkly mirthful. There were more than three. Suddenly a deep silence descended from above.

*****

Kamiko felt the sharp pull of doubt. There was nothing about the situation which could be seen as random or ill-conceived. She held no illusions about her own invincibility. She could be living out her final minutes. Whoever had taken Danae had done their homework and would be well prepared for Kamiko Hoshi and all that implied.

She'd had no alternatives in her approach to the lighthouse. It was built out on the edge of the canyon just outside of town where the terrain was too rough to build anything functional. And it was designed as a fortress capable of housing up to fifty men and provisions for two full months. Typically as it did now, the place operated with only a few men and women, paid employees with children and rent payments, no soldiers, and only a couple of city militia. She could see one of them just beyond the main gate. He lay motionless in the middle of the road, the whiteness of the snow around him speckled with fat splotches of bright red.

The huge stone and steel gate was drawn fully open, which, if not for the dead officer, was not that unusual. There was no reason to attempt hiding her approach. The broad paved roadway lay in plain sight all the way from the edge of town. She knew in her heart that everyone inside was dead. The officer was there in the open to make sure she understood the *how* of what was about to transpire. They had led her here to kill her, plain and simple, and were—doubtless—prepared enough to succeed.

"Fine." She growled to herself. "So be it." She drew the sword from her back, unbuckled the narrow barding, and let the scabbard fall at her heels. One of Felene's chastisements of a decade past echoed unexpectedly across her thoughts. It caused a brief smile to tug at one corner of her mouth. Felene was worried that Kamiko carried a long-sword on her back, when everyone with any sense knew it must be slung on the hip.

Felene! She could certainly use her help on this one. As she stepped toward the gate, thoughts and memories began cascading.

She was twelve. Butchers were roaming the streets of her small town, her domain.

She was not afraid.

Rachel

She was a good horse, but Rachel knew the feisty mare was a town-trotter not used to hard running. Still she had driven the horse mercilessly. The rising slope of the winding street was proving too much for the gentle beast. She slung her head and bucked slightly in protest as Rachel rounded the last long bend leading to the main gate.

The only flaw in the otherwise pristine snow was a single track of footprints passing beneath her, leading into the lighthouse complex ahead. Kamiko had arrived. Rachel drew the horse to a stop just outside the gate and hopped from her back where Kamiko's scabbard and barding lay partially submerged in the snow.

Without slowing to contemplate the situation, Rachel unbuckled the young nobleman's sword from the saddle, looped the reins safely onto the saddle horn, and rump-slapped the mare into motion, heading her back toward her rightful owner. All the while her eyes darted up toward and around the complex, taking in the details of the battlefield she was about to enter. A body lay just inside the gate.

Low light-gray clouds were forming in a slow-moving blanket, slipping over the land from the northwest. In the last ten minutes of the hard run through Flavin, the clouds had covered the sun, and the air turned from frigid to a bitter biting cold. She did not want to leave the young nobleman's fur-lined cloak lying in the snow to ruin, but she must not be encumbered by the bulk. His reaction, as she had commandeered his horse and sword, had been a curious mixture, both livid and gracious, bidding Rachel good hunting through clenched teeth, no doubt for the benefit of the young lady in his company. To his credit, he had offered Rachel the cloak willingly.

Dropping the cloak, the elder sister headed toward the prone body at a quick trot, pausing only long enough to check the pulse. Judging by the footprints, Kamiko had done the same. The pulse was irrelevant. His skin was like ice, and his still eyes wore the glaze of death. Kamiko's tracks led to Rachel's left, around the south side of a low wide circular barracks house and into a small open yard. Dominating the scene, the lighthouse jutted up from another low building connected to the barracks. A twenty-five-foot stone wall encircled the complex, cornered by cone-topped towers.

Another body lay in the snow, twisted and frozen into a shape wholly unnatural for a man. She didn't even bother to check him. Kamiko had discarded Felene's cloak nearby in a crumpled pile. From the spacing and lack of depth in the footprints, Rachel knew that by the time Kamiko had sprinted by the body, she was focused and fully immersed.

Kamiko's sharp bark echoed down into the narrow courtyard from the observation deck of the lighthouse, followed by a deep bellow of pain and the onset of ringing steel. As Rachel bolted for the door leading to the stairs, she caught sight of an odd motion above and beyond the wall on the cliffside. What, at first, appeared to be a large cocoon dangling out over the river resolved in her mind as Danae, tethered to the parapet of the higher observation deck.

Rachel could see no way possible to reach her from the top of the fortified wall. They had placed her in the exact spot to be seen but not reached. She bolted for the open door, drew the sword, and dropped the scabbard. She still had no idea who *they* were.

Just as she made it to the stair landing, a dense troop of fleet-winged birds engulfed and passed her by without so much as a single peep, pouring up the open stairwell in a tornado of dark feathers. Sounds of Kamiko in battle filled the large room from two floors above, her singsong chirrups and sharp barks amplified by the stone walls. Rachel pressed upward with all the speed she could muster, for one of those barks was the result of pain. Kamiko had been struck.

Danae

Danae could feel reverberations from heavy blows pulsing down the rope. She imagined someone chopping at it with a hatchet; though from the number of strikes, it would have to be rather dull or else poorly aimed. She had no doubt she would soon plunge to the icy river below and braced herself for the long drop. Siruis had told her to be strong and have no fear. In spite of the hood and her deafness, she could see and hear. The depth of the river chasm beneath her threatened to overwhelm her hold on fear, but she kept the sight of her protector in her mind and stayed calm. She could hear Kamiko's voice above all else. One shout lifted above the others—Kamiko had been wounded!

Both beings stepped back into Danae's sight. The messenger lifted its hand, and the tongue of flame flowered up into the air and flared briefly. Then the two angels shared a solemn look before the messenger turned and was gone. Suddenly the river below was no longer Danae's battle against fear, which, to her, was similar to disbelief. She feared for Kamiko's life.

A hard pulse rifled down the rope, and she felt the first moment of weightlessness as she began to fall. Suddenly she was surrounded by hundreds of birds, falling with her.

Chapter 23

Rachel paid no heed to the singular aspects of the grisly scene beyond what her mind automatically grasped. Half a dozen bodies lay in a tight semicircle, each pooling blood from mortal wounds. Only one remained afoot. The macabre oddity of what she saw caused that forbidden moment of hesitation. Each of the dead bodies was dressed in distinctly foreign garb, each one unique in outfit of weapons and armor. The one still standing was entirely covered in intricate designs of the darkest red. He alone wore no armor or clothing beyond a simple loin girdle.

Kamiko had her back to Rachel, and although she was standing at the ready, she held all her weight on her right leg, her left arm tucked hard against her ribs. Her back heaved with the effort of every breath. Blood pooled beneath her as well. She seemed not to notice the churning maelstrom of birds, intent instead upon keeping what remained of her broken sword at the ready.

The man in red withstood a steady—if ineffectual—assault from the swarm of furious birds with an aura of indifference. His back was to the open air beyond the parapet, and unlike Kamiko, he appeared wholly unscathed. As he lifted the missing part of Kamiko's sword, both Rachel and Kamiko moved.

To Rachel's surprise, Kamiko did not attack the man; instead she dove headlong to where the bare blade fell and severed the tether.

Kamiko snapped out her left hand with a painful howl and grabbed the trailing end of the rope a single moment before it slipped out of her reach. Danae's falling weight jerked her arm with a loud pop, but she held.

The broken blade rose swiftly in his bleeding hand, prepared to come down on Kamiko for the killing blow. Rachel's senses exploded in her head. She was too far away to block the chop. Kamiko was twisted and slipping toward the edge, and she would never be able to deflect the blow with her broken sword. Kamiko and Danae were about to die before Rachel's eyes. Still running hard, she leapt into the air and spun in full flight, releasing the young nobleman's ornate sword with all her might. She regained her feet without slowing and dove at the big warrior's face.

Kamiko

Fat snowflakes swirled in every direction. Were it a still windless day, they would float straight down in silence and staggering beauty, each a masterpiece and a reminder of perfection. Kamiko had always been driven by the swirl of heavy winds, had stayed aloft far longer than simple nature would allow. Death had called time and time again, had darkened her doorstep without relent. She could see death standing over her, raising the blade that would mark her final thought and bookend her life story. She would go there with Danae, her Karak-Tan complete.

She felt no fear and no anger. The Eternal would not be defeated by her death. She had served him without reservation, even in her times of weakness and doubt. And here at the last, he was reminding her of his perfection and glory, giving her the gift of swirling white pristine beauty. A snowflake was such a small thing yet as grand as the whole of the universe.

The rope was slipping through her bloody grasp. Her body slid toward the edge. She was bleeding out. The blade was falling.

Rachel

Rachel lived for the look on the man's scowling face. She'd seen it hundreds of times on the battlefield, the sudden blank focus of his eyes and the frozen sculpting of his face as reality congealed in his mind. The blade in his hand hesitated at the summit of his attack when the nobleman's finely crafted sword sunk halfway to the hilt in his rib cage. The pause offered her all the time she needed. Her outstretched hands caught him at the throat as her knee punched hard against the pommel, driving the blade to the hilt and out the opposite side. Her heart raced with the thrill of battle, the purity of her joy overwhelming her spirit.

It had been a good life. It would be a fantastic death.

Rachel drove him over the ledge, spinning out into the snowflakes. And as never before, she laughed.

Kamiko

Kamiko would not die without a fight. She lifted the hilt in defense, however inadequate it may be, unwilling to offer the smallest fraction of retreat. Then Sister Rachel, like an angel appearing from the ether, slammed into her attacker face-to-face, strong hands locked around his throat. A jeweled sword simply appeared in his side and then—they were gone. Rachel was gone. They floated out over the river and dropped.

As if on cue, Danae's dangling weight overcame Kamiko's grasp, and the end of the thin rope slipped from her hand. The fierce pain in her side gone from her mind, Kamiko rolled and lunged with her good hand, the broken sword falling away after the three of them toward the river. She landed on her chest at the edge of the stone parapet, looking down into the chasm. She'd had no real chance at the rope. Rachel would hit the water only a couple of seconds before Danae. The storm of birds passed her by and plunged down into the canyon without notice. Horror enveloped her soul. Her head swam with it, her vision watery and wavering from blood loss. They had killed not only her but Rachel and Danae as well. And she still did not know who *they* were.

Then far below, there was a strange motion, out of place but somehow familiar. A mass of white flesh lunged out from the black rock face of the cliff. Thick bulging arms akin to tree trunks plucked Danae gently from the air and drew her into their embrace, continuing the fall. Jerim rolled her into his mass just before they hit the water, seconds after Rachel and the painted warrior.

Where moments before Kamiko had displayed the strength to take six heavily armed warriors in close combat, she now had to summon all her will to simply draw breath. She found herself counting each inhalation, marking every exhale as final. She was well versed in death and could hear the rattle in her chest. The left side of her body burned fiercely and kept those precious few breaths to quick gasps. She lay sprawled across the top of the wide parapet, looking down at the dark river. The thickening swirl of snowflakes was mesmerizing.

Danae was alive. Rachel was dead.

Kamiko's heart slowed but was broken just the same.

The riddle of perspective assailed her. The mysteries of the past weeks, since she'd first encountered Siruis, folded inward and coalesced into a singular thing, as though she'd been seeing only individual limbs of an entire tree. She could now see the tree from the tiniest seed nut to the deepest of the hair-fine roots. The irony was almost too thick to believe. This would be her third death, the death of the body, the final dying. The first was her death as a child of twelve, where she was reborn as a butcher. The second was only hours ago, standing within the embrace of Mars Knoll, when she'd believed that no one alive could take her sword. Now she would die with the answer echoing in her mind, a useless victory.

She was both, Warrior and Woman, and she had always been wholly broken but fully healed. A dichotomy of flesh yet a single person. The memory of seeing her strange face in the mirror floated into her mind. Odd that she could recognize that face now.

She focused her will to a point and drew a shallow breath. The burn in her lungs slipped away slowly. Danae was alive. She focused her will, but her body could give no more. The breath did not come.

Perfect flakes drifting in silence pulled her downward.

Felene

The fury and quivering fear Felene felt had somehow infected Uila. Lord Merritt had dismissed her almost immediately, demanding she join her sisters with all haste. She'd not taken the time to saddle the mighty warhorse. She'd secured and buckled his bridle in one smooth motion and mounted with a leap. An angry-looking man in simple dress caught her attention, just outside the gate, and told her to go to the lighthouse. Without further question or doubt, Felene set the course and let Uila have his head. He seemed to know what was happening. She had never felt such power in an animal.

Still astride his broad back, they thundered through the main gate of the lighthouse, past two bodies in the yard, straight through the entryway, and even up the broad staircase. Felene had to lie flat against his withers to clear the door leading out to the balcony where they both scanned the aftermath. Both sets of eyes came to rest on one body in particular.

Felene leapt from Uila's back and sprinted to Kamiko's side. She was lying facedown in the snow atop the merlon, her head and right arm dangling over the edge. From the amount of blood covering her side and pooled beneath her, Felene could believe that she was too late. Uila was at Felene's shoulder, breathing hard and deep and angry. She gently rolled Kamiko to her back but held her greatest fear carefully in check as she pressed her ear to Kamiko's unmoving chest.

Nothing.

The rage inside Felene coiled anew. She needed to wail at the top of her lungs, wanted to butcher the dead spread behind her into shreds. Instead she gathered all her fury into a screaming hot ball and shoved it down into her gut. She would fight the way she knew Kamiko fought. She quickly unbuckled and lifted the barding over her head and threw her sword to the deck with a growl. She balled her fist and delivered three careful heavy blows to Kamiko's sternum, and then tilted her sister's head back and began breathing for her. She wasn't sure what good it would do. If Kamiko had already bled out, it was a useless gesture. And even if she could revive her, she would need serious attention immediately. It mattered little to Felene. She continued, Uila snorting at her shoulder.

Uila's chortling took on an angry menacing sound, and he turned from Felene's side. She spared a brief look between breaths to find Dairei standing atop another of the parapets, looking down at her. Felene returned to the cycle of breathing for Kamiko, pumping her heart, breathing, pumping her heart, even when Dairei's feet appeared at her side.

The woman dropped to her knees opposite Felene. She drew a pouch from a hidden fold, snapped out a small dagger, and cut Kamiko's shirt away from the wound. She pulled a wad of linen dressing from the pouch and forcefully shoved it into the deep slice between Kamiko's ribs. Felene never broke stride and no word was exchanged. Dairei opened a second leather pouch and removed a vial and a small black tube. She affixed the tube to the opening of the vial, then carefully squeezed until a single drop of clear liquid appeared at the end of the tube. A tiny flare of hope sparked in Felene's chest. The snow was coming in smaller faster flakes.

Dairei motioned for Felene to stop, tilted Kamiko's head back, inserted the tube into her mouth, then squeezed the vial flat. Felene's chest pounded fast and hard as Dairei withdrew the tube and flipped the vial over the edge, nodding to Felene to continue. Felene began the sequence with renewed spirit. Uila had grown quiet but for his breathing, again near her shoulder. Dairei pressed the heel of her hand against the wound.

"Where is Siruis?"

The quiet kindness in Dairei's voice caught Felene off guard and had the effect of quenching a smattering of the revulsion and distrust she felt for the thief. She was about to answer that she did not know when a gentle spasm rippled through Kamiko's chest.

Kamiko

So sleepy. She just wanted to sleep a while longer before starting her day. For the first time in many nights, she'd not dreamed of distant lands and strange faces, twisting realities or daemon hordes. It was only sweet, peaceful, silent sleep. Something of great importance tugged at her to awaken, but she had no energy for it. Her thoughts were still too muddled to grapple with it. She was cold to the point of shivering but felt no alarm at the realization. There was nothing uncommon about waking up cold for one who had spent a good part of her life sleeping under the open sky.

Yet a presence loomed over her, and a resounding pressure came down on her chest in a steady meter. Then warm hands were on her face, and warm lips were pressed to her mouth. They quivered and tasted of salty tears, and she felt air fill her lungs.

She knew well that she'd never in her life felt the touch of lips on her mouth nor the too-familiar touch of another person's hands on her breast. The warmth of closeness ceased, and the pressure on her chest returned. She fought to clear the mud from her mind. Something of great importance was tugging at her.

A sudden heat flourished in her face and a tingling burn like a mask of a thousand needles being laid in place against her skin. It spread down her neck in an avalanche, across her bare chest, and down her left side, exploding in a sudden flare of pain that caused every muscle in her body to harden with the fullness of her strength.

Her eyes popped open. Her breath caught short by the sudden intensity of pure burning pain in her ribs and a hard dull ache in her left arm.

Her last memory was of fat snowflakes falling down and away, drawing her into their slow wake as they bid her follow them to the river below. Some part of her spirit had obeyed and slipped out and down. Now she saw smaller flakes, in much greater number, coming from the sky, felt them stinging her hot skin, a mask of needles.

Felene

Hold her," Felene commanded as Kamiko suddenly bucked hard under her hands. "Keep her down."

"I've got her," Dairei assured with a quiet voice, cold but with the timbre of relief. She held Kamiko with one steely hand across her waist while the other held the blood-soaked linen firmly in place.

Felene spoke quickly and quietly to Kamiko, her hands holding her shoulders, her face mere inches away. "Hold on, Sister, be still. I'm here...You've been badly injured, and you've lost too much blood. We're in pretty big trouble, sweetie, and I need you to stop struggling."

At last Kamiko gained a small measure of control over her body and settled her arched back down to the stone. But she was trembling hard, and her muscles shuddered without relent. Dairei yanked the tie of her cloak and swept it off with one hand, the other never leaving Kamiko's deep wound. She flipped the cloak over to Felene, who immediately folded it double and spread it over Kamiko, tucked it under her arms, and nestled it around her neck. Kamiko's eyes were glassy and drifted slowly side to side, not focused on anything. Her face was ashen, her lips devoid of color.

Dairei winked at Felene and said, in a calm quiet voice, "You owe me a cloak, Sister." She added in a serious tone, "If we can't get her to a doctor in the next five minutes, this will have been for naught. We need Siruis now."

"No more tricks in that bag of yours?" Felene looked up at Dairei's scarred face, wondering why she would think to wish for Siruis and remembering her own recent encounter with the thief. Had Dairei witnessed the healing touch that ended Felene's paralysis?

"None good enough for this."

A silence settled as each of their capable minds searched for possibilities. There were no viable options. The silence was broken by a small sweet voice.

"There is no need for that, Master Thief."

Chapter 24

Siruis was standing close enough to Dairei to reach out and touch her sleeve. To Felene's surprise, the look that flushed upon Dairei's face was fear, and her body tensed, as if she might take flight. Felene felt a similar reaction flare in her own chest but was overwhelmed with relief.

"Blessed be, Sister," was all Felene could manage for words, and those came out small and breathy with the release of the stark fear she harbored for Kamiko.

Siruis was bundled sole to crown and was wearing a heavy woolen coat, the hood drawn tight around her pure white face. She wore thick pants tucked into short leather boots that had rolls of woolen fluff encircling the tops just above her ankles. Felene wondered for a moment how and when she'd had time to don such garments but lost the thought in a rush of rising joy.

Siruis slid her hand from one glove and leaned forward against the parapet, reaching for Kamiko's hand beneath Dairei's cloak.

Only then did Felene realize that birds had covered every surface of the parapets, stone window openings and benches and tables. They were set back from the women several paces, as if in respect for the serious nature of what was transpiring. Like the birds, Uila was still and silent.

"If you do not wish to see what should not be seen," Siruis warned both Felene and Dairei, "then do not touch her." Dairei's hand jumped away from Kamiko's ribs, and she scooted back a full pace, still on her knees. The wad of cloth bandage was soaked. She dropped it aside, absently scooped a handful of snow, and began scrubbing her hands.

When Felene hesitated to lift her hand from Kamiko's cold face, Siruis simply held her gaze for a few silent moments. The memory of her own encounter with Siruis's recent "gift" sent a shudder of renewed anxiety quaking through her spirit, and her hand jerked away from Kamiko.

There was no warning or preamble, no prayer for strength or wisdom, and no words that Felene could say. Siruis spoke three words, but they were gone from Felene's mind as soon as they had entered.

Kamiko

Someone with a warm hand grasped and lifted hers. Kamiko was confused by being both awake and still having the vision of a watery dream, unable to hold her eyes still. She could hear familiar voices but could not picture their faces. The whole of her body burned with fire but felt like ice. She wondered distantly if she'd somehow fallen into the Black River.

She could remember it was far below, could recall seeing Rachel and the strange-colored warrior hit the surface and vanish beneath it. She knew Jerim had leapt out from the face of the cliff to catch Danae, and that Sister Rachel had perished to save their lives. Her brilliant bright laughter as she passed overhead would never leave Kamiko's mind.

And then it happened. Siruis's distinct voice, such a small sweet sound to have unleashed such vast power, whispered over her, three words calling the gates of heaven to bear. She could easily recognize the being that appeared nearby and was not surprised when it touched her on the forehead. She'd seen the same happen with Captain Carthage earlier.

It felt as though someone poured warmed oil on her head. It spread from her crown, across her face, down her chest and back, rippled across her flaming ribs, and swept all the way to her icy toes. It washed away every pain and filled every pore of her skin with warm comfort. Strength returned to her body and clarity to her flailing mind in such measure she felt she might erupt.

She tried to rise but found no response in her body. Instead she felt the vibrant presence of another being, waiting in the shadows and holding her in place. Hun'jotzimon was engorged with righteous rage, teeming with violence held at bay by power that could not be fathomed. It was entirely focused upon Kamiko. It felt angry. She had no illusions that she could well be destroyed, body and soul.

As if in response to her thoughts, the presence of the sword grew still and silent in her mind.

She understood. She'd failed the Karak-Tan. It had not been Danae's crucible; it was Kamiko's. She'd been beaten by mere mortals while the power to wipe mountains away lay at hand unused. She'd brought every aspect of her existence to bear—steel, rage, skill, knowledge, experience, and wisdom—only to fail and be fatally pierced, losing Danae and Rachel in the process. Only Jerim's intervention had saved Danae. Rachel's death fell squarely upon Kamiko's shoulders, and the weight of that knowledge was immense.

Immense. The word stuck in her mind. The belief that she'd given Sister Rachel no alternative but to give her life was a weight Kamiko felt ill-equipped to bear. The call of the vast and powerful being she'd come to know was far greater a demand than what she was able to answer. She felt tiny, lost in a world of giants. It was a storm bearing down on her that neither skill nor rage could contend with. She would be crushed while still grappling with the sum of all her parts. It left her breathless.

Hun'jotzimon released her.

*****

Kamiko stood with perfect ease, the deep river chasm only two steps behind her. The worried wonder painted on Dairei's face and the blissful joy on Felene's was wholly lost on her. Kamiko's eyes were locked on Siruis. All the mystery was gone. Uila chortled and shook his massive head, stomping a front foot in the snow. As one, the horde of silent birds lifted into the heavily falling snow, flew around the balcony, and then disbanded in every direction.

For a moment, Kamiko could see, or rather feel, the broken shards, the final remnants of her old self—a twelve-year-old, a hard Warrior, a frail Woman, and a violent viper. They dissolved away like snowflakes melting on the surface of the river. The face in the mirror would never again be a stranger to her. She was whole. Relatively.

No one spoke a word. Rachel was gone. Felene and Dairei did not know. And both had Kamiko's blood drying on their hands.

Siruis's eyes held Kamiko steady. The veil of the physical world again shimmered as gossamer, drifting like a thin sheet in a breeze. The storm no longer raged across the ether in waves of darkness and explosions of light. The great shadow simply lay across the land, kept alive by gloom and fear, pain and hunger, but mostly by greed.

"The people of Cairistonia are no longer your charge, Kamiko," Siruis said. "You are needed elsewhere."

Kamiko felt the pull of a familiar presence and turned. Peering westward across the canyon, her eyes strained against the unbroken curtain of snow drifting across the gossamer sheet. They came into sight with sudden clarity, as if standing a mere stone's throw away on a clear day. There on the opposite bank of the river chasm stood Djinnasee, his hand stretched toward her, as if willing something to happen.

At his side towered the true colossus, the mighty Bartol. She'd known him since that barbarous day when she was twelve, had traveled and worked missions with him through the three decades since. She knew him as well as anyone alive, yet the simple sight of him still drove her back a step. The legend of Bartolamew Kane had been well earned.

His dark face was completely framed in a thick but flowing mane of jet black. Great strands of ice formed down the length of his heavy beard and around the crown of his head and shoulders, framing his darkness in crystalline white. He had just pulled his massive fur cloak around his shoulders and twisted the thick bone catches in place to hold it closed across his chest.

Kamiko had helped Bartol make that cloak many years ago. The shoulder cap and chest cover were of black rhino hide, lined and draped with a half dozen bear skins. The pieces were stitched together with long strips of mountain lion gut, twisted and cured into flexible rope the thickness of her finger. It covered him from neck to midcalf but had openings worked into the sides, just below the edge of the shoulders, to allow his arms freedom of movement.

More than once, Kamiko had used the great cloak as a shelter during their long excursions through the wilds. It took most of her considerable strength to lift it. The making had taken a full three months of hunting, skinning, curing, and forming and, at last, sewing together the great sheets of hide. She could easily recognize that as the best three months of her life.

Djinnasee had told her that Bartol shared the sentiment often. It was a memory Bartol held and recalled whenever he needed to remember something good, when the darkness of evil men loomed overlarge.

He looked up with dark eyes the size of Kamiko's fist, a profound sadness drawing his ice-flaked brow together. He grew still and peered, as always, into the very core of her soul.

The unexpected sight of her two dearest friends drove the building volcano of emotion into a full uncontrolled eruption of pain and joy. Her hands flew outward, and she shouted at the top of her lungs, a high wail that pierced the muffling snow and echoed down the canyon. She pressed all the air from her lungs, drew another deep breath, and wailed a second time. Bartol's massive hand lifted skyward, and thunder rolled out from his dark face to meet Kamiko's cries, meeting and joining with an eerie harmony—one high and filled with longing, the other voice deep with the natural timbre of peril and fury.

When their voices ceased, Bartol knelt beside Djinnasee and gathered something from near his feet into his hands. Rachel looked as small as a child against his mass. He lifted her empty body to his chest and stood. He'd been waiting for Rachel and had climbed the cliff face with her body.

Djinnasee's weathered face was the same as it had always been, bright with wonder, dark with burden. He gave Kamiko a sad smile for a moment longer before dropping his hand. The natural distance across the wide chasm returned, and as they turned away, the shroud of snow closed behind them.

Kamiko turned back, now speechless and breathing hard. The bite of the cold wind returned to her awareness and sent a hard chill from her heels to the crown of her head. She wore only her boots, pants, and thin shirt, torn and blood-wet. Dairei's tattered white overcloak lay at her feet. Kamiko lifted it with a billowing swirl and turned under it, letting it come to rest across her back and shoulders. The warmth was immediate.

Dairei and Felene dropped down from the parapet, and Felene knelt beside Siruis and put her arm around Siruis's shoulder. Dairei stood aside a few paces and was occupying her obvious discomfort by staring at the snowy deck near one of the bodies. Her fingers absently traced the indention of the scar across her cheek, drifting from the white starburst below her eye down the crease along her jawline. Her brow was furrowed, as someone distracted by warring thoughts.

Dairei's head cocked inquisitively to one side. She shuffled the snow with one foot, reached down, and lifted something in the palm of her hand. After a moment of reflection, her eyes came up to Kamiko's, all wonder and discomfort gone. She looked serious.

Kamiko stepped forward and dropped off the parapet to the deck. The master thief thumb-flipped what appeared to be a thick wooden coin through the air to land with a heavy slap in Kamiko's open palm. She knew it by the weight and feel in her hand before her eyes ever fell on it. It was a silver and bronze rendering of Koralilia set into petrified wood.

"My talisman."

End of Part 1

Chapter 1

Ravencroft City—Grace

The irony was not lost on Grace. She could easily imagine her dead body being found frozen into the gargoylian pose she was holding. She could not recall a time when she longed for the blistering heat of her homeland more than she did now. All of Ravencroft was buried beneath a thick blanket of snow. It mattered little that she was cocooned beneath layer upon layer of skins, furs, and thick leather wrappings, the cold knew no boundaries and had long since established what seemed to her like unhindered access to her dark sun-loving skin.

Yet she could not afford the benefit of movement to ease the cold bite. She required only her eyes to be clear. The snow covering her body was an essential part of her concealment. It made her one with her surroundings, an indiscernible lump of white amid thousands.

It gave her the distinct advantage. Those she was tracking would be on the move, trying to make up for lost time, and if they followed what she believed had become their nightly routine, they would pass within ten paces of where she waited. She would spring her trap, capture one or two—kill the rest. Their wanton butchery would forever cease tonight, even if it be borne of her own butchery. Tonight she was the natural reaction to their murderous ways.

Grace was seated on a small barrel with one foot back and one foot forward for the double benefit of keeping them awake and having a ready launch base. Her back was pressed against the low retaining wall encircling the perimeter of the cluttered rooftop she occupied. She had been waiting most of the hour.

At last they appeared, behind schedule and in a hurry. They gained the roof by way of an access stair bolted to the alley side of the building and moved, single file, through a maze of refuse, rusty stovepipes, dilapidated top sheds, and smoldering chimneys. They approached from her left. Six of them were trailed out behind a large beast of a man. The line passed within reach of Grace. They gathered around a trapdoor leading down into the building, just to her right, laden with ill-gained goods and reeking of innocent blood. The snow-muffled silence of the roof bolstered their confidence. Their tiny minds were giddy with the night's take. *Tis daybreak, and dirty hands itch for trinkets of gold and for silver coin*, she mused.

Four brigands would die with the greedy gleam still in their eyes. The big one she would save for questioning. The second would be used to convince the big one to talk. She was, in truth, gargoyle, a stone edifice, lying in wait. And the unwary had entered her circle and triggered the spell that would unleash her wrath.

Flavin—Kamiko

The snow was coming down in thick waves, falling at a hard angle out over the river but swirling and churning in every direction where they were gathered beneath the lea of the lighthouse. All the world seemed devoid of color, save for Siruis's bright blue eyes and Dairei's thick crimson mane. Golden-red strands were drifting up and around her head and shoulders like living tendrils in the twisting wind. Silence was all pervasive.

Kamiko looked from face to face. Felene and Siruis were staring at the talisman, obviously cycling through the few possibilities.

Kamiko said, "He was returning it to me, as a challenge. He said his name was Rendur-Kath, of Wroth, called me by name." Both

Felene's brow went up and then dropped into a deep furrow. Kamiko continued with a shallow grin, "Thought I'd finally lost that thing."

"How long?"

Her grin melted away. "Almost a year."

Dairei was more interested in their surroundings, methodically scanning every detail of the bodies, the crenellation, the deck, and even the dark sky lying fat and drifting, just overhead. Uila was standing in still silence to one side, from time to time shaking the gathering snow from his head and withers.

Dairei interjected from a few feet away, her voice distracted, "There was another one. He was standing here," she said, indicating a set of footprints off to one side. Although the snow was quickly filling the tracks scattered over the scene, it offered, for the moment, a distinct outline of every detail. She stepped toward the arched doorway leading back into the building but knelt while only halfway across the deck. Kamiko already knew what Dairei had found, and she drew a deep breath to prepare her heart for telling Felene what must be told.

"Smaller tracks lead in from here, a woman running," Dairei said as she rose and followed Rachel's footprints. "She jumped from here"—tracing the path with her finger, which then rose to point directly to where the warrior had been standing atop the merlon.

Kamiko kept her eyes on Felene's face as the dawning of possibility, then the dawning of reality, washed across her features. Her young face flushed red a single moment before she spoke.

"Elder!" Felene said quietly. "Kamiko, where is Rachel?" Her head jerked from side to side as her eyes searched, in vain, for any sign of the elder sister. Kamiko could see the wheels of thought churning by the hard set of her jaw and the tilt of Felene's head. Exhaustion masked her face, her eyes were swollen and red-rimmed from it. Siruis was still and silent, her eyes distant, as though expecting something. Kamiko's talisman was cradled in her small white hand.

Dairei hopped easily atop the merlon and looked down over the river, tapped the short section of rope still tied to a deck bolt with her toe, and cast Kamiko a questioning look. Kamiko had no doubt that Dairei had the whole scene figured out but was waiting to speak her thoughts out of concern for Felene. When in reality, Felene was drawing her own apt conclusion.

"Sister." She barked. "Where is Danae?" She stepped quickly up to Kamiko and grabbed her arms with no small amount of strength, squared off a mere handbreadth from her face, pleading with her eyes. The tattered cloak slipped from Kamiko's shoulders.

"Danae is safe with Jerim, my friend. The elder—Sister Rachel is gone." The words were like a kick in the chest for both. The flush of red drained from Felene's face as her eyes rolled up in her head. For the second time today, Felene fell bodily against Kamiko and into her able arms, who then lowered her gently onto the embrasure and leaned her back against the merlon. When Kamiko looked up at Dairei, she saw the look of warring thoughts had returned to her eyes, that she was again fingering the scar on her neck.

A quiet whimper from Felene called Kamiko's attention back, as her eyes fluttered for a moment, then welled with tears. She was not fully conscious but not fully unconscious either, drifting in the nether reaches of suffering great loss and living a nightmare. Kamiko was aware of Dairei dropping down to the deck beside her, just behind her peripheral sight, and called to mind Rachel's warning to watch the thief close. The recollection dawned a fraction too late.

Dairei swept her tattered cloak from the deck and laid it across Kamiko's shoulders, a seeming gesture of kindness against the bitter cold. Without warning, Dairei's arms completely encircled Kamiko's waist and then spun her aside, catching her off guard and off balance. She then lassoed a thin wire loop around Felene's ankle and flipped her bodily over the edge of the parapet, sending her plunging toward the river. Almost instantly, Kamiko felt the wire grab around her waist and felt Felene's full weight jerk her toward the embrasure opening.

Kamiko had no time to prepare for how she impacted the stone wall but to sprawl frantically with her arms and legs fully extended in the hope that she could hook enough body parts against the stone to check their fall. As fortune would have it, or by Dairei's design, the path of the wire was just near the inside corner of the embrasure so that Kamiko's body slammed and wedged neatly and securely against the wall face. Felene's full weight impacted across Kamiko's midsection like a mule kick. On the instant, all motion stopped. In the span of a single breath, Dairei had immobilized both Kamiko and Felene and was standing over Siruis.

Kamiko was pinned with her right shoulder and hip against the stone face, looking down at the snow-thickened deck. By turning her head leftward, she could see that Siruis was now lying on her back in the snow.

"I could have killed you both." Dairei stepped nearer Kamiko and knelt to where they could speak face-to-face, "You and the sister. Still could, Hoshi." She paused. "Remember that."

Kamiko's breath would not come without great effort. She snapped out her left hand, grappling for Dairei's face, but fell a handbreadth short in her reach. Dairei did not so much as blink. "I am taking her, Hoshi. But do not fret over it, she will be well kept. She is worth the king's ransom, ten times over, to me." She rose and dropped a small dagger to almost within Kamiko's reach. "Cut the sister loose if you wish to stop me. I will allow you to fight for the girl." Then she turned and gently lifted Siruis's still body from the snow and began walking toward the door.

Uila had approached but, with no order from Kamiko, stood in silent expectation as Dairei walked away. She stopped before the opening and turned. "I am truly sorry," she said, "for the loss of your elder friend. She was, without a doubt...the best of us." After a moment of reflection, while she looked plaintively upon Siruis's white face, the brigaunt again turned toward the door.

Calling Uila to action was not an option, though he would assail Dairei on command. She would most likely kill him outright, and he had brute force with little finesse, thereby a danger to Siruis as well.

Kamiko would not send Felene plunging to her death. The wire around her waist felt as though it was attached to a belt or a band meant to spread the impact of weight, undoubtedly part and parcel of Dairei's climbing and rappelling apparatus. It would take the weight without breaking.

She anchored her left palm against the icy granite embrasure wall and pushed with all her strength, loosening the weight which held her right arm pinned beneath her ribs. She then began drawing her right arm out to where she could get both hands against the wall. She felt the skin on her forearm and elbow being slowly stretched and torn but ignored the flare of pain and jerked hard. Her arm popped free, and she immediately slapped the palm against the wall and pushed.

Kamiko's body moved away from the wall enough to bring the dagger into reach of her left hand. With fluid-quick motion, she snatched up the dagger, cocked her arm, focused on a fingernail-sized point between Dairei's shoulders, and launched the weapon hard and fast. It was a long throw. The motion caused her right hand to slip under the combined weight of her and Felene, which twisted her body and altered the throw a fraction.

She knew she'd lost her precarious hold and felt a sudden surge of motion as Felene started the plunge, Kamiko tethered and in tow. Her right shoulder, her back, and the back of her head were raked painfully across the cornered edge as Felene's dangling weight dragged her across the embrasure. She managed to hook the fingers of her trailing right hand momentarily on the edge but without enough effect to even slow the quick traverse.

Just as Felene's weight flung Kamiko out into open air, her eyes caught sight of Dairei for a fleet moment. Still cradling Siruis carefully to her chest, Dairei was on one knee, the leather-bound hilt of the dagger protruding from her left shoulder. It would be a serious wound, from which she would never fully heal, a nagging bone-deep ache, forever marking the moment, not only in her shoulder but equally in her mind.

The plunge began in earnest.

The fall was long and cold, howling wind and snowflakes pelting her face from below. Yet the dark churning water was at her feet on the instant. Kamiko had only the time it took to *climb* the wire connecting her to Felene, bringing them together midplummet. Felene's bright eyes were open and alert, and she clasped one hand with Kamiko's. She would hit head and shoulders first, whereas Kamiko had used Felene's weight against the wire to pull her feet under her. Felene may not survive.

An almost childish notion swept over Kamiko, and her ire rose to fully vented fury. The bad guys would win! The odd warrior Rachel killed was simply an agent, his death mattered nothing to them. A warrior's cry of wild and furious abandon began quickly rising in her chest, her only remaining means of attack.

*****

Without warning, their headlong plummet paused, leaving Kamiko and Felene suspended in place for so short a span it may well not be counted. Yet for all Kamiko could tell, it may have been days' long.

There dwelt another manifestation nearby, and no simple ghostly specter but a being vastly more real than even those things "material." The irony drew Kamiko's thoughts and seemed to lend importance to the slowing of motion around her. She allowed her voice to speak the thought aloud.

"That I, a mortal fleshy thing, should deem the realm of angels somehow less substantial than our terra firma, simply because I cannot see it."

She could feel power coursing through Hun'jotzimon, could feel anger, pure and fierce, pressing against the very fabric of the sword. It was a brutal and wild thing yet not of chaos but of purpose. And in that fractionary moment, the still face of the rolling Black River within her hand-reach, it all clarified. From the outset, the sword had not approached her from another place, from some distant heavenly realm. She knew the anger dwelling in Hun'jotzimon intimately. It was her own. The odd face she'd seen in the mirror was less real to her than the sword and far less familiar.

She felt the silence collapse and anticipated the abrupt return of the onrush of motion.

*****

The cry on her voice returned as well and resolved into a single clear note. Hun'jotzimon responded to Kamiko's rage, to her readiness to use any means to bring about her will. The sword simply matched her tone and sang as well. And for that moment, the power of Hun'jotzimon flared hot in Kamiko, and she brought that power to bear in the physical realm of man and beast.

Simply she rebuked the material elements about her conspiring to bring their death. An observer, such as Jerim, perched against the rocky wall, or Danae, huddled shivering beneath the dark stones, saw only an abrupt halt in Kamiko and Felene's plummet. It was momentary. They dropped gently below the surface of the water and were swept away. Kamiko could feel the presence of Danae, Felene, and Jerim like roaring fires in a black night. Yet in her ears, only the rumbling quiet of being submerged in moving water and all around her the stillness that came with being one with that flow. Then Jerim's fierce presence engulfed them entirely, encircling them both with the steely bulk of one arm. He drew them to the surface with such ease they may well have been only rag dolls slung across his massive shoulder. Felene's eyes were again closed, her mouth hanging open. But she was breathing.

He stepped up the rocky embankment, into the wide throat of a fast-moving maelstrom of dark feathers and turbulent twisting wind.

The falling snowflakes were quickly shrinking in size and, in moments, became pouring stinging sleet, only partially blocked by the horde of birds overhead. The midday sun was lost behind the ever-darkening sky of thick clouds, and Kamiko heard the faint but distinct sound of thunder rumbling down the canyon.

Jerim set Kamiko on her feet but laid Felene's unconscious form gently on the icy stones of the rough embankment, then spread his wide mass above her to shield her from what sleet made it past the birds. Danae quickly but carefully scampered to Felene's side, obviously chilled to the bone, judging by the constant shuddering in all her parts and the pure whiteness of her face. Kamiko could see that Danae was struggling to simply remain conscious. She dropped to Felene's side opposite Danae and pressed her icy fingers to Felene's neck.

"Her pulse is very slow," she retorted to Danae, and immediately realizing her mistake, she quickly finger-spelled the word *slow*.

Danae had already begun working to free Felene from her soaked leather armor, growling and fussing in her wordless chatter. The clasp and banding holding the front and backplates together were freezing. When she understood Kamiko's word, a flush of panic momentarily colored her cheeks and clouded her eyes. On impulse, Danae put all of her weight into simply tearing the banding from the plate, a doomed and wasted effort. All three knew well enough—Felene was in mortal danger.

Kamiko knew that she and Danae would soon follow if they could not find warmth very quickly. She was still tethered to Felene with Dairei's cloak and wire, and though beginning to quake harder and harder from the cold, she quickly found the hook and eye that held the cloak about her waist. She had it off in a short moment and shook it hard several times. Most of the water soaked into the cloak had frozen and fell away in small clouds of tiny flecks that were drawn upward, vanishing into the maelstrom.

Danae's chin sank momentarily to her chest as her arms fell limp. Her fingers slipped from Felene's armor, and she fell backward but into Jerim's quick hand. The motion and contact was enough to jar her senses awake, and she bolted upright with a yelp, though her eyes were glassy slits.

As Kamiko flipped the cloak around Danae's shoulders, she became more acutely aware of the birds, noticing their numbers growing greater by the moment, much greater. They had formed an impenetrable barrier against the sleet but had churned up a strong wind of bitter cold.

This drew her notice to her own state of dress. Her shirt was in tatters. For all practical purposes, without the cloak, she was mostly bare-skinned from the waist up.

She caught the twinkling flicker of firelight from the corner of her eye, downriver. She looked up to face Jerim. They were not far from the first of the river piers of Flavin. Even with Jerim's help, it would be difficult to climb out across icy stone, and the cold would be unbearable. The warmest place she could think of, for the moment, was back in the water. This was the summer runoff from the highlands, not the ice-melt of winter.

As though from reading Kamiko's quick scan of stone and water, Jerim reacted to her unspoken idea and lifted Felene with both hands to his chest, enfolding her within his body heat. Kamiko quickly adjusted the cloak to better fit Danae and fastened the clasp at her waist. She then looped the lasso end securely about her own wrist, gathered the long slack between them into a tight coil, and handed it to Danae. The girl's eyes were blinking rapidly.

Kamiko signed the single symbol for *mount* and hooked a thumb toward her back, then turned and crouched low for easier access. Danae's darting quickness and nimble feet were gone. She moved with an awkward stiffness in her arms and legs, simply leaned forward against Kamiko's broad back and let her head drop against Kamiko's shoulder. The warmth between them was immediate. This brought enough spark to Danae that she scampered quickly onto Kamiko's back, arms around her neck, legs about her waist.

Without hesitation, Kamiko made for the dark water and climbed down into the churn on jagged rocks slick with snow. The pull of the river was immediate and strong against her legs, but it felt warm. As Jerim moved in close behind her, the horde above them began to dissipate and was gone in moments. The sleet returned in earnest.

"We must be away from this stony embankment, lest it beat us severely," Jerim's voice was deep yet with the tightness of lingering youth. He offered Kamiko his massive left hand, moving past her into deeper water. He held Felene's unconscious form lengthwise, drawn to his body with his right arm. "You hold to me that you may free yourself as you see fit. I will draw us out into the deep and back again. We float from here."

"It is not far," Kamiko said, "so don't take us too deep." She took his hand and let him lead her and Danae down into the water. It only felt swift for the moment it took them to be one with the current, then the world became very still and serene. The relative warmth of the water suddenly eased the quaking in Kamiko's body, and a sad bliss settled over her. The only sound was the quiet hiss of sleet on the water.

She looked over her shoulder to find Danae's bright eyes peering back from only an extra nose-length away. Her brow was high with anticipation, her head speckled with tiny flecks of ice. She no longer shuddered with the convulsions of cold, rather that of weeping silently.

Jerim was on his back, scissor-kicking gently with his legs, Kamiko and Danae in tow, and pulled them away from the danger of being dragged across the submerged perils of the stony bank. His face was a mask of calm focus, but Kamiko knew his thoughts burned for Siruis.

Her own concerns were divided between Siruis and Uila. He was without command. And though his training would send him back to the last place he was stabled, he would not perceive Dairei as a threat. She hoped the thief would not spend her vengeance on Uila.

The brassy deep moan of a bargeman's horn rolled across the surface of the water from downriver. In a few moments, the answer would peel back from the higher-sounding trumpet of the pier master. A languid calm opened inside her.

They would survive this. Dairei did not possess the power to alter Siruis's path. There were principalities at work which Dairei held no belief in, so she could not comprehend the magnitude of those watching over Siruis, neither their severity nor their size, and certainly not their numbers.

The downpour of sleet began to falter, gradually at first, and then it abruptly stopped altogether. Kamiko again turned to Danae and, with her free hand, pinched her nose closed as she pursed her lips and puffed out her cheeks. Kamiko figured her own head was as sparkling as Danae's, it felt just as frozen. She nodded vigorously and loosened the hold she had on Kamiko's neck and around her waist.

Kamiko felt Danae's chest swell with a deep breath just as she slid from Kamiko's back and down the length of her arm. The young girl nestled the crook of her elbow into Kamiko's and let their bodies separate. They sank below the wrinkled surface together, back into the quiet that was almost silence. Her head was immediately soothed by the warmer waters, and the last of the tension of cold faded. She could scarcely remember being in a more relaxed calm but understood with perfect clarity the overpowering effect of sorrow on her state of mind.

Thoughts of Rachel coiled and twisted through every part of Kamiko's fiber, her name echoing again and again in her heart. An odd irony struck her—floating motionless and weightless yet speeding through the belly of the canyon faster than she could run. It required only that she fix her sight either on the water or on the black canyon walls.

Rachel's death was squarely upon Kamiko's shoulders but only from a pointless, selfish perspective. Kamiko would not dishonor the woman's great and glorious life nor squander her sacrifice with meaningless guilt. She died as she wished. It occurred to Kamiko that Rachel had bumped the very path of history from one course to an entirely different unfolding. Not only Kamiko's impact, but Danae's presence in history would be significant as well. There was no doubt in Kamiko's mind that God had set Danae's path in place with great care.

Kamiko had been holding onto Jerim's open hand, her fingers hooked over his first knuckle, with her wrist and forearm across his palm. She felt his hand close firmly around hers, followed by a sudden jerk that brought her head abruptly above the water. The motion caused Danae's elbow lock to slip, which, in turn, set the girl scampering back up Kamiko's arm so that she exhaled with an easy puff of air only inches from Kamiko's ear.

Again all the world had changed. The dark gray underbelly of the clouds was now awash with shimmering bright yellow and rolling dancing red. The whole of the canyon, mottled in black stone and white snow, appeared to sway in the bright hues and jerking shadows of a massive inferno raging far above their heads.

Danae's arms encircled and tightened around Kamiko's neck, and she yowled like an adolescent lion, more animal than human. Kamiko's compulsion to shriek was no less potent, though hers was an open-throated yelp when she saw the enormity of the pyre burning above them. She carefully rolled herself and Danae around to where they were facing back up the channel, floating backward like Jerim. The fire was not directly above them, but it was all the way at the top of the canyon, hanging out over the water, and the distance from the fire to the water made it seem so. Jerim began scissor-kicking beneath the water again, and soon they had overtaken the current and were moving even more swiftly downriver.

"The lighthouse!" Felene's voice crackled quietly from where she lay on her back on Jerim's chest. Kamiko was fairly certain Felene was not yet aware of that fact.

The serene odd quiet of the river was shattered by the sudden blaring of many horns. Deep bellowing blasts issued from just downriver and were quickly answered by horns of similar depth from a greater distance upriver, three fast brassy howls in call and three in response.

High piercing trumpet wails began sounding from all directions at once. Kamiko knew them to be the Horns of Flavin, Lord Merritt's own trumpeter signal corps, echoing around the canyon walls. It was another in a long list of gifts from the wealthy lord to the people at large. Many of the signals were commonly understood by the populace and were posted at many places across the city. These calls were, to Kamiko's surprise, not only a call to fight the fire but a call to arms as well. Lord Merritt had seen fit to treat it as an attack, and with the two as yet unexplained fires, he was wise to do so. Besides the lighthouse was constructed mostly of carved stone, and judging from the sheer enormity of the inferno, it had to have been set and that with a great deal of effort.

Felene let out a throaty yelp of surprise, drawing first Kamiko's attention, and then Danae's. Felene's face and eyes were puffy with fatigue and from the cold, and she was all but standing on Jerim's massive chest, ready, it appeared, to dive into the water and swim for her life. Even swollen, her eyes bulged slightly as fear and understanding battled.

"Sister," Kamiko said in a gentle but humored tone of voice, "allow me to introduce my friend, Jerim."

Chapter 2

Ravencroft City—Grace

Odd that she'd carried it for so long, through mostly sleepless nights and darkly wicked dreams, only to feel it churning as if it were a new thing. Perhaps it was the recent and sudden surge of violence which drove it to the forefront of her thoughts, this indwelling sense of panic, that all of her meditation and prayer could not assuage. Her soul was jittery inside her chest, a swollen knot of constant doubt, distracted and angry. She felt how she imagined a blind woman must feel standing in a bustling noisy market, trying desperately to find the one person who was still and silent. She knew in her core that something was there, but she could find no single trace to support the notion.

Parzon was still more than two years missing, and Yannis, her second-in-command, was in custody. But someone was in control. Grace knew a feint when she saw one, and every move Dairei Parzon's crew was making smacked of stratagem too remote for them to see and understand. A single plan.

It was a distraction.

She doubted Parzon was dead. But if she was anywhere within news-shot of Ravencroft, she would have long since returned. And angry that return would be.

It was midday yet darkly overcast. The narrow space of air between the bottom of the cloud blanket and the multitiered spread of Ravencroft was crisp and clear, neither the slightest moisture nor the tiniest wave of heat to distort the vision. Frozen but by no means unmoving, the city lay in countless layers of white relief, as if chiseled into form by the very hands of God.

From Grace's elevated view, her own rooftop at the edge of the upper city, the lower levels of the wide valley teemed with the people of Ravencroft City. Being buried beneath a layer of snow was nothing new to the northland city. The snow had simply arrived far too early in the season and without warning.

Twelve centuries ago, Ravencroft was established as the northernmost city of the monarchical rule of Cairistonia. The city was built in the valley which opened from the only viable pass through the massive mountain ranges, giving the powerful merchant class access to the northern lands beyond. The Crown managed to hold the area under control for a bit over four hundred years before it relinquished the entire area to an oligarchical government, headed by the vastly wealthy Riplin family. At eight hundred leagues' distance, it was simply too difficult and costly to manage. Seven hundred and fifty years later, Baron Vladimir Riplin still maintained the Riplin family crest as ruler.

But she was not here to gander. Long ago, Grace had divided the city into distinct sections and certain patterns, relevant and known only to her. From her rooftop, she could see the entire southern area of the city, as if it was built in miniature on a plotting table in the war room.

As was her regular habit, she used the tip of her sword to plot the activity patterns of Parzon's crew, beginning with the most recent and working backward. Blood still staining the tip and working edge of her sword distracted her, and a sudden weariness settled in her shoulders and arms. She felt the call to still her thoughts and get some rest. It had been two days this time. Too long.

Just before she turned to head downstairs to hot food and warm rest, she lifted her sword and touched—if only in her line of sight—the next spot in the city, her area of engagement for the night. Baron

Riplin's crew would monitor the location until she arrived after nightfall. It had taken no less than six hard months to find it, Parzon's urban hideout. But following a series of raids, which turned out to be red herrings, and with a tidbit of information gained from interrogating Yannis, Sister Grace and Baron Riplin believed they had at last found the real one.

Tonight they would begin a two-part operation, first to investigate and second to eradicate. She needed Felene for this. Grace felt as though she was working with only half her facilities when Felene's might was not guarding her flank. More so, she needed the balancing effect of Felene's compassionate spirit. Out of recent necessity, Grace had become more brutal than she reckoned she'd ever been. Yannis would never fully recover from her visit with him earlier in the morning. Some other part of Grace would bear the scar of that conversation.

Sheathing her sword, she turned toward the door and lifted her fingers to the nape of her neck and pulled free a small tie-string. It was at one end of a long leather-crafted hair glove which was immediately forced open by the thick bundle of shimmering black braids it contained. She drew it completely off as her hand fell away and shook her head vigorously. Thousands of tiny but long braids splayed outward, like the end of a large frayed rope, before falling to rest across her back and shoulders and rising in a silken black springy mass over the top of her head. She'd had it pulled in tight since she stepped off this same roof two days earlier.

The sweet odor of home-cooked food met her three full steps before she pushed open the door to her dwelling and stepped inside.

Flavin—Kamiko

A third layer was carefully swept over Kamiko, Danae, and Felene, huddled together as they were. Two soft woolen blankets and the third an oiled canvas sheet. Already the oarsmen were pulling for the dock. Already blissful warmth was driving the hard ache of the cold away. Concerned faces, all of them stern, all cast in shades of gray and of shadows blinked in and out of Kamiko's sight in quick succession. Men rowing hard for the dock leaned into and out of view across the slight opening of the blankets pulled over her head and face. She held Felene, seated beside her but lying across her lap, and Danae, who was curled into a ball at Kamiko's other side. Both were unconscious. All fell quiet but for a single voice, softly calling cadence and oars working against wood and water.

A second deeper voice spoke a gruff but quiet word, "Faster!"

The speed of the cadence increased gradually, answered in kind by four oars acting as one.

The sisters were facing the rear of the small boat, and as the bow came to bear upon the dockward side of the river, Kamiko could see out into the deeper waters.

Floating like a great dark plank of flat wood, a massive river barge sat motionless. Spotters and guild hands had seen Kamiko, Danae, and Felene floating near the edge of the deep and set about to rescue them. They were in no danger. Jerim had simply submerged to avoid being seen. He was under the boat and helped when the men hoisted Felene's substantial weight out of the water. They found her to be surprisingly light until they got her into the boat, as her weight seemed to return to normal. Danae was lifted from Kamiko's shoulder by one of the scullers with a single muscled arm.

Just as Jerim's hand had come to press against the bottom of her feet, Kamiko remembered she was ill-clad for being in a boat filled with men. It mattered little, as no one was paying attention but the pair who helped her aboard. With Jerim's push, she appeared to have easily flipped her feet and legs up into the boat by simply pulling with her hands on the side. An unfurled blanket engulfed her from behind almost instantly, pulled down upon her head and around her shoulders, then clasped gently closed at her throat by a calloused and meaty fist.

A rising mist began folding in behind the boat, obscuring the sight of the barge. The fire atop the gorge was out, and all shades had returned to gray and black. The wind lay dead still across the water, and the chill of the air felt to have dropped suddenly.

"Head fer twenty-three," said the gruff voice.

"Aye, Captain," answered the voice that had been calling cadence. And though he fell silent for a moment, the scullers never slackened their oar strokes. He spoke quietly to the steersman at the rudder. "Point one six starboard and heave 'er inta two three at a run, all the way to the back."

She could hear the men mumbling quietly but could not make out what they were saying beyond a couple of punctuated words.

The captain replied quietly but gruff, his gravelly voice a mix of command and kindness, "Keep 'er steady, boys."

One of the oarsmen asked, "Who's upped the wind, Cap'n? Never seen such."

"N'er," another grumbled.

Silence followed the unanswered question like a creeping predator, seeming to mute even the chatter of the oars against wood and water.

Kamiko felt a large hand rest against her back and the captain speaking from behind her in a near whisper, "Keep yer-selves covered well, Sisters. They always be eyes tallyin' at the gates." He pushed gently against her back. "Fold over a bit, yer too big to pass without regard. You'd be better if you were a-layin' on the bottom, like a bundle of stock."

A wash of mild surprise passed over Kamiko. How did he know they were sisters?

"Forget that, Captain," she replied, more brusquely than she intended. She wondered if he knew them specifically, or if he only recognized them as sisters of the Order. She allowed the concern to pass. Felene, outfitted as she was in her armor, could be no other than a full sister of the Order. And Kamiko, in the tattered state she was in and the three of them floating down the river from beneath the burning lighthouse, made it a good observation on the captain's part.

"My apologies, Captain," she said and bowed her head. "My sister is in bad shape. The floor of your skiff would do her no good. And the little one here has seen enough for one day."

"Aye." He chuckled. "Take comfort, lass. I'll sneak you in unseen and unharmed. Care for yer'n sisters. Have no worries about it." And he patted her back before turning again to his duties. "Bastion, come back over from port and take us in at two six."

"Aye, Captain."

"And slow us down a bit," he said and paused, "long run to do with four."

Kamiko needed to know. "Captain," she blurted, again with more force than she intended. Her military habits were never far away and were by no means timid.

When his broad hand pressed again on her back, she started anew, with less of the command so easy on her lips.

"Captain," she said, "do you know who we are, who I am?"

He was behind them, so she could not see his face as he could not see hers, but she felt his eyes on her back in contemplation.

At last he spoke, very quietly and much closer to her, "Aye, Sister, I do."

The spoken cadence had resumed but low and quiet. And they'd slowed considerably.

"My eldest son was aboard the *Jacksail* when she was taken and went down under Wilam's pirate crew, eight year back. He was among them ye saved, Sister."

She recalled the night easily. It was a bad one. The *Jacksail* was one of many huge river freighters sailing the Antarius. She and Bartol had come upon the attack by chance.

"I remember, good sir," she said, nodding at the recollection. They had slain the pirates to the last man. "What is your son's name, Captain?"

The soft cadence stopped, and a second broad hand rested for a moment on her back. "I am Bastion, Sister."

The scullers continued their quiet oar work without interruption. From time to time, the bright peel of a trumpet or the sullen bellow of a deep barge horn wafted across the water and through the rising mist.

And though it was midafternoon with the day still freezing, dark and full of foreboding, Kamiko's spirit felt an unexpected wash of warmth and peaceful joy spread outward from the two hands lying gently against her back. It was then she realized, the mist was freezing as it rose from the warmth of the river, becoming the tiniest flecks of swirling frozen snowflakes and engulfing the low boat within a blanket of concealment.

Her thoughts flew at once to the madness she had felt upon her first encounter with Siruis, to the decades of misery and death Kamiko Hoshi had unleashed by her very lifestyle as a warrior. In that moment, those months ago, she had seen the tally of her life collectively in a single framework. The horrors had easily outweighed the joys she personally witnessed, encasing her life in brutality and butchery. The effect on her spirit had been devastating.

Yet here were the hands of a father and son against her body, love and joy like she'd never known pouring over her. And this was the result of her sword and fist coming to bear in careful but wanton butchery, on the deck of a burning and doomed ship. She and the mighty Bartol had saved fewer than fifty of a crew of almost two hundred souls. Captain and son returned their quiet attention to the duties of the vessel.

"Lord, God of all creation," she whispered under her breath, "thank you."

Danae was like a feather against her, curled atop a folded blanket with her arms and legs pressed against Kamiko's thigh, her head nestled into the crook of Kamiko's elbow and waist. Felene was seated closely against Kamiko on the other side. She had eased Felene down to lay across her lap when first seated in the skiff. They had chosen to remove Felene's armor before setting to oar to get her dried and warmed. It was to be a long row.

Felene's limp weight bore little more substance than had Danae's. She was not simply easy to move, she was light in Kamiko's hands, lying across her legs like a thin blanket.

Kamiko leaned forward over Felene and lay across her strong back. She drew Danae up into the bundled warmth and closed her eyes. She stayed in the warm darkness of blankets and breath, not allowing the sight of angels to open before her. She needed the calm sad serenity to last a bit longer. The presence of those *immortalis* beings had too strong an effect on her, calling the Warrior to the forefront, casting all but the one emotion to the side—the passion for victory. She longed to be the sister, to use her strength for comfort, as was Rachel's way.

From the moment Kamiko lost sight of Siruis as she plunged over the rampart, Kamiko had locked upon her powerful sister's spirit and maintained the connection without effort. She knew exactly where Siruis was. For all that either of them could tell, they sat side by side in a low deep cave across a newly built fire, opposite Dairei Parzon. No words were being spoken, nor had any sound transpired between them. Dairei's wound had been cleaned, stitched, and dressed, her shoulder tightly bound, all by Siruis's own hands. Yet without the healing touch. In Siruis's right hand, Kamiko's talisman burned with a twisting dancing silver flame. She recalled seeing it the first time, from three hundred leagues away, a glistening beacon. To find it was her first crucible.

Above Siruis, Hun'jotzimon hovered in shimmering silver majesty, hidden from mortal eyes. Should all the armies of the world combine against her, Siruis would know no harm. Dairei presented no danger, rather she was a palette upon which Siruis was blending the shades that would become, in full, Dairei Parzon.

Kamiko drew her breath slowly, sending a wave of calm from foot to crown with each release. The feel of the boat beneath her, of damp wood and rope, leather boots and raspy voices, the fish oil and river stink permeating everything, all conspired between those breaths, and a small sanctuary gently opened around her. For many minutes, she simply hung there in silence, Felene and Danae across her lap. Her body felt an exact kin to the blankets they were covered in, a simple and cumbersome garment, a vessel not unlike Uila, a physical mount for her true being, that of her spirit, to ride upon the battlefield of *Materiel.* In this small open place, she felt the separation in full. She was a tiny glistening speck upon the forehead of the golem known as Kamiko Hoshi.

And leaning against her in tranquil silence was Siruis. How they could be miles apart yet side by side—Kamiko in a slow skiff and Siruis at Dairei's fire a mere thousand paces beyond the lighthouse—was a thing Kamiko wasted no time pondering. She accepted it as reality based purely on faith, although, she reflected, the same was true for every living human.

"We are no mere actors on a stage." She recalled the words of Bartol. "But we have forgotten we are not in a real world. We are blinded by the very illumination meant to shine upon our faces, hiding all which lies beyond."

She felt a gentle shift in their course and drew her bearing back into the pitch-dark of closed eyes and smelly blankets. A broad hand lay momentarily across her back, Bastion's deep soft voice bidding her to lie very still.

"We be approaching the gate," he explained, "three minutes out."

Although muffled by the blankets and some distance, Kamiko could hear the long peel of a lone trumpet rise above the quiet day, bright and clear, a high sharp tone, nonetheless, sorrowful.

Chapter 3

Ravencroft City—Grace

As Grace slept, she was assailed with wild and vivid dreams.

She stares across a dark courtyard at a strangely dressed man, someone whose bearing is regal, the confidence of royalty even in stillness yet wearing the rags of a long and toilsome journey. A curved dagger hangs from his hand.

Sorrow enshrouds him.

A blink—he is no longer in sight. Her vantage is from above the city, though from some other rooftop than her own. A series of loud staccato pops begins in the distance and quickly draws closer to her, followed by bright blooms springing upward into the city night, fiery plumes cutting a straight line from the south near the river to just below her.

Another blink, and again her vantage has shifted. She is now crouched beneath the boughs of an aged willow, heavy with growth, watching some large feral creature as it hunts for her. All of time and motion slows, and beyond that moment, Grace can see—nothing. Abyssal.

Her own voice shrieking jerked Grace to full consciousness. She was flushed and hot beneath the covers and thrashed momentarily, until they lay in a pile on the floor beside her. As she grew still, her eyes fell on the door. The slight motion and sudden light of it opening a sliver drew her notice. A full open handbreadth below the handle, she saw a single large green eye peer through and dart around for a moment before coming to rest affixed upon Grace's eyes.

Even the deep weariness she felt in her bones and the odd confusion from such a strange and disturbing dream could not keep a grin from half-forming on Grace's dark face. As if her slight smile was his cue to act, Tilly, a small boy of three, pressed his face against the opening, just enough that his entire head popped through. His bright eyes appeared overlarge on his freckled white face, his mouth almost too small. Golden locks of loose curls completely overwhelmed him. The look he wore was of pure joyous mischief. Poking his head into Grace's room was certainly a breach of the house rules. Respecting a person's privacy was paramount in her house, as there were eight children and three other women living there.

Above Tilly's head, through the gap in the door, she could see the boy's mother as she spied the infraction. She looked just as Grace imagined Tilly would look at that age—bright-green eyes, freckles, and her mass of golden hair drawn into a large bush hanging from the back of her head. As if he could feel the power of his mother's eye, his face morphed into wide-eyed concern. He cocked his bushy golden head slightly, listened momentarily, and then bolted away, leaving the door to drift slowly shut.

The sweat, which had turned Grace's bedclothes slightly damp, cooled quickly, and retrieving the discarded blankets suddenly seemed like a good idea. Just as she was reaching for the pile, she heard a high shout of surprise, followed immediately by the sound of pots and pans being scattered across the stone floor of the kitchen. The number 1 rule of the house: when danger is imminent, make a lot of noise, preferably by banging pots and pans together. No louder alarm could be raised. Her feet touched the cold floor, moving fast. She snatched up her sword and was through the door before the noisy pans had stopped bouncing and sliding.

Every face in the room turned from the large bay window of the living area to Grace and back to the window. Bethany, a young initiate of the sisterhood and part-time resident of the house, had her short sword in hand and was waving everyone back behind her.

She did not wait for Grace to ask. "Someone at the window! A man…armed…going up," she said, pointing her sword at the top corner of the huge window.

The dark woman's movements were the perfect embodiment of her namesake. She was naturally possessed of a fluid grace, which was obvious in all her actions yet which belied her ferocity and efficiency when in battle. It was widely believed that Grace was Kamiko Hoshi's only equal in a fight. Whereas Kamiko Hoshi was known for her strength and her speed, Grace was possessed of a double portion of speed. She floated over the couch and a foot table and had her face to the window in an instant. It was late in the dark afternoon.

The two-story house was situated at the very edge of the cliff-ridge separating the ancient upper city from the sprawl of the lower-city masses. Grace had chosen the location for that very reason. She could keep a watchful eye on what she considered *her* city. She'd commissioned the addition of the large window and the roof-deck before she moved in.

She quickly scanned the side of the house where Bethany had pointed and saw nothing, then continued the search all the way around the perimeter of the window. Nothing. She looked back to the initial spot and stilled her eyes. After only a moment of focusing on small details, she got the sense that she was seeing something out of place but could not make it out.

Oddly her thoughts flashed to the decorative bushes currently overthrowing the front of her house. Through pure neglect, weeds had flourished among the flowering variegated shrubs, so they appeared to be single plants bearing more than one leaf type. Then she saw it.

After seventeen years living in the house, she'd never stood at the window and really *looked* at the outside walls. She'd seen every aspect of the house many times over but had never focused on the details. Now she could just make out a bulk of darkness where none should be. There was no sun to cast shadows.

As if made aware it had been spotted by Grace's lingering study, the shadow moved, and she could see every detail with ease. What she determined was a man, kicked out from where he'd been clinging to the side of the house. Instead of falling, he swung out over the 350-foot drop on a thin tether line, one arm already raised and bringing a hollow tube to bear on Grace's chest. Most would have hesitated and died. Grace sprang straight up, spinning and yelling an order to Bethany as the window shattered. Something tiny punched her in the side and spun her even faster, and blood misted momentarily from beneath her arm. It felt akin to a heavy spear, glancing off her ribs, a battlefield memory Grace would never forget. She knew it was not serious.

She simply spun freely with the extra momentum, adding another complete rotation to the circuit, and came down exactly as she'd intended. She snapped her head to the windowless opening and jerked back, interrogating the scene with a veteran warrior's glance in an instant. The wooden window frame exploded from a second shot close enough to cover her face with stinging splinters.

As ordered, Bethany cleared the large common room quickly, directing everyone into Grace's bedroom at a run. Grace heard the door slam, followed by dead bolts slapping closed. She dropped low and took another split-second look out the window. The assailant was grappling up the side of the house, making for the roof. She made out the shape of a narrow hilt on his back and a curved blade sheathed at his waist.

She bounded over the couch and sprinted for the stairway leading to the roof-access door. Still barefoot and in her thin nightclothes, she burst through the door and onto the snow-covered roof-deck. He had just gained the deck and was rising from a low crouch, drawing both weapons and chuckling down deep in his chest.

His entire body was covered in a mottled dark wrapping, only his eyes showing through a narrow opening. They were as dark as the rest of him. Yet Grace could sense no rage or malice, only the stance of determined confidence, the detached calm of a man simply doing his job. Judging by the language of only his body movements, Grace knew that he, like she, enjoyed his chosen profession immensely. He was in no hurry.

She felt no need to wait longer and advanced, her sword coming out of the scabbard with a quiet hiss that ended in a clear high ring.

Much to her surprise, he stepped back one measured pace, holding his dagger hand out in a signal to wait, bobbing his head a couple of times. His sword was down and behind him, giving Grace an obvious and great advantage for the moment. She stopped short but kept at the ready, her sword high above her head. He stooped slightly and dropped the dagger at his foot, then drew something from a fold in the body wrapping at his ankle, retrieved the dagger, and stood. She noticed three small jewels dangling from the pommel and marked the oddity in her mind.

By Grace's reckoning, he was only stalling for time. She stepped forward again, but again he only held up his dagger hand, imploring her to pause. Then in a voice she would never forget, and with an accent she'd never heard, he spoke, "Sister Grace," he said. Tapping his chest with the pommel of his dagger, he continued, "Cauldin-Kath of Wroth." He tossed the item he'd retrieved to the deck between them. She recognized it instantly. It was a cheap golden locket she'd had since childhood. She kept it in her bedroom in a box, locked in her dresser drawer. It had mysteriously vanished months ago.

He straightened for a deep breath before assuming a defensive stance, both weapons coming up. She bounded at him and leapt with a high shriek. Moments into the fight, she realized he'd been preparing for her specifically. He repelled an opening sword barrage that very few people alive could have survived and left her with a hard elbow punch to the nose for the effort. As she separated, he delivered a circle kick into her gut with such speed that she did not consciously *see* the move. She certainly felt the deck when she landed flat on her back and slid several feet.

Grace was on her feet with a twist and a kick, expecting to be hard-pressed by the strange assassin. Of that notion she held no doubt. She had been studied from the shadows for no small measure of time. The pendant was proof of that. But no attack was forthcoming. He was right where she'd left him, his feet together, arms loose at his side, his face tilted slightly skyward with his eyes closed. In that single moment, he reminded her of Kamiko. There was nothing haughty or derisive about his physical attitude, he was simply comfortable and calm. Something told her he was at the end of a long journey. He was contented, happy even. And without a doubt, he was there to kill her.

She allowed a one-sided grin to rise with the thought and spoke aloud, "Not so original!" She led back into the fight with what appeared to be the very same assault she'd opened with. This time, however, she had a smattering of observation to draw upon. They both knew he could not beat her without wearing her down first. And he'd likely never seen Grace engaged in real combat, only her interaction with common criminals. She projected rage and hesitation, holding her natural fluid speed in check. He drove her back again. But not before she slipped in close and delivered a hard palm-punch to his nose for payment in kind. He nodded his approval as blood darkened his face covering.

She forced a shift in her perspective. Overkill was the answer. She must engage this assassin as if she was facing both Kamiko Hoshi *and* Felene Dresdle. He fought like they did—from a foundation of strength, with years of not only practice but real battle. She lunged again, showing only a slight variation in her third attack. He turned her killing blow with a deft and powerful sweep of his sword, driving her blade low and out, her posture almost crouching on the deck. She unleashed her potential fully, explosive and violent fury. She expected his quick dagger strike, had set him up for it, offered a killing blow too sweet to bypass. She spun thrice, *fast*, on the rise.

His dagger-wielding arm whirled away from his body, severed above the elbow. The second circuit left a heart-deep slash across his chest. The third took him across the throat. Her feet had left the deck completely with the third spin, taking her straight up and right back down into her own footprints. She touched on her toes and rolled away to the side, both to avoid any death-borne slash he may attempt with his sword and to avoid the blood spray, and came up on her feet ready to continue the fight. He staggered backward until he met the low deck rail, his eyes darting wildly and already glazing over, and pitched over into open space. She leapt to the rail and peered over as his body tumbled in the air and slammed into the cliff face far below.

The blood in Grace's veins was boiling with ready fury, her mind fully engaged with all the possibilities of battle. She spun toward each quadrant of the roof-deck battlefield, scanning for his backup assassins, his company of lackeys waiting in hiding to clean up if he should fail. She saw a dark motion atop one of the snow-covered roofs of the buildings directly below, where the lower city was pressed against the foot of the cliff.

The shock of recognition assailed her mind with such force that the memory of the man in her dream momentarily overtook the sight of her eyes. She shook her head and returned her focus to the man in the near distance below. He was the same. His face was turned directly toward where she stood, though he was too far away to make out details. He raised his hand high above his head and slowly waved his arm, seemingly to draw her attention. Suspicion was still a churning ingredient in her chest. She quickly rescanned the close perimeter around her before turning back to the occupied roof below. He waved again but with greater insistence, an agitated motion which made Grace think more trouble was imminent. She returned the wave. He raised both arms over his head. She followed suit, her sword pointing directly skyward. Apparently satisfied, he sprinted across the rooftop to the very edge of the building and hopped atop the retaining wall. Even from the distance, Grace felt he was communicating an air of urgency. She spun again, searching for the danger behind her. Nothing!

She turned back and saw the dark figure below her touching his eyes with both hands, and then he pointed back toward Grace with one outstretched arm. She waved her sword overhead in acknowledgment. To her surprise and confusion, he lowered the arm but only slightly. She looked at the deck but saw nothing she considered to be a danger. When she looked back, he had dropped to his knees and was slapping the outside wall of the building he occupied. She suddenly understood and quickly leaned out over the deck rail and searched the spot where she'd first seen the assassin. Terror struck her to the core. A black box, roughly the size of a helmet, was attached to the wall of her home. The assassin's backup plan!

She shot the dark stranger a momentary look to find him standing again, his arm flying around his head fast. There was no doubt he was telling her to run for her life. She offered two single moments against the need for haste. The first was to salute the man by tapping her sword-bearing fist to her chest, the second to snatch her locket from the bloodied snow as she bolted for the door.

She made the living area at a hard sprint, shouting at the top of her lungs. The strong door of her room flew open, and Bethany sprang into action, her small sword ready for anything. The look of shock on the girl's face reminded Grace that blood was still trickling from her broken nose and had already covered her neck and chest. Grace was shouting, not with the air of panic but of command, and in a moment, Bethany had responded, and everyone was running for the front door. Tilly's huge bright eyes locked onto Grace over his mother's shoulder, his tiny neck reaching to the limit. Then they were on the frozen street, still running and out of her line of sight.

Bethany was the last to exit, shouting over her shoulder, "That's everybody! Let's go, Sister!"

Grace moved toward the windowless opening, where she'd watched over her city for seventeen years but stopped back from the window. Glass was everywhere and her feet were bare. She considering going for the box but instead cast a final glance to the rooftop below. The dark stranger was on his knees, his arms stretched heavenward, his head back, and for all appearances—he was praying.

Grace bolted away, sprinting for the front door when she heard a dull pop. Darkness and silence enveloped her.

Flavin—Kamiko

Felene turned from the window of the coach and offered Kamiko a tired but sincere smile. "It is snowing again," she said. They were moving without haste into the southern skirt of Flavin. The streets were bustling with a daily life infused by the adrenaline of catastrophe so near at hand.

It had been a bit traumatic when Kamiko awakened Felene upon their arrival at dock slip twenty-six. Felene came up swinging, scared and confused, and Kamiko now bore a tender bruise on her cheek in the shape of Felene's elbow. Felene's only apology had been, "I owed you one," delivered with a single raised eyebrow and one-sided grin. Kamiko only nodded her agreement, happy all the thrashing had not sent them over the side and back into the water. It had been no small affair to calm her down and convince her that she could indeed *walk*.

The captain's name was Ezra Kale, someone Felene knew by reputation but had never met. True to his word, he'd brought them in unseen. He'd bundled them into his private boathouse, ordered them without reprieve into the hot shower rooms, clothed them in clean warm clothes that more or less fit, and fed them fresh crusty bread, bean soup, and home-brewed ale, dark and warmed. Kamiko and Felene had fallen on the meal like starving soldiers taking a break from the battlefield, with no single word spoken until they stared into empty bowls. Danae nibbled at the edge of her bread and sipped a couple of spoonful of broth. Her eyes were distant and shimmering and never once lighted upon either of the two sisters.

Before they had finished brushing the crumbs from their mouths, Bastion respectfully ushered them to the carriage house where they climbed into the coach without concern for prying eyes. Felene was getting some of her energy back, though her eyes would glisten randomly, focusing on things not seen. Danae was downcast, though she was aware and responsive, just supremely sad.

They were alone in the carriage and sat in a row on the rear-facing bench, Danae between them. Felene turned back to the curtained window, peering through the small opening she held with her finger. After only a moment of her habitual surveillance, she turned back to face Kamiko. She touched Danae on the knee, drawing the girl's attention to her hands. She spoke in both tongues at once, for Danae's benefit.

"Sister," Felene asked, her voice dark and soft, her island lilt peering through, "how did she die?"

Danae's small white face turned up to look at Kamiko. Expectation, wonder, and pervasive sorrow all dwelt there without reservation. Felene was not asking what had happened.

Kamiko smiled at them both in turn, holding their eyes for a moment, Danae first. It took no effort for serene peace to beam on Kamiko's face. Danae's eyes lifted slightly, her chin rising.

Kamiko spoke with only her hands. "She was singing"—she paused and remembered—"and laughing." She laid her hand gently on Danae's face, then Felene's. "And more so now by far, singing," and she flourished the word expressively with both her hands, "laughing."

Danae's face brightened only slightly. She turned to Felene and back to Kamiko, lifted her small hands and told them, *I saw her.*

Kamiko offered no questioning look, such would project doubt she did not feel. She had seen Danae's cocooned form dangling over the river gorge and knew she'd been hooded as well. She asked simply, "How?"

Danae began her response immediately, but stopped before showing a single sign with her hands. Confusion danced across her young face for a moment before she started again. But again she stopped short before saying anything. She looked first at Felene, then up at Kamiko, apologizing with her face and a shrug of one shoulder. It was plain to the sisters that Danae could not form the explanation with her hands.

She drew a deep breath, shook her head, and then reached out and took a hand in each of hers, Felene to the left and Kamiko to the right. She took another deep breath and exhaled slowly, closed her eyes and lowered her chin almost to her chest, and became perfectly still. The two women shared a look over the top of Danae's head, each silently asking the other what was happening. Neither knew for certain beyond the notion that Danae was going to meditate a bit to gather her thoughts. Such was the way of the sisterhood at times. Patience was paramount.

Without warning or the slightest effort on either of the older sisters' part, the physical veil shifted, and the realm of angels flourished wholly into sight. All three sisters knew Danae had not done this, she'd simply prayed.

Even having experienced the shift once before, Kamiko reeled. Felene was unprepared. Though in truth, neither was Kamiko prepared for what they saw.

They were suspended in the belly of a slowly rolling maelstrom, the coach and the city almost too remote to recognize. A battle was fully engaged, eons ancient. The mode of operation, how the battle was being fought, was based upon authority and not the ability to destroy the enemy. For in this realm, only eternal beings exist, and death has no function, thus the sword is a meaningless tool. The dark spirits are already banished, there is no deeper pit, only levels of the one. Everything which plays out between the two forces would unfold here. For it is in the realm of men that the fallen dwell yet as bound creatures. And the presence of the Almighty was among men as well, that those called to worship him would likewise gain from his strength.

This day God's agents were busy. Eleven points of light billowed up into the ether and shone across land of Cairistonia—Rachel and ten sisters of the Order, including Kamiko and Grace. Kamiko perceived herself to be engulfed in a raging pyre of bright-silver flames, far greater in size than the horde of birds Jerim had called to shield them from the sleet. She knew that even in a place such as this, she was seen as fierce among the angels, both the banished and those still withstanding in the host. Felene and Danae were seeing her in this furious form and were afraid.

Upon hearing Kamiko's dark and silken voice, both sisters became still, their fear suddenly and completely lifted. "Take comfort, Sisters," Kamiko said and held her arms out for them to see the vibrant and wild flames pouring from her. She turned her palm facing upward and gently moved her thumb tip back and forth across her fingertips. Searing white energy dripped like honey from between them, pooling in the palm of her hand for a moment before sizzling away like water on a hot skillet. "God moves mightily across the land this day."

Kamiko, Felene, and Danae looked out over the entire kingly realm of Cairistonia, at its natural darkness, moral decay rampant. But as always, bright rivers and streams and pools of light veined the darkness covering the land in every corner of the kingdom. There were countless individual sparks borne of godly belief, twinkling across Cairistonia like the star field overhead, and eleven explosively bright flares jetting righteous fury into the realm of angels.

To both Kamiko and Felene's surprise, Danae spoke aloud, "Twas here I saw the elder, my sisters, when she fell." Her voice sounded oddly similar to Felene's, too deep for her small size. "She was singing," she said to Kamiko, "and laughing. Her arms were back, like a great beautiful bird."

Kamiko gathered from Danae's demeanor that something more was to come, as her sight turned to inward scenes, and a shudder passed through her. She continued in a very quiet voice, seemingly oblivious to the great and powerful struggle spread around them and spanning the whole of the kingdom.

"One of the angelic ones was waiting, a messenger, I believe, waiting for you, I thought, Sister Kamiko. But I was wrong, it was there for the elder…for Mother." Danae's voice was slowly changing and morphing as she spoke, rising and falling. "I saw her body fall to the river, but I saw the elder stop before the messenger, her body was already empty." The timbre of her voice had fallen to a depth akin to Jerim's and profoundly sorrowful. *She's never heard the sound of a voice speaking*, Kamiko thought.

After a moment, Danae continued, her voice more relative to her size, "She frightened me."

The scene around them pulled at Kamiko's attention, her own distraction drawing Felene's gaze in its wake. She realized that to describe all that was under her view would take years and many thick volumes to pen. The relevancy of size and space no longer held true, and for all the sisters could tell, the whole of the kingdom lay at their feet. They could see the interior of the carriage and the eastern bank of the Antarius with equal clarity. They could see the stirrings of every soul in the land or come to rest on a singular face. As if compelled, all three sisters focused on a single dark face, one contorted with rage, eyes fixed and all but ablaze—Sister Grace. She was far to the north, atop her cliffside home, overlooking the lower tiers of Ravencroft City.

Her sword was high in preparation for a hard attack that both Kamiko and Felene recognized as one of her most aggressive. She faced a miasma. Kamiko could make out nothing of Grace's opponent, only a compact shroud of dark vapor, roughly the size and shape of a man. The apparition appeared to stoop momentarily, and then a tiny trinket on a thin golden chain appeared at Grace's feet.

Felene whispered, "Is that…"

"Yes," Kamiko answered gravely. It was the same scenario that had befallen her earlier this very day. Assassins were calling on Grace and of the same lot and caliber as had beaten Kamiko.

Felene moved forward on impulse, attempting to aid her sister, to guard her flank. But though Grace appeared to be only an easy stone-throw away, she was over three hundred leagues to the north, and Felene was still riding in a slow coach in Southern Flavin. Danae watched in silent fear, her bearing that of someone unable to look away from a spectacle certain to be horrific.

Grace lunged but was driven suddenly and violently back, blood spraying from her nose, and landed on her back several feet from the coiling murk. She regained her feet and lunged again, this time separating of her own accord. With the third attack, both Felene and Danae were momentarily overcome with shock, and both of them yelped aloud. Felene's hand reached out on instinct as Grace was quickly driven to the snowy deck.

But Kamiko saw more than her two sisters could yet imagine and knew Grace had prevailed, even as she'd stepped into the third attack. Kamiko allowed the slightest turn of her mouth, the tiniest smile she could muster, and then nodded in affirmation when Grace rose from what appeared to be defeat. Her dark sister attacked with such speed and ferocity that her opponent's only reaction was to stagger backward and pitch from the rooftop.

Kamiko knew they could not *be* anywhere but where their bodies resided on terra firma, but they could perceive any place as easily as they could see their own hand. She concluded some things were hidden from her, as though she and her sisters suddenly slipped forward in time, like standing on shifting sand.

Grace was now running for her front door, following the rest of her household, who were ahead of her by a street block. Before Grace made it out of the front room, the sisters saw a fiery flash and felt a concussive shudder, but heard no roar of the explosion that erupted where Grace's house was perched. It mushroomed up and outward over the cliff in a spray of flaming splinters. The blast would have destroyed Grace but for the elder.

All motion slowed suddenly. Kamiko wondered if Rachel saw the shift in time happen, or if perhaps she'd caused it. Rachel fell from directly above Grace in a slow drifting motion. The wall of flaming debris advanced with no more speed than sunrise on approach. Yet Rachel timed her descent to arrive at the last possible moment before Grace's death, raised a silver sword and an embattled bronze shield. She took the brunt of the blast. She stood over Grace until all of the blazing shards had fallen. Then from three hundred leagues away, Rachel turned her face fully square with Kamiko's, locked onto her eyes, and lowered the sword toward the ground. She removed any doubt in Kamiko's mind that she'd effected the tangible motion of time.

The passing of time was sliced so thin everything appeared suspended, brought into still balance by God, the only One able to create and thereby manipulate such things. Rachel had simply tapped into that power by authority of the silver sword she held. Kamiko's thoughts touched briefly upon Hun'jotzimon, but she stored the now-lingering question with all the other mysteries gathering in her brain.

Rachel's eyes rested fixed upon Kamiko's, a timeless moment between them. Thoughts bloomed. Rachel knew Kamiko's quandary with Siruis's safety and silently bid her success. The elder appeared neither incorporeal nor wholly physical, but she was possessed of a fierce countenance beyond even the mighty Bartolamew Kane when his battle-rage was full. She wore the full accouterments of battle garb. Small wonder that Danae had been shaken at the sight of her.

Rachel flipped the sword suddenly upward and dove up into the ether. The three sisters watched her path to the remaining eight points of flaring white light. They saw her perfectly timed intervention for each of the powerful sisters stationed throughout the kingdom, as each suffered near-exact attacks as Grace and Kamiko. The whole of the operation spanned no more time than that of a single breath. Kamiko and Felene understood immediately that which Danae could not comprehend. The young sister's innocent question was answered by a small voice at Kamiko's side. No one saw Siruis appear.

"We are under a concerted attack, Danae," Siruis said.

"A well-timed attack."

"Yes, Felene. Kamiko first and Grace second," Siruis added.

"With roughly two hours between them," Felene said.

"Yes, and then all eight sisters were attacked almost simultaneously and"—Siruis raised a finger—"almost successfully."

Kamiko nodded and spoke softly, as if afraid that giving words to her thoughts might hasten the reality of their meaning. "And were it not for our elder sister, all ten of us would be dead. It has begun, my friends, the fall of Cairistonia. This was somebody's first strike."

Siruis continued Kamiko's sentiment, "Yes, Sisters, the enemy is revealed and has begun to move. Their time of watching is over. And now, as always, the Eternal moves in power across the land. The elder was granted this"—Siruis waved her hand to indicate what they'd just witnessed—"her final request."

On the moment, and like an angry storm, Rachel was hovering directly before them, thrumming the very ether with energy, even to her smallest movements. Kamiko's heart surged with natural excitement. The warrior adrenaline fired strong. The coppery taste of battle-born fury was suddenly bitter on her tongue. Long ago, the taste of blood, a mist upon the air of every battlefield, had imprinted on that part of her soul where the berserker dwelt and henceforth always filled her mouth when the berserker appeared. Some new part of her reached for Hun'jotzimon but drew short, knowing better than to call the sword without need.

The urge to drop to one knee and bow to Rachel was strong and almost had Kamiko kneeling on impulse. Felene caught Danae by the arm as the young girl all but fell on her face before the one she'd once named Mother. Yet for all her ferocity, the look on the elder's face was one of awe as she gazed singly upon Danae. After moments, she turned and held Felene in her gaze, in silence, not a sound uttered, her brow darkened not by reprimand but resolve.

Felene's face and posture rose and her body flexed, warrior-like. She nodded once, then cocked her head and offered Rachel a questioning look, a slight smile on her lips and mischief sparkling in her eye. After a moment more, Rachel centered on Kamiko and answered her recently pondered question.

The sum total of Rachel's life lay before them upon a single moment, and when weighed as such, it cast her as Kamiko's twin, her path just as brutal in nature. For the first time in all their years together, Kamiko could see how much they shared instead of being overwhelmed by their differences. And another piece of Kamiko that wasn't real flaked away; that Rachel had always been far above her in stature, grace, beauty, and charity, wise beyond Kamiko's natural ability to understand. But such notions were the false perceptions of a volatile twelve-year-old sword-wielding fury, which had never abated.

Kamiko realized that she'd calmed to an almost serene state. The wanton destruction boiling suddenly in her veins, only moments ago, had subsided without her notice.

When at last the elder's eyes came to rest on Siruis, they lingered for only a moment before her countenance grew serious. Rachel began slowly ascending, drifting upward and outward from the sisters. She'd made no sound.

Rachel still carried the sword and the shield and lifted each straight out to opposite sides, shield to the left, sword to her right. A sonorous trumpet sounded out a short but powerful blast from what felt like a place deeper than even this angelic realm. It was a single tone but laced through with harmonic resonance that exceeded the senses, both the high and the low range of what physical creatures may hear. This was followed immediately by the sound of hundreds of voices, not in concert, rather in conversation and lively excited banter at that. And on their lips was the name *Rachel*.

Without warning, a higher rank of the angels simply flourished into sight. Creatures of bright beauty, yet coiling with immense power, moved with the darting agility of schooling dolphins playing in the bow wake of a passing ship. They swarmed around Rachel, their voices gradually coalescing from many into one, and again on the instant, the whole mass came to an abrupt halt, just as their voices struck the harmonic balance of a beautiful chord. It echoed away on the ether as their song clipped abruptly off, and the chattering laughter returned. Every being in the mass was animated but stayed fixed in their respective positions within the meager gathering of some hundred-plus angels.

To Kamiko, the whole affair felt akin to a roomful of people whose conversation turned to laughter and whose laughter rose to the point of a cumulative shout of simple joy. She would not have been surprised had they raised goblets of wine.

They had formed a small sphere surrounding Rachel, Kamiko, Siruis, Danae, and Felene, three of which were still aboard the slow carriage drifting through the ghostly haze of Southern Flavin. Grace remained far to the north but watched the scene with an unwavering eye. Kamiko assumed Grace could see across the distance as well as the rest of them.

A cluster of fleet angels broke from the main body and descended upon the elder sister, like a swarm of frenzied scissor tail playing afield. The chatter from the living shell rose and fell in waves, as those attending Rachel dismantled her war garb.

A trio of the angels broke immediately away, lifted the mighty shield from her left arm, flashed out into the heavens, and were gone. Likewise helm, gauntlets, breast and backplate were lifted and borne away by tight clusters of fleet angels unto points unseen. All but the mighty sword still held out to her right. She was now dressed in the simple robes she'd always favored in life, flowing and light in the breeze. The intense ferocity of Rachel's bearing softened, and her movement slowed as her warrior spirit cooled, as Danae came once again to be the focus of her undivided attention. She let the sword drift slowly downward.

This time Kamiko clearly felt the ebb in the flow of shifting time, sensed it in her bones and saw it with her eyes. Every movement around them, angel-kin and mankind alike, slowed abruptly, and all fell silent. Only Kamiko, Rachel, Grace, and Danae were there. Felene was statuesque, and Siruis was no longer present, having left without notice. Kamiko sensed that the angels had simply drawn very still and watched with rapt attention, unaffected by the machinations of the sword.

Yet for all the building of the angelical gathering, the moment was fleet. Rachel simply pointed the sword at Danae, then slowly lifted it over her own head and released it. Even as her hand came away, the sword broke into a silvery mist and dissipated, only to coalesce and form again above Danae. A wave of awe whispered around the angelic ranks, though all held still and remained watchful. Almost immediately, the sword faded from sight, and the flow of time reinitialized, setting the whole of creation back to business. The troop of angels broke rank and scattered in clusters, then blinked out of sight right where they were. One of those clusters engulfed Rachel in a living cocoon, then tore away and was suddenly gone from sight, too far away to see even in terms of the heavenly realms. Kamiko hoped they were taking the long way home, the scenic route for Rachel's benefit. She knew Rachel could not yet enter the realm of God, that she was being taken to a place of waiting. Kamiko also knew she would never mourn for her friend again—she would only miss her presence.

Siruis was again at their side. Danae showed no sign of having seen the sword appear above her and likely had no idea what had transpired. Felene and Danae abruptly slipped out of the ether, now part and parcel of the ghostly material of nature's canvas. And scattered across that stage were ten blistering-white flares of fury, those sisters saved by Rachel's intervention, stoked to ferocity rather than butchered wholesale. And though they were spread across the vast kingdom, all of the sisters had seen Rachel, knew what had transpired, and were now gazing among themselves for those few moments before their sight darkened. All their eyes came last to rest on Kamiko, who pressed her fist into her palm and thus touched her forehead in silent salute, and then all of the sisters slipped from the ether, save Kamiko, Grace, and Siruis.

Kamiko sensed this was a formidable and unexpected shift in the tide of the war to come, ironically instigated by the enemy. The one who, in the end, would be most damaged had angered a serious hornet nest when he kicked the sisterhood.

Kamiko spoke his name aloud, "Rendur-Kath of Wroth".

Grace spoke another name aloud, "Cauldin-Kath of Wroth."

They shared a moment of silent thought. They would find this man—*Wroth*—and make his failure complete.

"One more thing you must see, Sisters, before you may rest and repair." Siruis lifted her finger toward the eastern mountain twin, Mount Elan, above Ravencroft, directing Kamiko and Grace to turn their attention to the icy peak. Perched on the sheer face sat the visage of a strong man clothed in simple robes, unaffected by the cold. He was colossal in size and physical stature and appeared carved from jade, bronze, gleaming silver and gold, and much onyx. And though dark orbs, his eyes were full of life and focus and were fixed upon the human mass filling the valley below him. His mighty feet were anchored to the stone face, and while sitting on his haunches, he was leaned out over Ravencroft City. His bronzen arm was outstretched, his golden forefinger extended to a singular point. In that place, the shadow which had been poured over the city by Luthain was held at bay. Authority. This one had greater authority than even Luthain, which told Kamiko he was the archangel, one who had a seat in the very throne hall of God. A shudder ran through her body. What this one had seen and heard and had done was far beyond anything she could imagine. She had little doubt he was aware of their attention.

A bright clearing covered whomever was beneath the spirit being's focus. Kamiko sensed someone there but knew beyond a doubt that they were being hidden from all eyes, friend or foe.

It seemed obvious to her. "He is a friend," she said, "one I have seen before. He came across the mountains from the north."

Grace nodded her assent. "Yes, a friend."

The angel faded from sight as Siruis lowered her hand. A moment later and without another word, Siruis's image slipped from the ether, Kamiko's talisman still in her hand.

Grace spoke first, "Are you okay?"

"I lost."

"Yes, me too."

"No, you took him down hard, Sister, beautifully executed. I cheered."

"He killed me back."

"Well, he tried."

Grace smiled at that, changed the topic. "I need Felene."

"I know you do, Grace. Soon, I need her a bit longer."

Grace nodded her assent. "Sister," she said, "I saw him."

"Who?"

"Our friend, the one we just saw or didn't see. He saved everyone in my household."

Kamiko liked the sound of that and smiled at Grace. They stood still, gazing across the frozen span of deep jungle between them, simply waiting in silence but in the presence of someone dear.

Chapter 4

Ravencroft City—Grace

The sight folded away, and Grace was alone, standing in the rubble and looking down at the lower city through a smoldering crater where her house once stood. People were running and shouting. The house on one side of her was ablaze on their adjoining wall, the house opposite was crushed and smoking where it neighbored. Fiery shards lay scattered a hundred paces in every direction. Grace was standing whole and unscathed at a point where everything around her was blown apart—wood, stone, and earth.

Rachel was standing over her, feet spread, leaning into the blast behind the great shield. All around them was the blazing fury of a howling storm and the elder shouting at the top of her lungs right along with it.

Grace bent her knees and lowered herself into a sit, only then to realize her sword was still in her hand. She could hear Bethany's voice, shouting, coming closer.

She was alive after the firestorm. And she'd just seen angels. Lots of them, and the archangel—she'd seen the *archangel.*

Bethany's hands were on her shoulders, rough, jerking Grace about. She stumbled and fell, collapsing across Grace's lap, trying not to shout, trying not to cry, and failing at both attempts. Grace's lips were numb, and her nose was throbbing. She wasn't breathing. *Can you forget to breathe?* she wondered as her chest rose with a deep draw of smoky air. She didn't know what Bethany was saying. Big fat flakes began drifting down in a silent torrent. Everything was slow.

She'd seen angels. Lots of them. She was so cold.

Flavin—Kamiko

The first thing Kamiko became aware of when her sight darkened was the door of the carriage banging open as Felene jumped out. And because they were traveling at only a measured walk, the driver easily brought the carriage to a stop when Danae leapt out behind her.

Peering through the open door, Kamiko saw Felene bolt into an intersecting alleyway and fall to her hands and knees in the snow, retching hard and fast. The wide walkways teemed with people bundled fat against the cold; round red noses, pink cheekbone faces, and wide eyes were the only flesh Kamiko could see. Her knowledge of the royal proclamation concerning her whereabouts kept her firmly planted on the seat. It made her jerk back out of sight as many of those faces were tracing Felene's path back into the open door where Kamiko looked out. The coachman riding on the backstand of the carriage had climbed down and appeared in the doorway, carefully blocking the curious onlookers.

"You okay, Sister?" he asked quietly.

"I am, thank you," she said with a nod and a wan smile.

He smiled and assured her, "I will tend to your friends, please remain inside." Then he closed the door with a quiet thump. He was a stocky young man whose build and face were almost familiar. And he was aware of exactly who was in this carriage—legend. The joy gleamed in his eye. It did not feel like greed, rather the jolt someone would get from a simple brush with fame. The "reward" for delivering Kamiko could be greater than he would earn in his lifetime. But then who would the captain entrust with Kamiko Hoshi's safe and stealthy transport? The answer was obvious the moment the door opened a handbreadth, and she saw his features again. He was the son of Ezra Kale, with enough of his mother's looks that Kamiko had little doubt she could pick her out in the room.

Danae slipped abruptly up in front of the young man and leaned her face into the doorway, hands extended and speaking very fast. Behind her, the man showed himself to be a gentleman and, graciously and with thoughtful tact, stepped aside, further blocking any stray sight lines from the slow-moving crowd. And by holding the mounting rail on the carriage and extending his arm, he had draped his cloak to form a heavy warm curtain behind Danae and across her back. She flicked him a sincere smile of gratitude, her hands still on the dance.

Kamiko had no idea what the girl was saying and patted her hands gently in the air to stop her for a moment. Danae went dead still for a four-count before one brow lifted, and her mouth tightened slightly. Kamiko signed "slower" with a smile and a nod. Danae's eyes darted left, right, left, then re-centered on Kamiko, and she spelled out with slow perfection every letter of "we are walking." Kamiko laughed aloud.

Kamiko twisted the button clasp at her neck and let the borrowed cloak drop from her shoulders, then rolled it into a bundle and passed it to Danae with a nod. All three sisters were bundled against the cold, but Kamiko wanted Danae to feel more than simple permission or acknowledgment. She was gleaning from every possible opportunity, a growing support of Danae making all her own decisions and that no questions or doubts were forthcoming, ever. She needed to be able to falter. *We have but to take a wound to learn to heal,* Bartol's words of long ago. Kamiko had no other means for teaching Danae how to recover than to let her fall. Or at least to fall short.

Then to Kamiko's surprise and delight, Danae pushed her fist into her palm, a handbreadth out from her face, and nodded her head slightly, her attitude serious, the Dead Fist. The bundled cloak slipped from where she held it in the crook of her arm. She snatched it from the drop so quickly Kamiko was barely aware she'd moved. With a flourish of her arm, Danae swept the young man's cloak aside and whisked away, already unfurling Kamiko's large mantle.

"I doubt the good sisters need me to safeguard them, I shall remain with the carriage," Ezra's son said. "We are only ten blocks from home." And with a smile and a look of familiarity, he added, "My mother is very anxious this day, and I shall be honored to present you to her and to my elder sister, Anje." He did not wait for an answer but closed the door after a nod and another broad smile. The carriage moved forward smoothly and built speed to a trot. They were short minutes from the Kale homestead.

Danae was her bright spritely self at the moment, when need dictated, when Felene required support. The morose-slowed awareness had been set aside but would return abruptly when Felene's need was fully met. Danae's eyes were rimmed in pink, and she held her brow high, as if by force of will. Kamiko knew then that Danae's training would begin as soon as she arrived at the Kale home. It was likely that Kamiko would never again have Danae in such a bedraggled state, expecting comfort and rest and time for mourning. She would be required to eat, take water, take her toilet, and report to Kamiko to begin—all within ten minutes.

For Djinnasee to have invoked the Karak-Tan meant Rachel had seen great success in Danae's training. Kamiko felt a small surge of sorrow flare in her chest for what the girl was about to be subjected to. In the years to follow, Danae would mark this day as one of the toughest. And as Kamiko pondered her own role, she realized it would rank very high as one of her hard days, and the thought weighed heavy in her heart. But the presence of Siruis was there as well and shared the burden, bolstering Kamiko's resolve to be the fire in which Danae would be tempered. They both knew Kamiko was the only one alive able to mentor the girl in such a way. And both Kamiko and Danae still carried the fresh heart wounds of the previous hours. A more ready stage could not be set.

In one carefully contained recess of her mind, the battle at the lighthouse looped incessantly, every move etched into her mind's eye. She could see the flaw that allowed the sword to slip through her defenses, followed by the sharp burn as it plunged between her ribs. It was the deepest wound she'd ever taken, the only fatal strike in all her years. She gently closed the door to that alcove and forced her thoughts ahead.

The captain's son had said his mother was anxious. Indeed Kamiko felt a strong sense of pre-planning at work—food, clothes, rescue, the ready carriage. And all with an uncanny precision which smacked of Djinnasee. They had fallen from the lighthouse little more than an hour earlier, floated unseen until the captain pulled them into the boat, and then were brought to this very point without pause, but to eat a bowl of soup and down a mug of warm ale. There was little time for a mother to be anxious, even if a runner had brought a message from the dock house, beside the fact that Ezra's son had not seen his mother to gain such knowledge.

"Aah," she said aloud, "and what does it matter? God provides as he sees fit."

It occurred to her that at the moment, she had not one single possession of her own. Oddly it was not resentment but comfort which arose from the thought because she was warm, well fed, safe from prying greedy eyes on her way to a household of godly peace. At the moment, she could think of nothing she needed. Of all her belongings, only Uila remained hers to command, though where he was, she did not know for sure. She believed he was on his way back to Lord Merritt's. She tried not to dwell on the fact that several hundred people would have seen him running naked through the streets, for he would be running headlong and thundering riderless and unsaddled. Word would spread, and the hunt for Kamiko and Siruis would begin in earnest.

Ironically Siruis was safe with Dairei but also because she was beneath the relentless gaze of Hun'jotzimon. Kamiko's mouth curved into a lopsided smile at the thought that Siruis was most safe with the notorious criminal. For the time being, no place in Flavin was better suited to her needs. And by now, Jerim would have made it to their grotto hideaway.

Kamiko shook her head and whispered to no one, "A gathering of giants."

The carriage slowed suddenly, and the driver brought it to a smooth stop. Kamiko could hear the strong clear voice of the son of Kale, casting orders to clear the way and to open the gates. Lesser calls echoed the order, and in moments, the carriage moved forward again slowly. She felt the carriage turn right off the main avenue, and in a pair of moments, the dim light escaping in through the curtained windows darkened. Kamiko's internal count kicked in and ticked off twenty beats before the light returned.

"A thruway into a carriage yard," she whispered, again to no one. As the carriage continued, so did her count. At fifty-five, the light dimmed again, and it sounded to her like they had come into a much smaller enclosure. The driver's handling of the rig was so smooth she hadn't felt the motion change. She didn't know they had stopped until the door opened. The first thing that struck her, besides seeing the driver and the son of Kale, was the scent of horse!

A deep abiding serenity settled down over her body and soul. She'd been borne of her mother's body into Djinnasee's hands who, in turn, placed her, swaddled, in a basket strapped upon a horse's withers. Her first twelve weeks of life were spent crossing a wilderness on horseback. She would whip a man to save a horse but only shoo a horse to save a man.

She came out of the carriage which what must have seemed abrupt, for both men stepped back on impulse and simply looked at her for a long moment. The driver's arm rose defensively, if slightly, and he retreated a full step, while young Kale's feet only shifted backward a handbreadth. The tops of their heads barely breached the height of Kamiko's shoulder. The driver's leather long coat, thick leather hat, gloves, and heavy boots were all of obvious excellent quality. His trim jet-black beard and thin mustache were perfectly groomed, and his teeth shone in even white rows through a nervous smile. He was stout but lean and dark of skin and shared no single feature with the young man beside him, his outward attitude notwithstanding. Kale wore his joy so openly, Kamiko half-expected him to break into dancing and singing, while the driver seemed far less certain. Yet the young Kale seemed to carry something lingering below the surface, a burden weighing on his spirit. He introduced himself with a slight bow.

"My name is Corti'deleno Rasha Kale, known to most folk as Cort. My comrade is Sir Johns Roland, horse master and trusted friend. Your presence is a closely guarded secret, Sister, and we are very happy you are here." As Sir Johns drew his hat from his head, recognition brought a sharp but pleasant memory to Kamiko's thoughts.

"We have met," she declared.

He looked genuinely and pleasantly surprised and, smiling broadly, nodded first at Cort, then at Kamiko, his voice not yet engaging. After a moment longer, he cleared his throat and said, "Yes, I spoke to you about your horse several years ago. He has long been the object of my interest. I must confess concern at his absence. It is widely believed that you seldom part."

She smiled at the comfortable humor of it, pleased that someone was concerned for Uila's well-being. "He is fine, I think. We got separated, but he was under no duress and likely returned to Lord Merritt's estate." And with a nod, she confirmed, "And we seldom part, of that I can attest."

"My apologies for bringing you in through the backdoor," Cort said. "To watching eyes, we are simply retiring the coach for the day." He clapped his hand on his friend's shoulder and added, "Hey, my father told me to get you in unseen best I could, and this is it, Sister Kamiko." He exclaimed with a broad smile, "Welcome, and let's head this way." The two men turned on their heels and stepped into a brisk, if nervous, walk, moving forward of the carriage past the draw horses.

Kamiko was less inclined to hurry, as her attention was drawn to the building they were in. It had a cavernous echo about it that the modest carriage tunnel they occupied did not offer. Her steps were in the opposite direction, into what became the open inner room of an enormous roundhouse. And though the building had several large windows encircling the uppermost walls, the gloomy dark of the day outside filled the room with shadows of gray and deeper gray. She simply stood in silence, looking around at the few details she could see. Her senses were tingling with the stark sensations left over from a childhood of being immersed in all things horse! That part of her soul was clanging like a struck bell.

"It is always quiet in here during the day," Cort spoke from where he'd appeared beside her. "Take a look around sunset, and it will look a whole lot different."

"What is this place?"

"Kale and Kale Enterprises, of which Sir Johns is a vested member, operates a joint business here. Sir Johns is the stable master while I operate a small but thriving carriage service. Anje, my sister, designs, builds, and sells custom leather riding tack, saddles mostly. And we are all partners in our own large animal clinic, specializing in equine, of course. Dr. Flynn Vesture joined us early on and has been running the clinic since."

"I know Dr. Vesture," Kamiko said, surprised at hearing so prominent a name from the young man. She looked over at him. "How long have you been in business?"

"Five years. And that appears to be the hump. We are finally getting all our feet on the ground, so to speak." His eyes were moving out across the dark room as he spoke, "We are up to twenty-six drivers, fifteen carriages, and somewhere in the neighborhood of 250 horses. We keep about forty here."

Kamiko turned to where she thought Sir Johns would be standing but found that he was nowhere to be seen.

"Mr. Roland was called away on business. He's been prattling on for days about, well, all this!" Kamiko felt the urgency bubbling in Cort, so she reined in her urge to explore the place and turned back to the carriageway.

"Please, lead on, my friend," she said with a nod, "I like your place a lot. I feel more at ease with horses than people, generally speaking." She stepped forward with him and spoke quietly as they walked. "I get the sense of being expected here—now. How is it that your mother could even be aware of me or that you and Sir Johns were waiting? He is not one of your drivers, and this is your personal coach."

They were just at the carriage, moving back through the passageway. It appeared flawless in every detail.

"Very clever eye, Sister Kamiko. I started building this craft one year ago this very day. You three sisters are the only passengers to date. I shall begin disassembly once you no longer require it."

"What?"

"Aah," he exclaimed with a laugh that Kamiko imagined was a normal part of his speech, "how else could it be my gift to you?" They passed the team of big twin chestnut draw horses, dressed in quilted warmth, and came into a large open room with a high ceiling of skylights, set in thick-beamed cross members. The very air thickened with the scent of horse, wood, paint, glue, manure, and woodsmoke and flushed her cheeks with warmth. To her left and stretched lengthwise against the far wall were a row of ten or twelve stable fronts, where no fewer than eight bright inquisitive faces, ears upright, and nostrils quivering, peered back at Kamiko and Cort as they strode into the room. To their right, in the greater part of the vaulted room, were three beautifully crafted carriages, each in a different stage of construction. But to Kamiko's surprise, there were no signs of any people but for the tools and wood refuse of a crew obviously given the day off. Cort never slowed and walked directly for a door near the corner of the building, his boots thumping a rapid cadence. Kamiko shortened her stride to match his step, lest her long legs outpace him and propel her into the lead.

It was obvious, Cort was not going to address her questions concerning the apparent preparation for her arrival. She anticipated no more than a single word in explanation from Cort's mother—*Djinnasee*. Some part of the notion bothered her, but she was not certain what part. Cort likely started building the carriage the very day Djinnasee came calling on the Kale family, as he said, one year ago today. Were her steps so perfectly placed by design or simply discerned from the past or future? As long as Kamiko's life remained an unfolding mystery to her perspective, why would she care that God had leaked some of it to Djinnasee beforehand? Was there some prerogative unavailable to God? None she was aware of.

Cort slowed only enough to turn the handle and draw the heavy door open. It swung inward easily upon wide oiled hinges, the sight of which triggered in Kamiko a moment of judicious searching through the eyes of a warrior. From the thick and band-fortified door, snug-fitted doorframe, and fat set bolts to the thick structure supporting and framing the glass ceiling, tall walls of stone with minimal-wood structure points, this was a fortress.

As they stepped through the door, they came out to an open courtyard, and her notion was confirmed. The whole of the property was walled. The smoldering gray sky was still belly-flat upon the city, but Kamiko could tell it was thinning, growing shades lighter. Icy wind was blowing hard and seemed to strike from every direction at once, but the snow had ceased falling. Thirty steps directly ahead, a small stone hut with a single door was nestled into a lone cluster of trees. Cort made directly for the hut.

At least one hundred paces to their left and fifty to their right, the main encircling wall stood tall and crenelated with long elevated guard platforms, also built primarily of stonework. That span across the whitened yard looked to be roughly half the length of the property. She had little time to peruse the grounds but saw that everything was orderly and that most all the spaces had been put to use. A few modest outbuildings stood between the big roundhouse and the main wall to her left, where she could see a heavily fortified gate leading off property. By her quick estimation, the walls would enclose a bit less than ten acres of land, but it was earth-torn straight across the middle.

It was the tiniest clipping from the toenail of a mountain, but the cliff face dividing the Kale's homestead loomed large and grand, almost straight up to a height of fifty feet at least. Their fortified wall to her left was built straight into the face of the solid rock and continued again directly above where it disappeared behind a stable yard house, nestled and fenced and shaded by a grove of trees. The land sloped down sharply from that high-walled border to within five feet of the level where they approached the door of the hut.

Beyond the hut and to her right, interrupting the course of the perimeter wall, Kamiko could see another small but heavily fortified building, round in all aspects, a half-sphere rising out of the ground. Cort noticed where her gaze happened to be as he reached for the door handle.

"That is the front door, Sister," he said as he pointed to the small dome, "which is directly west from right here." He pointed back toward the big roundhouse and said, "Go out through that door and to the right to go north." Then he pointed over to the gate she'd seen earlier. "Go through that gate to go south." He opened the door of the hut and led her into dim heat which smelled of warmed oil, scented with herbs. "Mars Knoll is over an hour on horseback, Lord Merritt is only about forty-five minutes or so, both northeast from here." His voice had become gradually softer, breathier.

Not three long paces beyond the threshold of the hut, the entire width of the floor dropped away and lighted steps of weathered but well-kept wood led down beyond sight. She could already sense the feeling of antiquity about the place. Cort fairly trotted down the steps with the staggered hopping gait of a lifetime of crossing. Kamiko figured that going up, he likely climbed the steps three at a time and closer to a gallop than a trot. She took them two at a time, also with a slight skip in her step, and came to the bottom of the wide stairs to find an anteroom. The side walls were lined with coats and strewn with boots and shoes, and what, at first glance, appeared to be a scattered mess resolved in Kamiko's mind as the ordered array of many people in a busy household. If the room was emptied of the coats and shoes, there would be nothing left but a few low benches and lines of many hook pegs on the walls.

There was a single door leading out the other side of the room, but Cort stopped short of opening it. He removed his heavy coat, hat, and gloves, which he dropped, already forgotten to one side. Kamiko could feel the warmth of the room on her face and followed suit. She was dressed entirely in the dark and baggy clothing common to bargemen, which was a layering of sundry and unrelated shirts, vests and tunics of sufficient number to bring warmth. She peeled all but two of the layers off at once and draped the mass across one of the benches.

Cort hooked, first, one bootheel into the boot puller, then the other, and then stepped into a pair of comfortable slip-on shoes better suited for indoors.

Kamiko got the impression he was now keeping his back to her, a notion confirmed when he turned around and faced her suddenly, as if by a duty, which was against his will. The bright and cheerful young man was gone, even to the point that his father's features had faded, and an entirely different person gazed back at her. Oddly the familiarity tugging at Kamiko's memory strengthened, and she saw an almost-forgotten face resolve in her mind's eye. But her attention was drawn to a canvas boot bag hanging from Cort's hand as he held it out to her. When she hesitated, though for only a moment, he set it on one of the low benches near Kamiko and stepped back. She could not tell if it was fear he was holding in check or anger, those twin sons. It was likely equal shares of both.

"It is a gift." He paused, his manner quiet and terse. "From my mother."

Kamiko easily recognized the bag as one common to the sisterhood. It was a boot bag of stitched hide and heavy canvas, treated with heated paraffin and handworked to a silky softness. She'd tried to make one long ago with limited success. It was a lengthy process which took many days to complete, if done correctly, but produced a bag that would last a century. Many sisters of the Order had made their own. This was the finest she'd seen by far, a very generous gift from a master at leathercraft. Before she'd lifted the bag to get a closer look, she knew it was not empty.

She sat on the bench, loosed the gather cord, and drew open the mouth of the bag. Inside she found a pair of boots made from dark soft hide. From the leg of each boot, she pulled a low-cut thin-sole shoe, also of the same soft dark hide. The cut and design were exactly that used almost exclusively by her sword sisters. The boots were soft and flexible but thick hide and tough underfoot and, when laced, would rise to just below Kamiko's calf muscle. The slippers were equally durable but designed for stealth and traction, with a toe brace between the first toes. They were designed for the assassin aspect of Kamiko's calling.

She pushed off the borrowed dock boots and scooted them under the bench with her heels. Even as she leaned forward to slip the shoes on, she knew the fit would be perfect, for the craftsmanship was flawless, and no such artisan would make one without the other. She expected the slight overtightness once they were on her feet. The same would be true of the boots—overtight for the span of a few days of wear while they were shaped by the natural pressure and motion of her feet. She knew of only two people who could know her by her feet, one being Djinnasee, the other being Bartol, and she'd never known the giant to be prescient.

"Djinnasee," she said to Cort, who looked on as if hoping she would take an hour inspecting the boots. He appeared to be avoiding looking at the door. "This has to be the doings of Djinnasee."

He looked perplexed and shook his head. "I'm not even sure what that is."

Kamiko smiled and said, "Djinnasee is a man," then added, "he is my father."

"Is he a cobbler?"

"No, he—"

"Well, he didn't make these, my sister did," Cort said. And though he caught the impulse, Kamiko clearly saw Cort's hand rise toward his coat, stop with a jerk, then roll into a fist as it dropped to his side. It felt as though the young man would rather push her through the door and shut it behind her.

"These are without equal in the kingdom, my friend, I am grateful." She stood and tested the feel of the shoes as she returned the boots to the bag. "And I am most anxious to meet your mother and your sister. And, Cort," she said as she drew still and faced the young man, "I am humbled by your gift to me. I know little of carriage-making, but I can recognize the time, work, and the skill required to build a craft of that quality." His troubled brow relaxed slightly, and she saw a glimpse of the other brighter Cort trying to surface.

She lifted the bag in her fist and said, "I tried my hand and made one of these when I was younger. It was an okay bag, but it was a tattered mess after about five years. I expect this one will outlive me several times over."

A slight grin broke on one side of his mouth, telling Kamiko he was on good terms with his sister. She decided to test the waters where his mother was concerned, to see if he darkened noticeably.

"I will be certain to thank your mother. I was in dire need."

The darkness which dropped like a curtain over his bearing was neither anger nor fear, but sorrow. His mouth was a straight line across his face, and his eyes thickened with emotional fatigue.

"She will not know…she does not remember," he said quietly, then turned to the door and pushed it open. Before he walked through, he looked over his shoulder, though not directly at Kamiko, and added in a flat dry tone, "My mother has been cursed by the sorcery of your sisterhood." Then he stepped into the expansive domed room which lay beyond.

*****

Felene eyed the driver with open suspicion. A lot of people were staring at them, something she could not afford. She was frustrated and did not plan on climbing back inside any carriage. She needed air and daylight and cold wind. She needed her guts to untwist and for her spine to flex from the wooden post it had become.

"Fine, let's get going then," she said to the dashing young man who seemed intent on giving her a ride. She closed the door with a muffled thump and motioned to the driver's bench. "But I ride up there with you."

He removed his hat and, with a slight tilt of his head, said, "Sir Johns, at your service, sister. You may ride where you wish, but it will be cold, as I intend a hasty trip."

"Sir Johns, I am Felene Dresdle, and freezing wind in my face sounds entirely grand at this moment." She climbed atop the carriage bench and moved to the far end to allow Sir Johns the driver's seat. Once he was seated and disengaging the brake, she said, "To the Knoll first, then back to Lord Merritt's. I need to be the bearer of ill news, lest rumors catch flight."

Her eyes were drawn to the pair of beautiful horses out beyond her feet, something which caught the driver's notice in turn. A broad smile spread over his dark features as he whistled and barked a quiet command to the team. They pulled forward, slowly at first, and angled out toward the carriage lane, a process requiring skill, patience, and a small handful of minutes. The crowd of foot traffic was not heavy, but neither was it sparse, and the capable driver made his way carefully.

"This is Boda," he said and opened his palm toward the horse on the left, then toward the one on the right, "and this is Ruda." They were silken black and thick with muscles and almost as tall as Uila at the withers. "And, Sister, these boys can run."

She'd noticed their hooves were rising almost to their bellies, as if there was no other way to travel so slowly than to make the stride as long and slow as possible. It gave a dancing appearance to their gait, though the cushioned seat she occupied was smooth and steady in the ride.

All Felene could manage was to nod and say, "They are beautiful."

She felt like she was standing on a glass tabletop, one already broken beneath her feet but still in that momentary balance between the breaking and the falling. The moment was frozen around her as the day just kept playing out. She should have awakened hours ago back home. It was not like her to sleep so long, to dream with such lucidity. She looked down at the horses, at their perfect blackness against so stark a white as new fallen snow, and knew only her mind was present. She believed her body was still lying in a low bed near an open window that overlooked the eastern ocean. Danae has been gone a little over twenty years. Felene has not seen Kamiko for forty years. All this Felene believed to be true, even as Sir Johns easily led the rig into the carriage lane and brought Boda and Ruda up to a slow run. She dared not attach herself to this dream any further, yet she dared not sleep nor close her eyes, lest she trigger the awakening into her numb meaningless body.

She'd forgotten the feel of having muscles, of wielding steel, or of thundering through the city atop one such as Uila. She'd never felt such sorrow as losing Sister Rachel or such joy as seeing Danae alive. But there were no events demanding valor, nor dangers to test one's courage awaiting Felene's return, only yawning years of creaking boards and rain spattering on the windows. That was her daily life, not racing through the whitened city trying to outpace imminent destruction. She'd been read hundreds of books rife with such scenes, especially before Danae had left, so it was no small wonder she was dreaming so soundly. And she had been missing Danae anew and strong. Felene's seventy-third birthday came and went, wholly unnoticed by her caretakers, something Danae would have never allowed. Her soul had sunk to a new darkness. Then something very hot had touched her forehead, and her eyes had opened at the Knoll, and she was back on the icy ground and back in her young able body.

The team slowed to a trot abruptly as Sir Johns prepared to make a turn. The motion shook her reverie just as a small glimmer of what looked like truth broke through in her mind. Siruis!

Felene could not have conjured Siruis to her dream, nor Jerim for that matter. Siruis's presence was like an anchor to what was real. The cold blast of air tightening the skin of her face felt suddenly sharp, and a warbling shudder rippled up her spine and spread across her scalp. She felt that moment, before she awakened as an aged invalid, churning around in her stomach, as though building to heave. She fought to stay in the dream, focusing her will upon the two horses now stepping into a full but cautious run up an ice-clad northbound carriageway Felene knew from both forty years ago and from last week, with equal clarity.

But her stomach did not empty, and she did not awaken. Siruis was real. The icy wind threatening to peel the flesh from her face was also decidedly real. Some part of her mind knew, and some part of her heart suspected that she was here to stay, that her gulag had been broken. The joy that threatened to rise was held hard at bay by the lingering and overpowering fear thriving in all her being. She must be very still lest the glass beneath her feet give way and drop her into the old, old woman she'd become, bone-thin and motionless, some 1,800 leagues eastward from Flavin.

Sir Johns had to nearly shout over the noise of the horses, road, and wind. "You look cold, Sister." Taking both reins in his right hand, he reached down to the edge of the bench with his left and slid open a deep drawer from beneath the seat, leaned toward Felene, and said, "Help yourself."

He was right. She was shivering. The multilayering of dockman's clothing she wore was suited well enough for the cold if one was walking or riding inside a fine carriage, but the wind made a mockery of the idea if one was riding outside at a dead run. The drawer contained a puffy fur-lined hat, which she tied upon her head immediately, a pair of heavy gloves, and a thick hide blanket which looked a lot like bear skin. The shivering subsided quickly.

"Bless you, my friend. You have earned my gratitude for life."

The smile that broke across his handsome face warmed her and stilled some of the shuddering in her spirit, and the surging tide of anxiety began to calm. The sky was dark and low, and the wind was coming straight at them from the north. It was only late afternoon in a day that seemed to have lasted a week.

Siruis had done more than just brought Felene back to that snowy midnight courtyard at the Knoll, she'd set something afire inside her. For all Felene could tell, it was a wild frenzied *thing*—a berserker. She shook her head at the thought. One thing which had always set her apart, even within the sisterhood, was her unwillingness to throw compassion to the wind and simply kill everything afield. Felene was not well suited to warfare. She thrived on chasing down criminals, the meaner and nastier, the better. It put the decision to kill right in her own hands, and she, in turn, placed it in theirs.

It appeared all such things were about to change. Siruis may have done that to keep Felene alive in the coming days. Perhaps it was time to embrace the berserker.

She took deep breaths and quieted the last of the nervous shuddering from the attack of pure panic and let her eyes begin to drift out into the sights around them. It had been forty years since she'd seen the streets of Flavin. It hadn't changed a bit.

*****

Cort's cryptic message was ringing in Kamiko's head like a gong as she stepped into the spacious room. If she'd had any expectations, they were certainly gone now. She did not take it too close to heart, many people thought of the Order as a gathering of misguided children or a gaggle of witches. Good witches, but witches just the same. Many people thought of Djinnasee as someone needing to be captured and institutionalized. Kamiko had been forced to defend the old prophet with the use of strength *and* steel too many times.

She could see all the way to the far wall where a long flat fireplace shone bright with a rolling fire behind long glass panels. There were a few standing walls enclosing a cluster of small rooms off toward her left, but the main body was all open. And big. Kamiko thought that with the floor cleared, she could fit a troop of five hundred men in here. She also knew that she could stand on this one spot for a week and still not see all there was to see. Some areas of the house were brightly lit while other areas were darker, but overall the light prevailed, and the whole room and domed ceiling glowed golden.

To her far right, an ascending stairway zigzagged up to another floor, which she believed was the roundhouse entry Cort had called the front door. She could see a passage leading down from the stairway landing as well, down into shadow.

Straight ahead was spread row upon row of thick-built and heavy-laden bookshelves. She followed Cort down another set of three steps to what turned out to be the floor level of the room and directly into a wide aisleway leading through the forest of bookshelves. She was walking inside an inverted bowl, amid what seemed an innumerable collection of books alone but whose orderly shelves were shared by like number of everything else one may imagine in a week of careful thinking. Toys, weapons, tools, jewels, strings of baubles and beads, bags, hundreds of hats, gloves, tiny shoes, more weapons, trinkets and small-framed pictures, stringed instruments of many shapes and sizes, like manner of drums and shakers, flute and horn, and many varieties of all things visible.

The shelves were arranged much like one might expect in a library—in orderly rows of long straight lines. But the aisles between were very narrow, with the shelf occupancy compacted to fill every possible shelf space. Even so there was no sense of clutter about the place, only the feel of great age baked into the very pores of the veined stone ceiling and all dwelling beneath it. At first glance, it had appeared the library was spread over a full third of the floor. They were halfway through the forest of shelves when Cort veered abruptly left into a well-lighted alcove set back into the embrace of a clearing in the surrounding shelf works. Low tables, three wide and deep chairs, and a short settee formed an open circle.

And there in the center of the alcove stood the mold from which Cort was truly cut. For the young man had turned as he stopped and was standing shoulder to shoulder with her, twin faces of different generations. The recognition that had flared moments earlier came to fullness as Matilda, sister of the Order, long retired, smiled at Kamiko with the knowing look of an elder of the sword. Cort bowed slightly to Kamiko and offered his hand to his mother, who took it and stepped forward a single step.

"Kamiko Hoshi, I believe you know my mother, Matilda Kale." His smile was natural and beaming, and before Kamiko could respond, he turned aside and raised his other hand to where his sister leaned against a tall heavy-laden bookshelf. "And this is my sister, Anje Kale. May you find peace and well-being while you are here, Sister."

Kamiko nodded first to Cort, then to Anje, and last to Matilda, who released Cort's hand and stepped toward Kamiko, stopping at arm's length. Matilda was younger than Rachel by only three years, but, like Rachel, looked fifteen years the younger. She was stocky and still looked strong enough to fistfight most men Kamiko knew. They had not seen each other since Kamiko's first year as sergeant in the cavalry, two full decades and some extra years ago. They had shared battle together for a time during a war. Oddly even now, Matilda stood with the warrior's flare of uncertainty, chest up, shoulders drawn back and tight, the look in her eye almost wary.

A moment of silence ensued. But it was more akin to the silence of dread anticipation.

Kamiko broke it with the oldest adage of the sisterhood she could call to mind. It followed a lost tradition where a sister of the Order would offer her protection to a dwelling, be it a cottage or a castle, by laying her sword across the threshold as the line no foe would survive crossing.

"Had I a sword, I would adorn thy threshold, Sister."

Cort barked aloud, as if heel-bitten by something with teeth, and took a full step backward, then grew very still. Anje moved quickly to Matilda's side, saying, "No…no…no…" under her breath. She looked more than simply worried. Long-brewed emotions were driving her. Matilda was staring at Kamiko with an open mouth, a battle of joy and confusion playing on her face. Anje gently, but with firm hands on both of Matilda's cheeks, turned her mother's face to hers. Kamiko imagined that if their unspoken thoughts were fire, the whole place would burn.

"Did you hear, Andi Jean, did you hear what she said?"

Anje released her mother's face, kissed her on the forehead, and turned the look of pure settling in shock upon Kamiko, and said, "How is that possible? How can any of this…"—she waved her hand around over her head a moment—"be possible."

Cort stepped quickly over to them, laid his hand on his mother's shoulder, and, in troubled tones, said, "That means the rest of it…"

Matilda cut him off gently, "*Yes*…that means the rest of it comes along too." She turned back to Kamiko and answered the question only just forming in Kamiko's mind.

"No, Sister, I have not seen the prophet for some ten-plus years."

"What?"

"She said you would say that," Anje blurted, though more from being shaken than from being unkind. She was the oldest of the Kale children according to Bastion.

"What?" Kamiko felt like a dull soldier, a helmet-head.

"She told us, one year ago today, that you would walk in here, and those would be the exact first words outta your mouth." Her voice was steady and even. She managed a smile and added, "She was right on it, Sister."

It clicked together pretty quickly for Kamiko. "She has said other things, I take it." And out of regard for Matilda's presence, Kamiko asked her, "Said other things, I guess?"

One corner of Matilda's mouth turned up. Anje answered for her, "Yes, I was asked to prepare a room for you, that you will need it now...and...I'm all...it's all ready." The shock they were feeling seemed to be waning, and as is often the course of emotions, it soon shifted away from dread. In short, the trio realized that Kamiko Hoshi was in their house and would be staying for several days. She actually showed up. And that much was a good thing.

Now it was Kamiko who stood mute from shock. Custom-fit shoes, an awaiting room, their very reactions to her presence. Was it Siruis then, if not Djinnasee?

The motion of Matilda's head slowly turning side to side drew Kamiko's attention. Their eyes locked for a moment that, at no surprise to Kamiko, encompassed far more than a mere moment would allow. This had nothing to do with following any words of Siruis or Djinnasee, this was all Matilda's doing.

Matilda stepped forward and took Kamiko's hand and said, "I first...*saw* you when you passed through Essen, midyear, as if you stepped from a fogbank into plain sight. I have been watching our sister of Marjan four years now. This very day, Sister Grace came into my..."—she glanced aside momentarily—"sight."

She trailed off as her eyes cut toward the stairwell leading down from the front entry and said simply, "Danae." She dropped Kamiko's hand, as though it had been forgotten and simply fell from her grip, and turned, looking for Anje, her motions jerking and nervous. Matilda asked Anje, "Is the room prepared? Are we ready? Is everything ready?"

The kindness and patience in all Anje's doings told Kamiko a lot about the woman. She cast her brother a look that set him into motion, taking Matilda's hand. Anje cast Kamiko a pleading look over her head, then spoke to her mother, "Everything is ready, Mama, I will take Sister Kamiko down and show her the room. Rasha, would you heat Mama's tea? I will be back shortly." She was curt and strong but so gentle with both Matilda and Cort.

"Yes, yes, I was just thinking...about..." Matilda's voice faded to barely a whisper.

Cort seated her in one of the deep chairs and lay a small blanket across her legs. Anje led Kamiko from the thicket of bookshelves, her hand on Kamiko's shoulder, gently urging her away. Kamiko noticed Anje looking at her new shoes as they walked and was pleased to see a shallow smile form on the younger woman's face. Kamiko said, "I love these, Anje. And I will not remove them for two full days."

Anje nodded and smiled and said, "I am—" but was cut off by Matilda's voice echoing into every space in the room, carried by the carved stone face of the domed ceiling.

"Just happy they fit, I had only my mother's word to the size and cut." Her voice sounded dreamy and breathy, reciting words without concern for comprehension. "I have a tin of ointment enough for the shoes and boots. I will…give it…" Matilda's voice trailed off.

Sad resolve was on her face, but Anje reached into a deep pocket and withdrew a leather pouch about the size of her fist and, dangling it by the pull cord, handed it to Kamiko. "Be careful," she said and paused a moment. Kamiko thought she was listening. "This stuff will stain anything it touches for life. It'll wear off your hands in about a year, so use the leather finger gloves in the bag. This will loosen the tightness and allow the shoes to form to your feet. That much should last about six months. After that just work them over with warm beeswax every couple of years."

"Well, I am amazed at your level of craftsmanship, Anje. Your brother said you design and build your own line of saddles. You must tell me about it when we have time to sit down and talk."

"Thank you, Sister." They had emerged on the far side of the library and followed the outer edge of the shelf rows as they made their way toward the zigzag stairway that led both up to the light and down into dark. Anje held up her hand and stopped them briefly and said, "My mother has been struggling, Sister, almost four years. When she commissioned me to make these shoes and these boots, she warned me to apply myself fully. I did. She convinced me you have a very long journey ahead."

"Was she…were those your thoughts she was speaking?"

"I believed it was so at first. Kamiko, every single thing she has declared has come to pass. What you saw just now is a smaller part of what my mother is doing. And yes, she is party to all our words." She took Kamiko by the elbow, and they moved forward again but slower. "She gave me all the measurements of your feet almost off-the-cuff. I think she actually waved her hand in the air when she was telling me, as though she was just making them up right there." She said this with a thin but genuine smile and nodding her head, spoke to Kamiko and, obviously, to Matilda. "I love you dearly, sweet Mama, but Kamiko, she is wearing us out." Her tone was simple and held no timbre of complaint or, for that matter, weariness. "And to answer your question, yes, she spoke my thoughts in general, but not in my own words nor details of what I was thinking."

"And the bag?" Kamiko asked with a big smile, holding it up in front of her face to focus on one of many fine details as they walked.

"That was my idea. Mama has one that is over a hundred years old." She hooked her thumb toward the shelved collection at their right. "It's in there somewhere."

"Anje, you are correct. I am going to be on the path for many years to come, it would seem. This gift will see every league of it, to the end of my days."

They had come to a curved banister before Kamiko realized they were on a landing with a stair, leading down on the left and another leading up on the right. The stairway leading down was lined with candles burning, close to the wall and with many shapes and sizes, each of them unique like everything about the Kale home.

Matilda's voice rose out over the room, "Danae…Andi Jean…"

Movement at the height of their peripheral sight drew both women's attention, and they looked up to see Danae's bright-red face peering down from the landing above.

"Your mother told you to prepare a room for me?" Kamiko asked quietly.

"Well, in a way. She said to get the hall ready for Danae."

Kamiko smiled at that. "Downstairs?"

"Yes, just follow the candles. Everything is ready, food and tea and…well, Mama gave me a list, so I hope all is as it should be."

"Ah, with food and water, all else may be improvised," she said and waved to Danae to come down. "Do you speak with your hands?

Deaf sign?" She noticed Danae appeared to be walking on her heels again rather than her normal toe-bounce gait. The girl was so tired.

"Umm, well, barely. I can spell my name."

"Would you like to learn?"

"I'd say I'm willing to learn."

"It's just that Danae has a vigorous young intellect," Kamiko said, "and she tends to press the language upon you."

"What is going on? What's about to happen? Why does she need the hall all set up?" Kamiko was coming to know that Anje was a peaceful person by nature, excitement held below the surface of calm.

"Training, my friend, very difficult training for a twelve-year-old girl." She thought a moment and added, "And a forty-two-year old woman." She thought a moment longer and said to Anje, as Danae was making the bottom of the stairs, "I don't know what to think about your mother yet. I believe you should act on her every word to the letter without question or pause. I assure you, I shall."

As Danae stepped up and smiled, it occurred to Kamiko that she was alone.

"Danae," she spoke and signed, "what have you done with your sister?"

Without hesitation, Danae answered, "Sold her for fifty gold buttons." Which Kamiko translated verbally. This drew a sharp laugh from Anje and left a lingering chuckle rumbling in Kamiko's gut for some minutes to follow.

*****

Felene

"The sisterhood? Disbanding? The Order cannot simply close their doors and walk away, Sister Felene. We depend on you being part of things, you do a lot of good." Sir Johns had pulled to the side and slowed the carriage suddenly to allow them to converse without shouting. They were moving at an easy trot, with Mars Knoll and the wind now at their back, so that the air was still but for swirling eddies tickling across her face.

His voice was calm, but Felene knew his thoughts were very busy. She said, "We were barely *banded* together anyway, we just do what we do. Don't trouble over it, Sir Johns, we sisters are still where we are, with or without a name or the Knoll. We serve God, not a king, a habit we will continue indefinitely. And something tells me my sword sisters and I are in for much ado...very much a part of things."

The Order was the leanest and smoothest operation in all the kingdom. By the time Felene and Sir Johns arrived at Mars Knoll, it was already being swept clean and was standing mostly empty. Sisters Talitha and Rose were going to maintain a presence until they were certain the news of both Rachel's death and the disbanding of the Order was universal knowledge among the sisterhood. In the interim, until the crown took occupancy, the Knoll would be opened to all needing shelter from the cold. Other sisters were on their way to local merchants who had always offered food and physical goods when called upon by need. Uila had not been seen. Felene and Sir Johns had left within ten minutes of their arrival. Felene felt no urge to go inside. None at all. They'd spoken to Talitha and Rose in the stable room and then left. Almost three thousand years, the Order had endured, to have ended in a meaningful embrace and a prayer for safe travels. Such was the way of the sisterhood.

"What are your worries, Sir Johns, what have you been hearing?"

"Tis Rasha...I mean Cort," he said. "And he says *many* things." He gave her a nod and held her gaze a moment before turning forward again. When he continued, his tone was a light banter, but the words were dark and held great weight. "Rasha believes the fall of Cairistonia is at hand. He told me half a year ago the sisterhood would disband, and that the sister would be here this very day."

"Kamiko?"

"Yes, her too. But I speak of the young one—Danae, if I am saying it correctly."

"What was that? He was talking about Danae?"

"Well, his mother, Matilda, is the one. Rasha only repeats to me what he hears from her." He held her gaze another moment and turned back to the road. "He was very worried that Kamiko would show up today. I've never seen him like this, all nervous and..." He looked again at Felene, twisted his face into a comical expression of disbelief, and said, "Bubbly!"

Felene felt the seat press harder against her back as Sir Johns loosened the reins, granting the horses their wish for a more comfortable running gait. Still he kept them at an easy run through the muddy slush, ice, and snow. They rode in noisy silence, each in thought. Around them, the city crawled almost unnoticed, out of focus to their senses, hush-like.

Felene's mind bounced around with thoughts of waking up young, seeing Kamiko's form ablaze in silvery flame, the angelic realm, Rachel, Danae, Siruis, and then back to Dairei, the effort neither digging her out of her morose nor deeper into it.

The day was beginning to wane, and though the clouds had lifted somewhat, the dusk was forming, and it would soon be dark. Felene and Sir Johns both saw the man on horseback move suddenly at their approach. He left a static position at the edge of the pedestrian lanes and headed directly for the carriage at an easy gallop. He was liveried as a messenger, with a small silver trumpet dangling at his waist. Even so Felene's fist impulsively tightened around a hilt she did not hold, and she could feel the exposure of sitting in open sight like liquid pressure on her skin, like searching eyes were about to find their awaited target. One need only find Felene and practice patience and no small skill to eventually find Kamiko Hoshi. Of the limited options open to her, Felene chose the simplest. She snugged the hat down to just below her browline, then lifted the blanket edge to the bridge of her nose, effectively hiding her face and her form. She felt no concern for the messenger, rather someone secretly following the messenger.

But the courier came up short and slowed to allow right of way to the carriage, or so it appeared. Felene was looking directly at the man when he turned to face their passage and held his clenched fist against his midsection for a long moment before turning his horse into a run behind them to follow. She could now see the standard emblazoned on his armband and knew him to be under Lord Merritt's employment. Sir Johns had caught the signal, one obviously meant for him. He leaned toward Felene and tried to keep from shouting. She scooted closer and leaned to meet him, still keeping her covering intact.

"Something is afoot," Sir Johns said.

"He flashed you a warning."

He smiled, broad and open, and said, "You are very observant, Sister." Two more riders outfitted in the exact livery as the first eased out from the edge of the carriageway and joined the steady run in the leading position. "When we stop, you don't do anything at all. Sit very still, hunkered like you are bone-weary from a cold day in that seat." She nodded against his shoulder. He continued, "We are picking up Lord Merritt. I believe it would be prudent to keep you as an unknown element from here on. If your influence is required, I would rather it be with the benefit of surprise."

"I am with you, Sir Johns," she said and leaned back to where she'd been, but she slouched forward into the concealing folds of the hide blanket.

Chapter 5

Kamiko

Danae had eaten the small meal of baked fish, dark rice, and two small honey-sweetened corn muffins quickly, downed a full cup of tea, and set a second cup to steep. She trotted to and from the curtained alcove privy and downed the second cup, casting a quick glance at a beautiful old mantle clock sitting on the floor beside a well-stoked fireplace. Kamiko watched her closely. Danae took care of everything Kamiko had told her to do within the first five minutes of her ten-minute allotment, including placing her dinnerware on the floor just at the top of the stair. Then she lay down on the stone floor before the fire and was asleep.

Kamiko was already seated in the center of the round room. This smaller deeper dome, also carved from solid stone, was higher and dark. The only other lights in the room, beyond the fireplace, consisted of three lamps, two on the floor near where Danae had eaten and a small one glowing golden in the center of the room with Kamiko. Anje had indeed set the room in order like a true sister. A small low table and single cushion for Danae's respite, three lamps, the clock, and a circular area in the center of the room, layered with seven rugs, was all that stood upon the polished stone floor. A single stone-carved carafe of cool water and two stone cups were the only other objects in the room and were on the low table near the hearth.

Kamiko sat cross-legged, soldierlike, with her elbows on her knees and her chin perched on her thumbs, fingers overlapped but not interlocked. A long night was about to begin. She would have a full thousand things in her mind at once if she allowed it. She focused her thoughts instead, if indirectly, upon Siruis. Kamiko held every certainty that Siruis was nothing more than a simple flesh-and-blood woman, who was acting on her godly belief with an uncommon fullness of expression. Kamiko's awe was struck twofold. She stood in awe of God in his might, but it moved her all the more that he would focus on so minute a point as Siruis, a small woman from an unknown place called Marjan, and offer to open the tap of his power where she, in human terms, may direct it. The story was fully enveloped by him, and he was actively helping his champions and supporting his agents afoot with real power.

The *thousand things* were not Kamiko's transcendent cause. She believed God wanted all of her focus on the current moment, not spread across countless possibilities. Such was God's own divine craft. Living in the present was the mark of mankind.

And so, she turned her thoughts to Danae. She would most likely be expecting combat and technique training. Kamiko was not yet convinced that combat was Danae's calling. Felene had told Kamiko that during her forty years of paralysis, Danae remained with her for two full decades. Who would do that? What kind of girl becomes that woman? She then knew exactly how to begin. Something Danae would never expect. That was crucial—to get her off any predetermined ideas from the outset.

Danae's form stirred. *Two minutes to spare*, Kamiko thought and allowed a slight and momentary grin on one side of her mouth and in the lift of her brow. The lithe girl rose to her feet, already at a trot, and disappeared into the alcove again. When she came out, she walked slower and joined Kamiko in the center. As she sat, her backside touched the rug as the minute hand on the clock moved, the tenth minute expired.

Now this is a student of Rachel's, Kamiko thought as she lowered her hands and straightened her posture, showing Danae every respect she would show any full sister, though as yet, Danae was not a sister. It occurred to Kamiko that Danae would never be a full sister with the Order breaking up. She waited until the girl was seated and still, then spoke without preamble.

"You will teach me how to speak better with my hands. I will teach you how to speak with your voice." The slow and broken manner of her visual diction made the point perfectly. Danae nodded her agreement slowly for a moment, her face passive but bright with attention. "You are responsible for your own decisions, starting now, and lasting for the fullness of your lifetime. I will give you no commands, only options. And the first choice before you is to join me for a run or to rest here on the carpet."

It was the most words Kamiko had signed in many years, and it was fraught with skips and pauses and ill-rendered wording. Without waiting for reaction or reply, Kamiko rose casually and slowly walked to the outer edge of the round room, gradually speeding up to a slow trot, testing the feel of the tight shoes. She did not look behind her as she rounded into the curve of the room, but she could see the carpet pad in the center of the floor was no longer occupied. She sped to a slow smooth run and began drawing deep breaths. Danae had only a certain amount of energy left and Kamiko needed to ration it carefully. But a good run would get her blood moving and her brain working well. It would also serve to allow Danae time to ponder the short directive.

Kamiko knew she had a lot to learn about the young initiate. Their entire history together was yet marked in only hours. Danae had been under Sister Rachel's tutelage for two years, so she would have some fighting skill with a staff and with short blades. Kamiko knew that also meant she was capable of physical endurance and spiritual tempering, and that she had deeper than a simple working knowledge of godly precepts. Rachel was Djinnasee's student for more than three decades, and Kamiko knew the elder's breadth of knowledge had been carefully spread over Danae's spirit. It would be a mistake to underestimate the young girl's talents.

Kamiko could just hear a whisper of sound behind her, a soft cadence almost twice as quick as her own long and steady stride. A few strides more, and the top of Danae's head formed at the lower edge of Kamiko's sight, as the girl moved easily into the lead. Then with what Kamiko could only perceive as a look of feigned innocence, Danae peered over her shoulder at Kamiko and accelerated. Considerably. Just before Danae's head snapped back around, she crossed her eyes and stuck out her tongue at Kamiko. But when her face recentered on what lay ahead, she leaned forward and bolted away from Kamiko at a hard sprint.

It took a moment for it to dawn on Kamiko that she was to give chase, but when the thought struck home, she powered her mass hard and fast and locked her focus upon the girl now way out in front of her. She kept her full strength in check, however, lest she get a mule kick of a cramp to the thigh. She would let Danae run her strength out.

*****

Felene

An armed contingent escorted the elderly lord from his receiving door to the carriage, and two of their number entered with him. For all Felene could tell by the exact meter of their boot strikes, only two people were walking across the brick driveway, Lord Merritt and someone heavy. The two men who entered the carriage were his ever-present attendants, bodyguards Oric Jinz and Jesse Turel, two of the toughest men Felene had ever known yet possessing no penchant for meanness or power. She knew they were cousins but knew only a little of their true past. Their family was bound to the Merritt family over thirty generations ago. It was a legacy both families bore with dignity and honor, and Lord Merritt treated them like sons, sometimes at the expense of his own sons. The line of Turel held no single connection to any bloodline of note, while the Merritt historical ancestry could be seen in bas-relief in one of the many halls of the king's own house. Felene had seen it for herself. One was bound to servitude, the other to lordship. The two gentlemen warriors watched over Lord Merritt of their own choice, bound or not, this Felene knew for a certainty.

The door slammed with a quiet thump. She cocked her head enough to see two heavily armed footmen mount the out seats on the tail of the carriage. Sir Johns simply clicked his tongue a few times, and the black horses stepped forward eagerly but with such ease Felene could barely feel the onset of motion. A childhood memory flashed in her mind of falling asleep atop her horse while it grazed the highland pastures of her father's realm, three times a week. It made her smile beneath the cover as she peered through the slot between hat and blanket.

And though her mind seemed to be wandering more than usual, she was keeping a vigilant eye and saw a motion that seemed out of place. Someone had been standing between the decorative embrasures of a building front ahead of the carriage and dropped out of sight suddenly.

"Did you see that?" she asked Sir Johns, indicating where she'd seen the motion. He offered only a nod and kept his attention on the road.

A pair of armed cavalrymen, outfitted in Lord Merritt's, were on station, waiting for the carriage, and spurred their mounts into a run that brought them into the lead, just as Sir Johns began letting the horses have their heads. The procession thundered onto the main carriage lane just as the day was darkening to night, and the countless flickers of lamps began sparkling across the frozen city.

*****

Kamiko

Kamiko could not easily believe it. She was bent at the waist, her hands heavy on her knees, her lungs pumping hard. It had been a long time since she was a runner. Danae stood thirty paces away, standing upright, and unlike Kamiko, she was not winded. Danae had thrown the challenge down, and Kamiko had been unsuccessful touching even a finger to the girl. *Well,* she thought, *I'm not done just yet.* But as Kamiko gathered her energy to resume the chase, she could see Danae bending her knees and angling her feet for flight. She muttered aloud, "Gonna be a long night." Then she lunged.

*****

Felene

Twice the lead horseman had turned in the saddle to flash Sir Johns a signal. Each was followed by a change in the direction they traveled. They had slowed considerably but only enough to accommodate the smaller streets and pedestrians. This was the third signal. The procession slowed abruptly, and the two cavalrymen split and took up station on both sides of a tunnelway, through the belly of a massive stone building. The long corridor was barely alight with a row of small overhead lamps and was large enough to pass a carriage thrice the size the one they were on. Sir Johns maintained a quick trot out of the night and into the dim light of the tunnel. At what Felene perceived was midway through, there came a sharp wooden triple knock near their feet, which Sir Johns appeared to have expected, as he brought the team to an easy but quick stop.

Felene sat very still and listened as the door latch clacked, though the opening door was silent on its hinges. She looked to her left just as Oric stepped out of the carriage, followed closely by Jesse and Lord Merritt. The elder man turned to look up at Felene and extended his hand to her.

"Sister, please come quickly." Felene moved immediately but cast Sir Johns a look before dropping down from the high seat in one bounding leap, leaving the hide blanket up top with him. Jesse stepped up to her with his usual one-sided grin and untied the thick fur hat, pulled it from her head with a yank, then turned and snugged it down over Oric's head, all the way to his browline. He clapped his kinsman on the shoulders and nodded toward the high seat. As Oric took Felene's guise beside Sir Johns, Lord Merritt ushered Felene into the carriage, then followed her in. Jesse bounded in a moment later and closed the door with a clack of the latch, then took the seat beside Lord Merritt.

Felene sat very still for a few moments, seeing if she could tell when the carriage began moving. She could sense that it *was* moving but did not feel the departure. When she saw the look on the elder lord's face, she gave him her full attention.

"I will believe nothing I have heard, dear Sister, until it issues from your mouth. Please tell me everything, for I am casting against hope that what I have heard is not the truth." His face was devoid of any emotion but keen interest, though he appeared to be holding out against fatigue. Felene knew the exact news he sought.

"Lord Merritt," she said and leaned forward to take his hands. "Anton, my friend. Sister Rachel is lost to us. All others are well and safe." She felt a slight flinch and a momentary shudder in his hands and saw the darkening of sadness in his eyes and in the set of his mouth. Jesse closed his eyes and lowered his head for a moment, then placed his thick hand on Lord Merritt's arm. A heavy silence settled over them and lasted for a span of many minutes. Four lamps, fixtured at the uppermost corners of the interior of the carriage, glowed dim yellow, with so slight a shine that the moisture in the lord's eyes twinkled like golden starlight.

"We will talk more about it later," the elder man said. "I wish to keep her smiling visage in my thoughts a bit longer."

"Then there is nothing to fear from hearing about it, my lord." Felene's islandic accent had crept in and rolled on her tongue. "You'll be smiling to the depths of your chest, elated by what has befallen our Sister Rachel. And you will sleep quiet and sound, bothered by no terrors." Both men's eyes came to rest on hers. "Aye, she was laughing, my friends, and singin', fierce and wild. And she fell into no pit in chains. I saw her carried away by a thicket of fleet angels into the realm of the infinite. We know well enough—her evening meal will be far better than our own." She fell silent and let the two men have their thoughts. When Lord Merritt's eyes finally came back up to hers, she could no longer hold her tongue.

"I have much to tell you, my friend, but foremost is this. This kingdom has come under attack. Nothing short of a declaration of war. And tis true, the sisterhood is breaking up, but we are not going to stop doing…what we do." She recalled the sight of seeing every sister in the entire Order spread across the kingdom. Each of them were as aware of what was happening as she was, had seen all that she had seen—Sister Rachel in the war garb of the angels, Sister Kamiko virtually erupting like a silver volcano, the attack on Sister Grace and the others. She opened her mouth and simply let the tale form, beginning with the outbreak of fire at Lord Merritt's estate. They were yet ten minutes from the Kale homestead when the course of her tale rejoined them in Sir Johns's carriage.

Lord Merritt wasted no time on silent brooding. "It seems we have an odd dichotomy before us. We have much to do, and we have little to do. A call to arms is a forgone conclusion and no small affair. Beyond that we continue hitting our daily mark, as ones who believe and trust to the hand of God. It is my opinion we are exactly as he has placed us, and we should stay on course until drawn to another."

Both Felene and Jesse nodded their silent acknowledgment.

Lord Merritt continued, "On that note, I shall promptly deviate from any norm I am familiar with. Jesse, if you please?" Jesse stood and turned toward the back of the carriage where he and Lord Merritt were sitting. A recessed shelf for stowage of bags and parcels was built behind the rear seat, and from this, Jesse retrieved a long and rather large flat wooden box. Even with his strength, he had to be careful, for the box appeared to be heavy and was unruly for its length. Lord Merritt offered a stabilizing hand as it came over his head. Rather than try to turn again with the long box in his hands, Jesse simply backed up and sat beside Felene, laying the box across both their laps. It was almost too long for the width of the carriage, and it was as thick as Felene's handbreadth. It was made of oak, by the look of the grain, stained dark red, and as wide as her arm from elbow to fingertip. What struck her, though, was that it appeared extremely old. And it had no marking, latch, handle, or hinge to make one think it was anything other than a plank of fine oak.

Lord Merritt scooted to the center of the bench and extended his hands to both ends of the box, then pressed the rounded corner of both. Felene saw a small wafer of the wood slide out under the pressure of each of his thumbs, and the top of the box popped up slightly. Before he opened it, he placed his hand over the lid and drew Felene's eyes to his.

"I commissioned the search for this three years ago. It arrived this very day." He held her gaze a moment longer. "Quinlan-Dunc. I have little doubt you are familiar with that name."

Hearing a name of such lofty prominence in her family heritage sparked a flame of home in her chest. "Yes, I know the name of Lord Quinlan-Dunc well. He was the king of Feldenland, my island home, over six hundred years ago, during the time of the Tartan siege."

He lifted the lid off and lay it on the floor between them, then drew away the silken cloth cover to reveal an enormous sword. The two men sat in silence and watched Felene's reaction. This was her weapon of choice, Lord Merritt knew well. And it was the ancient sword of her kinsman. She gasped aloud.

"Yes," he said, smiling. "And being a bit of an historian, I have come to know your centuries-removed kingly grandfather very well." He lay his hand across the broad crosspiece. "He led your ancestors in a successful campaign, which drove the Tartan Armies into the ocean. He made war upon the warlords, bandits, and pirate kings, seeming to cover all the land and sea, until he, at last, ruled the land in peace. He died aged 162 years." He paused to let Felene's eyes finally rise from the sword before he continued, "All with this sword in his hand."

The sword was set into a fitted form, carved into the wood and lined with thick and highly polished leather, of a size and fit to hold the sword in its sheath. Lord Merritt lifted the sword with both hands and held it up with a genuine reverence. "This sword was a vital part of your homeland gaining its liberty and keeping it these several centuries. King Quinlan-Dunc of clan Duncl. His castle still stands in the northern highlands like a great dark crown jewel. You have been there a few times if I am correct?"

Felene nodded, as memories of her home sprung from her fertile mind like a field of flowers after a spring rain. "Aye, my lord, I have." And oddly she could not turn her eyes from the elder man's face, though the sword called to her with only it's presence.

He said, "I have been there twice, my friend. Jesse and Oric were with me on the second occasion." To which Jesse nodded and smiled on one side.

Something occurred to Felene with a mild shock. "Lord Merritt," she asked quietly, "how have you come to own this sword? This is no collectible on a market shelf but a relic of foremost import to my kinsmen." She noticed that Jesse tried and failed to suppress a reaction, allowing one brow to rise dramatically. Oddly Jesse's reaction and her notice only served to raise a smile on Lord Merritt's handsome face.

"Truth ever marks the path of the sisterhood, Jesse," he said and turned to Felene. "My dear Sister Felene Dresdle of Clan Duncl, I have not purchased this sword, I am returning it to the rightful owner." He waited while Felene began turning over what she knew of her ancestral linage, looking for who the rightful owner may be. She could tell the sword was heavy for him to hold, yet his arms were steady as oak as he hefted the sword toward her, still flat across his hands. Her hands naturally jumped up from her lap, and one slapped midsheath while the other found the hilt. It fit perfectly in her hand. Jesse chuckled under his breath and was smiling with both sides of his mouth.

Lord Merritt said to his young charge, "Well, my friend, and so it has been done." To Felene's puzzlement, the two men slapped their palms together and squeezed and laughed aloud like old friends over some secret victory. She understood the implication clearly enough.

"My pardon, Lord Merritt, but I think you have run aground in your search for the rightful owner, if you think I am even on the list." She knew better than to cast a single hope. "The smattering of royal blood I may claim puts many people between myself and the bloodline of King Quinlan-Dunc. This would better serve in my father's house."

"Your father is not among those with claim to this sword, rather your mother. As you know, she is daughter to Lord FeDun of Keinsland, whom I personally researched and vetted as a direct descendant of the king, which makes you a direct descendant too. But you are correct to assume that you would not be foremost, if there were a list. However, there is no such list," he said with a smile, "but you have been declared rightful owner by those with the fullness of Quinlan-Dunc blood in their veins. Tis yours henceforth, until you part ways with this world altogether, Sister Felene, with the blessings of not only your father and mother but the entire standing council as well."

For the first time in her memory, Jesse spoke, "I got the feeling your activities in their war against the pirate warlord were not soon forgotten."

She looked over at Jesse. "You were there? At my home?"

"I was."

"They called a council over me?"

"Not exactly," Lord Merritt answered. "The council was called because my agents found and acquired the sword. Jesse made the trip on my behalf."

Felene lifted one brow and smiled at the gentleman. "Found and acquired?"

"Yes, it vanished more than three hundred years ago. No one is certain exactly how or when. But I discovered evidence it has surfaced more than once. Well, it recently surfaced again, in the hands of one of those crazed desert warlords of the eastern Goli-Ben, a ruffian named Rulith Bean and his band of gypsies, and so…we acquired it." He shared a look with Jesse, who raised a single brow in answer. "He met our agents there to return it to the council, and left it with them. They sent it to me of their own accord."

She looked at Jesse. "You took this to my home?" Indicating the sword by lifting it.

"I did. I took my lodgings in your brother's old room," he said with a sheepish smile, "overlooking the westering mountains, with their feet out in the sea. Your father and mother offered to host my stay."

"How long?" she asked, hesitant. Feelings of home churned to sudden and full life. Forty years. She'd never returned home again from her crippling day—yesterday. Felene had never known why the sisterhood had not taken her home then.

"Six weeks."

"Six." Her last visit home lasted two and a half years, half of which was spent fighting a war, the other half rebuilding from its ravages. She'd returned to Mars Knoll six years ago, then continued on to Ravencroft.

Jesse continued, unprompted, "We shall sit over a keg and a pile of food, and I will tell you every detail, my friend. You may question me to no end. I met and conversed with many people who have sent their prayers and tidings. You shall have them all."

"I should like that very much."

"Please mind the words of Lord Merritt," he said. "The sword is yours by vote of the Council of Princes. And it was a quick and unanimous vote at that, Sister. I was present for the session and can attest to a deep and abiding gratitude they feel toward you. And I heard the history of your deeds from many mouths, in many forms, with wings in one particular tale."

Her eyes had returned to the sword when she felt and heard the slightest drop in the speed of the carriage.

"Where are we going?" she asked, looking at each man in turn.

"To the Kale establishment. I am hitching a ride," Lord Merritt said. "I have business with Master Ezra, and I desire to see Kamiko." The carefully contained sadness crept across his eyes again.

Felene tilted her head slightly and asked, "How—"

"Djinnasee," he said and nodded, his brow darkened now, furrowed. "Three years ago, he set upon me the task of finding this sword. He also gave me further instructions, which I am following now." He pressed the palm of his hand to his forehead and closed his eyes for a moment. "His words have been flawless, Sister, down to the fine details. For three years, I have hoped you would be on this carriage this night, as Djinnasee declared plainly you would be."

The carriage had slowed and slowed again. They heard Sir Johns's strong tenor voice call out a command and, moments later, call the command again with increased vigor. All three of the passengers were now focused upon that single event, and they waited in silence for the next. When the carriage lurched to a hard stop, Jesse was out the door, thumping it firmly closed behind him.

The carriage was of excellent quality, designed for a quiet and smooth ride. In the short moment the door was open, a row of excited voices was clearly heard that, once detected, Felene could still hear after the door was shut and the enclosed quiet returned.

"What is this, my lord?"

"I'm not sure. Both Kamiko and Siruis have been seen by many people at Mars Knoll and at my estate, word is out. Uila came thundering to my gate with only his halter intact. He was enraged, I am told, and would allow no hand near his body. They simply opened the way to his previous stall, where he collapsed and slept."

The door opened only enough for Jesse to enter and was quickly thumped closed behind him. The carriage moved forward, smooth and sure. Jesse had returned to sit beside Felene and resumed his hold on the long box. He shared a look with Lord Merritt that ended with a slight nod.

"Sister," the elder man said, "there are roving bands of mercenaries, citizens, and opportunists spread across this area that will be quickly converging on Flavin, all of them looking for Kamiko and her charge. There are also bands forming to stop them. Half the kingdom wants the *witch woman* killed on sight, as they believe it will stop the fall of Cairistonia." His voice reflected his spiked disdain for the statement. "The other half believes Siruis to be a prophet of God and will see her defended." He shook his head and continued, "Everyone fears her, Sister Felene, everyone." He paused for a moment. "But no one will harm her. The sheer enormity of the reward for her living undamaged self will protect her."

"And this?" she said, and hooked her thumb toward the door.

Jesse answered with a one-sided smile. "A roving band."

Felene smiled at Jesse and drew her homeland accent to fullness. "A roving band, is it? So ye jest step out the door, and whoosh, off they scamper, eh? And they say a reputation is nay a good thing."

He chuckled and said, "Funny thing that…but yes. And the presence of Oric and the twelve armed horsemen guarding my flank. There was a bit of profanity and then a general scampering from the path," he said with his half-smile. "I believe Sir Johns is going to take a roundabout way to the southern gate of the Kale estate." His face grew suddenly stern, and he looked at Lord Merritt and said, "They are searching for Kamiko, my lord."

Chapter 6

Kamiko

She held no misconceptions. If Danae had been fully rested at the onset of the chase, Kamiko would never have caught her. Sheer fatigue made the girl falter, and Kamiko barely managed to drag her toe across Danae's hip, ending one of the greatest challenges Kamiko had faced in a long time. They were lying on their backs atop the rug pallet, still catching their breath from a short but potent fit of uncontrollable laughter. It had taken Kamiko well over an hour to finally catch Danae, and something about that had triggered a giggle, which quickly grew and suddenly calmed. And thirst.

Kamiko rose with a start, making for the water pitcher, as her throat dried to stonecutter's dust. But Danae flashed past her, snatched up the pitcher and one of the cups, filled it, and held it out to Kamiko as she stepped up. Kamiko nodded her thanks to Danae and raised it in thanks to God for the contents, then downed it in one slow draw. She handed the cup back to Danae, who filled it and likewise took her own portion.

The fire had burned down by more than half, and the room had dimmed to a dark glow. The lamps were pools of yellow light too weak to cast into the darkness of the ceiling. Motion at the stairway caught both their eyes as Cort appeared from above and quietly stacked an armload of wood on the bottom stair. A smaller boy, roughly half Danae's age, placed his burden of a hefty jug and a small box on the second step from the bottom, then turned and sprinted up and out of sight. Cort followed at a much slower pace but cast a brief parting look over his shoulder at Kamiko.

Every time she laid eyes on Cort, a different emotion played on his face and colored his movements. This was a young man who was fighting inside. Years of hard work were finally paying off for his carriage business in spite of the lunacy his mother was seemingly under, which spoke of an uncommon resilience in the man. Kamiko had not spared a minute trying to imagine what the past few years had been like for the Kale household. She could feel the love that was inherent in the place. It was tangible, a palpable taste in her mouth, as though generations of laughter, peace, hope, and the love of godliness had been baked into the very fabric of the stone. The emotion most often etched into Cort's face was fear. Matilda had most likely told him, and all of the Kale family, that this would soon be coming to an end.

At her side, Danae had grown still, and Kamiko thought the girl was also momentarily seized by a wave of contemplation. It lasted only short moments before the girl set the cup down and walked toward the stairway, her movements still quick but dulled by the fatigue borne of a day filled with tremendous difficultly. Kamiko felt more strength of muscle and vitality of spirit than she could call to mind since she was Danae's age. *Since*, she thought, *Siruis's healing touch.*

For a moment, Kamiko saw a man standing nearby, again in the garb of a commoner. In the outstretched palm of his hand danced a small tongue of fire which flared brightly, and then he was gone. Kamiko saw herself as the twelve-year-old warrior, sheen with the blood of a hundred brigands, standing side by side with Danae. She saw two statues, one of shimmering onyx, the other of glistening silver. The onyx bore the perfect resemblance of the fierce Warrior vision Kamiko had carried since that terrible day of blood, the silver that of the timorous Woman she'd contrived alongside. A sudden flare of heat, white from the sheer intensity, reduced the statues to swirling black dust instantly, leaving the two twelve-year-old girls in their places. In that moment, Kamiko knew that Danae's destiny was far greater than being a sword-wielding warrior. She also fully understood that the nature of the woman she'd contrived did not represent weakness at all, rather strength of spirit, one who battles demons, one able to stand against the likes of Luthain. Her breath quickened and her nose flared, tingling as the awareness came to full fruition. Danae was a giant. At best Kamiko would be her steward.

The vision cleared as suddenly as it had overtaken her, and she found they were no longer near the stair. They were seated in a small circle in the center of the room on the carpets, Matilda with them. The fire in the hearth had been fed, and the lamps glowed brightly with replenished oil and newly trimmed wicks.

Kamiko had been the first to open her eyes, followed by Matilda, then Danae. As the girl looked around in obvious confusion, Matilda reached over and touched Danae's forehead with two fingers. The girl yawned hard and long and stretched her arms over her head for a moment before she slumped gently to her side and was fast asleep.

Well, Kamiko thought, *a change of plan must be in order.* Matilda nodded her agreement with Kamiko's silent thought and, using her hand, signed the word *Felene,* then hooked her thumb toward the stairway.

*****

"My family has been here for 135 generations," the elder man declared, quietly and seemingly to no one in particular. "My ancestor, Von Delben Merritt, was a citizen of the great sojourn from the west and witnessed, if not the actual cataclysm, the global aftermath which followed." His gaze and his hands rested upon a flat long wooden box lying on the table between them. One hand was casually placed and moved as he spoke. The other he appeared to hold carefully in place, as if to cover something he wished to conceal for the moment. Kamiko got the sense he was speaking mostly to her.

"Before the death of King Romas Phiemus, Titus's father, I witnessed with my own eyes, Lord Von Delben's signature on the original charter of Cairistonian kingship, penned in CR year 1."

Felene stood in silence at Kamiko's left, Matilda at her right. An almost incorporeal visage of Siruis stood alone at one end of the long table, which separated the elder lord from the three sisters. Only Matilda had reacted to Siruis's presence. Kamiko was certain that neither Felene nor Lord Merritt could see her. The cavernous domed room was otherwise completely empty of souls and was soundless, but for the quiet man's soft voice.

"Based upon information irrelevant to this discourse, but obtained by the personal order of King Romas, I now know we Merritt's are the last remaining bloodline still intact of the 170 patriarchal founders who signed the charter."

Kamiko felt her mouth open of its own accord and saw Felene's do the same. He slowly raised his eyes to meet Kamiko's. She deliberately closed her mouth and held very still. "Lord Von Delben made the sojourn with Djinnasee, Sister Kamiko, had meals with him, took rest with him, and walked those 1,100 terrible leagues at his side. He counseled the elders and the masses to heed Djinnasee's words, to homestead when they arrived at the place we now call First Colony. He stood at Djinnasee's right hand when the schism formed, and they sought the prophet's life. He pleaded with them for sanity as the people split, and war preparations were begun." He grew silent for a few moments, holding Kamiko's gaze with a steely intensity colored with *mischief.* A shiver of anticipation crawled up the full length of her spine. "Then he drove them into the sea, without sparing any living thing among them, be it man or beast, mother or child. He returned home victorious but mortally wounded. Djinnasee sat at his bedside and prayed for seven days and nights that the Eternal grant Lord Von Delben's dying wish. He declined to save his own life, instead praying for his many sons and their progeny that they know godly fear and should enjoy unfaltering belief in the Creator, for all of the Merritt generations to come."

At the end of the long table, Kamiko caught sight of Siruis stepping forward and turned to look at her. Kamiko's talisman rested in her open palm and glistened with a low crackling white fire, which danced around her hand as sizzling energy. She felt Matilda's hand close around her wrist and turned back to see the same glistening sheen, dancing around Lord Merritt's unmoving hand, where it was laid atop the box. It was a tiny cloudless lightning storm, again unseen by Felene and Lord Merritt.

"Von Delben's sons took it upon themselves to watch over and protect Djinnasee and pledged every generation of Merritt-born menfolk to God for this purpose, for all of time or until God commanded them to do otherwise." This history was wholly unknown to Kamiko. "In the year CR 1352, Djinnasee gave that very order and released us from that duty forever." This was spoken with the timbre of sadness. "It was the day of Delia Mars' birth and the institution of the Order." Kamiko's breath stopped altogether. "Undaunted, the sons of Merritt simply transferred that obligation to rest upon Delia Mars and all her bloodline and have continued, as before...until this very day." Again the seasoned diplomat paused to allow emotions, reason, and shock to coalesce and settle into the very souls of those listening. Now his eyes burned upon Kamiko with genuine ferocity. "You, my dear Sister Kamiko Hoshi, are the very end of Delia Mars' bloodline. There shall never be another."

Before the words had fully formed in Kamiko's heart, the room seemed to implode, leaving nothing in her awareness but her own body, Lord Merritt, and the crackling storm beneath his firm hand. It pulsed and danced out over the box several inches, growing agitated, excited. "Delia Mars lived exactly three hundred years to the day. Upon that day, those many generations ago, my ancestral grandfather was given the charge to hold this in trust, until such time that history made it necessary once again." He simply lifted his hand and stepped back one full pace, his arms floating out to his side, palms up, with his head bowed in the attribute of prayer. "As they marked the beginning, thus we mark the end. The sisterhood is—"

A miniature volcano erupted from where Lord Merritt's hand had rested. It was no dancing twisting silvery flame this time but a blast-furnace roar of howling white intensity, whose sudden light filled the entire room, washing out every color. But the illumination was borne within the ether and cast its glow upon the faces of those who dwelt there. And for several moments, Kamiko, Siruis, and Matilda were in the presence of many others. Felene and Lord

Merritt showed no outward sign they had seen the brightening of the light or the appearance of the others. As before, Kamiko could now see all the way across the expanse of the kingdom. She got the impression that thousands of godly messengers had been busy at their assigned tasks but were distracted for a short time by the flaring light from Lord Merritt's wooden box. They were being called to pause and bear witness. The message was clear—this moment in Kamiko's life was providence.

"…no more." Lord Merritt's voice had not paused. The sight had unfolded between the moments and then folded back away and was gone.

Kamiko knew the others had not ceased to exist simply because her eyes could no longer see them. The tiny storm was gone from the box, as well as from the talisman in Siruis's hand. Now Kamiko could clearly make out the silver wire inlay of Koralilia set into the wood of the box, in exact duplication of her talisman. With what Kamiko felt to be an external compulsion, some other hand lifting her arm, she placed her right palm on the sigil inlay. It had turned to dust. She had no expectation but would never have imagined the result. Wood and silver simply rotted away, as though 2,500 years of decay had been held in check until her skin touched the surface. And there under her palm, the sword of Delia Mars rested in waiting. She glanced at Siruis and saw that her talisman had also dissolved into dust. She had been carrying the key to the box for two and a half decades unawares.

"Oh." Felene cooed quietly, to which Lord Merritt slowly nodded his agreement.

Kamiko lowered her hand down to rest with her palm over the crosspiece and simply gazed upon it for several minutes. The pommel and crosspiece were unadorned, common to a working soldier, pure function. And to no surprise, the grip was a flawless fit in her hand as she lifted the weight of the sword with a firm squeeze. Well balanced, not too light. She looked more closely at the metal of the blade and saw the long curvy vein-edges of a thousand folds, giving not a silver reflection but bright gray, almost green in hue.

She stepped back from the table and lifted the sword, though not pointed upward in the style of the soldier, but lying flat across her upraised hands, balanced only on her fingertips as high as she could lift it, in the way of the sisterhood. And just as she'd hoped, it was Lord Merritt's voice offering a brief prayer of thanksgiving to the unseen God.

*****

Felene saw a look come over Kamiko's face she'd never seen before, like a child with a chance-found fancy toy. Her face brightened with a flush as the sword dropped from her fingertips and into her palm. She backed away from the table several steps, turned around, and drew very still, the lowered sword resting in her gentle grasp, almost letting the weight slip. Felene understood that Kamiko had passed the initial emotion and was already delving into the feel and weight and balance of the weapon, from the perspective of the greatest sword-sister alive, likely in all of their history.

Felene spared a glance at Lord Merritt and Matilda, who, in turn, shared a brief contact. Kamiko's back was to them, and her head was slowly nodding as she gazed down at the sword. She turned her head and cast a glance back at Lord Merritt, which seemed to convey speechlessness, her mouth open, but unsure which sound to utter first. Kamiko lifted the sword with a snap, pointing it straight up, arm fully extended and brought her heels together, then rose to her toe tips and drew rigid as a post. Her other arm was extended flat horizontal to the tips of her fingers. Kamiko looked like a finely crafted statue in a perfect moment, captured by a master artisan.

The reflective nature of the large domed room cast faint shadows at odd angles and fell across Kamiko's back and shoulders from above. Felene had never been around Kamiko when they were not suited for a fight, had never paid any heed to her natural form other than her greater height and build.

Felene could clearly see why Kamiko's strength bordered upon legend. Her back was a stone wall of long thick cords, which gathered in boulders around her neck and along her shoulders. Her arms were carved heavy with strength yet without the bulging muscle girth of masculinity. It was not adoration or desire that triggered Felene's thoughts, rather respect, one warrior to another. Kamiko was a powerful woman, more so than Felene had realized.

She looked up at the sword and saw that Kamiko was not holding it in her hand, rather it was perched in perfect balance on the tip of her extended thumb. *Well, of course it is*, Felene thought with a half-smile and one raised brow.

*****

Kamiko could feel Hun'jotzimon's volatile presence above her, much like one feels the sun, midsummer, middesert, midday. And whereas that great being had exuded intense anger when Kamiko had drawn her sword within the walls of Mars Knoll, she now felt excitement and anticipation. And just as she'd come to recognize Hun'jotzimon's anger as an extension of her own, she felt the urgency mirror her thoughts and emotions, as when she had released a hundred thousand warriors upon an enemy stronghold. Preparations of a millennia and a half were coming to fruition as the sword of Delia Mars now rested firmly in her grasp.

Yet Hun'jotzimon remained aloof. She could feel the separation and the intention to remain so in her bones. Hun'jotzimon would continue waiting, but for what, Kamiko did not know. She could not see the ethereal sword, and Siruis was no longer in sight, only earth and stone, flesh and bone.

She turned toward the trio and returned to the table with the blade cradled against the underside of her forearm, the grip reversed in her hand, with the dark blade trailing behind her. She spoke to Lord Merritt, "Thank you, my friend. Sincerely…deeply. Your family has maintained their honor for nearly four thousand years." Beside her Felene glowed with adoration for the elder gentleman. Kamiko thought it good that Felene's forty-year gulag had not taken the love from her heart.

Felene said to the group, "We know what this means."

Lord Merritt nodded and answered into the near-silence of the cathedral room, "We have a serious fight coming."

Chapter 7

Ravencroft Pass—Grace

The cloud blanket had risen beyond the reflective glazing of the lights of Ravencroft City, so the night was dark and hard cold. Innumerable dim lights glistened from countless points, but without the moon and stars to lead the assault, darkness won the canvas of the vast cityscape below her.

Against all odds and reasoning, Grace was alive. What had happened could not have happened. What she saw could not have been real. Yet in her heart, she knew it could not have been *more* real. She need not even close her eyes to *see* the angelic colossus in her memory, the single being holding his hand over a single man. There was nothing illusional about it. She could have touched hands with Kamiko, they were so close. Grace's unknown savior appearing in her dream just before he saved her life meant that was no dream. The sisterhood was not disbanding. They would become something far greater and were simply dropping what was, in essence, a useless decorum from what was now the old way.

The night was bitter cold, but Grace was warm and well fed, fully suited and geared for shadow urban warfare. A thin opening across her eyes was the only gap anywhere in her garb, light gray and mottled in white. She was standing in the exact spot where, four days earlier, Sister Rachel had saved her life, the rubble of her home scattered where it had fallen. She held a blazing torch mounted on a long pole in her left hand, the butt of the shaft on the ground. Her sword was in her right hand, and her feet were spread in a set of defiance. She knew *they* were watching, and she wanted her message to be clear.

"My turn." She growled aloud.

Kamiko was right. Grace had won her fight, on the enemy's terms and with all his devices in play. And it had taken six of them to defeat Kamiko. No, the sisterhood was not scattering, they were gathering. God was pulling them together and preparing them, collectively and individually, with strength and skill. To what end, she could not know, but she could draw a pretty good conclusion. Grace felt it was unlikely that Djinnasee would send the sisterhood into whatever battle or war was looming, rather they would protect someone or some group of people specifically. Which meant Djinnasee had long since started the wheels turning to bring people together somewhere, a gathering of souls with courage enough to still believe in God and follow his lead.

From that well of knowledge, which comes from decades as a crime fighter and a battlefield warrior, Grace knew they would return to her with greater numbers to try again. She decided that the name Wroth was at the top of their command chain and was acting on ego rather than intellect, else the greater force would have descended on her with a larger unit instead of allowing one of their elite fighters to show his superiority. She could not suppress the urge to smile when her thoughts brushed over what she imagined *their* evening debriefing must have looked like. Wroth's initial affront had been a total failure. She hoped their spirits were doubly bruised by the fact that a group of women had handed their champions back to them with their heads on the proverbial spike! She had no doubt that they were to have continued to secondary and tertiary targets, with a wave of their lesser comrades breaking cover in their wake. It was obvious to Grace that the first-assault group was already deeply embedded in-country and were positioned in each of the cities where the sisterhood had been attacked. It would not take them long to regroup and reinitialize their maneuvers.

She had confidence that every other sister who'd been attacked was doing exactly what Grace was doing—sending this same message and mustering every sister in the kingdom to readiness. God had shown them the attack in real time, and the sisterhood was not in the habit of ignoring such blatant providence.

A sudden flare of twinkling firelight sprang to life atop one of the building roofs below her and quickly grew to a controlled but sizable blaze. She immediately recognized it as the same building and the same stranger she'd seen before—the one who had warned her to run and had saved everyone in her house in so doing.

And though the rooftop he occupied was below her at no small distance, she could see his features with enough clarity that it seemed at odds with reason and possibility. Grace believed that angels were becoming more involved and were likely bending the physical laws on behalf of her and the other sisters. They were committing war to the degree they were allowed.

There was very little clutter on the roof he occupied, mostly piled at the very edge on one side. The man was stationed in the very center near where the fire burned inside a large barrel. He was holding a thick curved knife, like the one the assassin had fought with. Every surface was rose-colored from the dancing flames but the man standing near the barrel. He was dark and covered entirely in clothes which could easily mark him as a beggar in the streets of Southern Ravencroft.

It occurred to Grace that she may be reading the situation very wrong. She had assumed the great archangel was covering this man, when the equal possibility existed that this was simply the next challenger who intended to be the first, and thereby thwarted the backup plan of the first.

Such was a common trait among warriors vying for the glory kill, history being replete with examples.

Yet there was something in his bearing and his movement that made her think, this was a man who did not carry the burden of dishonor in his soul. She tried to focus on his face, as he appeared to be looking directly at her, but the fire blazed behind him, and he was cowled in thick furs, so his face was submerged in shadow. He held the odd knife over his head for a moment as he cleared a small patch of snow from the roof-deck with sweeps of his foot. Then he knelt and drove the tip of the knife into the roof, stood, and pointed at Grace with one hand, while pointing to the dagger with the other. In that moment, with his arms extended and the happenstance angle of the light from the fire, Grace caught sight of a thick hilt and the body of a sheathed sword bound to his back but slung inverted, drawn downward from the waist.

As he stepped back from the dagger, he spread his arms and bowed to Grace, then with the same nonchalance one might snuff a candle, he turned, drew the sword, and passed it over the blazing barrel. Grace immediately doubted what she thought she saw. The roiling fire was drawn fully into the blade, and darkness re-enveloped the scene entirely. Mystery stacked upon mystery.

She spent no more time staring down upon the dark rooftops. She leaned the tall pole torch out to her side and let it fall where it may, then sheathed her sword as she turned and broke into a trot, back up out of the rubble to the street level. Bethany held Grace's horse in waiting, while six other full sisters awaited her, already mounted on horseback. They were barely discernible from Grace, all dressed in gray mottled with white. Six pair of eyes glared back through narrow openings in their battle dress, angry and anxious to begin the hunt. Grace mounted with a single leap and immediately led the sword sisters along the sloped street toward the gate leading down into the lower city.

Grace meant to have that assassin's blade. Now she had the missing element, the cohesive force behind all the madness which had descended upon Ravencroft City over the last two years. She'd been right—it was all a feint, a ploy designed to allow them to observe and measure response and methodology. Baron Riplin had been apprised of the situation, both concerning Grace and concerning the well-being of Ravencroft. He'd dispatched a unit to find the body on the cliffs. The enemy was not at the gate; they were already here. And Grace had a good idea how to find them.

But first, the knife.

Flavin—Kamiko

"Again." Kamiko barked aloud and with her hands. Danae obeyed without pause and set her feet, then drew still for a metered ten-count. She held a bamboo short sword in each hand. With her arms extended level with the floor, she leaned forward, bending at the waist, and simply walk-flipped her legs over her head, and with a midflip turn, she landed facing back the way she came. Kamiko watched only the swords. The right was holding level, but Danae's left hand was dipping during the turn. She fell backward into a simple roll and came back to her feet, both bamboo swords flat with the floor, then rose directly to her toes and into a slow spin, again dipping the left sword slightly. She dropped out of the spin into a crouch, one sword directly in front of her eyes and the other across her back at the waist, both dead level with the floor. She held the crouch for an exactly measured ten-count, then stood with her arms loose at her side, looking at Kamiko and awaiting the same command.

Kamiko spoke with only her hands, "Dipping still…left arm…in turn…chest…leaning into turn."

Danae lifted one brow and shook her head, effectively halting Kamiko's wrecked sentence with a look of pure pity for what Danae had come to refer to as *helmet-head*. She tucked the bound bamboo shafts under one arm and spelled out, "Left arm…what?"

Kamiko spelled, "Is still dipping."

"Then say that."

Kamiko looked at Danae's face, bright with determination and purpose and saw that the girl was indeed taking her role in the apprenticeship seriously. She also knew she must give Danae every consideration as the role of teacher switched between them. It was obvious that Danae had readily snatched the baton from Kamiko for the moment. They would teach each other how to speak in their respective languages during the course of this training. She decided to test Danae's resolve with a tiny pull against her. She ignored the girl's instruction, clapped her hands, and signed *again*, holding Danae's gaze with her own determined look.

The girl hesitated just enough for Kamiko to get the message that her acquiescence was a momentary thing and voluntary. She began again, but not until she had punched her right fist into her left palm with a slight nod of her head. The Dead Fist. Kamiko smiled and watched only the bamboo swords.

CHAPTER 8

Ravencroft—Grace

It had taken nearly an hour to make it to the rooftop. She'd split the group in two, sending four of the fierce sisters ahead to scout an area of town where the bulk of the mysteries still held. Grace, Shel, and Dor had come in search of the curved dagger, planning to meet the others as soon as time allowed. It was exactly where the stranger had left it—near the cold fire barrel in a cleared spot in the snow.

Before Grace turned her full attention to the dagger, the trio scanned the dark neighboring buildings and searched the perimeter of their own for anything of interest or threat and found nothing of note.

Except they found a total lack of any evidence that the mystery man had been here, and beyond the presence of the curved dagger, all appeared normal. The ankle-deep snow blanket was pristine and undisturbed but for the place he'd been standing by the fire barrel. No tracks leading up to or away from the barrel could be found. The night was dark, even though every surface was white.

"Sister," Dor's husky voice called from where the refuse was piled at the edge of the building's roof, "take a look over here." As Grace approached, Shel shifted her vantage to near the center of the roof and took up a guarding post, scanning carefully for the subtle movements often associated with the springing of a trap.

Dor had her sword in hand and was using the tip to lift what turned out to be the corner of an old rug, thrown over the top of a pile of wooden crates, all of which was made common by the covering of snow. The whole stack appeared to be a randomly piled bunch of trash, roughly waist-high. As Grace stepped up to Dor, she could see that the rug was a flap concealing an open space inside the rubble pile. Dor had also been careful to avoid messing up several distinct footprints in the snow, newly made and connecting her discovered hideaway to the very edge of the building. She lifted the flap with her sword until she could easily reach it with her other hand, then drew it back enough to where Grace could see into the dark recess.

From a pouch at her waist, Grace retrieved a small tube, half the size of her little finger, which she squeezed, breaking the diaphragm inside and allowing the contents to mix. The result was that a dull-yellow glow appeared at one end, producing only a slight wash of light. This Grace shone into the opening.

There was nothing of interest. Only a pallet of dirty blankets and straw covered the floor. Grace could tell there was an opening at the far upper corner of the piled-up structure. She crawled in just enough to verify what her thoughts were adding up to. The opening was a sight window for watching her house. The crater of burned rubble at the top of the high ridge was centered in plain sight in the window. This was where the assassin had been keeping tabs on her coming and going.

She backed out and kept low, using the luminous tube to study whatever details the footprints offered beyond leading to the roof perimeter wall. There she found a set of steel pegs, hammered directly into the stone wall and offering an easy climb to the window below. She knew what was there.

"Cauldin-Kath of Wroth," she said loud enough for Dor to hear. Dor stepped over to Grace and peered over the side of the building.

She said, "Yeah, good chance this was him, I'd say." She nodded toward the window below. "You want to check that out?"

"Maybe later," Grace replied. "I want this Wroth character," she said as she slipped the dimly glowing tube back into the pouch at her waist. She and Dor walked back to the center of the roof and turned their attention to the dagger left by the stranger from her dreams. Again she retrieved the light from her pouch, but she kept the shine closed in her fist until she'd knelt within reach of the strange weapon. She opened only one finger slightly, allowing a sliver of yellow light to cast out in front of her. Dor knelt beside her.

She recognized the weapon. A trio of jewels hung from the end-cap on thin silvery wires.

"This was his blade. I remember the jewels. I thought him arrogant for putting them on this...what would you call this thing, Dor? It looks like a mini scythe, but the handle comes straight off from the shank." Dor simply shook her head in answer. Grace reached out and gripped the handle and worked the weapon free of where it was stuck in the roof.

"What's that?" Dor asked as Grace lifted the bladed weapon. Impaled on the tip was a small sheaf of colorful paper, which Dor carefully removed by slipping it off the end of the blade. It was roughly a square of a size to cover three of her fingers, and it was completely covered with drawn designs: a face, a row of symbols which could have been letters or numbers, an ornately drawn border, and something resembling fine red glitter, lining three edges. The remaining edge was obviously torn.

"Looks like some kind of bill." Dor offered near Grace's shoulder. "Maybe foreign money."

"Yes, and torn in half," she said and turned her attention to the weapon. She opened her hand only enough to bathe the scene in the dim yellow light. Upon closer inspection of the blade itself, she saw it was serrated with tiny scallops along the entire length of the working edge. She spoke her thoughts as they filtered through her mind. "Sister, this is an assassination tool, a decapitator"—and held it up for Dor to see as she added—"and our mystery man left it here for me to find."

"Sister Grace," Dor asked with a serious demeanor, "are you certain *he* isn't just another one of these guys?" And she hooked her thumb toward the hideout at the edge of the building. "Maybe *he* is staying downstairs and not this Cauldin-Kath," she said quietly and pointed at the weapon in Grace's hand.

Grace closed her hand completely around the glowing tube and drew the blanket of dark over them. "I thought of that myself," she said to the ghostly outline of her sword sister. "Still keeping it up front a while longer too."

She could see the ghost of Shel appear beside Dor, who gave the order to evacuate the roof. "We've been here too long." Grace nodded into the dark and followed her sisters across the dark whiteness of the roof at a trot.

Flavin—Kamiko

Siruis returned at dawn after their first night spent at the Kale home. She'd simply appeared in the anteroom of the upper house, the front door as Anje had described it, with a white ferret peering out from beneath her cloak. Siruis, Kamiko, and Danae descended the stair, then never left the cavernous lower room for four days and nights.

Felene was well versed in the ways of the sisterhood and took no offense at being excluded. She joined Jesse in establishing a defensible perimeter within the homestead's fortified walls. She'd greeted Siruis and brought her into the subterranean home, gathered her coat, gloves, and cloak and introduced Siruis to Matilda, an event which happened in complete silence. Matilda had led her to the stairway down.

Kamiko hadn't realized how relieved she would be to have Siruis with her again. They had been separated for only a few hours, and then only physically apart, but after almost a half-year in constant company. Kamiko had grown more than simply fond of her. She loved this sister deeply and completely, and she knew Siruis held the same kinship for her. She felt strengthened by her presence, physically and spiritually, a calm lucidity which drove all remnants of doubt and unrest out of her soul.

Siruis's only explanation concerning Dairei letting her go was that the master thief had had a change of heart. She said Jerim had brought her to the Kale estate and would be nearby.

To Danae's disappointment, the ferret offered her no notice at all. It scampered from Siruis's shoulder when her feet touched the stone floor of the lower room and commenced a detailed search of every nook, niche, and cranny that was so thorough, two full hours passed before it leapt to the mantle above the fireplace and took up a watchful post. Only then did the ferret look at Kamiko. It held her gaze for several minutes, its head high and with a look on its face which showed far too much comprehension for a simple creature. Just to be certain, Kamiko nodded to the ferret and lifted her left hand slightly, then suppressed a chuckle when the ferret mimicked the motion exactly. *Jerim!*

By then Danae was exhausted to the point of collapsing, having succumbed to Kamiko's relentless and vigorous training, which had spanned the entire night, with only the single break Matilda had imposed. Yet the young girl had already begun to unravel the secrets of Kamiko's unique style of melee combat. Danae was wholly unaware that would be the ultimate outcome of the forms she was learning, that the pattern of the exercise was the very form of Koralilia. Kamiko's own private constellation was the pattern basis of her own private fighting style. Danae would be the only other person alive versed in *this* way of war.

By the close of the fourth day, Danae had turned the routine into an amazing fierce dance, full of graceful slow flips and fast spins and perfect leaps that left her afloat. And all the while, her bamboo swords drew flat level with the floor. Kamiko thought she'd seen Danae's eyes closed for a span of the routine. The girl was not a quick study, she wasn't even gifted; she was something else, something far greater. Her very motions were beyond normal, as though she was waiting for time to catch up to her hands. She already showed more grace and dexterity in the routine than Kamiko ever had, even when she was still turning it daily.

And mixed into the physical training, at every level and at all times, was their agreement to vastly improve their communication skills. Kamiko had finally managed to help Danae connect breathing with making sounds and helped her learn how to make her vocal cords work. Danae would first hold her finger against Kamiko's throat, then on her own throat to *feel* what she could not hear.

Kamiko never once touched the sword. It stood leaning against the wall at the foot of the stairs until the day they withdrew. Then she strapped it across her back as usual, as though she'd carried it all her years.

On the morning of the fifth day, they emerged to find the Kale homestead under siege. Anje met them at the top of the stairs and led them directly to a long table. Gathered around one end were Lord Merritt and Matilda, Jesse, Oric, and Felene. No one was speaking as Kamiko, Siruis, and Danae approached and joined them. Anje went to stand by Matilda and rested one hand on her mother's shoulder. Every face was solemn. She expected to see Cort and was surprised he was not there.

Lord Merritt spoke, "It seems the time is upon us, my friends." He looked at each of the sisters in turn, his eyes coming to rest on Kamiko last. "We hold to the words of God as spoken to us through his prophet Djinnasee, and heed the command to quit this place." Kamiko was signing his every word for Danae, her hands now smoother and quicker and, most of the time, accurate. She wondered why no one reacted to the decree. Was she the only one who hadn't expected it? "My estate and all my holdings in Flavin have been foreclosed upon by the Diamond Trust company, for dispersal among the citizens of Flavin Precinct. I and my household leave for Essen, as soon as we disperse the rabble outside the walls."

He spared a brief look with Jesse, who reported, "Soon, my lord. Within the hour."

Lord Merritt looked back to Kamiko and said, "It is the general belief out on the street that you two are here, Sister."

When Kamiko tilted her head in question, Felene answered, "It was me…we figure."

Now it was Danae's head which tilted.

"She's been spotted twice that we know of for sure," Oric answered Danae through Kamiko's hands. Then he said, with a nod toward Kamiko and Siruis as well, "But no one out there knows for sure that either of you are here, so they should be easily persuaded to break up. There is no fire in the spirit of a man who does not believe in what he fights for. Beside that, we have two hundred battle-ready men here," he said, pointing up. "And another unit arriving within the hour."

Jesse leaned forward toward Danae, knotted his thick fist in front of his face, and spoke to her directly, "And, little Sister, we pack a mean punch." Then he gave her a wink and his half-grin as he sat back in his chair.

To everyone's astonishment but Kamiko and Siruis, Danae reached up and laid one finger across her throat, just where it curves into her jawline, and hummed a short sound. Then she spoke to Jesse in clear even words, "I bet you do, big bro-ther." She looked up and smiled at Kamiko, who gave her the sign for *flawless*. The odd placement of levity and no small wonder, in the otherwise grave gathering, had the leverage to draw smiles from everyone present.

Kamiko knew that if her eyesight brightened to include spiritual sight, she would see white light pouring from Danae's spirit right now, strengthening the resolve of godly people and confusing the hearts of those bent upon evil. She thought of Cort and prayed he would see his true gains and not the total loss of everything, as it surely appeared to him.

Kamiko asked Lord Merritt, "You said Essen? We passed through there a few months ago."

"Yes, we know of your time in Essen. Most of my family has already arrived there."

"We digress." Matilda offered quietly, patiently.

"Yes," agreed Lord Merritt, "you must leave at once. Anje will lead you safely and discreetly away from the estate. Captain Ezra Kale awaits you, my friends. He will transport you downriver."

"Captain Kale?" Kamiko asked. She did not bother to ask where they were heading. She had placed her journey to the throne room in God's hands and intended to watch the path unfold in his good time.

*****

Kamiko, Siruis, Danae, and Felene trailed out behind Anje, Kamiko with many questions bounding around in her head. They were warmly dressed, with what few possessions they held between them. Kamiko's new moccasins were forming perfectly. She felt nothing on her feet, as if the soles of the shoes were attached magically to the bottoms of her feet. The white ferret sat atop a small knapsack Siruis wore on her back. Now that she took the time to notice, Kamiko could see that Anje was also dressed for traveling, though she carried no pack or obvious provisions for a journey. She wore leather breeches, which disappeared into the tops of tightly bound boots midway up her calf, a tight leather vest brimming with woolen fluff at the arms and throat, a dense wool scarf around her neck, and long thick sleeves of heavy cotton which covered all the way to her knuckles, with a hole for each thumb. Her hair was braided tight against her head.

To the sister's collective surprise, Anje led them down into the lower room rather than up to the courtyard, where Kamiko had assumed a carriage would be waiting. The presence of brigands threatening an all-out assault on the street level made that notion almost useless. But since no one had shared the plan of escape with them, the sisters simply followed where Anje led and wondered how things would ultimately unfold. Anje asked them to clear away the stack of rugs in the center of the room, while she moved to stand near the fireplace. Felene grabbed one corner of the pile and gave a hard pull, sliding the mass with a quiet hiss, then Anje pushed against a carefully located stone in the mantel. The section of floor which had been hidden under the rugs began to slowly and almost silently drop away. At first a large dark hole opened in the floor, but as the floor fell deeper, dim light appeared, illuminating a vertical stair carved into the stone. The stair led down to a doorway, open to a tunnel, also dimly lit from an unseen source.

Anje said to Kamiko, just before she climbed down the stairs, "I will take us in if you would pick up the rear guard." She paused a moment and added as she descended, "Though we won't be pressed from behind, I'd wager."

Only once everyone was down the steps did Anje venture into the tunnel, and then only far enough to allow everyone to step out of the hole they'd climbed into. Then with a nod at Kamiko, she called to her quietly, "Pull that lever, halfway down." To which Kamiko complied, pulling down the only lever she saw halfway. The giant plug of stone began slowly rising until the doorway was closed solid.

Anje backed further into the tunnel and motioned for the others to do the same, as she instructed Kamiko further, "Now push it all the way down, hard, until you hear a pop." Which Kamiko did without hesitation. It was not lost on her that Anje appeared to be concerned for their safety—for *their* safety—when she continued leading them away from Kamiko. "Now"—Anje had to speak at a low shout—"shove it all the way up kinda hard, like you are trying to break it off, and then get over here quick like." To which Kamiko answered with a blank stare, her hands poised to do the deed. Before Kamiko could even form her objection to speak, Anje led the others on into the tunnel at a brisk walk. First Danae, then Felene, and lastly the ferret peered back at Kamiko, with concern in their eyes.

Kamiko flexed her jaw and twisted some traction into her new shoes, set her feet to lunge and shoved the lever up hard—Kamiko-hard—and snapped the handle off clean with a loud crack. She leapt forward as it fell from her hand. She'd also felt a heavy thud hit her feet through the stone floor and knew something had been triggered. By her third step, the second impact slapped her foot, but with only enough force to sting a bit, accompanied by a wash of air from behind her and a scattering of small stones raining down for a moment. She caught the line of retreating sisters quickly and called them to a halt, as the rumble was only momentary and the danger had passed. She scanned the surrounding passageway as she asked Anje, "What was that?" Her eyes finding the young woman with the last word.

"Yeah, not sure about that," Anje responded, "I was just following instructions. But I'm pretty certain you just sealed that passage forever." A thin cloud of dust had billowed up behind Kamiko and now drifted, settling in the air currents still swirling about. The ambient light was coming from a row of openings running along the corridor near the floor.

The hallway was obviously carved into the stone, as the walls, floor, and ceiling were hewn flat and what appeared to be exactly square with one another. And it ran straight away through the stony flesh of the firmament, a dim-lit hole. Kamiko drew her heels together and lifted her hands out from her side enough to feel the balance centerline of her body and thereby knew the floor was true flat-level, no upward or downward incline.

"Well, then," she said to Anje with a thin smile, "let's be about it."

Anje nodded and then took a moment to look over everyone in the small party, her eyes resting on Siruis a bit longer than the others. Then to Kamiko, she asked, "Are we fit for a run or…"

Kamiko understood clearly enough, Anje was asking if Siruis could handle it, or would they be walking. It dawned on her that she did not know the answer to that question, she'd never seen Siruis even walk a long distance, much less run. With runners. "I…well." She started, words failing her after that.

Danae had been watching their words and clapped her hands sharply, turning every eye to her with a matched jerking motion. She ignored everyone but Siruis and, with a smile, silently asked if she was fit for running, or did they need to walk. Anje had no idea what had been said and stood silently by. Her palms were hanging forward at her side, the stance of question, while Siruis signed to Danae to set any pace desired, that she would keep up. Danae simply peered up at Kamiko, who nodded to Danae and Siruis, and, with her own questioning smile, said to Anje, "We run, my friend."

Two hours later, Kamiko was finally getting used to the odd form Siruis had taken. When Anje had first struck the tentative trot along the hallway, Siruis vanished from sight. Moments later, she reappeared just behind Danae and keeping pace. Kamiko had to sprint to catch them. The only word Kamiko could contrive to describe Siruis was *ghostly*. She was a wraith straight out of the old stories, walking leisurely, as though she had to slow her pace so they could keep up. Even when Anje had accepted the fact that she could set a faster pace, Kamiko was sure Siruis had actually stopped walking more than once, waiting on them to catch up to her. She had no idea how Siruis appeared to the others, but no one seemed to take the slightest notice.

Kamiko was impressed with Anje all over again. She'd set a hard pace to hold for two hours and had not slacked off. Few there were who could still do that. Nonetheless, when she slowed suddenly, then stopped at the closed doorway marking the end of the tunnel, everyone was winded. Except Siruis. She was standing to one side, waiting in silence while everyone else fought for breath. Kamiko was glad to see her in full form again.

The ferret was still sitting on her knapsack, but it was busy cleaning its feet. On impulse, she tested a notion and whispered, "Jerim." The ferret froze with a toenail still between its teeth, then turned and looked straight at her for a moment, then went back to the toenail. Little reason left to doubt. A slight smile broke across Siruis's face, but she kept her eyes forward.

Anje went to a wall panel near the door where five short levers were mounted. One at a time, she pulled down all five, but in what Kamiko reasoned was a specific sequence, and was rewarded with a dull *thunk* as the door broke open slightly. A wash of icy air drifted across their faces. Anje nodded back at the group of women, as if to make sure everyone was paying attention, then leaned against the stone and bronze door and pushed it open.

They followed her out into a dark day, the air so cold it slapped Kamiko's head, face, and hands with a sharp bite. She was immediately grateful for the heat built up from the run but knew they were not dressed to endure much time out in it.

They had come out into a brick-built alcove, aged and crumbling, about twice Kamiko's height to the top and thirty paces across, open to a sky of low dark clouds moving swiftly. Anje pushed the door closed behind Kamiko with an audible *clack* and a heavy thud, which told Kamiko this was a one-way passage, meant only for escape.

As Anje led them out of the alcove, the backend of an odd-looking carriage came into view. Kamiko could make out that a horse was out front, but the carriage faced directly away from her vantage, so she could tell only that the animal was big, off-white, and probably ugly. She admitted to herself that her assessment was based upon the ragtag look of the carriage.

For all intents, it was a gypsy wagon, down to the covered porch and proper steps leading down from the doorway on the back of the wide boxy rig. It sat tilted a few degrees to the left and was painted with a stunning regalia of colors, in an impressive array of shapes and figures. Curtains and beads hung at the corners and were draped to random spots on the walls in a spangle of color and texture that was somehow uncluttered. Several sizes and shapes of glowing paper globes dangled from like-number of bamboo lengths all around the perimeter of the roof, like a fluttering golden crown. One other thing she noticed, a cone-topped chimney with smoke coming out. Warmth!

Anje led them to the carriage quickly, and just as they approached the rear entry, the door swung open, and Cort hurried out. At that same time, the driver dropped down from the driver's seat, trotted back to the sisters with a nod, specifically to Felene.

"Happy to be driving for you again, Sister." Sir Johns's voice came from behind the high thick collar of his long coat and from beneath a heavy woolen hat. He had another long coat hanging on his arm and a woolen hat in his hand. He offered them to Felene. "If you want to ride up there with me." She stepped up and grabbed them without hesitation, unbuckled her sword, and handed it to him. He studied the sword while she spun the coat on.

Anje's hand on Kamiko's elbow distracted her from the two.

"C'mere a second, Sister." She led Kamiko forward as she continued, "We gotta be out of here quick, but I wanted you to know—" And she stepped aside so Kamiko could see the horse.

Uila's big dark face turned back toward her as Kamiko stepped up, and he immediately started grumbling and shaking his head at her, as though he was fussing at a wayward child, his short tail beating at the rigging. Kamiko felt a sudden wave of calm at the sight of her old friend. Her parts were coming back together again. Siruis and Uila were within her physical reach, and the sword was on her back. She strode around to the front of Uila and stepped right up under his thick face, where he stilled but pressed the side of his mouth against her cheek. Her hands rubbed up the sides of his long snout, around his dark eyes, and up to the base of his ears. There she focused the blissful kindness of a good deep scratching, while she mumbled the words and sounds of comfort common between them.

Yet the need for haste was pressing, so she backed away to arm's length and held his furry warm chin in her palm for a moment. She dropped her hand and allowed a bit of command into her voice. "Uila," she said and raised her right hand, "company guard." Then she lowered her hand. She was answered with a low grumble and a single hoof strike on the ground.

She turned to follow Anje to the back of the rummy wagon, only to meet Sir Johns heading forward to the driver's box. She stopped him short and said, "He's not really meant to be used as a draw horse, Sir Johns, hasn't been trained to a harness and has not been conditioned to a load." Then she softened a bit and added, "Though I am grateful to be back with him. Were you his steward?"

"Yes, I have been working with him four days now." He held his hands up. "Four amazing days!" He smiled up at Kamiko. "He is a very special horse. I discovered he is trained in dressage and also well versed in combat commands, so between those two disciplines, I was able to teach him to drive on the first day, Sister. He is smarter than even Rasha!" To which Anje nodded her agreement. As he turned to continue to the driver box, he assured Kamiko, "I have been very careful with your comrade, Sister Kamiko, he remains a warhorse of renown." Then he bounded up to the driver seat and began setting himself, ready to leave.

Kamiko was just turning to again follow Anje to the back when someone in a thick long coat, a fluffy woolen hat, and heavy body mass impacted her shoulder to shoulder with enough force to knock her aside a full step. Felene's distinct accent was doubly thick as she turned and growled at Kamiko.

"Oat o'th way, ye sniv-ling weakling, afore I tarn ye out like a beggarly whelp."

The smile which broke across Kamiko's face was triggered not only by the attempt at humor but for the swell of joy that Felene's spirit was beginning to heal. Her fear of waking up as an elderly cripple was waning. She was getting her fire back. The only things beyond her voice, recognizable as Felene, were her dark-brown eyes, twinkling at Kamiko through the thin slot between coat and hat. Otherwise she appeared exactly as a bigger version of Sir Johns. They were a gypsy coachman and his burly nephew. This was a good ruse.

"Try that again, ya worthless bushwhack, and I'll strap you to the next barley wagon headin' for the asylum."

"*Ha.*" Felene guffawed. "They keep a room for me…just in case."

Felene extended her gloved hand, and Kamiko immediately slapped her own hand into it with a hard squeeze. After a pair of silent moments, they parted ways. Felene mounted the gaudy wagon top, while Kamiko and Anje moved to the backdoor and climbed inside.

The wave of heat was so heavy it felt like stepping into hot water. Siruis and Danae had already shed every layer of clothing possible, and Kamiko could see a sheen of moisture forming on Danae's face.

"Don't worry," Anje said, answering the look on Kamiko's face, "it won't stay this hot once we move out of the alcove and get into the wind."

The interior of the wagon held no resemblance to the outside. Neither the floor nor the walls showed the tilt she'd clearly seen from the outside, and the colors were muted and earthy, more dark leather and canvas. And everything in sight was neat and in orderly stowage.

Kamiko felt the slightest shift in her body weight and knew the wagon had begun to move. Cort was leaning against the wall to her left, and Siruis and Danae were seated on a low couch to her right. Anje had moved past her and was at the very front of the wagon, busy opening a long but narrow wooden lid. Kamiko stepped forward and lowered her mass to the couch beside Siruis. Something about the scene was seriously amiss. Cort had an expression on his face she had not yet seen—regal confidence with a set of general disdain about his eyes. However chatty he'd been when they met, he was stoic now.

"It is good to see you again, Cort," Kamiko said. To her relief, his smile seemed genuine, if subdued.

He said, "Yes, Sister, welcome to Anje's real home." And he nodded at Danae and Siruis. "Sisters." He seemed little concerned about the ferret and only glanced at it in passing.

When Anje turned back around, it was as though a different woman stood before Kamiko. She had donned a fitted leather belt and had strapped on a small fitted chest plate of leather, reinforced with darkened bronze and steel strips, with a simple leather support band across her lower back. She was just attaching a sword to the belt as she turned, and the mild-tempered woman who had attended Matilda was gone. Her eyes shone with purpose. She appeared years older.

She spoke to all three sisters as she explained, "We are not going to meet my father at the river," she said. "We felt it necessary to go with an alternate plan and take you down another route. I want to stay as far north of the Bos`Jin Sea as is reasonable. The river would take us too far south. We'd end up skirting the seacoast for the entire trip. Instead we will be traveling with a merchant train. I and my company have three wagons, plus this one in the train. We will be safe, and you may remain unseen."

There was the problem. No one had asked Kamiko where she meant to go next, yet Anje thought she knew enough to plot a course. Even Danae did not know that secret yet. "Where are we bound, Anje? You seem to have set a path to where you imagine we are going. I'm just wondering where that is." She could feel sweat forming on her face and brow.

Anje grew very still for a few brief moments. Then she stepped forward and knelt down in front of Siruis and asked her, "Do you know what she plans for you, Sister? She believes it is her duty to turn you over to the king." Kamiko let the statement go and remained silent. Siruis was fully capable. "There is a kingdom-wide decree that declares you to be a witch and orders you captured, gagged, bagged, and boxed so you may be brought before the king and executed." She glanced up at Kamiko for a moment, then back. "Myself, my brother, and everyone alive that I know wants to keep you out of his hands, except my mother…and Lieutenant Marshal Kamiko Hoshi, Titus's right hand."

"And what did your mother tell you?" Siruis asked.

"Simply that," she said, "Kamiko must bring you before the king, and I must take you there."

"And in doing so, you become party to my death at the hands of King Titus's axman."

"Yes."

"What would you have me do?"

"Run. I can help you. We can get you to a safe place without anyone knowing," she said. "Go to the Seven Clans, to King El`Thorn. There is a crossing at Kell's Landing, I will take you there."

"And would you then deliver the message I carry to King Titus?"

Anje just looked at her.

Siruis continued, "Do you believe I am a witch, Anje?"

Kamiko watched the woman closely. Her eyes were dancing back and forth between Siruis's, but she showed no sign of the debilitation Kamiko had felt when she'd first gazed into her eyes. She was glad to see Anje weighing the question. Her answer would be honest.

"No, Sister, I do not believe that. Nor does Rasha." She took Siruis's hands in hers. "We believe you to be a prophet of God, a far scarier thing than a crazy woman from Eten."

"That is good and very true. You should fear my words, fear hearing them. But trust in God and fear nothing. I have a message for the king, nothing more."

"You *want* to go?"

"Kamiko is my guardian, not my captor." She nodded and added, "I must go."

Chapter 9

Ravencroft—Grace

"We have two very distinct mysteries to unravel, eh, Sister?" Dor asked in a deep hush, careful to keep the whisper from her voice. Shel turned up one side of her lip and nodded her agreement to Grace. Three other sisters were down on the street level in hiding, on guard. The seventh sister of her crew was on her way to Baron Riplin for a briefing. It had been six days since the last.

Grace answered in low quiet tones and into her palm, "Who is *he*," she said, then pointed into the dim room they had discovered but had not yet entered. "And who are *they*?"

Shel leaned in closer and pointed to a chair positioned in front of the door, several paces into the room, then opened her palm upward in silent question. When Grace focused her attention on it, she saw that a dark bag, bundled with its own pull cord, was sitting on the seat. She did a third scan of the perimeter of the room and was satisfied no other information could be gleaned without going in. With a nod from Grace, Dor stepped inside and moved to the left. Grace followed her in and covered the right. Shel walked straight to the chair and stopped.

It had been dark for many days, and the unlit room was dim, everything cast in shadows. It was a single room, rectangle, the entire fifth floor of a small abandoned building, blackened windows all the way around. Near the far end, some thirty-odd paces away, the floor had been cleared of the rubble of a rotting building. As Grace drew closer, she could see that it was sectionalized in even squares, and that each square resembled all the others in the items she saw. This was not mercenary or roguish, this was military discipline, plain and simple. Bedroll, pack, and a bundle of small-bladed weapons were neatly arranged in each corner, a single low table and stool in another. Beyond that, nothing. Twelve equal spaces, with one of them empty, making a unit of eleven. She wondered if Cauldin-Kath was number 12, or rather, number 1.

She turned and strode back to where Shel was just opening the bag. "This is a bivouac," she said, "and I think these guys are military, or of similar bent. I make eleven occupants." It turned out to be a common burlap grain bag with some weight to it. Shel rolled back the opening to reveal a whole stack of the curved daggers, each exactly the same but for one small individual contrivance, making each one unique. The handles were all clustered together, and Shel split them roughly in half and spread each half out just enough to count them at a glance.

Grace looked up and said, "Eleven blades here, and eleven beds over there. Now what could that mean to us? Did our friend just take down this entire unit?"

"I don't know, Sister," Dor said. "Seeing a bag full of their weapons doesn't tell us as much as seeing eleven bodies. It could still be a ruse. But"—she cast a look at Shel—"he has been helping us all along, so he is either working both sides, or he is on our side. And if he did take this cell down, then I'm callin' him a friend." She shook her head and added, "He must be one tough cookie."

Shel and Grace were both nodding as Dor spoke. Grace said, "We have no choice but to try and make actual contact with him and to trust him, until we see reason to do otherwise." She looked at each of the sisters. "Think about what this unit was about to unleash upon Ravencroft City. Our man saved hundreds of people from being butchered. We should also assume this was not the only unit in place. He had my locket for a year, my friends, a year."

"I agree," Dor said quietly. "And if they are gathered in units this big, then we need to form larger patrols."

"Yes, we do," Grace said. "Which means it is time to get Baron Riplin on point."

"Agreed."

Shel nodded her silent accord.

"Shel," Grace said, still with the habit of their quiet-speak, "get the word out. We muster in this very room at dawn. Full house!" Shel nodded and backed away, then turned and trotted out the door. To Dor, Grace said, "We set station 1 here. I need you to—"

Dor interrupted and finished Grace's order. "Set up four more houses along the Jayd Street corridor, two north of here, and two south."

"Yes, it looks like we could be in for a long stretch." The sisters looked out over the deserted room, each feeling pressure in their gut and in their bones from the inherent and unknown danger. "I will go see Baron Riplin," Grace said.

Kamiko

"You need to get me out of this wagon…*now*!" Kamiko assured Felene. "Sixteen days out of Flavin, Sister, and I've been out of this bucket three times. And how is my horse? Is he being a gentleman or a helmet-head?"

Felene stepped the rest of the way through the door and closed it behind her. "He is a perfect creature, Sister, and no, you may not go outside. Too many people about." Felene looked very swashbuckle. She'd taken to the culture of the gypsy merchant train with ease and had traded wearing her armor in favor of a dark leather vest over layered shirts, with long sleeves of colored cotton. She'd also donned a dark and warm woolen cloak with a deep cowl and knee-high boots, with heels for riding with stirrups. And she had not been separated from her great sword for a moment. With one hand, she unclipped the sword from her barding and leaned it in the corner.

In her other hand, she held a fat bamboo steam basket and carried it to the far end of the wagon, where she placed it on a small fold-down table left permanently open. The smell of cooked food, heavily spiced and still smoky from the cook fire, filled the small room and set Kamiko's stomach to burbling with anticipation. Siruis was on her feet, opening one of the many narrow cabinets lining every wall, nook, and cranny. She retrieved three bowls and set them on the table as Kamiko opened a drawer and set out a knife and three spoons, a small one and two larger serving spoons. Felene moved back to the doorway and began shedding the warmest layers of her garb, while Kamiko and Siruis prepared the table. Danae had been out since dawn and would likely not return until late afternoon.

Kamiko could easily see that the look on Felene's face was strained, one eyebrow seeming stuck in the lifted attitude of Felene when her mind was distracted. As she stepped back toward the meal table, Kamiko asked her a mundane question, "What is Danae into today?" The surprise which flittered across Felene's face disappeared just as quickly, but Kamiko could tell it took a little effort to draw her mind to the question.

"She got a job," Felene announced distractedly. "The trail master caught wind that Danae could use handspeak and asked if she would be willing to teach it to him and his family for one silver coin per week."

"Ha!" Siruis chirped quietly, then added, "Good for her. She needs purpose in her life right now." She filled a bowl with dark rice and handed it to Felene. "See if you can find something for this one to do," she said with a wry smile and a tilt of her head Kamiko's direction. "A bit of wagon fever."

Felene side-grinned at her as Kamiko ladled hot broth over the rice and then laid a slab of steaming grilled fish atop that. Felene moved around Siruis and took a small stool at one end of the table, while Siruis handed Kamiko the second bowl of rice. Felene raised her bowl slightly and whispered a quiet prayer. Kamiko could easily picture the angel lifting away from Felene with a golden censure, smoldering with her petition. Kamiko knew the messenger would not stop until it knelt before the throne of heaven and delivered the desire of Felene Dresdle, as sweet incense before the great One. The thought made Kamiko shudder.

Felene set the bowl down, snatched up one of the large spoons, and began stabbing the fish down into the rice soup. Siruis spooned a small dollop of rice into her own bowl and held it out for Kamiko to add a bit of broth and a small piece of fish, then took the stool at the other end of the table. Once Kamiko's portion was filled, she sat on the corner of the low couch near Siruis, looking across at Felene.

They ate in hungry silence until Felene had all but finished her second helping, then Kamiko jumped in all the way. "Okay, first tell me about Uila. How is he acting? Did Sir Johns mess his mind up with all that wagon-pulling nonsense? And who is riding him now? Just you and Danae, that's it, nobody else."

Felene spared a look of feigned wonder at Siruis, who nodded and smiled in response. Then Felene said to Kamiko, "He's fine, Sister. Trust me. He is well disguised and, for the life of me, seems to be playing the part, as if he knows just what is going on." Kamiko and Siruis shared a look. "And he pulled the wagon maybe two leagues, Kamiko, just until we met the merchant train. He's been with either Danae or me since then. I took him out for a good hard run yesterday…and saw Jerim." She bounced her eyebrows at Siruis, who smiled. "He was shadowing us but stepped out where I could see him a couple of times." Kamiko knew Felene had no idea about Jerim's connection with the ferret, with Uila.

"So what else is going on out there? You are concerned about something."

Felene held Kamiko's gaze for a moment. "A company joined the train this morning, two dozen wagons. They brought a warning to avoid Drakes Pass, and they were actively looking to hire arms." She let Kamiko have a moment to process the news. "We reach Drakes Pass in two days. They intend to side along the main body for another day, then they will veer eastward and cross out into the open plains before turning south again."

"What is going on in Drakes Pass?" Kamiko asked. She noticed Siruis had suddenly become very still, facing straight ahead, with her hands resting in her lap. Felene noticed too.

"Hard to say. Sounds like a skirmish may have flared up between two citizen groups, right down in the center of town. There were a few deaths."

"A *skirmish*? You mean like two-armed-groups-doing-battle kinda thing or just a really big bar brawl?"

"I got the feeling it was more organized than a street fight, but I was just one of twenty people listening to the conversation between the trail masters. He said the report came from a royal courier."

They sat in silence for several moments. A royal courier was as good a source as any Kamiko could think of. It also meant the word *skirmish* was the military usage, which meant it was a leading battle between standing and armed forces, one testing the resolve or defensive worthiness of the other before committing to a hard fight.

"Did they discuss what caused the fight?"

Felene held very still for several moments, keeping her eyes on Kamiko's, until she finally nodded once toward Siruis.

"What?"

Felene only nodded, her face dark with grave concern. Siruis had her eyes open and, for all Kamiko could tell, was listening intently. The ferret lay curled on a low shelf, eyes open, ears forward, its small head following the conversation. Kamiko's first thought was that they had been discovered, but the folly of that thought became quickly evident. The skirmish would have happened here at the wagon. This was a larger portion at work.

Luthain. Kamiko saw Siruis's eyes cut her way and looked over to meet them. *And King Titus.* Siruis dipped her chin one time.

Felene continued unprompted, "Rasha and one of Anje's hired arms volunteered to ride ahead and see what they can find out. They should return by morning."

"What do you think this is about, Sister Felene?" Siruis's voice was barely a whisper, but both sisters flinched when she spoke. Kamiko watched Felene's face as she sat in silence, turning the question in her mind. A single brow lifted just before she spoke.

"It has begun. The kingdom is splitting." She paused a moment, then looked from Kamiko to Siruis. "Cairistonia is tearing apart over you, Sister Siruis." Siruis nodded one slow time.

Kamiko wanted to ask how such a thing was possible, but she knew the answer even as the question formed in her mind. "Fear, Sister Felene. They fear what she has said, and they deem it to be her fault. But they also refuse to acknowledge God's place as her source of the knowledge. So they hate her because to them, she is false, but they also hate her for bringing destruction down by her prophecy. It is double-minded madness, thus demonic in origin." Her mind flashed momentarily to the memory of Luthain atop Mount Oman, pouring his decree out upon Ravencroft City. She also recalled the visage of the archangel on Mount Elan, covering a solitary man down in that same city.

"Fear and hate are fruits of the same tree," Siruis said, now in her full voice.

Felene said, "They are going to find us, Sisters. This guise will not bear even casual scrutiny if someone is looking for us." She nodded. "And everyone is looking."

"I agree with that," Kamiko said. "I think we may break off, here and now. You know how people are when they want to be dangerous. This entire caravan will suffer for it if they find us here."

Felene stood. "I will send Danae back here to you, then I'll speak to Cort about three more horses." The look on Kamiko's face checked Felene for a moment. "I will find us some mounts along the line." She stepped to the back of the wagon and layered vest, coat, and cloak back on, then pulled on a pair of dark leather gloves and picked up her sword. "I'll be back in one hour." Just before she opened the door, she pulled the deep cowl over her head, and her face sank into the shadows. Then she was gone.

Outside a pair of horses thundered by, a thing so common Kamiko barely registered the sound. The train was a big one, more than two hundred wagons, most of them heavy. She could feel the danger of the situation should the next skirmish include these people. An angry organized armed mob would make short work of the meager security force guarding the train. She had seen this kind of outraged insanity plenty of times before. Many of them had no idea why they were so angry or afraid, they were just swept along by those who desired strife and had silver tongues. Truth was rarely even a consideration, much less a driving force.

"Or," she said to Siruis, "we stay right here and be ready to protect the caravan. All this is about you and I—you mostly—so I am going to have to defend you no matter what. A presence from the sisterhood may be enough to keep this train safe. Not to mention what Jerim could bring to bear, if things get out of hand."

"There is something else to consider." Siruis stood and walked to the center of the small room and turned toward Kamiko. Danae had woven Siruis's wild mane into a tight but thick corded rope, which lay down her back to her waist. To Kamiko, Siruis's face looked longer and older now that it was framed by her hairline and not the bushy mane which normally engulfed her upper half. "As soon as you come out in the open, our mysterious adversary will try again."

"True. And we know they are going to try taking us *all* again." Kamiko pushed back deeper into the couch and let her weight sink, totally relaxed, her head lying back. It took a couple of deep chest-swelling breaths for the tension she'd been holding to fully release. "We are traveling too slow. We need out of this wagon. It has been twenty days since the attack, which may be enough time for Wroth to have regrouped from his disastrous opener."

"Kamiko, where would you go if we need not see King Titus?" Siruis asked as she moved to where a small alcove held the makings for tea and coffee. A water kettle remained permanently filled and heating on a small stove set in the corner.

Kamiko thought for only a moment. "To King El`Thorn, straightaway." She nodded the affirmation as she said, "The moment our task here is done, I will be leaving to join the Seven Clans." She folded her hands over her belly and loosely interlocked her fingers and spoke partially to the ceiling, "I have a growing suspicion that King El`Thorn and I are facing the same enemy."

"That has been true before."

"Yes, it has." She thought about the vision of El`Thorn she'd awakened from in Lord Merritt's library. They were not savages that gave chase in her mind that night but seasoned and hardened warriors. El`Thorn need not flee savages that had gathered less than fifty of their skinny brothers to challenge him. And why had she been unconscious? She knew it was no mere dream, which meant it would be made known when she needed the understanding most. She was looking at the ceiling, her mind suddenly twenty years in the past.

She was in King El`Thorn's realm, climbing down Mount Hileah. She'd made the climb to the temple of the Order and then back down every single day for nine years. That was the first time she wore her pack, weapons, and traveling gear. The king of the Seven Clans was waiting for her midway down the mountain with a flask of cool crisp wine and food for the journey. They'd shared a parting drink and watched the sun fall away from a cloudless sky.

Kamiko said absently, "You know, Sister, Per El`Thorn once asked me to be his queen." She could still recall the bright tartness of the wine and the chill wind of the mountainside. "Three times on my way to Castlehaven, I turned around to go back to him." She still wasn't sure if she regretted following her duty to continue. She had never known mind, body, or heartfelt desire since. She cast her look toward Siruis. "And here we are." But she forced no smile where none wanted to rise.

She'd seen the king many times in the years to follow, hunting with his sons and daughters, fighting his enemies, traveling his vast wilderness. And she willingly admitted to a stronger kinship with the Seven Clans than with the Cairistonian Kingdom. The Seven Clans were strong, clean, and healthy and lived in peace, unlike the savages who thrived on strife and were ever on the brink of starvation. *Barbarian* was a word never used by El`Thorn's people, it was a moniker for the wilderness tribes only in Cairistonia.

Siruis set two small steaming mugs on the table and turned her attention to clearing the meal. Kamiko let the melancholy dwell in her chest and allowed her thoughts to imagine what life as El`Thorn's queen could have been like. It was a common musing that would be with her all her days.

"There is one thing yet to pass before we see the king, then we will make haste to Mount Hileah," Siruis said.

Kamiko had just turned to look at Siruis when the door swung open, and Danae bounded in. She heel-kicked the door closed and dropped a large canvas bag in the middle of the floor, then immediately began stripping off layers of cloak, coat, gloves, jacket, scarf, sweater, and long-sleeve shirt. When Danae had shed everything but her last layer of wearing clothes, her quick motion stopped cold, and she stood there with her arms out, while she took a pair of deep breaths. Siruis and Kamiko shared a silent grin and waited until Danae had gathered her bearing.

Siruis asked her, "Did you see Felene?" To which she nodded she had, as her gaze fell on the food still on the table. Kamiko eyed the canvas bag and scooted to the edge of the couch, then made to reach for it. Danae checked that with a swipe of her hand at Kamiko, followed by a steady forefinger pointing straight up between them. Kamiko drew her hand all the way back to her chest and laid back on the couch again, already grateful for Danae's bright nature, dissolving the melancholy from her chest and throat. Danae kept her finger raised until she saw that Siruis was indeed taking down a clean bowl, then the girl cast a sly grin over Kamiko.

She dropped to her haunches and began removing what turned out to be a neatly folded stack of clothes. She quickly sorted them into three distinct smaller stacks and laid one across Kamiko's lap with a wink and a wide grin. The other two stacks she portioned to Siruis, and lastly to herself. Kamiko thumbed down through the stack and saw, to her delight, that Danae had managed to find insulating top and bottom undergarments that would cover all the way to ankle and wrist and were woven whole. These she separated and set to one side. What remained was common to the gypsy lifestyle, colorful and flowing.

Kamiko held the tunic up by the shoulders and declared, "I am *not* wearing this!"

*****

The hour passed cold and gray as early afternoon dragged on. Felene did not return. The wagon lumbered quietly along. Danae's brightness had at last overpowered Kamiko's resolve so that she was now wearing the colorful clothes Danae had so carefully picked out—just for her. In truth, now that she'd been in the outfit a little while, it was growing on her. She was doubly surprised and pleased that it had all fit. The material was unlike any she'd ever seen, tough but very soft to the touch. The collar had a rise to it that she was not used to and was edged in heavy gold-colored thread which had an unusual stiffness to it and held the collar in shape. The pants had a wide waistband, were loose fit, and gathered at the ankle, and like the shirt, the material was soft but dense, made to endure both time and abuse. She had to admit, it was nice to be swathed in color and comfort, though once she was dressed, she could see that the colors were simple accents and less vibrant to the eye.

A group of horses thundered by, as with many times before, but something automatic triggered inside Kamiko. She slowly and quietly began packing her few belongings into Anje's gifted canvas bag. Siruis had long since taken charge of Danae's formal education, and they were sitting at the table in silent but animated conversation over an open book. She heard the next group of riders as they approached and let her mind simply draw an impression, a conclusion, from what her ears could hear when focused.

Recognition was instant, one of her deeply ingrained familiarities. It was the rattle of weapons amid the hoof strikes, the clamor of armor above their thunder. Siruis was still now, her hands flat on the table, looking at Kamiko. Danae was occupied reading from the book. Another troop of horses—this one larger, judging by their time in passing—rumbled by, moving the same direction as the others—toward the head of the caravan. From the sheer ferocity of the hoof thunder, Kamiko knew the riders were driving the horses hard. It sounded like a muster of arms was underway. She heard the distinctive presence of Siruis's whisper from inside her own being, *Yes.*

The sisters paused for a single second longer before wordlessly moving into swift and exacting action. Siruis placed her hand over Danae's study text, as Kamiko turned and tied her canvas bag high on her waist, then layered on her coat and cowled cloak. She had already donned the long garments when she'd dressed in Danae's gift and had even laced up her new boots to check the full fit and function. She was standing ready at the door, her sword fixed loosely on her back within a ten-count, just pulling her gloves on. When Kamiko turned around, Danae was already fully winter-clothed, with gloves and her ample hood pulled forward, waiting. Kamiko knew she could easily be convinced that Danae had a different relationship with time than anyone else.

Siruis buttoned the last three clasps on her overcoat, then placed her hand on Danae's shoulder and urged her closer to the front of the wagon, away from the door. The ferret was coiled around Siruis's shoulder but kept its eyes on Kamiko, watching her every move, as if waiting for a cue. Jerim was nearby and keeping close watch. Following Siruis's urging, Kamiko stepped back from the door. A moment later, she heard Felene's distinct voice speaking quickly, approaching the door. It swung open with enough force that it slammed against the outside wall. Anje practically leapt into the room, with Felene on her heels and Cort right behind Felene. Only when Sir Johns trotted up the steps and closed the door behind him did it occur to Kamiko, the wagon was still moving.

Anje was red-faced, with anger or exertion Kamiko could not yet tell. No one spoke. The look of strained patience on Felene's face hinted that she was trying to let Anje have the lead role. Was that blood flecked on Felene's cheek?

"Anje," Kamiko prompted, "what's going on?" Even as she was speaking, she felt her weight drift more fully to her left side, as the wagon veered off the line.

Anje's mouth broke open with a near shout, "The train is coming under attack. We are breaking off to the east. We are out of here, now." With that formality out of the way, Kamiko looked at Felene, who answered without further prompting.

"We just repelled a unit of about fifty men. Rasha and Raul never made it to Drakes Pass. He said they came upon a big force moving this way."

Cort was nodding at Kamiko and picked it up. "I saw about a hundred horsemen, but I don't really know how to tell infantry size, Sister. It was definitely closer to five hundred men than a hundred. We turned around quick, but they saw us and sent a unit to chase us down."

"I guess they did not catch you," Kamiko said with a slight smile.

"Ha!" Cort said without humor. "No, Sister, they won't be catching any horses from our brood." He hooked his thumb at Sir Johns.

"How far out?"

"Maybe two hours," Felene answered.

"Did the trainmaster call for a muster?"

Felene's face darkened, and her mouth twisted, but she nodded. "Only about three hundred, Sister, almost all of them on horseback."

Kamiko said to Anje, "If you peel out from the main body, they will just track you down."

"Not so," Anje said. "There are thirteen companies leaving the train, all right now. We are scattering in every direction."

Felene interjected quietly, with grace, "That won't work, Anje. They will simply split the company and hunt you all down at once. I can tell your arms men are tough and know how to handle themselves in a fight, but could they take ten-to-one odds?"

Anje looked at Felene, then at Kamiko, then back to Felene before she turned again to Kamiko and said, "Yes. With you and Felene, I believe we could handle greater odds than that." The tension which sat down over the room was akin to the sensation of seeing a hornet nest drop and watching it fall toward the ground.

After a moment of frozen silence, Kamiko stepped closer to Anje, now looking down from her natural height. "Anje, we are not going with you."

Both Cort and Sir Johns said, "What?" Anje's mouth dropped slightly, and her eyes grew pained.

Felene answered all their questions with an easy statement, "The only way to stop the caravan from being attacked, and to keep you and all the rest from being hunted down, is for them to find us here…now."

Kamiko nodded her agreement with Felene's thoughts.

Anje held her ground under Kamiko's gaze. "What about her," she said and pointed at Siruis. "How do you think she will fare, if they get their hands on her? Do you care about that at all? Have you not heard what they will do?"

Kamiko could sense Felene's ire rising at the same rate as Anje's, although Felene's eyes were on Anje. Kamiko's heart was easy in her chest. She understood the woman's frustration all too well. Anje was someone who knew Kamiko only as a legendary figure, standing at the literal right hand of the king, the strong arm. She was the *one who must be feared* when Titus, the *one who must be loved*, failed. To Anje, Siruis was in Kamiko's clutches, with no hope of escape.

Kamiko took one more step, which brought her standing close enough for Anje to feel her breath. She spoke kindly, quietly, "My friend, you do not want to witness what will happen if someone tries to take Siruis where she does not belong. It would be a nightmare from which you would never truly wake." To her credit, Anje did not budge. But Kamiko could feel her trembling, from rage, from fear, and from helplessness. She had little idea how to help the woman. "Thank you for your hospitality, Anje. You and your family have offered charity to us without reservation. Your mother is a great sister, and she is blessed to have children who love her as you do. You may travel in peace without looking over your shoulder." Kamiko was pleased to see both Anje and Felene gather their emotions underfoot.

Siruis said, "Anje, you are a protected woman, you and all your party. By the prayers of your mother and from you, the heavens respond, have always responded. You are blessed."

Kamiko resisted the automatic urge to move back from towering so close over Anje. Siruis's voice had softened the tension in her face, her anger challenged twice with kindness.

"What do you mean protected? You are talking about angels."

Kamiko answered, "Yes."

"Here, now."

"Yes."

"Angels flying around all over the place, fighting demons and casting them into hell, while the demons try to destroy all the people by turning them into pirates, whores, and drunks." She said it flat-toned, as if reading from a book.

Felene piped in quietly, "Well, she got the first word right anyway."

"It doesn't really work that way, Anje," Kamiko said as she began moving around her toward the door. "There is probably only one here, now. They are mostly messengers."

"Just messengers?"

Siruis said, "Yes, but they are the ones who deliver the decrees of heaven down here in Drakes Pass, and for that, they are vast and powerful beings to be sure." A picture of the archangel flashed in Kamiko's thoughts.

Felene backed toward the door and stood with her hand on the latch handle. Siruis pulled her hood forward, tied the throat strap closed, and also moved toward the door, drawing Danae along by the elbow. Cort and Sir Johns were crowded against one wall, being very quiet, both looking as though they wished they'd stayed outside. Anje looked torn between frustration at losing control and a growing rage at Kamiko, for reasons Kamiko was only just coming to understand.

She turned toward Anje suddenly, causing the her to step back with one foot, and asked, "Anje, what has you so angry? I am no threat to her. You must believe I will be standing at Siruis's right hand, not Titus's, when we present ourselves to His Majesty. And you may rest assured, Siruis will be in no box or bag or shackles."

"I don't believe you, Lieutenant Marshal, plain and simple," Anje said. "I think you are taking her to her doom. It's what you do."

Kamiko could tell her ire was still burning, even though her voice had gone calm. Anje turned, and with the same visible tightness of control, said to Cort, "Turn back in and take us to the front of the train, as quickly as possible." The two men moved immediately. She stopped Cort with a hand on his shoulder. Sir Johns hopped out the door Felene opened for him. "Rasha," Anje said to her brother, "you rig a fresh mount, one with legs." She held his gaze for a few silent moments and said, "You will *not* be here when that force arrives. Get us to the front, then you and Sir Johns gather every horse not attached to the drive detail and head for Essen. Take your whole crew too, everyone. Now go."

Cort nodded once and stepped through the door, just as Kamiko felt the wagon began to speed up. Moments later the turn came, as they altered course and headed to the front of the caravan. Moments after that, Anje pulled on her thick hat and stepped out without another word. The four sisters sat on the couch and remained fully ready.

CHAPTER 10

Ravencroft—Grace

The snow had been coming and going for days, but the clouds had neither parted nor lifted once. The day was dark, and a still and bitter cold seemed to crackle in the air. Fat flakes drifted down in a slow-moving mass that cast a hush on the already-quiet street, three stories below where Grace stood, looking out a building window. Behind her Dor and Shel stood at battle ready, swords drawn, with their eyes locked on the object of Grace's attention. Yet her own hand remained empty, even in the presence of Dairei Parzon.

They were in one of their five Jayd Corridor houses taking a much needed break from many days on patrol. The dwelling housed almost thirty children, sixteen women, and four men, most of whom had been, until recently, living on the streets. The sisters had taken food and rest and were spending a few minutes comparing notes and rehashing their collected information, when the sound of a small rock striking the window drew their attention.

The building was originally an upscale inn built over three hundred years earlier. Seven floors and a steep roof made it the tallest building in the area during the first fifty years of its heyday. Now it was dwarfed by the density and height of the city growth pressed upon it from all sides. It was currently home to the poverty-stricken indigent commoners of South Ravencroft City. The sisterhood had maintained a community home on the third floor for decades to aid the men, women, and children, whose only crime was to be utterly poor in a society of extreme wealth.

The sound of the rock had drawn the three sisters out to the balcony where they found Dairei, perched in an open window across the road, out of reach. Dairei spoke first, "What have you done to my city, Sister Grace?"

Grace decided now was not the time to argue ownership of Ravencroft. "We've been cleaning up your trash, thief."

"I hear you have Yannis."

"Yes, we do."

"I heard he gave me up."

Grace offered no answer. "What do you want, Parzon?"

The question seemed to bother Dairei. She was completely covered but for a tight oval opening for her face, from the lower edge of her bottom lip to just above her browline. Grace had encountered Dairei only twice face-to-face, so she could not be certain how to take the troubled look which clouded Dairei's eyes or her hesitation in answering. At last her fiery eyes rested on Grace.

"I am—" She began but stopped abruptly. She took a deep breath and started again. "I have been instructed to seek you out, Grace of Leary and…" She paused again, reluctant. "I am to offer you my services."

Shel laughed once and bounced her sword in her hand.

Dor growled quietly. "What?"

Grace simply stared at Dairei as if she'd lost her mind, her mouth open with a slight half-grin. "Yeah?" she said finally. Dairei glared hot but held her tongue. She decided it was not a good idea to push someone as dangerous as Dairei. "Who?" Grace asked simply.

"Siruis of Marjan."

Drakes Pass—Kamiko

The northern towns of Cairistonia were only well-defined points of civilization within a vast wilderness, connected by thin strips of roadways and cart paths. Great oceans of grasslands and forest groves spread two hundred leagues to the south. Much of it was covered in farmlands and home to large shepherd tribes with migratory herds of livestock. The only town of substance, further north than Drakes Pass, was Flavin, before crossing the northern border of the kingdom at some ambiguous point a few leagues inside the greater jungle.

Kamiko had agreed that Anje needed to avoid the southern route along the coastline of the Bos`Jin Sea. That was some of the most densely populated territory in the kingdom.

The wagon had been sitting motionless for several minutes, and still no one had returned. Felene was taking the three paces to and from the door again. She'd decided to stick close, no reason to start out separated if things got out of hand. The ferret sat near Siruis's shoulder and watched everything.

Kamiko said to everyone, Danae included, "We still have one problem to overcome."

"One?" Felene asked with a chuckle.

Kamiko smiled back at her and said, "Yes, and a very big one." Then she turned to Danae and asked, "Any ideas?"

The girl thought for only a moment before signing her answer, "You are under an oath of summons, and Sister Siruis will be arrested on sight."

"Yes," Kamiko answered. "We are stuck inside this wagon." She pointed her finger at Felene and said, "And you as well."

"You will be pressed to keep me here, if things start getting rough out there."

Siruis said, "Well, eventually someone is going to open that door and probably sooner than later."

Felene added, "Yes, but we need to already be out there when that force arrives, that is crucial. You must ignore the summons, Kamiko. We need to get out there now."

Kamiko thought about the oath and the consequences of disobeying the summons. The message she would send both king and kingdom would be that of rebellion, of open disobedience. Kamiko had been one of the officers of the Crown tasked to write not only the statute of the summons but the punishment for ignoring it as well. It gave a certain amount of control to whosoever bound her. Kamiko would be obligated to follow them to the throne room without resistance or delay. Or not, which meant she would either be forever an outlaw or a prisoner for a full decade.

She remained an officer of the court and a sister of the Order, but even as a simple woman, she would never consider such dishonor. At the present, she was fulfilling the summons because she was on her way to see the king. Captain Rath had first made her aware of the summons, but he hadn't bound her. Lord Merritt intended to bind her but choose not to in light of events. But now anyone could serve the summons anytime they wanted. And it was common knowledge that, if they delivered Kamiko personally and straightaway, the king would show his gratitude in gold.

"I am at a loss as to how, Felene. I will not refuse the summons, and it will get served within the first ten minutes of stepping out the door."

"Look," Felene said with firm kindness, "right now your influence is needed to stop a massacre perpetrated in Siruis's name. The summons can wait. I will tie up whoever serves it and leave them here until we get past this, but I gotta have you out there on Uila."

"Sister," Kamiko addressed Felene directly, "if I am served the summons, I will be bound. We need to plan on that being a factor and act accordingly. Which means I stay here."

Siruis interjected, "Come and sit, Felene, let us recall God's role in all of this, lest we forget the outcome does not rest in our own hands but in his." The ferret hopped up and scampered to a small shelf Siruis had padded with folded cloth.

Felene had a look on her face that spoke of having been convinced on the sly. But with respect for Siruis, she stepped away from the door and sat on the low couch. Kamiko was grateful that Felene had never lost her willingness to listen and carefully consider ideas that were not her own.

Siruis continued, always including Danae in the discourse, "Sometimes we forget our most potent strength." She held each of the sisters with her bright blue eyes for a moment, then asked Danae, "What do we do now while we wait?"

As was her way of things, Danae answered simply, "We pray."

To which Siruis smiled and nodded.

*****

What time they spent in prayer went quickly, for in short minutes, a tumult of voices was heard approaching the wagon. Siruis spoke first, "See, Felene, the answer comes swiftly." Before Kamiko even had time to consider what Siruis meant, the door was opened, and no fewer than twenty hard faces peered in. Puffy clouds of white breath drifted from every face, pale skinned and splotched with the red from a cold day, every brow furrowed with worry.

Cort and Anje were standing in front of the group, and Anje immediately motioned for Kamiko to step outside, her face dark. Felene rose and was out the door in an instant. She stopped almost nose to nose with Anje, looking down at her from above.

"What are you doing, Anje?"

The smaller woman was clearly intimidated but glared up at Felene, then, through clenched teeth, said, "Step aside, Sister, this has nothing to do with you."

Kamiko called from where she stood in the doorway, her head bent down slightly to allow her to pass through. "Felene, it's okay." She closed the door behind her and stepped briskly down the steps. Kamiko placed her hand on Felene's shoulder and spoke loud enough for everyone present to hear with great clarity. "I need you to guard the wagon. And, Felene," she said, peering at the gathering for a moment, "kill anyone who puts a foot on those steps." She paused a moment as a quiet gasp rolled around the small group. Kamiko held Felene's eyes a moment longer before she hooked her thumb toward Cort and Anje and said, "Even those two." At this

Anje's stony demeanor wavered, and a sick look slipped over her face. Felene nodded to Kamiko and stepped backward toward the wagon, drawing her big sword slowly, pure menace showing in all her movements, a dark look of promise in her eyes. Kamiko knew Felene well enough to know, the fierce woman now considered herself to be at war—with *everyone.*

Kamiko stepped in front of Anje and said, "I am here, Anje, do what you must do." She could see that the instructions to Felene had stunned Anje with a hard dose of terrible reality. Anje was shaken, and by her hesitation and the emotions battling across her face, she was seriously doubting her idea. "It is too late for doubt. Do it now, Anje." The kindness and complete absence of command in Kamiko's voice bolstered Anje, and she stepped forward.

She reached into her belt pouch and withdrew something Kamiko recognized immediately—a gold badge with Titus's royal symbol emblazoned in the center. She was an officer of the court. The many faces of Andi Jean. This would have more teeth than a simple summons.

Anje raised the badge so the gathering could see what she held in her hand, and then spoke in a loud voice, "Lieutenant Marshal Kamiko Hoshi, I place you under arrest for failure to maintain the oath of summons."

Teeth. Indeed.

Anje then reached into the same pouch and withdrew a leather strap, roughly two fingers in width, an arm's length, with a weighted ring attached to each end, and held it out toward Kamiko.

Felene stepped forward and growled, low and menacing. "No, you don't, woman." She did not brandish her sword at Anje, but her free hand was a granite fist, held low to one side. The wagon door opened, and Danae came bounding out and sprang from the second step, covering the gap to Kamiko's side in one long floating stride. She stepped between Kamiko and Anje, punched her fist into her palm, and took a ready stance.

Anje looked like she'd been caught by a bear but had not yet been bitten. She held the badge in one hand and the wrist hobble dangling from the other. Kamiko could see her knees bend slightly and her weight shift to her toes, but she did not move from the spot, and for that Kamiko, smiled at her and nodded her approval. Then she laid her hand on Danae's shoulder and eased the girl around to face her. She spoke only to Felene and Danae, using the silent language.

"Sisters, what were we doing just before the door opened?" Felene and Danae looked at each other, and their anger began to fall away by degrees, but neither spoke. "Our prayer was answered, even as we were praying." She let them think for a moment or two. "I am very intrigued by what will happen next, and I recommend we put all of our faith in God's desire to answer prayer well." The dim day was quiet, and the gathering was nearly motionless. The air had been still, but it was beginning to rise, this time straight up from the south and reeking of dirt and moisture. While still dictating to Danae, Kamiko spoke aloud to Felene. "What do you imagine Anje could do to take me from the path I am on?" Anje's head tilted slightly, and her brow tightened.

Kamiko then said to Anje, "Let us see what part of providence God has placed into your hands." She held her wrists out and showed what kindness could be offered on a weathered warrior's face. It did not surprise Kamiko that Anje was still doubtful and hesitated. Everyone present knew the hobbles were a symbol of shame, adding insult to the injury she was placing on Kamiko. It was also well known that Anje could choose to not use the bindings.

Anje stepped forward, but Felene stopped her again. She sheathed her sword and yanked the hobble from Anje's hands, then turned to Kamiko. Time slowed with anticipation as Felene worked the strap through the rings, making a slip loop at both ends. Kamiko sensed those watching had been holding their breath, as they collectively exhaled when Felene looped them over Kamiko's wrists and pulled them snug. She again drew the sword as she glared down at Anje, and stepped aside. Being a symbolic shackle not meant to physically restrain someone, the length of the binding between Kamiko's wrists allowed her to easily function.

Cort's eyes had not wavered from his feet since she'd first stepped out of the wagon.

She called over to him, "Cort, would you fetch Uila for me?" She felt a lightness about her. She realized she'd been imprisoned for days in a wagon home, and before that, a windowless underground dungeon, since she'd last ridden her trusted companion. She'd not been on Uila since their arrival at Lord Merritt's. Cort was hesitating, waiting for a reaction from Anje by his body language. Anje was statue-still, her eyes on Kamiko's smiling face in a serene shock she'd not expected. The mightiest warrior in the land was under her authority, wearing her hobbles. Anje's monetary reward would be life-changing in the extreme. By the look on Felene's face, Anje's present serenity would be short-lived.

When no one moved, Kamiko put a little of the command back into her voice. "Cort, bring my horse...now if you please." This time he did not wait for his sister's nod and stepped quickly past Kamiko. The young man bowed his head slightly as he approached her and met her eyes as he strode by, a plaintive smile on his face. She doubted any of this was his idea. He had the look of a man being pressed along a path he would never choose on his own.

She turned to Danae and asked her to remove her sword, then held her arms out to allow the girl access to the buckle. She complied instantly. Once the barding and sheathed sword were in Danae's hands, Kamiko instructed her to which Danae nodded a vigorous agreement and skipped into motion.

She set the whole bundle on the ground at Felene's feet and carefully, but with sure confidence, drew the sword. Kamiko saw she lifted it with ease, knew it was almost weightless in Danae's hand. Kamiko also noticed that Danae's grip was in perfect form for the larger sword. Two years with Sister Rachel had left a wide river flowing in the girl. She turned and sprinted for the wagon, veering around it in a broad circle, dragging the sword tip, and cutting a well-defined line in the ground. She made seven such fast laps around the wagon and draw horse, cutting seven deep grooves in a single unbroken line. And without slowing her headlong charge in the slightest, Danae connected the end of the line with the beginning and lifted the sword, rendering the line infinite.

In that moment, Hun'jotzimon shimmered into sight. Kamiko felt a surge in her chest, of what, she was uncertain. It was the sudden swell of emotion which leaves you breathless in the ascent, and again breathless in the plunge to follow. Elation and horror in a single harmonic chord. How would this being interpret her intent? What degree of control does an infinite creature possess? At what point do minuscule and catastrophic become one thing? Perspective was ever the soothsayer of truth.

She knew no one else was seeing Hun'jotzimon and feared for them, for what she was about to declare into existence. She knew people would test it, that many would die. Danae came to stand between Felene and Kamiko with the sword tip on the ground, her hands folded casually atop the pommel, which was at chin-level to her.

It had to be done. Kamiko stepped forward and spoke in a loud voice, "I declare by my word and my belief in Almighty God that anyone attempting to cross that line but my three companions and I will be destroyed. I suggest you make that widely known, and please heed the warning."

A murmur wafted across the small gathering until one voice rose above the rest. "We must see her." Before the words had completely died on the gusting wind, the door of the wagon opened, and Siruis stepped out, walked down the steps and over to the circle where she stopped. The pure white ferret sat curled on her shoulder, glaring out with as much menace as a tiny face may muster. The hush fell over them again.

Felene leaned over toward Kamiko and asked quietly, "So I don't need to guard the wagon anymore?" Kamiko offered Felene a shallow grin and shook her head.

"That was a bit of an impulse," Kamiko whispered back. "I needed to make a point."

Felene stepped forward, again moving toward Anje, and spoke over her shoulder to Kamiko, "You know, Sister, I'm feeling an impulse myself. To make a point." She stopped one short pace from Anje, who had moved back closer to the gathering, and spoke loud enough for everyone to hear.

"Here is *my* decree. If *any* of you attempt to add more dishonor to my Sister Kamiko, or further sully the sisterhood with the bitterness in your hearts… I will kill you. You would do well to remember that I am not bound by you or anyone else and shall act as I please."

Anje's face flared hot, and she retorted at a near-shout. "I am under orders from the Crown, and I'm just doing my—" Her voice was cut off by Felene's thick hand clamping down on her throat, not hard enough to choke or even hurt her but with strength enough to feel. The bear had bitten.

"Now you slander the good name of duty by placing it upon an act of greed." She released Anje after only a moment's hold. "Go about your plans, Andi Jean, I will see to the disposition of your prisoner and guarantee her full cooperation with the law."

Kamiko let it play out. Felene needed no help figuring out when a show of strength was called for. Anje was well within the right for the arrest but had gone too far with the hobbles.

Sir Johns and Cort appeared on Kamiko's right, leading Uila and a dark brown muscle-bound beauty, with black mane and tail. She noticed that neither horse was held by a lead rope; they were following the two men by command. This meant the other horse was also a destrier, and if Kamiko had correctly assessed the two horsemen, he had been carefully chosen for duty alongside Uila.

As soon as Uila laid his eyes on Kamiko, he practically barked and broke into a fast trot, nudging Sir Johns aside with gentle force that almost knocked him down. He trotted right up to her, his short tail standing straight up while his head bounced around dramatically until he stopped abruptly with his massive forehead pressed against Kamiko's chest. She immediately encircled his head with a firm hug as he chortled and nickered his relief. She allowed exactly ten seconds of the blissful blessing before the immediacy of the situation demanded action.

She stepped back from Uila, raised her hands, and gave him the hand signal that had been the most difficult for him to learn in all his years of training. It was not a single command for a specific action, rather a concept meant to encompass many commands. It was the command to *war*. It told Uila that a battlefield loomed nearby they were meant to occupy, and that no commands were forthcoming. He was to act as a free agent. His entire bearing changed. His dark face hardened, and he lifted his head, flared his chest, and flexed every visible muscle on his body, then drew still but for his slow chest bellows.

Sir Johns gasped quietly and pointed up to Uila and said, "He just got bigger, Rasha." Cort was silent, gazing at Uila like everyone present—Anje, Danae, and Felene included. The other dark warhorse stopped when Cort stopped and stood waiting behind him in much the same attitude of Uila but without the sheer mass.

Kamiko was doubly pleased to see, not just her own saddle and tack but her pack, bedroll, and even her short three-legged stool tied to the saddle. She turned to Felene and Danae and spoke in silence.

"Felene, I need you here with these people. Danae will ride with me." Kamiko knew Felene needed no explanation as to her plan, they'd drawn the same conclusion in reading the situation. "I want to put Anje in charge of the caravan." There was a slight motion beside Kamiko, and when she glanced over, Danae was already sitting atop Uila's dark companion, with Cort adjusting the stirrups to accommodate the shortness of her youthful legs. "If things go bad here, you pull back into the wagon and let the train make a run for it. Siruis is who they are looking for, and I need to know you will be at her side."

Felene signed, "Inside the circle?"

"Yes."

"Why? What did you do?" Felene cut her eyes toward the wagon. Siruis was still waiting where she'd stopped, a pair of paces inside the line.

"Not sure about that yet," Kamiko said aloud.

"*Destroyed*...that's what you said." She cut her eyes back to Kamiko, her distinctive single brow lifted high.

"I did."

"What if someone breaks that line in the dirt?"

Kamiko looked at Felene for a few moments, trying to figure out what the question was about.

"Will it still work?"

"What, Sister? Will *what* work?" Kamiko was at a loss.

"That thing you did, the *destroyed* part."

Kamiko could only stare at Felene. At last she managed words. "Sister, I have no idea what will happen, but the groove in the dirt is probably irrelevant. This is not some heathen spell. Anyone trying to approach the wagon will be judged, swift and terrible. Do not be deceived, Felene, and do not allow anyone of these folk to cross that line."

"Only the four of us."

"Which means no one else may follow you through that judgment safely, even if the enemy is on you. You must let them go, Sister. It would be far better for them to die the simple death of a sword than to find out what happens if they try to cross." Kamiko turned her gaze on the gathering, still silent and attentive to every detail before them. She knew they were listening.

She raised her voice only a little and told them, "I hope you are listening." She turned on them and stepped forward and said, "If any of you have even a shred of belief left in the Almighty, you should look to it now."

She was pleased to see the reaction on Anje's face. It reminded her of the first time she'd put a saddle on Uila. The ride had lasted only twelve seconds before she was airborne. Anje looked like that now. She was strapped onto a wild animal and felt no sense of the control she'd previously imagined. Kamiko would help her anchor a bit.

"As lieutenant marshal to His Majesty, the king, I appoint you, Anje Kale, as my deputy and charge you with the well-being of this train." She stepped a little closer to Anje and said, "That means you are the boss. If anyone disputes that, just send them to Felene." She could tell that Anje had harnessed her anger but held it close to the surface. Now her face was softening, as it dawned on her what Kamiko had done.

Kamiko turned to Felene and said, "Would you rig my sword to Danae's saddle?" And she lifted her hobbled hands. "Looks like I'll be useless in a fight."

Felene picked Kamiko's sheath from the ground as she spoke, "Well, you always were easy to whip in a fistfight." She continued as she stepped to Danae's side and retrieved the sword, "Maybe you should stay in the wagon, have a cup of tea..." She trailed off into a chuckle as she affixed the sheathed sword to the saddle.

Kamiko took one more silent glance over the gathering before she leapt all the way into her saddle and found the stirrups. Felene stepped back from Danae, just as Kamiko nudged Uila into a trot, and the two headed south into the darkening afternoon. The wind was being drawn from the warmer south, up into a building storm pushing down from the north, as if the weather knew this was to be a terrible day and was gathering strength for a suitable backdrop.

She laid the reins across the saddlebow, retrieved her gloves from her belt, and pulled them on. After a brief glance and nod at Danae, who saluted with the Dead Fist, Kamiko nudged Uila into a hard driving run. She would enjoy the roar of his rolling thunder like never before. With a glance to her side, she saw Danae standing high in the stirrups but leaned over the horse's neck, with the bit loose in his mouth, driving him faster. Here they were, just before a fierce storm, racing across the plains on powerful horses in pure bliss. Let them thunder!

CHAPTER 11

Felene

No one moved until Kamiko and Danae had been enveloped by the blowing haze and vanished into the gray light of the failing day. A false warming of the air told Felene that moisture was being drawn up into the storm and would soon be hurled back down in the form of ice.

She felt someone at her shoulder and turned to find Anje, shielding her face by holding her hood tight with both hands. "Where are they going?"

"To commit war."

"What?" Anje almost shouted. "Just Kamiko? She can't—"

Felene cut her off. "Can't what? Get herself killed and blow your chances at being a rich little tart? Think she can't handle a thousand-to-one odds? Anyway Danae is with her, so she's not alone. Ah… but think about her chances, now that she is hobbled at the wrist and forbidden to draw her sword." Felene turned and walked briskly toward Siruis, Anje taking up on her heels.

"Where are you going?"

"To get ready."

"For what?"

Felene stopped and turned on Anje. "To commit war." She held Anje's eyes for a moment and said, "You should be doing the same, boss."

Now Anje's face went ashen, and her tongue fell still. Felene let the woman bake in the fear running through her veins for a solid ten-count. A little heat for the tempering of her spirit. She knew Anje's mind was an empty void of ideas. Finally Felene stepped closer to Anje and placed a big hand on her shoulder. Anje's head came up with a snap.

"First, send anyone who questions your authority to me. I promise it will only take one. Got that?" She moved closer and let her arm slip around Anje's shoulder and cast her voice low. "Second, go ahead with your plan to scatter the train, and to get Rasha and Sir Johns outta here. You make sure he doesn't come back, Anje. With Siruis and Kamiko staying here, they will not be chased by the main body. Still, though, tell him to pack heavy and be ready."

"How do you know that?"

There was a moment of silence before Felene continued, "The trainmaster and everyone in his company are to remain and provide the muster call. Form circles with the wagons like spokes, wagon tails out, horses facing in. It is time to don the armor, my friend, and drop your empty sheath at your feet. Go, see to those things right now, and I will meet you out here shortly." She pointed at the gathering. "Make them see what must be done, then order them to the task. And, Anje." She turned to look at the smaller woman face-to-face. "Get Rasha and Sir Johns out of here."

Kamiko

"Cort needs to learn how to count," Danae signed to Kamiko, who could only nod her head in response. It had been a short ride over a pair of low hills.

"How many?" Kamiko asked.

Danae looked out over the mass of men moving slowly up the long valley slope. "Difficult. They are in one big group and waddling along, so not Royal Militia. One thousand. More."

"Yes, a little more than one." Kamiko nodded at Danae and signed, "Good eye. And about a hundred horsemen."

They watched the slow progress with only the sound of the wind in Kamiko's ears. They were still too far to tell details, but Kamiko could think of nothing more she needed to know. She asked Danae, "Why did we come out here and what should we do next?" The girl looked at Kamiko for several moments, while thoughts whirred in her head, then looked down over the army, then back at Kamiko, still thinking. Then she grinned and motioned for Kamiko to follow, as she turned her mount into a run down the slope but behind the ridge, and thus, out of sight. Kamiko moved with her and saw where Danae was likely heading. They had avoided using the main road in hopes of coming up beside the force. Now Danae was making for that very roadway. She'd come to Kamiko's own conclusion exactly.

When Danae reined her horse to a hard stop in the middle of the road and turned to face the oncoming company, Kamiko was certain. They were all being shown the same things, the entire sisterhood. Kamiko and Felene had just planned and enacted a small-war strategy without speaking a word. Kamiko's sword sisters of the past always had an uncanny sense of timely arrival, but something stronger was at work. The impulses Danae, Felene, and Kamiko were feeling were so similar in nature, they had to be coming from a single source. She felt a small flourish of inner excitement, anticipation of what was about to unfold, with the forces of God moving over the land. They sat in silence and waited for a small army to descend. Behind them, a winter storm had finally gathered enough strength to become angry, and the wind in their faces stopped.

It took many minutes for the leading edge of the mass of armed men to reach Kamiko and Danae. To both their astonishment, no one appeared to even notice they were there. It was obvious they were seen because the company parted and flowed around them, close enough to brush against their legs. But no single mark of recognition showed on any face. So they sat very still and watched the men walk by, most of them in silence. They were armed brigands and no small number of curious townsfolk, no doubt, being led by a handful of greedy fanatics. As yet she'd seen no one she could pinpoint as being in command.

Danae touched her arm and pointed off to their right. There another smaller group of people also marched, keeping pace with the larger company. They appeared much more timid and were carrying their weapons in hand, as if they expected trouble at any time. This group was gathered behind one man in particular, a big man who Kamiko saw was a soldier. He wore a breastplate of dark steel and had several weapons hanging from his belt.

An odd sensation passed through Kamiko then, and her eyes were drawn to the place right in front of Uila. He grumbled quietly. Someone had stopped not two paces from his nose and lifted a hand, as if in greeting. Then a round and very dark face, with eyes a deep rich chocolate, shone out from beneath the ample hood of an old and weathered cloak. Even had Kamiko not known Joon-tae Boruhn, sister of renown, she would have perceived her as a sword sister by the feel of her spirit. She had never donned weapons or armor, but she was fierce and dangerous.

Joon smiled and asked with only her hands, "Are you ready?" Kamiko nodded in response and reached up and pulled her own deep cowl back and off her head. Several sets of eyes turned to look at her, but they were only passing glances without recognition. Joon stepped up to Uila and simply laid her hand gently on his nose. For all intents, this was the trigger which caused everyone to finally see Kamiko for who she was.

Without warning, bedlam broke in an outward pushing wave, with Joon, Kamiko, and Danae at its center. Now recognition was immediate. Every face was contorted with surprise, and weapons sprang into the air as those closest to her pushed and shoved and shouted their way deeper into the crowd, away from Kamiko. A wide circle opened around them quickly. Kamiko knew she was about to find out who was in command as soon as the general tumult settled down.

"Joon-tae Boruhn," Kamiko said aloud, "Your timing is good, Sister."

She smiled up at Kamiko. "I have been watching you for many days." They spoke casually as if an armed company was not taking formation all around them.

"You just improved my odds a great deal, my friend. Have you been following me?" Kamiko asked with feigned suspicion.

Joon laughed bright and clear, in spite of the horsemen shoving quickly through the crowd from one side of the formation. "No, not follow...*watch*," she said. "Your spirit is like one of the great pilot fires of old. I can see you from a thousand leagues, Sister Kamiko, and have journeyed to be here in your time of need."

A sudden hush fell over the field, and Kamiko turned in her saddle to see what everyone was looking at. Six men on dark horses had stopped behind her, just inside the wall of bristling weapons. Kamiko focused on the only horse wearing a few pieces of armor and looked up at the one riding it. He was an older man and grim, with the dress and haughty air of wealth. She knew him by reputation—Rubio Pollard III, a wealthy man who rarely bathed. One of the lords of the Drakes. His companions were likely sons and nephews.

She turned back to her seat in the saddle and spoke in a loud voice over her shoulder, "Have you come here to talk then?" She imagined them exchanging looks. She could hear him clicking to the horse and heard him moving around on her left, circling at the border of the clearing. She kept her eyes on Joon even after he answered.

"We've come for the witch, Hoshi."

"You will need more men, Pollard."

"Someone has been sent to that very end." He'd moved into her peripheral vision, but she offered him no notice.

A voice rose up from somewhere in the back of the pack. "She is there!" Which triggered a hushed din of whispers, punctuated with low shouts, some angry. Kamiko heard the word *prophet* more than once and *witch* repeatedly. Joon nodded toward Danae, whose face and features were still concealed in the cloak and hood.

Using one hand, Kamiko very subtly called Danae to attention, to not move until further instructed. She would see how this played through with the chance deception in place. Three unarmed sisters against a thousand. Easy odds with Uila in the foray.

A commotion erupted where the shouts of prophet had come, and the crowd began parting from the back for a mountain of a man who strode unhindered, a heavy battle-ax hanging in his fist. Kamiko recognized him as the leader of the smaller group. When he stepped out into the clearing, a hush fell over the whole of the scene but for the rattling of many weapons in unsteady hands. He stopped near the edge of the crowd and simply looked at Kamiko for several moments, then with the casual swagger of a dangerous man, he turned and strode toward Pollard.

Kamiko was more than a little pleased to see Pollard's crew rush to his side with their swords drawn. It told her all she needed to know about the man with the ax. He never spoke a word and strode by the six horsemen with complete disregard. The silent message was loud and clear, and the younger men bristled and spat insults. The big man turned his back to them, lowered his eyes to the ground, and walked to Kamiko's side. He looked up and simply lifted the axe her way momentarily, then took his station two paces out from Uila. His hair was close-cropped and black as tar, his face shadowed with black stubble.

"What do you hope to achieve, Rubio Pollard?" Kamiko asked. "You don't really want this girl, you want the money. But money will do you no good where *I* am sending *you*." She let the weight of the simple statement ripen with silence.

The rider nearest Pollard growled to him. "Father, look, she is bound. We must take them...*now*." His companions looked less certain but grumbled their agreement and brandished their weapons in the air. She briefly lifted the hobbles for all to easily see.

Joon remained at Uila's nose and turned to Kamiko and signed, "No more words. Let them come." Kamiko's very thought. She nodded to Joon. Sure enough, Pollard drew his sword and backed his horse several paces, while his sons and nephews formed a line in front of him, weapons held high. It saddened her.

Kamiko could not tell the source of the impulse—whether from her own intuition or from one of the unseen messengers—but she acted as if by command. She simply leaned her weight onto the heels of her hands on the saddle horn, then lifted her body up into the air, high enough to bring her feet into the seat and then stood upright in the saddle. It had the effect of freezing everyone in place from anticipation.

Joon took several quick steps out in front of Uila and turned back toward Kamiko. Then, and in perfect concert with Kamiko, Joon raised her right arm up from her side and pointed her fist straight up, as if she was holding a sword, in the call to arms stance of the battlefield. As Kamiko's fist reached the summit, both she and Joon released their cloaks and let them fall to the ground.

Now chaos broke in full force over the entire assembly. But not before several moments of stunned silence held everyone in their tracks. Kamiko and Joon were not alone in the salute. No fewer than two hundred silver swords slipped up out of the crowd in exact unison with Kamiko, with like number of shabby cloaks dropped, as though timed. The sisterhood had been summoned. The chances of surviving just rose for everyone involved. Then the clearing around Kamiko, Danae, Joon, and the unnamed warrior grew by more than triple, leaving Pollard and his five horsemen alone in a field of angry sisters.

Once it had quieted enough to hear, Kamiko called to Pollard, "So we will call this matter settled then." It was spoken as an absolute, not a question. Even in the cold, she could see sweat covering his face in rivulets. Several droplets flipped from his nose as he nodded nervously, his breath coming in short gasps. By his demeanor, he was expecting a rain of steel on him, his sons, and nephews and looked doubtful when the sisters offered a passage out. The parting look he gave Kamiko before they turned their horses into a departing gallop was gratitude. The gathering quickly dispersed and moved in a large broken mass back to the south, toward Drake's Pass.

Kamiko lowered herself to the saddle, as the gathering of sisters lowered their swords and stood waiting in silence. Kamiko had won battles with half this number.

The second smaller group was undaunted and began filtering through the sisters carefully, making their way toward who they assumed was Siruis. They had abandoned their arms, so there was no single weapon among the lot of them, thus the sisters let them pass.

The big warrior stepped around to the front of Uila and watched them approach. They numbered roughly one hundred.

"They would not be refused, Sister. They came here prepared to die to the man, to protect the girl. I could not abandon them." Joon moved around and faced them as well, completing a small circle of four.

The man looked up at Kamiko and said, "When last I saw you, Sister, I called you Captain Hoshi. I followed you into six major battles. Riklund Dunning, but you knew me as Helmet."

She said, "I remember you, Helmet. Did I ever once see your face?"

He smiled and shook his head. "No, Sister." He looked at the folks gathering a few paces back. "They believe she is from God. For that, they and their families will be made to suffer."

"Their sacrifice would have been wasted, Riklund Dunning, this is not Siruis," Kamiko said and signed to Danae to come out of hiding. She untied the drawstring and pulled her hood back and smiled out at the group of mostly men, few women. Kamiko was fairly sure none of them had seen Siruis, but no one thought she was a twelve-year-old girl. The hope on their faces drained away.

Riklund asked, "Where is she? We have a desire to see her, to hear her words. We do not fear them."

Kamiko heard a sound she'd come to know since she met Jerim—many birds in fast flight. "No," she said abruptly, "you must go quickly from here." The sisters spread afield began looking to the sky, as if searching for an elusive sound. Kamiko heard it plain. "Gather every one of these people and all their families and get them to Essen." The horde of silent birds was on them, a mass of thousands. They came straight and fast, but the column shot upward and curled in on itself and twisted and turned, then reformed and tore directly back the way they came, toward Siruis. Jerim was calling her to come running.

"To Essen, Helmet. Give them one day to prepare, and then you leave." She was reining Uila around as she spoke, then kicked him into a hard run, Danae right on their heels. The whole troop of sisters broke into a run with them, all on foot.

Chapter 12

Felene

Felene was pleased it was sleet right at the outset instead of rain. Freezing cold was better than freezing cold and soaking wet. She had prepared the wagon for Siruis's comfort, assuming her safety was already secured by whatever Kamiko had done. The fire was built with wood to spare, and the draw horse was secured on the leeward side of the wagon and entirely draped with a large tarp Felene had attached to the wagon. She had even tied the wheels to the frame in case someone clever figured out to lasso the wagon and pull it out of the ring.

Then she'd entered the wagon and prepared for battle. She had bathed her extremities with a warm moist towel and scrubbed her face with hot water. Then she'd layered her clothes for not only warmth but mobility. At last, even after her low boots were bound tightly about her ankles, she donned her leather breastplate, the only remaining piece of her armor from the times when she'd served on the battlefield. Siruis had helped to get the thick straps oriented and fastened evenly behind Felene, so the worked leather armor hung on her snug and comfortable.

Then she'd covered all with a large canvas poncho, treated with the dank reeking lanolin from sheepskins. It was a gift from the trainmaster upon discovering she was a sister of the Order. She intended to show him her gratitude and keep him and all his family alive.

Last had come the sword. *Her* sword. The sword of her ancestors yet bestowed with no more magic than what comes with the inspiration of wielding it. All else was excellent craftsmanship and Felene's knowledge of its employment.

Two bands of wide heavy leather, one laying over each shoulder, met and clasped in the center of her chest, then continued down each ribcage, met again and fastened to the thick sheath-plate band lying along her spine, up to between her shoulder blades. The great sword was affixed slightly cocked, to offer the hilt at Felene's right shoulder, but low to allow the sword to be easily drawn with the length of her arm. She hoped beyond reason that she would see no cause to wield it today.

When she stepped out of the wagon, the sleet was a quiet roar on the canvas hood, even with the woolen hat pulled tight over her head. The wind was suspiciously calm, and though the cloud cover had lifted higher, it was growing darker by the minute. She scanned the area around her as she pulled her gloves on. She was pleased to see the train had been disbanded and was in the process of reforming in the circle Felene had described, a thousand paces back up the roadway. People and horses were scattered everywhere, all moving with the haste of driving fear. Anje had gone with Rasha and Sir Johns to help get their herd moving. Felene hoped that whoever showed up would focus their attention on Siruis and leave the fortified caravan alone.

It struck her as odd that the thought of *their* fear had driven her eyes down to the ground at her own two feet. The seven-layered circle in the dirt had sparked something dark in Felene, a gnawing fear that the physical power of God would come into play this day. Kamiko had done something. *Destroyed*, Kamiko said. She stepped across the line with a shudder from toe to crown.

Felene drew her sword slowly, with reverence in her heart, and prayed in the simple terms of a warrior, "Give me victory, even if I stand alone against giants, for I declare the Everlasting as my strength all the days of my life. Show mercy, oh God, in your wrath, even to my enemy." Two men appeared, both clad like Felene but with no weapons between them. One moved to stand near her right hand, the other moved to her left. As they took their places, they passed again from Felene's sight, as if they wanted her to know for certain she did not fight alone. She lifted the sword to her forehead in salute. It felt light in her hand. Then she turned to the business at hand.

She set her sights on the tumult that was the caravan and took a first long stride—then stopped short. He had formed out of nothing, standing right in her path only a dozen paces more. Even so she had to raise her eyes to find his face and lifted her sword on pure instinct. He was a giant—a true giant—and not just a very big man. And he was entirely covered in hides, fur, and canvas so that even his face was hidden in the shadow of his great cowl. Only when Felene could see that a few locks of his golden hair had escaped at his neckline did she allow the sudden fire to calm. She'd forgotten Siruis's companion, Jerim. Now that fire turned to joy, and she trotted forward. He lowered to a hunkered crouch and drew his hood back slightly and met her eyes as she stopped.

She sheathed the sword and reached out toward his hand, just as a single distant voice shouting emerged in her mind. Both she and Jerim turned to the east and, in the distance, saw Anje and Rasha on horseback, running at them as fast as they could drive the beasts.

Anje's hand flew out to her right, and as Rasha veered in the indicated direction, the two riders split, Anje heading straight for Felene, Rasha heading for the caravan. As Anje pulled her horse to a hard stop, Rasha was just making it to the edge of the activity at the caravan. He rode through the people, shouting at everyone he encountered, causing them first to stop cold, then to run hard for the circle of wagons. Felene's gut was churning, even as Anje bounded from her horse, her words a fast torrent.

"They are coming...*now*! A body of men at arms, Sister, bearing from the north and east." Felene turned to cast a look at Jerim but found she was alone with Anje. "We are under attack."

Without hesitation, Felene ordered Anje with a sharp but quiet command, "Go to the wagons quickly, Anje. They are not yet ready to repel an assault. Then you stay with the trainmaster inside the ring. Let the hired arms earn their pay today. Now, go, go..." Anje bolted for her horse and mounted with a single leap, already kicking the beast into a hard gallop. She'd closed the gap by half when Felene's heart felt as though it stopped cold in her chest for a long moment.

She saw hundreds of glistening flecks of dull light appear from out of the haze of sleet, which, as they came closer, formed into a line of polished helms and long spears and men on horseback. Then another line and another formed as they rode at a slow gallop. She spotted the command flag then, and her heart dropped into her stomach. It was the signet of royal military command in the rank of colonel. Two other color-bearers flanked the royal banner and the colonel on either side. They were just close enough that Felene could make out that one banner lowered slightly to the left, the other to the right. The advancing horsemen split into two bodies, each following the officers in either direction, one to the caravan and one toward Felene. If she was reading the command posting correctly, this was a light brigade of two thousand trained warriors, being led by a cavalry of over five hundred strong. The horsemen would need no help from infantry this day. If it came to blows, the caravan was doomed.

Still the one ingredient Felene had not heard was the trumpet call for a full attack.

Felene! She heard Siruis's voice in her head and on the wind together and turned toward the wagon. Siruis was standing on the small porch before the open door, the ferret draped over one arm. She motioned for Felene to join her and stepped down the steps. Felene wondered if it was even possible to refuse any request or command coming from Siruis. She turned and walked briskly to the wagon, slowing against her will as she stepped over the line. Siruis joined her midway between the line and the wagon, and both women turned to watch as the king's own army descended.

As they drew closer, Felene could clearly see that only a small fraction of the force had been dispatched to the wagon, with a captain at the lead. The main body, now plainly five-hundred-horses strong, began the calm deliberate encircling of the caravan, the colonel at their lead position. She could tell that the wagon circle had not fully formed, but she understood clearly enough that against the royal military, no defense they could mount would be strong enough to withstand.

Siruis's arm came up and pointed to a place out away from the caravan. Almost immediately, Felene saw Anje, still on her horse and still running as hard as the animal could manage. Again she was making directly for where Felene and Siruis stood silently waiting. She would be hard-pressed to make it before the captain's company cut her off.

She looked down at Siruis and said, "I am here to watch over you, Sister, not Anje."

"Yes."

"Jerim is here," she said hopefully. "He would not allow them..."

"Jerim may not save her, Felene." Siruis stroked the top of the ferret's head gently but held Felene in a stern gaze. Felene could only nod, her eyes locking again onto Anje.

Had the captain so desired, he could have intercepted Anje. But he allowed her time to get by before he turned the column in behind her. She kept the horse at a full run to the very last moment and dismounted without bringing him to a complete stop. Felene was worried Anje may cross the deadly line without meaning to and stepped forward with her hand extended. But Anje's eyes quickly scanned the ground and found the layered groove, now outlined in gathering sleet, and she stopped just outside. The horse simply kept moving and trotted out into the field, then stopped and turned, his sides heaving great columns of white breath.

Anje was standing facing Felene and Siruis, her own lungs working as hard as her horse's. Her face was contorted by a combination of fear and anger, which rendered her features almost maniacal. Her eyes began darting back and forth among the captain, Felene, Siruis, and the mysterious groove in the dirt. She saw her predicament as easily as Felene saw it. She could not find sanctuary inside the demarcation, and even with Felene at her defense, they were outnumbered by far too great a force to hope to survive a fight. Under normal circumstances—

"Be still, Anje," Siruis called to her gently. "Wait with us and see the hand of God." The young woman nodded vigorously, willing to attach to any shred of hope offered.

The captain had the troop in place quickly, and all motion came to a sudden halt. He scanned the scene only until his eyes came to find Siruis, then he lost interest in all else. He raised his hand in signal to someone behind him and was immediately answered by two horses moving forward to join him at the front of the company.

One horse carried an armed soldier, his sword out with the tip pressed into the ribs of the other rider. This one was in chains and shackles. His head was exposed to the sleet and his face was swollen, blood-caked and bruised dark. He looked at no one.

The captain's first act was to cuff him across the face with his riding crop. Felene saw the pain twist the prisoner's body to the soles of his feet and knew he'd been tortured for days, that his entire body was likely as bruised as his face. The rage which sparked in Felene's chest was a new sensation to her, more of a wild beastly burn than simple anger. Was this the berserker Siruis had released, at last finding a reason to wake?

The captain simply pointed the riding crop at Siruis, then turned a questioning eye upon the prisoner. Felene felt her legs engage but also felt Siruis's hand come to rest on her arm, somehow locking her feet in place on the ground.

With slow obedience, the haggard beaten man lifted his eyes to Siruis and gazed at her for several moments. Too long. He shook his head *no* and grumbled something to the captain, which Felene could not make out, then lowered his gaze to his saddle horn. The captain nodded to the prisoner's guard, who twisted the sword back and forth and slid the tip just into his flesh with a sharp bump against the pommel with his free hand. The man's face came up with a contained growl, sleet thickening on his head and shoulders, him refusing to submit even a shout of pain. He shook his head *no* again, emphatically this time.

Beside her, Siruis wept in quiet sobs, but she kept her hand on Felene, who knew she could not move a muscle if she tried. The rage boiled in her chest, but her breath was slow and deep. Siruis would release her when it best served. Then her breath would quicken, and her blood would boil without restraint.

The captain cuffed him again, then called an order over his shoulder. A trumpet immediately blared a short call three times. The captain pointed the crop at Siruis and pronounced doom he could not begin to fathom, "Seize her."

To his left, a tall flagged pole was raised. The horsemen moved as one, spreading their bulk outward into an enclosing circle. Of those sweeping around behind them, several followed protocol and, to affect an approach from behind, moved into the circle toward the front of the wagon. Felene watched their physical elements burn away in no more time than it takes a sword to strike. At first no one seemed to notice. Then there was confusion as to where they went, and other riders moved into the space their comrades were to have filled. This time, half the company saw their bodies, all their possessions, and their mounts dissolve in a momentary flare of heat. There was no more sound than a brief hiss, though it was followed by many shouts, curses, and heathen prayers.

Other soldiers had moved to obey the captain's order and climbed off their horses. Six men in exact dress, armor, and weapons, four toward Felene, two toward Anje. Siruis released her arm. Felene strode forward suddenly, briskly, and moved directly at the center of the six-man team. She punched her fist into her hand. She would draw her sword only when they forced her to. When Rachel spoke to her before, when she was taken, she spoke of compassion. These were working soldiers with families, not enemy combatants or even criminals. Felene whispered aloud but to the two unseen men she knew accompanied her, "Without killing them…"

The captain called another order, and no fewer than thirty soldiers leapt from their horses and began to quickly converge on Felene and Anje.

"Fine," Felene said aloud and then over her shoulder to Anje, "you get to your knees and be very still. And do not lift your head, Anje." This the advancing soldiers heard with clarity, followed immediately by the deep ring of Felene's enormous sword clearing the scabbard. The lot of them knew the great sword to be one of the most deadly weapons known on the battlefield. Had they known who was wielding it, they would have given pause. Yet a soldier of the crown has no such luxury. The command was given, and Felene joined them in a battle. Felene's sword was back in the sheath before reality had even found a foothold in the captain's mind. Thirty-six men lay sprawling, broken and bleeding, but all alive.

The captain's mount pranced sideways and backed away, based solely upon the horse's perception of the man riding her. To Felene this was a sign that the captain abused the horse with the crop, and that he was a fearful man. The horse was accustomed to a hasty retreat after feeling such a shudder. It was dawning on the captain that he could be facing a sister of the Order, though Felene's features were still hidden.

He cried his next order aloud, like a desperate man keeping a shallow hold on his fears. "*Take them*!" The result was far from what he could have expected. Fifty men dismounted and charged Felene and Siruis at a run, most heading for Siruis. And like a great stampede of plains bison flowing headlong over the edge of a deep cliff, the men faded from sight in quick succession, as the last man in the file passed Kamiko's line unawares and dissolved into nothingness.

Likewise Felene's sword rang and was sheathed, and the horrific silence of hissing sleet returned, far too abruptly for the attempt which had been made. Anje had not moved in the slightest. Felene knew the woman now understood the order with staggering clarity, as the sword had passed over her head many times in only seconds. This time men had died. Felene saw the wounded men crawling away around her and recalled the simple prayer she'd made. Felene knew in that moment that she could take the whole company, if the captain pushed her to it. She was not alone. She could feel her two companions moving with her, bolstering her strength and speed.

She noticed that the prisoner's horse had wandered away from his guard. The man was slumped all the way to where his face was against the horse's neck, and the horse was aimless. Then several trumpets began sounding, as the colonel arrived with the main force of the cavalry.

Motion off to her left out in the field caught her attention. It was the sudden appearance of an enormous flock of birds in flight, which first drew her eye low to the ground in a thick churning cloud, fixed to one spot like a tornado. For all she could tell, they were circling some large object. Just as that thought congealed, the tornado broke form, and the flock erupted toward the dark sky, then turned and tore over Felene with the speed of fleet birds in haste. As the leading end of the mass passed her, the trailing end was just lifting away from—Jerim. One last creature remained aloft, drifting in a slow circle around the giant, a great white owl. A moment later, it followed the host, but no faster than the slow glide it already maintained. It stroked its broad wings a single time and drifted south.

Jerim lifted his finger toward the prisoner on the horse, who was now drifting slowly in a direct line to Felene. Then he pointed at Anje and nodded. Felene whispered aloud, "Yes! Get ready, Anje."

The horse broke into a sudden trot and then stopped abruptly where Anje could hop over Felene's slain and climb onto it's back. She immediately checked the prisoner's neck and nodded to Felene, then pulled him into an embrace from behind, as the horse headed directly toward Jerim at a quick trot.

Seeing this, the captain snapped up his crop and ordered men to intercept. A unit of fifteen cavalry broke out of the rank and charged Anje on horseback, long spears coming to bear. But now Anje was out in the open. Felene was about to spring toward her at a run when she heard a small quiet voice, not in her head but whispered in her ear, "Wait," Siruis implored. Felene did yet with her eyes fixed upon the potentially horrific scene.

At first she thought Jerim had yawned, and for that moment, she was stunned. But he rolled his head back, let his massive arms drift outward and bellowed up into the building storm. The horses bearing quickly down upon Anje simply fell to the ground, the entire unit at once. Men and horses were scattered.

To Felene's ears, the tone Jerim roared was sonorous and beautiful and moved as a sadness within her. Every horse Felene could see was having a terrible reaction to the bellow, as if deep predatory instincts were being challenged, and their worst fears were rising.

Many of the horses across the whole of the field simply fell to the ground, senseless and writhing. Most of the others broke and ran, distinctly and directly away from Jerim. Those few remaining had commenced war on every living thing, whether man or beast. The only two exceptions she could see were the horse bearing Anje and the prisoner and the draw horse tied to the wagon. Jerim let the bellow dwindle down and stop, then crouched to one knee to see to Anje and the prisoner.

Felene had not moved and turned and walked back into the circle to rejoin Siruis and the ferret. They stood together in silence as the cavalry fought to overcome the mad horses. By her quiet estimation, over half the men were out of commission as well. She asked Siruis what seemed like an obvious question, "Did Jerim make them do that?" She was pointing out at the carnage. Siruis simply nodded.

She could see the colonel, the captain, and their aides attempting to restore order. Even with Jerim having gone quiet, the horses were not recovering. It made Felene wonder if he'd done more to them than was obvious. Or, she thought, the fear had to run its course, like any ailment.

It mattered little. The colonel would be in a spiteful and deadly mood. The people of the caravan would be used as pawns. Innocent blood was one of the only threats anyone could offer the sisterhood as leverage in scenarios such as this one.

In the distance, trumpets peeled long and high, announcing the arrival of the infantry. The captain was standing at crisp attention as the colonel shouted orders into his face, pointing, first, toward the caravan, then back toward Siruis. The captain saluted and ran at a hard sprint toward the caravan. The colonel turned to face Felene and Siruis, still a hundred paces away where he'd fallen from his horse, and glared as much anger and hatred as a handsome face may manage. Felene hoped he could see her smiling. A group of several hundred soldiers was gathering behind him, with sharp military efficiency. The thrashing horses had all been put to the sword, so the field was a bloodbath.

Felene noticed the clouds were dropping, and the sleet was letting up. It would soon return as snow.

Siruis's voice gave her a start. "Felene, there is something you must know. May I command you, Sister?"

She turned to look down at the small woman beside her. "Are you asking my permission to give me an order?" She smiled. "That is very original. And yes, Siruis of Marjan, I am yours to command, now and always."

"You will go to Ravencroft City. Grace is in dire need of you there. I am taking Kamiko and Danae from you for a short time, and I need you to go to Ravencroft to prepare for them."

"Them? Not you?"

"Oh, yes, I will be there. But my task is at hand, Kamiko's task awaits her there. It is for her you will prepare."

Felene was facing Siruis, gazing on her for several moments, feeling as though her life was written on a page and left for Siruis to read in fullness at a glance.

When Siruis spoke, it was to Felene's inner secrets and turmoil, "You have not imagined that thing which haunts you. You are reborn, Felene. The old woman you awoke from is forever asleep."

The declaration almost stunned Felene, but the question was never more than a thought away. "What did you do? Was I healed?"

Siruis reached up and took her hand and stepped a little closer, as if to conspire over a secret. "I did not heal you, Sister. You died at Dairei's hand."

Died.

Felene decided not to take Dairei killing her to heart, best not to dwell. "How did I end up paralyzed? You say that was not just in my mind? How is this possible?"

Out in the field, the banners had finally been found and raised in the center and at both ends of the colonel's line of aides. Cavalrymen were still finding the last few places in the formation, though devoid of living horses, forming up among the dead ones. The sleet stopped, and the wind began to rise, blowing straight down from the north.

"Rest assured, Sister," Siruis said, "you will die at peace, the mother of many generations. You have a long life before you, Felene Dresdle of Clan Dunc. It is my belief you will wear a crown one day. And you carry the sword of kings already."

Felene was trying to let that sink in when she saw a cloud of birds coming at them in a dark twisting mass.

"They are returning to Jerim?" Felene asked Siruis.

"Yes, he sent them to bring Kamiko." The feathery horde churned past between them and the colonel in a tight column, which appeared to further unnerve the man and all his aides. It continued out of sight toward where Jerim had been standing.

"We may be here a while, Sister," Felene said.

"No, we will not be delayed much longer. Kamiko and Danae are here, Anje is safe, and the caravan is contained but has not been attacked. Everything is ready in both spirit and firma. The battle may commence." As Siruis spoke, the first deep peals of thunder rumbled quietly in the belly of the dark clouds. Fat snowflakes began swirling in the wind, giving the sense that things were suddenly moving fast.

*****

Kamiko and Danae drove the two warhorses right up to the insignia banners before they stopped hard. Uila danced nervously for only brief moments before Kamiko nudged him into a full run again, Danae on her heels. The colonel had staggered away from Uila and would have fallen to the ground had his ready aides not caught him.

Felene climbed the steps to the tiny porch so she could follow the two sisters' progress with her eyes. Kamiko charged in the direction of the caravan and took Uila and Danae on a circuit all the way around. They passed from Felene's sight behind the encircled wagons. The infantry had arrived from the northeast and were forming into large blocks of silver helms and twinkling spearheads, on the east side of the field. Trumpets blared without pause, back and forth over the whole mass, and to the untrained eye, sheer pandemonium ruled supreme. But Felene saw order and discipline and knew that at any moment, all the bedlam would cease, and silence would settle over the field.

"I find it ironic, Siruis. The bulk of these troops know what they know because of Kamiko's martial influence over the past two decades. Now they take formation to walk into the wake of her destruction. Some foul thing is at play here, something beyond the colonel's ego." She hopped from the porch to Siruis's side and dove into those crystal-blue eyes. "I have seen beyond this canvas once already," she said softly, tapping her chest at the word *canvas.* "I would see that way again…now."

Siruis held Felene's fierce brown eyes for several short moments before she said, "Sister, present your sword." Felene stepped back and drew her weapon out of the scabbard with a clear ring and held it in both hands, with the sword tip pointed straight up. "I do not know the full result of what we are about to do, Sister. We are dealing with beings who take their direction from God and no other."

Felene was ready to answer. "As do I, Siruis, as do I."

"Then hold your sword aloft and present it there…" she said as she pointed overhead to a space directly above the wagon. Without question or hesitation, Felene lifted the mighty sword and found she was pointing it directly at another sword, one suspended in the heavens but dwelling in the firma. Her heart pounded in her chest. Was this what Kamiko had done to protect Siruis?

It felt as though someone grabbed the tip of her sword but made no effort to take it from her, someone holding it in place. The blade began to hum and to resonate, through her skin and into her bones, and, with a sudden rush, filled her entire body for one instant. Then she felt her sword released to her full control again. Something like transparent scales fell from her eyes, and the world around her suddenly became far busier.

Felene's eyes were already upon the belly of the blackening clouds beyond the hovering sentinel. This was no storm. A dark and angry face peered down at Siruis from directly above her. It was drawing the elements around it's body like a living coiling cloak. It turned its demonic gaze on Felene, and she knew she was now present in the scene fully. Siruis whispered a name to Felene, "Luthain." She heard the colonel's voice, as if he was standing very near instead of a hundred paces away. He spoke a simple word to his second-in-command, *archers.*

In that moment, Felene saw the others. A dark being stood pressed against the colonel from behind, one arm wrapped around his chest, the other gripping the top of his head. Heart and mind. A thick volley of arrows sailed up and over the span of ground between them. Then a second and third volley arched up into the deep darkness and churning snow.

The first volley fell at them as insubstantially as wind upon castle walls, in hundreds of tiny flashes, which looked like momentary stars against the dark cloud field above. The second wave of arrows dissolved as it fell, and the third. Kamiko's protective sword hovering overhead allowed nothing to pass.

Felene watched as the dark being behind the colonel lifted its hand from his head and squeezed hard against his heart. A look of confusion swept over the man's face, replaced quickly with despair and heavy beads of rolling sweat. He looked to the soldier to his right, but the dark one turned and whispered, and the soldier stammered and pointed back at the wagon, nodding yes. The dark one placed his hand back atop the colonel's head, who then raised his riding crop and dropped it. The volley began again.

"Felene." She heard Kamiko's distinctive voice and turned to see her sister looking directly at her. Kamiko and Danae were just coming around the far side of the caravan, with a wall of wagons and people between them, but Felene locked onto her eyes for a long moment. Even as she knew it was impossible to see Kamiko with her eyes, Felene was face-to-face with her.

Kamiko was a cauldron of power when seen with the sight. For all Felene could tell, it was white fire that all but roared with Kamiko at the center. Danae had her horse close against Kamiko's left flank, running all out. Behind, before, and beside Danae, a trio of angelic beings ran afoot in darts and streaks, watching over her like protective and powerful kinsmen. Felene was to meet Kamiko out in the field.

She stepped forward and began moving toward the center of the field. She need not rush, her timing would be perfect. She was beyond Danae's line in the dirt when the first volley arrived. She was ten paces beyond when the third volley was released, as the second volley began to rain. She clearly heard the colonel add the word *combatant* to the order to fire and knew that every single archer had aimed at her. This she knew with her mind.

Her heart felt only calm resolution. The dark one holding the colonel was looking directly at her now, glaring with obvious seething hatred. Above her thunder rumbled and rolled. The volley of arrows came down with the precision of the laws of nature. Felene's pace never sped or slowed as hundreds of shards fell from the sky. One of her angelic companions reappeared, walking a few paces ahead of her, the other walking close behind. No single arrow even fell in their path.

A surge of dread began growing in her gut, as silence fell over the awestruck soldiers and the speechless colonel. It was time to unveil and enter the foray. She worked the chest buckle open and let the heavy barding fall away and lifted her sword clear of the scabbard. The world was strange to her, everything she knew was gone, everything new in its place. She kept her feet moving, and with her free hand, she pulled the poncho off her body and dropped it on the ground, then yanked the woolen hat free and slung it aside.

The colonel's face was contorted with confusion and fear, as the dark being shoved it's fingers all the way into the man's head and squeezed, whispering in his ears. Another of the dark ones appeared in the ranks of the men and began chanting. Felene could hear nothing of its voice, but the result was where the import lay. It sowed fear into their hearts.

Kamiko and Danae thundered up to them from across the field, drew their mounts to a hard stop, and leapt from their saddles. With a brief and knowing glance at Felene, Kamiko stormed straight up to the colonel. The dark angel scampered away from Kamiko's brightness but came quickly back and crouched behind the colonel.

Felene moved up to stand with Danae, who had stopped several paces back from the colonel. Uila pranced and grumbled for a moment before falling still behind Kamiko. Then he stood with his sides heaving and his head up. Felene checked for Siruis over her shoulder and saw Jerim standing next to her but outside the line Danae had drawn. Birds covered the entire wagon.

Kamiko stood over the colonel in silence for several moments. His aides had backed away and were fidgeting with their slung weapons, weighing the risk of drawing arms on their own lieutenant marshal over disobeying a direct order from their commander. Felene knew they would die to the man if so ordered.

"Colonel Dorin," Kamiko said at last, "what have you done?"

He was almost blithering, "I have done…I…" But the dark one at his back was under compulsion it could not resist, even in the presence of Kamiko and Danae's protective trio, and it stood behind him again and hugged tightly around his chest, then it squeezed his heart with bitter contempt. And whispered.

The colonel seemed to snap out of his confusion, and his face grew suddenly stern. He took several steps straight back and said to Kamiko, "We shall see what I have done, Hoshi." He turned to his right and ordered the aide, "Full assault, kill everyone bearing arms, destroy the caravan, and bring the survivors to me here." The aide saluted and stormed away at a fast trot. When the colonel next spoke, Felene thought she heard a distinct change in his speech and mannerism.

"You will kill them all for me, Hoshi. They are my blood sacrifice to God. See how I have them eager to be led to your slaughter? See how many you have slain already?" The fallen angel was peering over the colonel's shoulder at Kamiko, sneering at her, but the colonel's tongue was moving. The trumpets began blaring, and troops began shifting around, splitting to the two tasks.

Then Felene saw Jerim's great white owl float swiftly overhead and dive down over the caravan. The colonel's voice said, "We will destroy all the world with slavery and with suffering, and mankind will curse God, Hoshi."

"Silence, demon," Kamiko commanded, "release the colonel."

But even though it grew agitated, the dark one did not retreat. Another voice peeled down from the cloud, "You have no authority here, child. Your *jurisdiction* does not extend into my realm."

Danae was at her saddle, working the buckles open that kept Kamiko's sword attached. Felene absently wondered if the royal army practiced attack formations for just three people. She wasn't entirely sure why she felt no fear in the presence of the demon or from the voice thundering overhead.

"Vested authority, Luthain, I need no jurisdiction," Kamiko answered quietly. With that she raised her bound hands over her head. The sword Felene had watched guarding Siruis appeared in Kamiko's hand, sleek and simple in form but humming with anxious power. Now the reactions were immediate and wild.

The dark one began peddling backward, physically dragging the colonel along. The black cloud suddenly coalesced into hundreds of churning fingers, which dropped straight down into the mass of moving soldiers. In the blink of her eye, Felene now saw that dark beings were spread over the entire army and had begun shouting and chanting. The soldiers broke rank and turned toward Kamiko with a thousand lances. The demon may be right; they could be forced to kill them all.

Felene stepped forward to her side as Kamiko lowered the sword, looked over at her fierce sister, and said simply, "Into the breach."

Kamiko smiled at Felene, her calm slow certainty beaming, as though all the world was not collapsing atop them. "Go to Siruis, my friend, there is nothing you can do out here."

Felene spared one look at the sword and decided that Kamiko was asking for room to fight. She nodded and turned to trot back toward Siruis and Jerim. Danae had affixed Kamiko's sword to Uila's saddle and was just leaping up to the stirrup to mount the other dark warhorse. She moved alongside Felene and offered the stirrup to her. Felene swung her leg over behind the saddle, and Danae nudged the horse into a slow run, as the mass of soldiers moved toward Kamiko in force.

They made it to Siruis and Jerim as the army came down the low hill toward them. Danae dismounted, leaving Felene in command of the destrier, then Felene and Jerim stepped further out from the wagon.

Felene lifted her ancient sword to heaven again and prayed in silence. Noise and motion drew both their notice, as a formation of sword sisters charged into view, near the southern flank of the moving company. The body of sisters drove laterally down the royal flank line and flooded into the space between Siruis and the building foray, where Felene joined them at their lead.

As the sisterhood formed into rank and file and prepared to meet them in battle, Felene saw an odd and telling reaction spread across the ranks of men. Those dark demons moving in their midst began shifting back away from the formation of sisters, and the resolve of the soldiers began to falter. Military discipline had all but vanished when the dark ones dropped down from the cloud, and now their forward progress stopped abruptly, as confusion and fear swept through their ranks. Every combatant in the field understood that even though they were outnumbered ten to one, the sisters were in no way overmatched. But Kamiko was standing in her saddle now, and the reluctance in the hearts of the soldiers was doubled by the sight.

The shimmering sword in her right hand was pointing straight up into the belly of the black cloud, which was squatting down over the battlefield. A thick column of the cloud plunged straight down at Kamiko, but appeared to be kept at bay by the sword she held aloft. The column punched down on Kamiko with pulses of force, each time causing her to shudder and strain. Her face was washed in running sweat.

Felene knew Kamiko well enough to see the change come over her. Her spirit howled and roared, and the volcano she held in her chest came blasting out into the ether as silver fire. Her face colored over with darkness, and she closed her eyes. She released the powerful sword, and it shot into the cloud and tore an enormous hole through to clear blue sky, darkening in the twilight. The being in the cloud wailed and shrieked, and the soldiers on the field regained their ferocity and pushed forward suddenly. Thousands of the dark demonic beings darted around the ranks of men, shouting fear and madness and driving the battle frenzy higher and higher. It was inevitable that innocent men would die this day, maybe a lot of them, Felene thought, perhaps all of them.

The sword hovering above Kamiko began waging war on them with spits of fire, and a hundred men fell dead in their tracks. The demons in their ranks shouted rage and confusion and pressed the men forward against the will of their hearts and minds. They pressed down and around Kamiko and Uila until they had completely encircled them. Kamiko knelt atop the saddle for long enough to draw her real sword from the scabbard, then stood again and simply held it aloft over the battlefield. The effect was that doubt reasserted in the hearts of the soldiers, and again they paused from an uncertainty of their actions. More dark beings dropped from the churning cloud, and the battle for the will of the soldiers rose to a new frenzied height.

Felene wondered that no one else was seeing or hearing this happen, surely Kamiko and Siruis.

She felt a hand on her leg and looked down to find Siruis. "Go to Kamiko. Take all the sisters and go to her. She needs you there, Felene, go quickly."

Felene did not need to be told again. She thrust her sword high and kicked the dark horse hard, sending him leaping into the air as he lunged. She shouted at the top of her lungs, "*To me… To me*!" The sisterhood fell in behind her as she thundered forward, and they filled the chasm she made as she drove the horse mercilessly into the press of soldiers now attacking Kamiko. The back ranks turned as the new threat began killing them from behind, and a gap opened. Felene thrashed the horse hard with her heels and drove right over the top of the remaining blockade, just as spears were reaching for Uila's ribs. She broke into a shallow clearing between Kamiko and the mass of soldiers. Many of the sword sisters sheathed their swords and snatched up the spears of the fallen soldiers

Now she could see the ethereal sword overhead wage war on those coming within striking distance to Kamiko. A wave of more than a hundred men dropped where they stood, and a wider gap now encircled her and Felene completely. She believed no one else could see the sword hovering there, only her and Kamiko.

Felene plunged her sword into the ground and clamored to her feet in the saddle. Kamiko's sword was drooping, and her head was back, but the pulsing cloud had not yet driven her down. Felene felt anger and hatred hit her like a battering ram. The sisters poured into the gap and immediately surrounded Felene and Kamiko, driving the soldiers back and widening the clearing. Felene stepped over to Uila's rump and threw her arm around Kamiko's chest, grabbed Kamiko's right hand—sword and all—and thrust it skyward. Felene felt it this time. Everyone in the field was bolstered once again to reject the demonic influence, and many of the soldiers let their weapons fall, then ceased the advance altogether, backing away in terror. The dark destrier Felene had been riding fell to the ground at Uila's feet and writhed in death. She could see a hilt protruding from his flank that had been meant for her leg.

The opening in the cloud above them had begun to close again as dark beings dropped to the ground. However, now they fell upon the fighting sisters and entered fully into the physical realm, a thing forbidden to them. Felene saw the first sister fall as a result of a demon knocking her weapon aside to allow a fatal spear-thrust to find its mark. Then another, and another sister dropped to the ground, dead. The wind was howling.

Felene could see the other sword still hovering high overhead. She was standing with her mouth only inches from Kamiko's ear, so she fought the urge to shout. "Call the sword, Sister. Call it down."

"No," Kamiko said quietly, "no, I must not. Felene, it will destroy everything."

Felene spoke words she had no reason to know, "No, Sister, not if it is in your hand. You must call it down. It will heed your heart and act accordingly. Call it."

Another sister fell and another right atop her body.

"Hear me, Kamiko. Trust in God Almighty. Do not listen to Luthain."

Kamiko turned her head slightly and looked at Felene from the corner of one eye. She nodded once, then switched her metal sword to her left hand. She lifted her right hand up toward the hovering sword. It dropped to her hand instantly. When the sword touched her flesh, the ground shook and thunder exploded in the cloud above and echoed away in deep rumblings. Angels far too numerous to count swooped down through the gap in the cloud and tore across the field on foot. The mighty captain who had been watching over Danae dropped to the ground and stood like a statue over the field. Its eyes were closed, and dangling from a golden chain in its right hand, a thurible of heavenly incense smoldered with thick white smoke.

The dark ones scattered in every direction, their fleshy soldier golems forgotten. Those fallen beings who had only whispered in men's ears were driven away. Those who had entered the physical foray were driven to the ground and chained. Felene could only marvel that the whole affair was unseen by anyone else in the field.

But Kamiko was not yet finished. She dropped from Uila's back in the clearing the sisters had opened, looked around one time, then plunged the mighty sword into the ground. Nothing happened until she gave it a sharp twist.

Kamiko

The wind and the chaos, the reeking bodies, Uila's presence beside her, angels at war on the ground, the great subcommander of all demons drifting in the elements above, her very soul, the very fabric of firma—all felt the impact of Hun'jotzimon. Even as she twisted to release its great power, she prayed for mercy. She begged for the lives of the soldiers and the colonel. Every single creature standing but Kamiko and Siruis was flung into the air. Only Jerim landed back on his feet.

But Kamiko had to summon her rage before she could wield Hun'jotzimon. And it had to be justified and righteous, not just simple anger. Her anger was with Titus, sovereign king. His orders of madness could only bring madness. If Luthain was here, then he'd been with Titus as well. That the sword had come in response to that particularly strong wave of anger struck Kamiko as important.

The blackness of the cloud withdrew in a howling wind and tore away southward like a great angry beast. The storm became only dark and foreboding, as the clouds took their natural form. The wind dropped, and the fat snowflakes drifted in slower swirls. Uila righted himself and shook his body hard. All around them, soldiers and sisters began standing, no weapons or fighting, only confusion and shock. One of the sisters helped Felene to her feet, who then retrieved her sword. Everything on the field had been punched into the air, living and dead alike.

Kamiko watched in silence as Felene brushed herself off, then began checking Uila over for damage. Felene grew still when she saw Kamiko's hand tightening on the hilt. Kamiko saw all the sisters around her do the same, bracing with anticipation. They had all just flown higher than Kamiko's full height and were prepared for another jolt.

She drew the sword from the ground and held it aloft, then lowered it when nothing happened. The ancient sword was still in her left hand, Hun'jotzimon in her right. It had not gone away. They were not finished.

Danae had sprinted from the wagon all the way up to Kamiko, with Felene's heavy leather barding over her shoulder. She dumped it unceremoniously at Felene's feet and offered to help her put it on.

"Felene," Kamiko said quietly, "Would you find Sister Joon for me, ask her to come down to the wagon?"

"Of course," she said as she buckled the chest clasp. "Who is Sister Joon?"

Danae climbed atop Uila and began peering around at the destruction surrounding them. Her young face was unreadable, but her mouth was slack and her eyes wide. She slowly sat down atop the great horse.

Kamiko said, "Joon carries no weapon and wears no armor, and she is very dark and quite rotund."

Felene nodded and went to the task, sliding her sword into the sheath as she departed. Kamiko clicked to Uila and began walking down the slight hill to Siruis. Uila trailed dutifully behind, with Danae sitting cross-legged on his broad rump. Both looked exhausted. Kamiko caught sight of the colonel sitting amid the carnage, with his head in his hands. The fallen angel that had been tormenting him was gone, for now.

She must be very careful. The sword was responding to her anger with Titus and echoing it back into her, whispering in her ear to experience real destruction. It wanted Titus, wanted him now. She attached her thoughts to the notion of now and fought to control her mind. Djinnasee's words of warning, from so many weeks earlier, sounded in her thoughts, *Without compassion, the world and all that dwell upon it will perish.*

As she stepped up to Siruis, she asked, "Are you ready to go?" To which Siruis only nodded. Kamiko's body felt stiff as a plank, and her movements were almost twitchy, her nerves were ragged, and her spine felt much like a rusty bow-saw blade. Hun'jotzimon was a thrumming storm in her fist, almost daring her to release it. There was still a separation between them, two beings coming to tenuous terms rather than one will of sharing. The sword could act on its own.

She looked up at Danae, still sitting on Uila's rump and leaning heavily on Kamiko's traveling gear. She had the look of someone trying to recover from having been stunned, again and again. Her mouth was open, and her eyes, though distant and shimmering, were following Kamiko's every move.

The sound of horses running fast turned Kamiko around. Felene and Joon had located a couple of mounts that had not escaped during Jerim's fury and were heading down the easy slope from the caravan. They both dismounted, while the horses were still moving, and trotted over to Kamiko and Siruis. Joon stopped short when she saw Jerim sitting on the ground behind Siruis, but upon seeing Kamiko and Siruis standing next to him without concern, she joined the group. Once there, however, Joon could not take her eyes from Siruis.

"It is you," she said quietly.

"Yes," Siruis answered. Joon nodded and smiled and seemed satisfied.

Kamiko still had both swords in her hands and the hobble on her wrists when she spoke to Joon, "I need your help, Sister."

"Anything within my power, Kamiko." Joon's eyes kept flicking from Siruis to Hun'jotzimon.

"Take Uila and ten sisters with you to Mount Hileah. King El`Thorn is in need of our help. I will meet you there as soon as I am able. And, Joon," Kamiko said, "we are all outlaws now."

"I will do it, Sister, this you know."

"Thank you, my friend."

The sisters in the field were beginning to drift down the slope in groups, from every part of the battle-ravaged field, and soon converged at the clearing around the wagon. No one approached and all remained silent. Seven bodies wrapped in long cloaks were laid side by side, and sisters took up stations around them, with swords drawn in silent salute. Many of the soldiers had retreated over the hill, but many were still in the field. The gathered sisters kept a wary eye upon the now quiet battlefield.

"Felene." Kamiko turned to speak to her but was forced to stop as the well of emotions in her chest drove all the way to her throat and clenched it shut. Tears drifted over her eyes and slipped down her face. She continued at barely a whisper. "You are my soul and my strength, dear Sister Felene. I would have collapsed along the way without your beautiful heart propping me up." Words then came to mind she had no recollection of learning. "Take half of these sisters to Ravencroft with you, Baron Riplin will allow us sanctuary for a time. Bid all the others go to Essen." The weight in her chest was easing slowly. She handed the ancient sword to Joon, who then could not take her eyes from it. Then with Hun'jotzimon held carefully above, she drew Felene into an embrace of kinship, of sisterhood deeper than sword sister. Felene remained silent.

And in those few moments, Kamiko saw the grand matron Felene. She was standing on the high porch of an ancient dark castle, looking south down the length of her great homeland island. A simple crown of plaited golden rope lay on a small table. She was strong and fierce, though she was very old.

When they separated, Felene's mouth hung open, and her chest heaved, and her dark eyes bore into Kamiko's. "I…*saw*…" Then she composed herself with a deep breath and a shake of her head. "And Siruis told me." It was all her voice would manage.

"Make your farewell with Danae, my friend. We will join you in Ravencroft some weeks from now." Joon returned the sword to the sheath on Uila's saddle, then held her hand to Danae. The young girl took it and dropped from Uila's rump.

Kamiko stood at Uila's head, his massive chin in her hand. "Fear not, my friend, I will be waiting for you." He chortled and pressed his forehead against her chest and grew very still.

For a few short minutes, many of the sisters came down and mingled with Felene, Danae, and Siruis. And almost without exception, they were introduced to Jerim, who fidgeted as though he had ants crawling around his armpits. Kamiko had seen Anje standing alone at the corner of her wagon. She pressed her face to Uila's for a moment, then walked over to her.

"Where is Cort?" Kamiko asked, for he was truly her only remaining concern.

"He is uninjured. The caravan was not attacked."

"I am pleased, Anje." The sword thrummed with great impatience, and for a moment, she thought it had grown hotter in her hand.

After a short span, Anje began. "All I really wanted was to see those hobbles on you." She paused and looked at Kamiko's bound wrists. "Now." Her words were coming with difficulty. Kamiko knew she could not help her. "I can see the shame I put on my mother and on my father and on Cort." She looked up at Kamiko. "Especially Cort. You…had it coming." She stood and faced Kamiko and showed her bravery once again. "You were the king's pet and the one person who'd never been put down. I never even considered you human." She shook her head. "I had a Kamiko Hoshi doll when I was a child. Rasha always said he was going to take it and burn it. Bastion stood up for me."

She stepped forward suddenly and said, "If you will allow me"—and she reached, as if to Kamiko's wrists, to the hobble—"I will end this debacle. Forgive me, Sister. I have wronged you, and I have made an enemy of Felene, and for that alone, my heart will never recover. But to you, Kamiko, I owe my life." Kamiko thought for a moment about leaving the hobble for her audience with the king but decided against theatrics. Releasing Anje from her guilt was far more important.

"You may, but you must cut the strap. If you try to pass the hobble over this sword, you could be killed, maybe worse."

"There is worse?"

"Most assuredly."

Anje's dagger was sharp, and the hobbles fell away.

"Anje, my friend, I will no longer be lieutenant marshal, I am no longer a sister of the Order. The king will strip my account and foreclose on my dwelling. I have only fine boots and a fine sword to my name. I will be at Siruis's side if I must destroy half this kingdom," she said and lifted the sword. "Go in peace, make amends with Felene. You are the bravest woman I know, Andi Jean Kale."

Kale was still on her lips when a hard shudder hit her hand. The sword began to ring like a deep old bell the size of a house. Every eye in line of sight turned to look.

The bell was struck again. An image flashed in Kamiko's mind. Titus! Luthain was with Titus! She turned and ran to Danae, holding the sword above her head. She was pointing at Uila and said to Felene, "Sister, my sword, quickly." Hun'jotzimon was rumbling aloud. Kamiko had no idea what to expect.

Felene

Felene leapt to it and had the sword free in seconds. Kamiko simply extended her hand, and Felene tossed it to her, as she and Danae trotted to Siruis and Jerim. Felene leapt quickly to Uila's back, drew her sword, and thrust it skyward, followed by the more than two hundred sword sisters surrounding them. As one, the war cry began, low at first, but then it quickly built to a fierce yell which, as was the sisters' way, coalesced into a single powerful note, high and strong.

The raging storm in Kamiko's right hand rumbled with thunder Felene could feel on her face through the air, like drums being beaten harder and stronger but without a set rhythm. The moment Kamiko and Danae came alongside Siruis and Jerim, everyone heard a loud crack and the sound of rending metal. Then a fiery mass swooped down from the sky in a long fast arch, and engulfed Felene's four friends. It shot skyward with a loud pop, and they were gone in the span of a breath.

The war cry ended abruptly as Felene lowered her sword, followed by a profound silence which lasted only moments. The calls for help and cries of pain from many wounded warriors triggered a wave of movement across the gathered sisters. They turned upon those they had fought, though now with help and comfort.

When Felene sought out the colonel, she found him unable to speak an entire sentence without being distracted and losing his thoughts. None of the officers from his command could give a sound description of what had transpired or could explain why they had attacked a caravan or had fought the sisterhood. The consensus among their ranks was that they had been subjected to sorcery or witchcraft and that the sisters had broken the spell. As Felene considered their perspective, she realized they were not far from the truth of the matter, not far at all. If Luthain was anything, he was that very thing—a sorcerer.

The night passed with Felene and Joon sitting around a rolling fire, with Anje, Rasha, and Sir Johns, Uila fast asleep nearby. No one spoke and no one slept, and dawn broke easy upon a field of silence, covered in a blanket of snow.

Chapter 13

Castlehaven

Kamiko was certain Hun'jotzimon had not brought this about, for it continued to rumble and to resonate in her hand. They had been swallowed by what Kamiko thought was a ball of fire but without the heat. As they lunged up into the sky and passed through the clouds, it took shape. Kamiko, Siruis, Danae, and Jerim were equally struck with awe. They rode in a large chariot, drawn by seven pairs of horses. The whole of the carriage and the draw-horses were carved out of living fire. She could see depth beneath her boots but could not see all the way through the floor. It was easy to see that this was not a burning chariot, rather it was crafted from fire by a master. The charioteer was a common looking man in the robed garb of an earlier age in history and appeared to feel no more of the heat than Kamiko. They were heading south. She assumed to Castlehaven.

She had never imagined such speed was possible. The flaming horses were running hard. They moved many times faster than horses could run. The wind was a hard roar around them, but they felt very little buffeting as they tore through the deep blanket of clouds, which covered much of the kingdom.

Suddenly Hun'jotzimon grew hotter in her hand, and she felt a distinctive pull, as if it wanted release. Both Jerim and Danae had been keeping their eyes on the sword much of the time. A sharp peal of thunder sounded off the flat of the blade, and it popped out of Kamiko's hand, then sped away straight ahead to the south and was quickly gone from sight. Jerim made no attempt to hide the relief he felt at Hun'jotzimon's departure. Both he and Danae had the look of being ready to leap from the back of the chariot and take their chances with a long fall. Now they relaxed a little and turned their worried scrutiny to the flames at their feet and to the open air around them.

Kamiko's heart was racing from being thrust high into the sky in a flaming chariot with no warning. Her mind had not yet accepted her circumstance and was locked in numb disbelief. Too many impossible things were happening too quickly. Everyone present was intelligent enough to understand that something serious was unfolding. The recent and abrupt rise of direct interaction from heaven's gate spoke volumes to them all, and the anticipation of what lay ahead overcame their trepidation. Kamiko could see it in their faces, as both Jerim and Danae stared straight back into her eyes as she looked at each of them. She turned and lingered on Siruis.

She was staring down into her empty palm, her fingers curved as if she held an invisible ball. After a few moments, Siruis flinched and yanked her hand back and rubbed that palm on her thigh, her mouth slightly open but barely breathing. Her eyes darted back and forth at nothing, then turned abruptly toward Kamiko.

Kamiko began to speak but realized the howl of the wind was too loud to converse, so she asked with her hands, "What did you see, Sister?"

After a short pause, Siruis spoke aloud, and even Danae tapped her ear that she'd heard her voice. "I saw…" She hesitated for a long moment, then said, "I will show you." And she pointed ahead. Kamiko sensed Siruis was struggling, her worried features and downcast eyes spoke of difficulty. She was nodding her head and said to Kamiko, "Yes, a great burden awaits me before the king. I have no desire to be the mouth which speaks the words he must hear, the eyes by which his vision will come. I have seen what he will see"—she lifted her palm and gazed into it—"and it is fearful to behold." Her words were plain, even over the sound of the driving wind.

They were interrupted by Jerim's quiet deep rumble. "Turtle Star, look there."

The clouds had broken, and the vast kingdom opened far below them like a great quilted patchwork, where the green lands met the dirty yellow sand of the Goli-Ben Desert. The charioteer directed the team into an easy descent, but rather than slowing, he called them to go faster, and the wind roared higher and louder. And just ahead and below them, Kamiko saw the first ridge of the southern coastal mountains come into view, where mountain, desert, and grassland met. To the east, the desert wilderness stretched out of sight without discernible features, other than golden yellow, mottled and streaked with dirty stains.

Below them and spreading west farther than Kamiko could see, the masses of Cairistonia's populace had grown and, to a limited degree, had thrived for almost four thousand years. Kamiko had never considered what the kingdom would look like from such a tremendous height and saw it in a sudden light. She recalled Siruis's effect on her at their first meeting and how Kamiko had seen her whole life pressed into one gaze. She saw the kingdom this way now, all at once, the history of its expansion, measured in layers of growth, wealth, and poverty.

The wealthy had always tried to overshadow all other classes of society with sheer size and built high towers and lofty statues and spires and great, walled fortress. But the masses were too big for any shadow the wealthy could cast, and people covered the land. So the wealthy had gathered their forces and set out to enslave them by helping some rise to an imaginary wealth status, while driving others into privation.

Kamiko knew Djinnasee started the Order, in large part, to help protect the common man from the wealthy classes. Such had been the case countless times over the centuries. Kamiko was one of only a few sisters in all that time to join the royal military, to be a ward of the Crown. In general, the sisterhood maintained a distinct separation between the Order and the throne. And many of the sisters kept their residency in Ravencroft to avoid the ever-changing laws and whims of the royal family. For although Baron Riplin was the head of the powerful reigning oligarchy, he did not have absolute authority, and Ravencroft was ruled by a standing council instead of a single man, as in Cairistonia.

Danae and Jerim were in awe, and both were smiling and were, at last, becoming attuned to what was going on. They were flying over the land in a speeding flaming chariot. This would never be forgotten. When Jerim turned and smiled at Siruis, his almost child-like demeanor changed to concern. Kamiko turned to see what he'd reacted to and saw that Siruis was again gazing into her hand, seemingly oblivious to the chariot and their circumstances. Even though the wind was howling around them, Kamiko could hear Siruis whispering what sounded like mumbled gibberish. Her brow was knotted, and her eyes were brimming with tears, and even with the odd sounding words, Kamiko sensed a pleading in her tone.

Kamiko reached to lay her hand on Siruis's shoulder, but Jerim stopped her by gently taking her wrist, then he shook his head slightly. "Leave her be, Sister, it will do no good." The concern on his face was colored with practiced patience, as though he had seen Siruis in this state enough times to have grown accustomed. One peculiar word Kamiko heard repeated often, spoken with the inflection of a name, *Terilaximea-Behethquid.*

Danae's quiet yowl drew her attention back to the scene below. They had skirted the edge of the mountains and were passing over some of the most densely populated territory in the kingdom. Here the buildings, homes, and roadways totally covered the land surrounding the fabled Cancellu City, where the massive fortified Crown Gate and thirty leagues of wall separated the kingdom at large from the Valley of Kings. At the center of the valley, but overlooking the Bos`Jin Sea, lay Castlehaven, city of the king. Only those of royal blood were allowed to live in the valley.

The heavy wall had already passed beneath them and now lay far behind the speeding chariot as they continued to descend. Kamiko had no need to look upon the wealth strewn about in the Valley of

Kings and turned back to Siruis. Danae followed Kamiko and knelt beside Siruis in silence, her young eyes full of wonder.

Jerim was crouched over Siruis, looking down at her as she spoke strange words into her cupped and empty hand. Kamiko could tell that Siruis was repeating a long phrase, ending with the words which sounded like the name. She could also tell that with each recital, Siruis appeared to be gathering her strength. Her eyes cleared of moisture and her browline unfurled, as her face grew serious and determination settled over her bearing. She drew her shoulders back, lifted her chin, and raised the invisible manifestation in her hand, speaking directly to whatever she was seeing there. Kamiko heard the name again, *Terilaximea-Behethquid*, but this time, Siruis growled the name with vehemence and flung her hand upward, like she was releasing a bird into the air.

After a moment longer, she whispered, "So be it," and looked up at Kamiko. "It is done. The beast will come." She no longer looked afraid, only concerned and angry. "We are here, Sister."

Just then, the chariot dropped into a steep dive that sent Kamiko's stomach all the way into her throat and left her feet barely touching the flaming chariot floor. Both Jerim and Danae yelped aloud and, on impulse, grabbed Kamiko by the arms, Jerim on one side, Danae on the other. All three were still crouched beside Siruis and simply stayed put, grappled together, as the charioteer drove the team almost straight down. Suddenly and with a throaty howl, the flames grew and folded over them completely, and for a long moment, they were engulfed in cool fire. But just as suddenly as it had scooped them up, the chariot left them standing on solid ground and shot skyward. It was gone from sight almost instantly.

Everyone was breathing hard but Siruis, who appeared to have failed to notice the chariot altogether. Kamiko knew Jerim and Danae's hearts were pounding like hers and figured her own face was as flushed with excitement as theirs. It took a few moments for Kamiko to register where they were, but then she recognized the place intimately. The charioteer had dropped them off on one of a thousand massive porches, overlooking the glistening face of the Bos`Jin Sea and looking down on the sprawl of Castlehaven. And where Danae was staring out over the vista in complete awe, Jerim had the look of one who, like Kamiko, had seen it enough times to find it commonplace.

For more than two millennia, the kings of Cairistonia had poured vast wealth into their city. It was a city of castles, pure and simple, with brightly colored domes and spires creating an enormous forest of handmade extravagance. For several centuries, the trend for the royal family had been to build *personal* statues so that an entire swath of the massive city looked like an army of stone giants had taken residency. This day they stood over the city in silent witness.

Siruis turned away from the porch and began walking quickly toward tall open doors leading into the king's hall. They followed her in without hesitation. Kamiko knew right where they were. Had the chariot dropped them at the opposite end of the cavernous hallway, it would have taken two full hours to walk to the spot where Siruis stopped. Kamiko, Siruis, Danae, and Jerim stood before the towering gold and ivory door to the king's audience chamber. And though Hun'jotzimon was no longer in her hand, Kamiko's arm ached, as it did following a long battle of continuous fighting.

She held the sheathed ancient sword in her left hand and touched the surface of the massive door with her right. To go before the king so armed was grievous. The door moved like it was floating on air as it swung inward, silent and slow. Incense and perfume immediately assailed them and turned the smell of cooked food sickly on Kamiko's nose. A rally of animated voices clipped off in stages until no words could be heard.

She strode into the room, with Danae at her elbow, Siruis and Jerim three paces behind. A long rectangular table beheld a feast of exaggerated opulence, with hundreds of choices of rare and exotic table fare. Kamiko knew from experience that no less than a thousand servants had been required to produce the meal. Around it sat a gaggle of roughly fifty of the wealthiest men and women alive, many of whom Kamiko knew remotely. They traded not in properties but in property barons.

As each of them looked upon Siruis, their eyes lost focus and relaxed in their sockets, and their heads drifted down to their plates, fast asleep. The long line of elite guardsmen, Kamiko's own corps, also fell into a deep sleep and dropped noisily in place. Several men burst into the room at the clamor, but as soon as their search took in Siruis's face, they fell where they stood. Kamiko was relieved when the queen lay back into her large chair, her mouth open and breathing quietly, instead of flopping facedown into her food. The king received no such pardon. He was fully awake, his breathing shallow and quick by the time Kamiko stopped at his right side, her legitimate place in his court.

She had no words but drew the sword, so King Titus understood the full depth of her purpose, then stepped back to allow Siruis to step up. Jerim reached to the center of the table and picked out a large bowl of sugared gelatinous fruit and turned it up like a flagon, taking the contents in one gulp. He then walked to the enormous glass doors leading to a long wide porch and pushed them open. The Bos`Jin Sea lay two thousand feet below. Cool moisture and the natural reek of the sea flooded the room.

King Titus saw none of this. His eyes were transfixed upon Siruis. Her declaration was brief.

"Titus Phiemous," she began, already omitting the royal obeisance of *Your Majesty*, "you have failed to heed the call and spiritual discernment of the Eternal through the words of his prophet Djinnasee. The kingdom has become a common harlot, steeped in corruption and deceit, whose heart has been torn from her soul by avarice and the worship of self. The Eternal has held his anger for twelve generations of your forefathers but will be appeased by the prayers of the prophet no longer." Thrice the king sought to interrupt, and thrice his tongue failed him. She continued, "The line of kings is ended, and Cairistonia will fall before your eyes," she said, as she opened her hand toward the door leading outside to the balcony, "right there."

Kamiko turned and glanced out the door and saw two beings, one floating midair over the Bos`Jin Sea and one standing, perched atop a carved marble baluster at the edge of the wide porch, Hun'jotzimon and Luthain. Both appeared to be waiting in anticipation of Siruis's actions. Luthain was as Kamiko remembered him from her first encounter, bent toward the right side under the weight of a heavy black hilt with no blade. His mangled left hand was kept hidden beneath his cloak.

Siruis motioned for the king to follow her and then turned to proceed out to the porch. Kamiko thought Titus was walking against his will. He kept trying to stop. He was wailing for mercy, he tore his robe away, he ripped a vast wealth from around his neck and threw it across the room, sending gems and jewels and fat diamonds skittering across the polished marble floor. He leaned against the doorframe and clung to it but slipped past and, at last, found his feet at the thick stone-carved banister and wide open sky. It was the highest man-made vantage in all the land.

Far below, hundreds of boats dotted the water, like trash floating after a storm. Across the sea, the uppermost spires of First Colony twinkled, as though they were tiny candles blinking in the fog. The free lands of King El`Thorn lay just beyond sight to the northwest. Kamiko longed for that wild country more than ever and wanted little else but to leave this king and kingdom behind her forever. She knew then and there that if the only way out was to leap from the balcony, she would do it.

Siruis swept her hand out over the great vista, and the king's breath caught with a high gasp. A sharp line of destruction pushed across not only Ravencroft and Cairistonia but the land of the Seven Clans as well. And what looked strangely similar to a wind-driven grass fire was, in fact, a flood of red helms and black spears. It first flared in the western reaches of the north highlands but filled every space in Titus's great kingdom with a smoldering blackness. Smoke rose from every city, as long trains of people were led away under whip and chain, driven north and west. The path of the flood was checked at the wall of the king's mountain fortress, and there it remained for one full year, beating at the legendary city gates below without success.

A deep and mournful bellow pealed down from the northern mountains above Ravencroft City. A windstorm like a hurricane washed across the kingdom, from the mountains in the north to the Broken Coast. Now Kamiko's breath caught, and a catlike howl slipped from Danae. Jerim's head was down, and his eyes were closed.

Siruiswhisperedto Kamiko, breathless, "*Terilaximea-Behethquid*."

Mount Oman, the towering western mountain overlooking Ravencroft City, cracked at the crown and a massive golden shard appeared to fall toward the city below. Just before it struck, two vast fleshy sails opened, one on each side. They grew tight and long, held outright and taut on bones the size of the towering cedars of Ledon. The glimmering shard drifted southward like a kite on the hunt, scanning every blade of grass for telltales of its prey. It came to rest far below, in Cancellu City, in the midst of the red flood assaulting the Crown Gate.

When the apparition settled and drew still, its true form became apparent. It was no mountain shard on wing. This was a creature of power and destruction, the likes of which had never before been seen alive in the world of men. Great claws grappled the top of the massive gates and ripped them from the fortified walls, then flung them with a casual toss out into the sea. Then the creature leapt up into the air and glided to the base of the castle, where it began to climb, every strike of its gargantuan legs setting the firma quaking.

Danae's hand closed hard on Kamiko's arm, and she began trembling. Kamiko looked at Siruis, who was also watching Danae's reaction. She bowed her head slightly, and Danae fell limp against Kamiko, who caught the girl and eased her gently to the stone floor.

As Kamiko's eyes came back up, the shimmering golden creature made it to the high porch and peered over the edge. Its head was the size of a three-mast ship, and each of its eyes were the size of an elephant. It wasted no time. The giant maw opened slowly, serpentine, and a forest of massive teeth gleamed with silvery perfection. Then with the blinding speed of a viper, it struck, taking the king and most of the porch into its cavernous mouth.

The king screamed and fell straight back to the stone floor, vomiting down his chest. He thrashed and sprawled in the mind-bending agony of fear. Then he scrambled to his feet and ran screaming for the guards and was gone. The world below them remained as it was supposed to be, the vision having been fulfilled.

Luthain held the sword hilt aloft, as if he was signifying a sure victory. She watched him straining beneath the weight, but he kept it there. It occurred to Kamiko that Luthain could no more see into the future than she, and he had likely come here for this very purpose—to see the culmination of his dark plan in the vision.

As his dark eyes came to rest on Kamiko, a hard shudder rolled up her spine. Hun'jotzimon was still waiting out over the sea behind Luthain, when the demon spoke, "Titus Phiemous is no longer your concern, sister of the Order." His voice was not what Kamiko expected. It was gentle and persuasive. "I shall watch over him..." He paused as he slowly, painfully lowered the empty hilt. "Until the day of wrath, Hoshi. He is mine till judgment come."

Kamiko had no intention of speaking to Luthain and stood waiting and listening. He continued in a deep voice, much louder than before. "I require the sacrifice of blood from you," he said and slowly lifted the empty hilt to point at the sleeping soldiers. "Their blood." As if by Luthain's command, the sleep Siruis had induced began wearing off, and the soldiers began stirring. Kamiko noticed the lords, the ladies, and the queen remained as they were. "Your *legend*," he hissed, "will grow a thousandfold." He drew his withered left hand out of his cloak and turned his palm upward.

The king's guard were just beginning to get to their feet and shake the confusion from their heads, when Kamiko saw the first group of Luthain's minions appear. Roughly two dozen were moving among the recovering soldiers, already whispering thoughts of fear and hatred, envy and anger. She knew the names of many of the men in the unit, and she knew they could not see Luthain or his lackeys, only her and her three companions.

A loud klaxon shrieked to life, followed quickly by many trumpets, barking fast and furious commands. This was not a simple call to arms, it was the muster call for warfare. The doors flew open, and a unit of one hundred battle-ready warriors began flooding the room. They surrounded the dozing party and removed the queen while she slept by lifting the whole chair and trotting out the door. More of Luthain's demon ranks appeared and spread among the soldiers.

The bulk of the men paid no heed to the sleeping guests and pressed out onto the porch, weapons ready to strike. Luthain was driving them into a frenzy. He meant for her and Jerim to do battle and to kill them all. They were trapped. Luthain was correct. If she fought these men, word would spread like wildfire across the entire region, and she would take Dairei's place as the most sought after criminal in all of the history of Cairistonia. Under Luthain's influence of deceit and pride-mongering, it would continue to grow to include the whole sisterhood, and they would be hunted down or driven out.

However, if she and Jerim did not fight them here and now, then at the very least, Siruis would be tortured and executed and, likely, Danae with her. Just as Kamiko began to draw her ancient sword and set her feet, she saw Luthain moving slowly along the top of the bannister toward where they were standing near the midpoint of the enormous porch. She stopped her draw but kept her hand on the hilt. Only Siruis reacted to Luthain's presence. Danae and Jerim were focused entirely upon the soldiers flooding the throne room and forming ranks on the porch.

Luthain lifted the empty hilt and leveled it at Kamiko's chest. It was as though he took aim at her very soul. Her mind darkened with dread, and she heard his deep voice resound in her thoughts.

"Have you forgotten who you are...*good Sister*?" The appellation hissed like searing meat, and around her, all motion slowed to a near stop. "Have you come to such a certain antipathy? The sister witch has shown you the truth of your bloodlust, yet you cling to piety as if you are blind, as if that is all which is required to pardon your sin. *Denial*."

Without warning, memories flourished in her mind. At first it felt exactly the same as when she met Siruis, with cascading memories of battle, of her father, and of taking down criminals, sometimes by the score. Yet now a different perspective was woven into the fabric of her life, and a new emotion emerged and quickly grew in her chest. Joy—of battle.

"Yes." Luthain's voice sizzled in her mind. "I will not let you forget your joy, Hoshi, will not hide it from you as your sister witch has done." He twisted the empty hilt, and Kamiko felt that same adrenaline charged joy well up inside her, multifold. The thrill of battle. She'd denied it her entire life, but it was there and just as real as the dread of butchery. "Are you not the greatest warrior this kingdom has ever known? You are no butcher, rather…a savior." Then he added, "*Good Sister*."

She'd not imagined him capable of speaking truth. For all the slave lords and murderers she'd killed, many innocent people had been saved. It was the simple nature of the thing. She called to mind how Jerim had spoken to her of entering the jungle as a hunter. Simple nature. She was the lion. Titus was the goat. Everyone else—simply sheep.

Luthain had lowered the hilt. He slowly drifted back to where he had been standing atop the wide bannister, as motion began returning to the porch and throne room. Her thoughts became suddenly muddled with uncertainty, and her sight darkened with confusion. Men with spears, shields, and swords were advancing on her. She felt Danae's fingers dig into her leg as she awakened with a start and rose from the floor.

Kamiko was remotely aware that she was again slowly drawing her sword and twisting her feet for traction. Her heart was calm in her chest, her gut devoid of the tightness of either dread or joy. Battle was a simple thing. No different than harvesting crops. The sharp tang of copper filled her mouth, as a hundred spears were lowered to point at her chest, as her sword came clear. A strong voice she should recognize was shouting orders. Men were about to die in waves. Their spears were useless against her and would soon litter a bloody floor, like a forest of felled timbers.

She raised her sword over her head and bent her knees in the final preparation to attack. Chaos and fear would soon reign supreme in the dying kingdom. Then she heard a soft dark voice.

"Turtle Star." Like a mirror shattering on a stone floor, her dark reverie was broken, and light flooded into her soul in a torrent. The cascade of memories began again, but this time with a distinctly different feel and resultant spiritual response. She was a small thing in the company of giants, a simple warrior in the midst of people of monumental purpose. Beginning with King El`Thorn, she saw the faces of those she knew to be the guideposts of her life's journey, no scenes or circumstances, only their faces. The list was much longer than she'd imagined and included the colonel, currently gathering his resolve to order her death. She met his eyes across the narrow gap, hedged in ready spear tips, and lowered her sword. His wife and children had dined in Kamiko's castle dwelling on many occasions. She knew Colonel Cho, knew he would lead the charge from the front line, and she knew he counted the remaining moments of his life on one hand. He had no choice in the matter. He, like Kamiko, was a soldier. As the tip of her sword touched the stone floor, Colonel Cho raised his hand to stay the attack. The moment froze between them. She knew in that brief span that she would not engage these men in combat. She would trust God to answer prayer well.

"Sister Kamiko." Jerim's deep voice was almost a whisper. She spared him a brief glance. He and Siruis were standing near the banister, looking down at the sea far below. Jerim was pointing down and nodding to Kamiko. Siruis turned to Kamiko, her bright blue eyes glistening with a mischievous joy.

"What are you about to do, Sister?" Kamiko asked, certain the answer would not be to her liking. Siruis peered over her shoulder, looking out over the Bos`Jin Sea. Kamiko followed her gaze and saw Hun'jotzimon was still hovering out in the big sky. She shook her head at Siruis, who, in turn, simply smiled and stepped into Jerim's open hand. She said to Kamiko, "Remember the Karak-Tan!"

Kamiko said, "No...Siruis, you can't be—" But Jerim was gone. He took one massive step and jumped.

Danae's mouth was all the way open, and she was slowly shaking her head at Kamiko. But the soldiers were awaiting the command to attack. To the man, they recognized their legendary commander, had trained under her eye, had grown strong and ferocious under her hand. They believed they were doomed.

She sheathed the ancient sword of her ancestor and held her hand out to Danae, who took it immediately. Karak-Tan indeed—they sprinted the few steps to the banister and leapt with all their might, out over the churning anger of the Bos`Jin Sea.

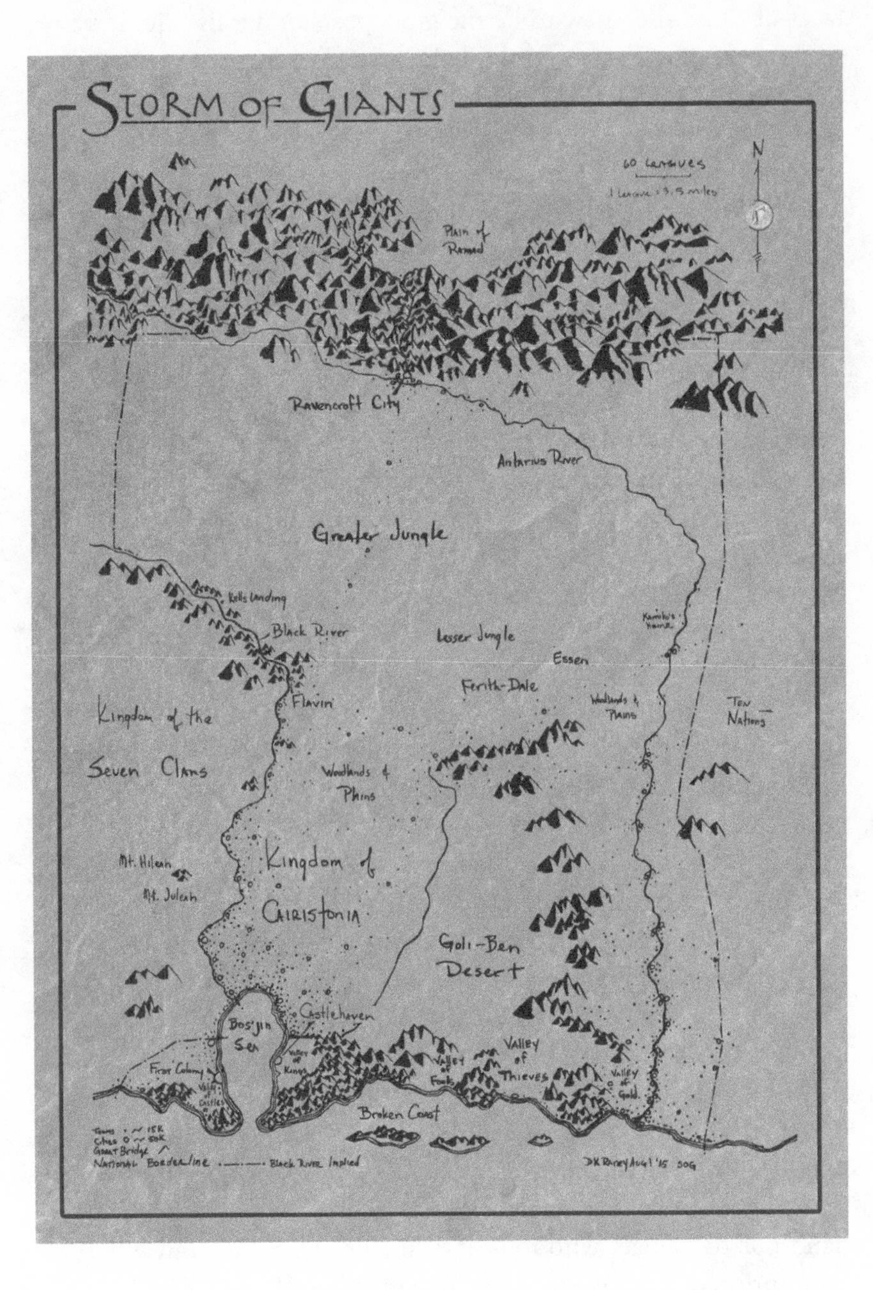

Storm of Giants
60 Leagues
1 League = 3.5 miles
N
Plain of Ravaged
Ravencroft City
Antarius River
Greater Jungle
Kells Landing
Black River
Lesser Jungle
Essen
Ferith-Dale
Flavin
Woodlands & Plains
Ten Nations
Kingdom of the Seven Clans
Woodlands & Plains
Mt. Hilean
Mt. Juleah
Kingdom of Chiristonia
Goli-Ben Desert
Castlehaven
Bos'jin Sea
First Colony
Valley of Thieves
Broken Coast
National Borderline
Black River Implied
DK Raney Aug 1 '15 SOG

CPSIA information can be obtained
at www.ICGtesting.com
Printed in the USA
LVHW041204230322
714164LV00001B/123

9 781638 815495